The
DARK
THORN

By Shawn Speakman

The Dark Thorn
The Everwinter Wraith*
The Splintered King*

Edited by Shawn Speakman

Unfettered*

*Forthcoming

The
DARK
THORN

To Jason –

Beware the fairies!

SHAWN SPEAKMAN

With Magic,

Shawn Speakman

GRIM OAK PRESS
SEATTLE

The Dark Thorn is a work of fiction. Names, characters, places, and incidents are the products of the author's imagination or are used fictitiously. Any resemblance to actual events, locales, or persons, living or dead, is entirely coincidental.

Copyright © 2012 by Shawn Speakman.
All rights reserved.

Dust jacket artwork by Todd Lockwood.
Interior map by Russ Charpentier.

Book design by Rachelle Longé McGhee.

Signed, Limited Edition ISBN 978-0-9847136-2-2
Trade Hardcover Edition ISBN 978-0-9847136-0-8
eBook ISBN 978-0-9847136-1-5

First Edition, November 2012
2 4 6 8 9 7 5 3 1

Grim Oak Press
PO Box 45173
Seattle, WA 98145

www.grimoakpress.com

For Richard and Kathy Speakman,

Who Loved

For Terry and Judine Brooks,

Who Believed

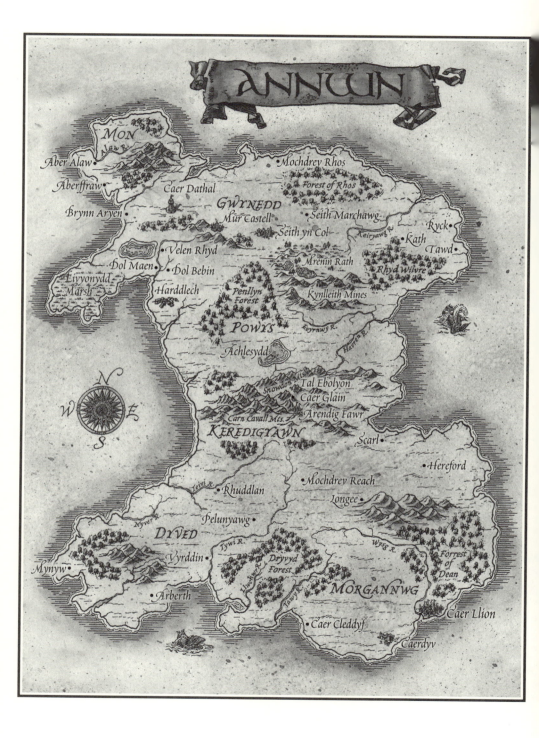

"Better to reign in Hell, than to serve in Heaven."

—John Milton, *Paradise Lost*

"We each owe a death, there are no exceptions."

—Stephen King, *The Green Mile*

The DARK THORN

Chapter 1

The rat glared with beady black eyes at the broken man's approach before scurrying away into the darkness, a lone vestige of life among the dusty bones of death.

Richard McAllister ignored the rodent's departure and probed the deep shadows of the tunnel ahead, a ghost given the substantive aspect of life. All was still. Faint light from the city filtered through squares of purple glass set in the sidewalk above, revealing the subterranean remains of unhinged wooden doors, rusted steel beams, and piles of dirt and mummified refuse. Brick from the turn of the previous century lined the building's wall on his left, its windowless panes gaping maws of mystery; on his right, the retaining wall of the city street's foundation was thick and mortared, unyielding. Dust and aged spider webs covered all.

The drip of distant water was Richard's only assurance that time had not frozen altogether.

He grew more accustomed to the weak light. It had been weeks since he had been called to the depths within which he now stood, but it was as it had been for the twelve years he had watched over it—a forgotten world by all save a few.

And those who existed in Annwn.

Wiping sweaty palms on his dirtied jeans, Richard moved forward to catch unaware what had entered his ward, his tight-laced boots barely a whisper on the uneven concrete floor. Despite wearing thermal underwear and a thick flannel shirt, a chill ran down his spine. In all the years he had guarded the city, it never got any easier.

Richard took his time down the passage, eyes seeking, body tense and ready for anything. He peered into every darkened cranny. He found nothing. Something had come through at midnight though and he would not let it pass. Couldn't. Only two had during his tenure and he regretted those failures every day of his life.

"Where are you?" Richard hissed.

No response came. The air was as dead as when he'd entered.

He had come into the city warrens through a door at the bottom of a staircase from the sidewalk above. With a word and a touch the door unlocked, giving him access where others would not go at night. The dark building embraced him as he left behind homeless wrapped in sleeping bags, the odor of stale exhaust, and watchful police. The world that had all but disappeared with Seattle's rebuilding after the Great Fire greeted him and, with the exception of an underground tour during the day, no one ventured here. The world of employer and employee, government and political party, kings, presidents, dictators, and subjects was left behind.

No such hierarchies existed beneath the streets. You were either hunter or hunted—or dead. The roles changed, even the last one at times, but they were the only ones that existed.

He gave his life to keep the two worlds separate.

He was about to turn the corner of the tunnel to continue on, navigating the debris on what used to be Seattle's sidewalks, when the echo of deep voices reached him from behind.

He cursed inwardly. In his haste, he hadn't relocked the door.

And put innocent lives in danger.

Two thin shadows separated from the gloom, hesitantly stepping into view.

"Ya down here, Rick?" White eyes gleamed from a black face

bearing a scraggly beard.

"Leave, Al," Richard growled. "You too, Walker. Now."

"Letz git outta here, man," Walker squeaked, his haggard pale face smudged with dirt, his drug addiction plainly marked upon him. "Dis place givin' me jeebies."

"Shuddup, Wakkah," Al said. "You a gurl or sumthin'?"

"You do not know what you *do*!" Richard said firmly, moving to escort them back to the surface, a cold sweat springing up on his skin.

"Whatcha doin down here then?" Al questioned, ignoring Richard and looking around. "Nuthin down here but big ole rats. Warmah though, spose."

Richard had almost reached them when the sharp scraping of claws against stone chased him through the air, followed by a low, reverberating growl. He spun, unsure of what he would find, his eyes probing the darkness ahead for the sound's maker. It wasn't evident; all appeared as it had for years. But the odor of new fog coupled with dewy grass, purple lilacs, and vibrant growing vines and trees filled the air, overwhelming the underground's century of misuse, the precursor to what he knew was coming for them.

The growl came again—nearer—painful to Richard's ears with its implications.

"Whatz dat?" Al warbled with fear, taking a step back.

"Get the *hell* out, Al!" Richard yelled, his focus fixed on the tunnel before him.

As his order echoed throughout the underground, he caught movement where the passage veered, a sooty smudge that grew impossibly large as it came into their tunnel.

"Little man thingsss," a deep voice snarled. Its features were still hidden by the gloom. "Where do you leave to?"

"Nowhere," Richard replied, planting himself between the creature and the two homeless men. "And neither are you."

A mewling hiss punctuated the air like released steam, a mocking laugh of self-assurance. Richard did not like it. The outline of the creature became more distinct as it entered the purplish light: broad shoulders and thickly muscled haunches, rounded head with stubby ears, long limbs covered in short black fur. Its large padded paws bore it silently across the floor like a prowling tiger, each languid step filled with power. Blazing from its barreled chest was a white mark like a crescent moon. The creature was alone; it was a beast that hunted alone. Richard knew what it was—had fought its kind before and had the scars to prove it—and he knew he wasn't going to have an easy time of it now either.

"What da fu—" Al whispered behind Richard. Frozen, Walker sobbed.

"Shut up, both of you!"

The cat looked past Richard with keen interest. "Brought fresssh meat, I see."

Richard kept his gaze firm. "Begone, cait sith."

"No weapon," growled the creature, grinning fangs like daggers. The cat's ears flicked at every sound as if they had minds of their own. "You are overconfident or faithless. Both see you dead."

"Return to your world," Richard ordered. "This one is no longer yours."

"And you hold no authority over me, *knight*." This last word came out as a cursing spat. "I serve—"

"A master who has no authority *here*." Richard braced his need and prepared for the inevitable. "Not any longer."

Two pinpricks of sharp crimson light flared in the beast's eyes, live embers ready to consume.

"You know not who I serve, fool."

Richard said nothing. There was nothing else to say.

But something plagued him—something not quite right. Cait siths were cunning and intelligent but rarely spoke. They preferred lethal action to words.

What was going on? Seconds ticked by.

The cat growled low then. "You are weak. I sense it."

"Find out," Richard shot back.

The cait sith's tail flicked infuriatingly as muscles bunched in knotted patterns beneath its black coat, its eyes never leaving those of the man before it. A part of Richard acceded to the creature's insult. He was weak. He knew it. The faith needed to sustain him came and went, a light bulb with a short in its electrical wiring. Now could be a time it went dark.

As if sensing his fears, the giant cat leapt into motion, a dark blur of rippling fur and terrible promise. Giant paws clawed at the concrete, its fangs bared. Gimlet eyes bore into Richard as the hulk of muscle, bone, and fury came on.

Richard took an involuntary step back but then held his ground. The tunnel with its dead air dropped away. The screams of Al and Walker—even the cat's growls—melted into a rush of white noise. The beast and the feral gleam in its eyes were all that remained.

He reached across the tenuous fabric between the two worlds, a call of heart that was his right—that had been bestowed upon him by Merle many years earlier.

Nothing happened.

He barely had time to react. The cat was immediately upon him, leaping with claws extended. Richard dove to the side, letting the beast fly past, his scream of fear mixed with defiance inhuman in his own ears. Searing pain flared to life along his left arm as he spun like a top from the slashing assault, knocking him backward and to his knees. He gritted his teeth and in a fluid motion turned to again confront his foe.

The cait sith bounded through a window in the brick building, melting into blackness.

Al and Walker cowered fifteen feet away—the former with a crazed look while the latter continued to weep.

A rumbling laugh filled the underground.

"Weak knight," his enemy mocked, gone from view. "I was told you would be. I will drag your corpse back with me through the portal as a trophy."

Richard straightened, still on his knees. He would not fail. Not while his only friends had need. Ribbons of liquid fire ran along his arm, soaking his shirt, but he barely felt the wound. A white-hot pressure arose inside, quick and sustaining, coming from the depths of his chest, mind, and even from without. It blossomed as a tingling sensation and spread outward into his limbs. The pain dulled; the shock disappeared. It was not anger or vengeance that came over him. It was the calm that came with the Yn Saith's service—giving up his own desires to protect others.

He reached back into the other world.

Where empty air had filled his hand a moment earlier, Arondight materialized into existence, the hilt and blade of the broadsword marked with ancient druidic runes, its length smooth and polished, the silver filigreed handle cool under his grip.

Magic encased him like an invisible armor and sent azure fire through his being.

Fearing the change in their friend, Al and Walker backed away.

"Don't move!" Richard screamed, regaining his feet.

It was too late.

As the homeless men passed a derelict window, the cait sith burst through the opening to kill.

With a thought, Richard struck, the runes flaring to life and blue fire lancing from Arondight. The magic hammered the creature in midair, tossing it aside like a doll before it could reach the men. It crashed to the heavy stone floor, howls of pain and anger filling the tunnel.

Back on its paws before its burning fur was extinguished, it charged Richard instead, knowing its true enemy.

Richard brought his power to bear. Blinding fire filled the passage again. The cait sith dodged it, faster and more nimble this time, and with a great leap pummeled him against the brick wall with its immensity.

Richard collided with jarring force, his eyes darkening for a second. The cait sith was on him, tearing. Gritting his teeth against the pain, Richard kept his focus on the sword before him, keeping the fire that ran along its length between himself and his foe, a protective shield of his soul's making.

The cat tried to fight through the defense even as its fur singed, the reek of burning flesh thick and pungent. Despite its ferocity, the cait sith's raking claws and fangs could not break through Richard's magic. It pressed inward, the glare from its maddened red eyes burning into him; it would not let him free and would die to see him destroyed.

But even as Richard was protected, his strength waned. The called fire took a toll on him physically and emotionaly, sapping his strength.

He had to end this.

The cat was nearly close enough to rend Richard's neck when its head suddenly jerked as if struck from behind. The creature's weight left the knight.

Behind the cait sith, Al stood, his black skin glossy with sweat, conviction raging in his eyes. In his grimy hands, a long, heavy pipe was poised for another strike.

"Get off 'im, devil," Al screamed, swinging again.

Enraged, the cat knocked the pipe from Al's hands and pounced, leaving Richard free. The homeless man's screams soon changed from anger to the anguish of one being torn apart.

It gave Richard the freedom he needed. He sent Arondight's fire raging into the back of the beast with all the magic he carried within, his anger fueling his power. It knocked the cat off the helpless man and slammed it against the thickly mortared wall.

The hollow crack of breaking bones filled the passage.

Richard was on the beast in a moment, a surge of certainty giving him strength. With the tip of his blade, he pinned the creature to the rubble at its neck but Richard knew it could not feel the heat or the blood he drew. The cat had broken vertebrae. It was no longer a threat.

Behind him, Al wept in agony, his clothing rent and bloodied.

"I'll make this quick, *cat*," Richard grated. "Why did you come through the portal?"

"Too late," the cait sith wheezed. It bled from dozens of wounds, and most of its chest and forelegs had been reduced to smoldering flesh. Its right hind leg twitched weakly. "You failed. The death rattle of your faith in the Word is beyond you. Behold."

Richard followed the cat's eyes. Where the stairway to the city above began, four furtive shapes not much larger than robins flew in the shadows around the rusted pipes of the arched ceiling. Instinctively, Richard cast fire toward them. The tiny beings rushed forward, chittering with sudden fright. Lagging behind, the last creature burst into flame as if doused in kerosene.

The rest escaped. They would be in Seattle proper within moments.

Fairies.

The cait sith had been a decoy.

"Where do the bastards *go?*" Richard rasped, twisting the blade's tip deeper into the cat's neck. "What is their intent?"

"Go to your hell, *knight*," the cat spat.

"I'm already in it," Richard growled.

He sent magic coursing down through the weapon, surging into the immobilized creature. One moment the cait sith was there; the next, it was reduced to smoldering ash and dust. It didn't make a sound. All that remained was a large blackened scorch mark on the floor.

Richard probed the surrounding warrens. Sensing nothing else had come through the gateway, he let Arondight and its fire evaporate into nothing.

He turned, feeling decades older than he had fifteen minutes earlier. His left arm ached and, remembering what the cat had done to it, he inspected his slashed checkered shirt. The claws had cut his bicep deep; his arm still bled but it was slowing, the flesh around the wounds angry and hot to the touch. He grimaced. He would take care of it as best he could for the night, and the next day visit the bookstore to have it looked at properly.

Behind him, Al clutched at his abdomen as he lay in the middle of the passage; yards away, Walker rocked back and forth, his arms crossed over his chest, reduced to the timidity of a four-year-old.

"Dat ting," Al whispered as Richard knelt. "What was—"

"It was nothing," Richard answered, peeling back the black man's clothing to view the bloodied shreds of flesh. The cat had sliced him to his ribs but he would live. "That was a brave thing you did, Al," Richard acknowledged. "I won't forget it."

"I won't evah," Al said through clenched teeth, beads of sweat gathering on his brow.

"Walker, get over here," Richard ordered.

The drug user's eyes refocused suddenly, and with palpable

uncertainty he also knelt next to Al, never deviating his gaze from Richard. He kept hugging himself. "What *are* yeh, Rick?"

"I'm your friend," Richard said sadly.

Before Al or Walker could say anything more, Richard grabbed their wrists.

Both of the men's faces slackened; their anguish and dread became Richard's. He went deep into their minds, where their memory existed. He reduced the last half hour to an alleyway knife fight with drug dealers, ordered Walker to help Al find the nearest police officer for medical attention, and demanded they never enter the underground world of Old Seattle again.

He watched the destitute men slowly leave, Al on his drug-addicted friend's shoulder, their horrific night erased and their eyes glazed as though they had just been hypnotized.

Richard wished he could be more like them.

Chapter 2

With dawn lighting overcast skies and his arm throbbing feverishly, Richard unlocked the door to Old World Tales and entered the bookstore on silent, uninvited feet.

No alarms screamed, no warnings sounded. Instead the old-fashioned bell tinkled in welcome as he closed the door. Richard adjusted to the dark; the store had not changed in his absence. Two windows displayed antique volumes, their wares cloaked behind sable blinds during closed hours. On the right, a counter supported the register; to his left, plush chairs surrounded a table bearing a chessboard. Rows of oak shelves vanished to the rear of the store, holding thousands of books. At the back of the shop, a set of stairs ventured to the owner's hidden apartment above.

An open cage hung from the ceiling. Within, Arrow Jack rested peacefully upon his perch, the merlin asleep despite the intrusion.

The familiar odor of smoked tobacco lingered, comforting and haunting at the same time.

He suddenly hated how weak he felt in returning once again.

"You should have come earlier," a familiar dry voice whispered.

Richard froze, suddenly unsure. All but invisible in the darkness, the faint outline of a figure shifted in one of the chairs. White light suddenly flared, blinding for a moment, before the table lamp revealed an old man with a short white beard clinging to a face lined by age. Icy blue eyes bore into Richard's own, the gaze weighted from a man privy to all, but who shared none himself. In his hand he cradled an unlit pipe carved with swirling runes, an affectation Richard knew was never far from its bearer.

"I couldn't come earlier, Merle," Richard stated. "Work to be done."

"I know," the other said. "You do realize, though, wounds notwithstanding, the role you fulfill cannot be done if you are dead."

A wave of intense annoyance crested within Richard.

"Maybe *you* should stop trying to control the world."

Myrddin Emrys tamped fresh tobacco from a purse into the bowl of his pipe and lit it. The odor of cherry and vanilla intensified.

"It was genuine care, Richard."

"You knew I would come here tonight."

"I suspected," Merle said, pulling on his pipe and emitting a cloud of smoke. "And I knew I must be ready. Some things are more important than a warm bed, even at this hour." He gestured at one of the chairs. "Please, Richard, long months have passed since we last spoke. Sit with me."

Richard nearly balked at the invitation; he wished to receive aid for his arm and nothing more. He instead took a seat across from the bookstore owner, a chess match in mid-play between them.

"What came through?"

"A cait sith," Richard said. "Killed it. But not before three fairies slipped by."

"Hmm, fairies," Merle said. "Mischievous creatures."

"The cait sith was a decoy."

Merle frowned. "How so?"

Richard explained what had transpired hours earlier in the ruins of Old Seattle. Merle did not interrupt but smoked his pipe dead while listening, intent on the knight and what he related.

"The war between the fey and the Word of the Church has ever been rife with passion and thoughtlessness, and each new battle begins without clear indication of who has renewed it. Even in the most peaceful of decades, one grievance gives rise to retaliation," Merle said finally, shaking his head. "The cait sith's pronouncement against the Church cannot be ignored. It is apparent the *fairies* are the aggressors here in some larger plot."

"Three fairies are barely an annoyance," Richard said. "Hell, the crows in Pioneer Square will probably *eat* them before they cause harm."

"True," Merle said. "But even the smallest creature can be a pain in the ass."

Richard had to concede the point. In his knighted tenure as one of the Yn Saith, he had seen the most innocent-seeming fey threaten lives and destroy property.

Annwn and its inhabitants could never be taken lightly.

"The failure of last night may bear fruit," Merle said. "You must pay special care to your service in the coming months. The fairies have been sent through for a specific reason—of that you can be sure—and while they are mostly impotent as you say, do not forget the persuasive magic they carry."

"It would take an idiot to fall prey to the whims of a fairy."

"Or the cu sith that slipped by you mere months ago."

Anger at mention of his failure rushed through Richard.

"Just be aware," Merle said, raising placating hands. "'Tis all I ask."

"Who could plan this?" Richard asked, cooling. "The Morrigan? Cernunnos?"

"Or quite possibly Philip."

Richard snorted. "Why would Plantagenet care? His crusade is not finished."

"The Morrigan has far more pressing quandaries to deal with than this world, namely Philip," Merle declared. He removed the ash from his pipe and began to tamp fresh leaves anew. "Cernunnos has never been interested in the war, choosing to keep the Unseelie Court in their shadows. Could be a rogue witch. Or perhaps a freed demon? Doubtful, although I suppose I should not be so quick to dismiss such notions. Whatever the case, it must be an entity with resources unimaginable to so brazenly enter this world with a plot—no matter how minor—and that fits Philip above all others."

"He *should* have died long ago."

"Yes, he should have," Merle agreed as he relit his pipe. "One more reason to be cautious. There will come a time when what he has acquired in Annwn will no longer serve. He will want more. It is in the nature of such men."

"Plantagenet would never use the fey."

"Would he not to gain an advantage?"

Richard thought it over. He had seen such men do just that. People in every aspect of life—whether in government, business, religion, or even on the streets—became corrupted upon gaining power and used whoever they could to retain it. Richard had spent years ignoring the demands of such men in the Church and in Seattle's homeless area known as the Bricks—and doubted it would ever change.

Philip Plantagenet could not be ignored.

"Have the other portals seen activity?" Richard asked.

"I do not know."

"That is not like you, Merle," the knight said, darkening.

The old man shrugged. "Regardless, it is what it is. The other knights have not reported activity to you, have they?"

"No. They haven't."

"Well then," Merle said pointedly.

"Dammit! Don't mince words, Merle," Richard growled. "You always know more than you share."

"We have had this discussion before," the store owner said flatly.

"And never finished it!"

"The past is for the dead," Merle said. "The present is for the living. That's you."

"Don't spin your philosophies to mollify me, old man," Richard spat back. "I am beyond your games, now that I know of them."

"The past can consume a soul, Richard. Do not let your own destroy you."

Richard wanted to explain that it already had.

"I know differently," Merle continued, as if he had heard the knight's thought. "You would not be so eager to attend to the portal, not so willing to put yourself in harm's way every day for years, if there were not a worthwhile spark still within your soul."

Richard shifted uncomfortably, weariness from his wound helping to rein old lingering anger. He suddenly wished he were outside on his streets. It was hard coming into Old World Tales and being confronted with painful memories; it was harder to hear that Merle still believed in him. The certainty in the other's ancient blue eyes drove a fresh spike through his heart, easily penetrating walls he had purposefully put in place. Richard took a deep breath. Despite the qualms he held for the bookstore owner and how Merle made him feel, the knight had not come to Old World Tales to fight.

"Is there anything you can do about the fairies?" Richard asked.

"Without a Heliwr? Or you running across them? No. I am powerless."

"You *aren't* powerless though," Richard admonished. "Why have you not appointed a new Heliwr?"

"It is not yet time," Merle said simply.

The knight's emotions boiled anew. "Well, when *will* it be time?"

"All things in due course, Richard," the old man answered, looking to the ceiling.

"That's not good enough!"

"*What is going on?!*"

Richard was on his feet instantly, Arondight a call away.

Where the light of the front room met the darkness of its rear, a boy of around twenty years old stood like a tensed creature ready to attack—hair wild, green eyes flashing challenge. He wore only a pair of gray sweatpants, his frame sinewy and strong. With both hands he gripped a large hardcover book like a baseball bat, ready to swing and strike if need be.

Richard relaxed. The youngster was no threat.

"What do you plan on doing with that?" Richard demanded.

The boy didn't back down, but uncertainty filled his eyes.

Then Richard saw the book's cover. A golden rose emblazoned

on the leather flashed in the weak illumination, its five petals opened and inviting readership. No title or author name could be discerned. It was an old tome but well cared for, its cover still supple despite its obvious age, its binding resewn by Merle numerous times.

Richard knew the book well.

"Did you just pick that book up?" he asked. "Or was it given to you?"

The boy frowned, a fight still written on him.

"Given."

"Relax, gentlemen. Sit, Richard," Merle said sternly. "Nothing to be on guard about here."

"Are you all right, sir?" the boy questioned.

"Bran, meet Richard."

Richard looked into the boy as he approached, surprised at what he had initially missed. Cold, untrusting eyes. A pursed, soured mouth. Distrust in every movement. Deeper within, a rod of steel existed, one tempered in hellfire most would never know.

The boy had seen hard times and they had left their mark.

"I heard raised voices . . ." Bran started.

"Go back to bed," the bookseller said. "Richard and I were discussing . . . old wounds. I am fine and you should be resting for the work on the morrow."

Bran hesitated, his eyes stubborn. Giving Richard a once over and a departing frown, he vanished into the darkness of the store.

"Have a new apprentice, eh?"

"Now, Richard—"

"Don't patronize me," the knight said curtly. "I know you better than you think. You do nothing without intention, invite no one into your life you cannot use. The boy would not be here out of charity or good will. Especially with that book. Do not believe me daft now as you once did so long ago. And do not ruin another life for your games."

Arrow Jack stirred in his cage above but remained asleep.

"Actually, Richard, the boy lived on the street—like you," the old man countered. "I have given him a place to lay his head and have put him to work. Mayor Dimes has treated the homeless terribly. You know that better than anyone. No, Bran is better off now than he was a month ago when I invited him to work the stacks."

"Riddles within riddles," Richard grumbled.

"I have never told a lie, Richard," Merle said. "Ever."

Richard gritted his teeth. Like the chess game in front of them, Richard and Merle were in the middle of an old battle, but this one with words. Chess was about misdirection and entrapment, making your opponent believe an attack was imminent from a horse rather than a conquering pawn. Merle knew how to play chess like no other, and it showed in how he related with Richard and the other knights; if the bookstore owner made a point to share information, it often had consequences far beyond any surface meaning.

"I saw the book, Merle," Richard said finally. "Don't treat me like a child."

"I am completing his education. Nothing more."

"Nothing more?" Richard scoffed.

"Just so," the bookseller answered. "Many have read *Joseph d'Arimathe* by Robert de Boron. I would think you, as an educated and scholarly man, would appreciate trying to broaden a young man's mind with the larger world about us all."

"*Joseph d'Arimathe* is a rare text few college professors assign to their graduate students, let alone to a boy his age," Richard argued. "There is only one reason you'd give him that book and it has nothing to do with a lack of quality education."

"For a learned man, you assume much," Merle stated, his eyes darkening.

Richard snorted, unable to hide his derision. No matter what Merle said, the story of Joseph of Arimathea was not common reading. Considered a minor literary work in Arthurian lore, it recounted how a man of some import and wealth named Joseph watched the centurion Longinus pierce the side of the crucified Jesus Christ with a lance to discover if He was dead. The Bible accounted blood and water spilled forth, but later de Boron wrote that Joseph caught the fluid in the cup Christ drank from at the Last Supper. With the aid of a staff given him by God, Joseph fled the Holy Land with his family, made his way to Britain where he kept safe what would become known as the Holy Grail, and helped Christianize the Misty Isles by founding Glastonbury Abbey.

Since most of it was cannibalized by later Arthurian writings, no one had reason to read *Joseph d'Arimathe*.

Except those who needed to know the history of the Heliwr.

"If your intentions toward the boy are truly only altruistic, what kind of work does he do in the stacks?"

"He helps me about the store," Merle said, shrugging. "Does what you once did."

"And look how that turned out."

Merle leaned forward, his eyes softening. "I know our past has never made our present an easy one to naviga—"

"Do not lecture," Richard interrupted sharply.

"I will," Merle insisted. "What you do not know has always hindered your judgment, especially where I am concerned. That will change with time, sooner than you think, I wager. That I know to be true, Richard McAllister."

It was Richard's turn to be quiet. He did not trust Merle, no matter his sincerity. Merle had a résumé full of completed machinations, ones that had wounded innocent people—like Richard—in their execution. The bookseller had always attempted to control events around the world for the betterment of mankind. Yet every attempt yielded casualties of the body, heart, and mind. For the old man to directly make such a bold statement about Richard's immediate future left the knight feeling more leery than ever.

When Merle began telling Richard unveiled truth, the knight would give him the benefit of the doubt. Until then, he would keep the wizened man away from his heart.

And maybe not even then.

"My own counsel will I keep," Richard said finally.

"As you should," Merle said, gaining his feet and placing his pipe back in his pocket. "Now, shall I have a look at that arm? Or should I let you keep bleeding into those filthy, stained clothes?"

Richard followed Merle into the depths of Old World Tales.

The knight didn't say a word.

Chapter 3

With the alley shadows draped about him, Richard waited like a wraith for its prey, and watched the light of Old World Tales wink out.

The boy did not immediately appear.

No one was about. The late rush hour had finished, tourists had gone, the fall sun had set long before. After Richard left the bookstore in the early morning, he had spent the day walking the dirty streets of Pioneer Square, searching for any sign of the fairies. He had found no trace; the tiny fey creatures were adept at hiding. Every flight of fallen leaves, every furtive movement the crows made, drew his attention. But no matter where he looked, the fairies were nowhere to be discovered.

It left him disconcerted but there wasn't much he could do.

Now he took a deep breath and shifted in the gloom, wincing. The arm Merle had bandaged still ached but the infection was already dissipating. The bookseller's administrations had hurt like hell, and Richard had gritted his teeth throughout them. But he knew by the next morning he would be greatly healed.

Even though it galled Richard to admit it, Merle was still deft at his craft.

Just when the knight was about to give up his vigil and head to his alley bed, the door to the darkened bookstore opened. Bran emerged into the night.

Richard stood still, watching.

The boy locked the door behind him. He wore a dark sweater and jeans, his hair as wild as in the morning. At first Bran did not move. Then with furtive eyes scanning his surroundings, he hiked a brown knapsack upon his shoulder and moved southward along First Avenue.

Richard separated from the gloom and followed.

The knight kept at a safe distance, thinking. Myrddin Emrys was a sneaky old bastard. He never made a choice that did not suit his ends. The boy had some role to play in Merle's plans, and Richard could not—would not—let another innocent become a pawn. Richard no longer cared if the old man had a well-intentioned purpose or not; the knight had witnessed firsthand what that meant and wished it on no other.

He would learn all he could about the new worker for Old World Tales.

And decide how best to progress with Merle.

Never deviating from the shadows, Richard watched Bran cut deeper into the heart of Pioneer Square. The knight hung back far enough to not be observed but close enough to keep up. He had no trouble; he knew every street, alley, and niche. The tall spire of Smith Tower lorded overhead, its white stucco gleaming, the light at its apex blazing amethyst over blocks of squat brick buildings. The night was mostly silent. As the boy avoided those leaving bars and traveled deeper into the Bricks, Richard passed bundles of sleeping bags, blankets, and flattened cardboard jammed into almost-hidden spaces. Homeless addicts, the mentally handicapped, criminals—or worse—they were the underbelly of a city that largely disdained them.

No matter the new clothing he now wore, Richard had a great deal in common with the denizens of the Bricks.

The self-contempt he carried in his heart made it so.

Within the bowels of the building he walked passed, the portal to Annwn thrummed, a reminder of his duty and why he tracked Bran. Pioneer Square was the oldest part of Seattle, but in 1889 a great fire had decimated it, giving the city council of the time an opportunity to improve it in the rebuild. It had originally been built upon tide flats that flooded twice daily; as a way to fix the problem of backed-up sewage, the council decided to sluice a nearby hill into the flats and raise Seattle above Puget Sound. The business owners could not wait for the project to finish before reconstructing their stores, resulting in thick buffering walls between the buildings and the dirt. The entrances to the businesses soon vanished beneath the modern-day street level.

The ruins below Richard's feet were what used to be the first floor of Old Seattle.

Much later, the portal to Annwn had been placed there where few ventured, a concrete defensive cap encasing the entry into this world from the fey one.

Richard exhaled sadly. He had watched over the portal for years, ever since graduate school. It felt like a lifetime ago, and the memories he carried seemed to be those of an entirely different man—one who had dreamed, hoped, and loved.

Merle had destroyed all of those things.

Bran turned down Second Avenue and passed Waterfall Garden Park, remaining in the shadows as much as possible. The boy was being careful, but for what reason? Was he on an errand of import for Merle? Or was he on his own after-hour venture?

"Come on, kid," the knight whispered. "What are you doing?"

As if hearing Richard, Bran paused, head tilted like a wolf catching a scent.

And then disappeared.

Richard blinked in shock. He pressed himself into obscurity, unsure of what had just happened.

One moment Bran had been in clear sight.

The next, the boy had vanished.

Long minutes passed.

Richard peered deeper into the gloom where Bran had last stood. Two buildings sat next to one another. No alley existed between them, no doorway he could discern. Nothing presented itself.

The knight was about to investigate when movement stopped him. Two police officers walked out of an alleyway farther down from where Bran had vanished. They were young men, new to the force, Richard wagered, placed on night shift in one of the darkest parts of Seattle. They spoke in hushed tones as they passed where Bran had been and beyond where Richard hid, laughing at some shared joke before entering the next block.

After the cops had strolled on, Bran reappeared as if by magic and traveled on.

Richard frowned, curious, and approached the spot where the boy had disappeared. A gap not a foot wide separated the two buildings, a tiny enough space for Bran to hide from the police.

Smart lad, Richard thought.

The knight followed anew, knowing to be more careful. Richard had never seen Bran in Seattle but the boy knew the Bricks well. Bran had to have come from the derelict and disenfranchised part of a different city.

The Bricks changed, became darker, the distance between the street lamps increasing even as the buildings fell into greater disrepair. Richard kept alert. Pioneer Square could hide any number of evils and become a dangerous wild creature if one was not careful once the sun had gone down. Bran did not seem to mind the change, never deviating from his direct path, and he crossed into an empty parking lot where two buildings joined to form a bordering ell.

An orange light glowed ahead, fighting against the night.

Richard slowed and angled to get a better view. At the base where the two buildings met, a small fire flickered lowly. Specters in ragged clothing huddled around it, unmoving, stealing the flaming light and its warmth. The scene was muted like a cemetery in winter.

Bran walked straight toward the group.

Richard hung back.

The boy approached without hesitancy. He was only a few feet from them before a gaunt man turned, the hint of a downtrodden soul peering from black eyes that lit up in greeting. Then the others turned—two bearded older men, a stringy-haired blonde woman with palsied hands that shook like Walker's, and a round black man—and all welcomed Bran with smiles and warm words.

Richard frowned. He did not know these particular homeless.

Bran unslung his pack, withdrew tinfoil-wrapped objects that glinted in the weak firelight, and tossed them to the group. Some of the homeless tore into their offering; a few came over and patted Bran on the back first.

It could only be one thing, Richard thought.

Food.

Bran sat with them for a few minutes, embracing their reverence and the fire, before saying his farewells and leaving. Richard sank back into his shadows; he was unwilling to confront the boy just yet. The streets were tough and he didn't know enough about Bran. The harsh conditions forced homeless men and women to form bonds of kinship out of a necessity to survive. Despite Richard choosing to live a life alone, he still relied on others like Al and Walker, people who—like him—endured through collective companionship. The knight found it curious that Bran, at such a young age, had developed such selfless responsibility for others.

It meant the lad had been on the streets a long time and knew these people well before joining Merle at Old World Tales.

Bran walked through the gloom as he had before, furtively careful. He did not return the way he had come. Richard watched him take a corner on the far side of the lot and disappear, on his way to a different part of the Bricks.

The knight was about to follow when his instincts screamed.

He froze and waited.

The itch at the back of his consciousness grew, a preternatural warning given life. The knight looked about. Nothing presented itself, but he knew better. Someone or something was watching, and the prying eyes held ill intentions. He had been in his role long enough to know the difference. But Richard did not know if it came from the fairies, the police, or another entity entirely. It did not feel alien—just angry, watchful.

He moved from his place of hiding, frowning darkly and peering into every crevice he passed as if it held a snake. Naught became apparent. He was a match for anything that might appear, but he would not be careless. To be so could lead to death. Arondight thrummed just beneath his skin, always a thought away from materializing, the ancient sword an assurance against being attacked by even the most formidable opponents.

If his life were in danger, he would have no qualms calling the blade into being.

But the night continued to hide its spy.

Bran visited two more groups, none of which Richard knew. The boy gave more food away until his pack was limply crumpled. The knight watched him, keeping his other eye on whatever pursued them from the shadows. Nothing presented itself. No matter what tracked the two, Merle's assistant seemed to be unaware of it as he aided those who were not as fortunate in life as he had become.

Richard stepped into the light to catch up to Bran, to confront the lad and notify him of the danger he was in from Merle and whatever watched from the shadows, when a sound came on the chilly air that stopped him short.

It was a chittering Richard knew well.

The knight sank deeper into the night, watching. He did not have to wait long. The hum came again, more urgent and excited this time, whirring overhead from several directions at once. Richard kept quiet. He watched to differentiate whom the buzzing creatures were after.

"Come get some," Richard whispered.

The shadows dropped like stones but not toward the knight. Instead they went for Bran, too colorful to be bats. His worst assumptions about the boy made clear, Richard scowled.

The fairies had found their prey.

Chapter 4

Bran Ardall strode through the vacant, dilapidated streets in the area he now knew as the Bricks, the city of Seattle hiding him beneath a mantle of darkness.

The damp avenues were like many others he had traveled.

Even though he had not lived in the city since before the death of his parents and had never been in the Bricks to his knowledge, Bran felt he knew Pioneer Square. Every city possessed a quarter where the less fortunate converged—an area a bit darker but available, more run down but with a soup kitchen, perceived less clean by the locals but with enough people to beg change from. The name of the city did not matter. Bran had been up and down the West Coast from place to place, but wherever he roamed he was prepared to survive because it never changed.

He hated living in such conditions.

To be homeless was hardship he wished on no other.

It was a difficult life. Food was hard to come by. The winter stole warmth and the summer scalded. Sleep was fitful and rarely replenishing. Danger strolled the streets in the form of aggressive drug dealers, meth heads, and thugs from every background, all of whom fought for imaginary turf. Thieves were rampant; liars were everywhere. Despair was a tangible entity, able to kill if one let it. Disgust from those who passed on their way to lives of importance permeated this world, gazes of contempt left unchecked.

Bran wondered when such looks would not wound.

Now nineteen years old, Bran hoped it would no longer matter. He had settled. Merle had given him an opportunity, looked past the grime of the streets, and Bran planned on taking advantage of his generosity.

Bran had been discovering what type of businesses existed in the Bricks, when he stopped in front of Old World Tales to scan the volumes in the windows. His father had loved books. As a nine-year-old, one of the last memories Bran had of him took place in his father's library, watching him pore over various tomes. Bran could not touch them; many were quite old, bound in leather with foreign letters stamped into the spines. When his father was not traveling, Bran watched him closely, fascinated by what he deemed so important.

At times, the odor of parchment and ink from that library returned to Bran from buried memory, thick in his nose, reminding him of a past before the streets, a past when he was happy and loved.

No matter what city he found himself in, the memory accosted him anew when coming across a bookstore.

While staring at the books, lost in reverie, the door had opened. A white-bearded man wearing a white collared shirt and khaki pants stood at the entrance and breathed in the warm late summer air before his eyes settled on Bran.

"Love books?" the man inquired.

"I do," Bran said, nodding. "Just something about them."

"Magic."

"Excuse me?"

"Magic," the old man repeated. "Nothing like a book, really. Nothing like a book can help a person become who they have always wanted to be. Nothing like a book can return us to our childhood. A book can hold amazing magic."

Bran looked at the man. Icy blue eyes penetrated deep, but his face held warmth and understanding.

"Looking for a way to get off the streets?"

Bran frowned. Trust was a luxury he had a hard time offering freely. Homeless rarely benefited from such unions with more respectable members of society. But there was something different about the man in the doorway, an innate goodness like his father had possessed.

"You own the store then?" Bran asked.

The other smiled. "Maybe."

"Then *maybe* I am looking to get off the streets."

"My name is Merle."

"Bran Ardall."

Merle nodded and, pulling a pipe from his pocket, welcomed Bran into the shop.

It had been a month since they met, the summer giving way to fall. Bran helped in the bookstore, dusting shelves, aiding customers, cataloguing books Merle acquired, and giving Arrow Jack—a temperamental merlin who watched with beady-eyed curiosity—occasional freedom to hunt outdoors. At times Merle also disappeared for days, leaving Bran in charge; it was that kind of trust that made Bran respect Merle all the more. The owner had one condition only—read the books he supplied to gain an education. It had been hard at first but Bran had read seven already, most about European history. It was easy work for a wage and the chance to sleep in his first bed in years. Now Bran tried to use his new life to help his few friends still on the street.

It was all he could do. As a high school dropout, he had limited options.

Bran had just begun to make his way back toward Old World Tales and an evening of reading in his warm bed, when instincts honed during his life on the street screamed like sirens.

He slowed, looking about.

The night was as secretive as before. The Alaskan Way Viaduct loomed in front of him, its double-decker highway blacker than the midnight around it. Light from the occasional streetlamp created vast puddles of dank shadow.

Danger could come from anywhere.

The face of Merle's visitor flashed in his mind—the haunted eyes, the emaciated frame. *Richard*, the bookseller had called him.

Was it that man out in the gloom, watching Bran now?

Bran didn't think so. Whatever followed him felt different. It was not the police, a thieving addict, or any of the commonplace threats that used to confront him daily. With the feeling came a stabbing hatred, one not tired like the streets, but fresh and vibrant.

A shift of gloom at the corner of his eye raised his fight reflex. Heart racing his mind, his feet picking up the pace, he probed the world.

Nothing.

The movement came again, closer, accompanied by a high-pitched whine. It came once again from two directions, and he understood with stunning clarity why he hadn't caught sight of his pursuer earlier.

It was in the air.

Bran ducked self-consciously as tiny flying shadows materialized. They were gone just as quickly, darting back into the night. Bats would buzz people, but with autumn come, the bats had gone into hibernation. When the fast-moving creatures came again, crossing over his head almost at the same time, Bran got a closer look at them—and couldn't believe his own eyes.

They definitely weren't bats.

They were something else entirely.

It was enough to set him running. The things came again, swooping in on sleek dragonfly-like wings of gossamer that shimmered in the weak light. They were each the size of a bat, but any other resemblance disappeared with their human-like arms and legs and tiny leaves sprouting in patches over cocoa-colored skin.

Panic quickening adrenaline, Bran dove behind a parked car, keeping low, watching. He was still several blocks from the safety of Old World Tales. What he had seen gave his sanity pause and his fear rein. Uncertainty pulled him in multiple directions—run, scream, fight, or all of them.

The chittering returned and he picked out intelligible words.

"Here, here, here!"
"Kill, kill, kill!"
"Feed, feed, feed!"

There were other words, but Bran couldn't make them out. The dark twittering litany increased from all directions. As they swooped past his head again, Bran bolted. Shoes pounding the sidewalk, he tore through Pioneer Square, his confusion and fright lending him strength. The buildings passed in a blur. Each breath burned in his lungs as a fire, every nuance of the world acutely emblazoned on his awareness.

He would fight until he won safety.

He was almost back to Pioneer Place Park, Old World Tales only two blocks away, when one of the creatures slammed into his head. Revulsion flashed hotly through his body. Clawing and scratching, the enraged fairy kept at him, spitting curses into his ear. He fought the thing, stumbling into an alley in a panic to get away from the creature, hissing like a cornered cat.

The fairy leapt off suddenly.

Breathing hard and worried at the next attack, Bran searched the air frantically. The fairy flew to join its brethren in the middle of the alleyway. The three floated on the air, chattering excitedly, their wings a blur and voices echoing and shrill.

Bran turned to flee down the alley—and froze. There was nowhere to go. Three brick walls prevented exit.

It was a dead end.

As Bran cursed his mistake and turned to flee, he skidded to a halt on the graveled pavement.

A creature from nightmare blocked freedom.

"What the hell?" Bran breathed.

The thing was wolf-like, its red eyes glaring malice. It was larger than a mastiff, with patches of coarse black hair like spikes growing out of dark green fur along its shoulders and hindquarters. Its hair bristled as it came deeper into the alley, the muscles beneath thick and rippling, its tail a braided mass sweeping the night like a whip. Slaver dripped from its fangs, evidence of its thoughts.

Trapped.

The fairies suddenly lost all importance.

Bran backed away. The unnatural hound's large paws were silent on the gravelly pavement as it crept toward him, its muzzle pulled back against canines. Sweat broke out in hot beads over Bran's body, infusing him with wildfire.

The only thing he cared about was escape.

The dog boomed a bark, spraying saliva everywhere.

Manically, Bran ripped the area apart, looking for a weapon or escape. Two doors with steel screens were closed and locked, the windows nearby covered in bars. A dumpster pushed against a wall wafted its damp contents. Freed bricks, wet cardboard, and a scurrying rat were his only other options.

There was nowhere to go. It was over.

The beast knew it. Eyes burning like coals in the darkness, it took slow steps forward. It grinned its intentions, pointed ears twitching in eagerness.

Dread threatened to overwhelm Bran. Alone and without a weapon, it was only a matter of time before the huge demon creature rent him asunder. Rather than cower in fear, fierce anger as he had never known rose within him like a tidal wave. It swelled until it crested, setting him in motion.

He grabbed up the only items he found at all useful. Two broken bricks.

And waited for the beast to attack.

"Get away!" he screamed, brandishing the weapons.

"No," it growled lowly.

"You speak?" Bran asked, surprise mingling with his fear.

"As thou do, child of man," the creature mocked darkly.

"What do you want?"

"Thy death," the creature salivated.

From a window ledge above, the fairies watched what transpired, goading the beast forward with squeaky voices and glee in their eyes.

"But why?!" Bran yelled, his heart pounding.

The animal stopped. The light in its eyes dimmed briefly before flaring anew.

"Because I must."

"Come then," Bran growled shakily, and raised his bricks like boxing gloves.

Ready for the coming battle, Bran's heart froze in his chest when a new shadow entered the alley behind the hound.

"Not. Another. Step!" a man's voice thundered.

Eyes narrowing, the canine spun, ears flat against its head.

"Knight shyte," it snarled. "I know thee, thy stench."

The man stepped deeper into the alley, unafraid, his hands balled into fists, his clothes ragged. He appeared the same as the last time Bran had seen him. Richard. The Old World Tales visitor from the previous night.

"Help me!" Bran shrieked.

Richard said nothing. The man was wholly fixed on the dog.

"Why protect him?" it whined. "He is nothing."

"He is innocent, cu sith," Richard said. "You are not."

"Thou knowest nothing," the dog growled low.

"The fairies above have twisted *you* to their will, cu sith," Richard shot back. "And you will not attack this boy nor survive to try."

A spark of hope entered Bran, although how a homeless man planned to defeat such an obvious threat, he didn't know.

The barrel-chested dog gave its enemy a final glance.

Then leapt at Bran.

Bran barely had time to bring his bricks to bear.

Before the hound could reach him, a powerful burst of blue light pummeled into the thing's hindquarters mid-jump, sending the beast reeling against the wall. Bricks and mortar broke free from the impact. Bran shrunk from blast. The green foe yelped shock and pain as it tumbled to the wet pavement, its fur disheveled and eyes surprised.

It was slow to regain its paws.

Bran pressed up against the rear alley wall, breathing hard.

Richard stood on the other side of the animal, a flaming sapphire sword in his right hand. His eyes burned with conviction, fixated on the struggling animal. With the fairies raucously cursing from above and shaking their wings in fury, Richard charged and brought his weapon up, driving its blade at the struggling dog, his ferocious intent unmistakable.

The canine jumped aside the last moment.

The sword cut into the wall as if it were made of paper.

With dexterity that belied any injury done to it, the dog jumped at Richard. It raged against the blue fire that accosted it, the smell of burnt hair filling the alleyway as it fought to reach the homeless man. Gritting his teeth, Richard backed away before the assault, the snapping jaws and massive paws of the cu sith returning the fight. Bran could barely see Richard, the man lost in a swirl of sapphire. The two continued to tear at each other, one with protective fire and the other, quick and shredding teeth. The time for words had passed.

The victor would be left alive and the other dead.

Bran wanted no part in it and awaited his chance at freedom.

As the minutes wore on, the dog appeared to be failing. Both hind limbs limped as it circled its foe. The man followed the hound's movements, steady in his steps, poised to take the advantage. Whatever damage had been done to him Richard did not show it. He was as indomitable as a mountain, moving fluidly, the muscles of his neck, shoulders, and arms corded knots. No growls emanated from the two enemies; with the exception of the angry chittering from the fairies above, the world had gone still.

Weakened and harried, the green beast leapt at Richard.

Richard moved like silk.

He stepped to the side with nimble ease—and rammed the blade of his flaming sword through the side of the hound's chest.

The dog gave a weak yelp as it landed limply on the ground.

It didn't move.

Richard did not stop. In one fluid motion he raised the sword above his head, hilt first, and brought it down with pure vehemence. The blade hammered through the neck of the canine and continued into the asphault of the Bricks like a knife through warm butter. Blood and gore spurted, sizzling from the heat.

His arms splattered with crimson, Richard straightened, breathing hard.

"Who are yo—"

Before Bran could finish question, Richard sent the fire of his weapon skyward.

The fairies tried to leap away. They were too slow. Screaming rage, they erupted into ash that sifted down like snowflakes.

The sword disappeared.

Richard and the carcass were all that remained.

"Bran," Richard said flatly.

"Who the hell *are* you?!" Bran questioned, suddenly angry.

The rail-thin man walked toward him, his haunted eyes growing darker with each step, his lips a severe line. Even in the darkness Bran could see Richard was tired. With pale skin and shaggy hair, the homeless man barely looked alive, a walking zombie.

"I am no one to worry about."

"No, seriously," Bran pushed. "Who the hell are you and what was that thing?"

"It *was* a mistake."

"A mistake?"

"Yes, thank you," Richard scoffed. "No more, at least." He peered down at the dead body of the cu sith. "The cu sith got lucky once. Not tonight though."

"What were those things?" Bran reiterated, pointing where the fairies had been. "And that dog thing?"

"*That* is none of your business."

"The *hell* it ain't," Bran hissed, still fueled with adrenaline. "I want answers!"

"Answers, huh?" Richard mocked. He offered his hand. "Leave the Bricks, boy. Get your things and get out of that store. You are safe, for tonight. But not from Merle."

An unidentified chill swept through Bran. Merle's visitor smiled in assurance but there was no warmth in it, the offered handshake a mechanical act. Bran sensed danger in touching the man's hand. He didn't know how he knew. He just did.

Bran rebuffed the hand.

"Why shouldn't I trust Merle?" he said instead.

"Don't come back down here—at night at least," the disheveled man said, ignoring Bran's rejection and turning to leave. "Mark my words. Stay away from that old man. He is nothing but trouble."

"Hey! Wait!" Bran shouted.

"Go back to your street friends," Richard said over his shoulder as he left the alley. "They are safer than Merle ever will be."

Leaving the dead cu sith behind, Bran chased after. "Stop, you assho . . ."

But out on the sidewalk, Richard had vanished.

Still leery of the night around him, Bran hurried the last few blocks to the bookstore. He didn't know what to think. Creatures that looked like fairies had attacked him. A giant green dog had spoken to him and then tried to kill him.

Either he had been drugged or it had really happened.

And Richard, a friend of Merle, possessed a sword that became vapor at will.

While unlocking the door, Bran peered through the night back the way he had come, angry at the fear still rushing through his veins and his inability to uncover what had truly happened.

For an instant, he thought he saw a flash of brilliant azure light.

Then darkness fell once more.

Chapter 5

Cardinal Cormac Pell O'Connor sat in the warm glow of several lamps and placed the phone receiver back onto its cradle.

He was not pleased.

Through the arched window, the silver light of the pregnant moon bathed the dome of St. Peter's Basilica and its neighboring Vatican buildings in frosty relief against a sky of diamond chips. Rome had a peaceful majesty at night that transcended its hectic daytime hours. It was rare for the Cardinal to watch the sleeping city with nothing but the tranquil view—he tended to retire early and, as so many others, rose with the sun—but it was rarer still to sleep within his Vatican City apartment and be awakened by a phone call made half a world away with such dire complications to his life.

Cormac sensed turbulent days ahead.

Picking up the receiver again, he dialed four numbers into the old phone. The click of connecting lines followed by a loud squeal met his ear.

He sighed and hung up once more.

The Cardinal leaned back in his chair, waiting and thinking, the simple red robe he had thrown on a smear like drying blood in the window's mirrored image. Rome glimmered outside but his superimposed ghost image stared back, face carved deep with wrinkles and hawkish blue eyes surrounded by heavy bags of darkness. The man within the glass looked haggard. He barely recognized his own reflection anymore, his disheveled red hair whitening, the apparition exuding weariness and grown older than he could account for.

But a fire still blazed in his heart despite the early hour, a driving need to fulfill his duty.

There just never seemed to be enough time.

Cormac turned away from the aging man, thinking how best to counter the information he now possessed. The call from the archbishop watching over the Seattle portal disturbed him; it forced his hand in a way with which he was not entirely comfortable.

The consequences of his decision could undo him and the power he had spent a lifetime acquiring.

The possible dominion likely gained though made it worth it.

While waiting for his summons to be answered, he picked up a framed photo that sat at the corner of his desk. Black and white, it displayed a smiling middle-aged man bearing a striking resemblance to Cormac, his arms wrapped around the shoulders of a woman and a girl in her teenage years. In front of the trio stood a grinning boy, his hair chaotic.

The background desert met the horizon and nothing else.

The Cardinal smiled sadly, remembering. The Middle East had been a harsh climate filled with a hardened people; Cormac had been a boy on the adventure of a lifetime, bringing the Word to new regions around the world.

The Cardinal Vicar of the Vatican barely remembered that boy.

The day to come would be like all others—filled with a mass, multiple meetings with delegates from around the world, and writing letters of import for the Church and its denizens. The Cardinal Vicar oversaw the daily spiritual operations of the diocese of Rome, a position once held by the Pope before his duties expanded to encompass the wellbeing of the greater Catholic world. Cormac was one of the youngest Cardinal Vicars in the history of the

Church, and at fifty-eight years of age, he still had several decades to bring light to the darkest places.

After twenty minutes, a sharp knock came at his office door.

Cormac straightened, letting the full authority of his mantle settle back on his shoulders before clearing his throat.

"Enter please."

The door opened and a tall man with short blonde hair strode into the room. Unlike the Vatican Swiss Guards he commanded, Finn Arne wore black pants with matching thick sweater devoid of symbols. The dead orb of his left eye peered at the Cardinal like a phantom moon. No evidence of disrupted sleep touched him. He was a captain with daily duties similar to all Swiss Guard but like the Vicar, Finn Arne had secret functions he carried out.

"Captain Arne," Cormac greeted.

The visitor inclined his head and sat in one of the offered chairs. "Your Eminence."

"It is early," the Cardinal said. "I apologize for waking you."

"The Lord knows neither sun nor moon," Finn said, his accent shadowed by Germanic. "How may I best serve you, Cardinal Vicar?"

"I have received a disheartening phone call."

"From?"

"Seattle, Washington, in the United States." Cormac folded his hands within the sleeves of his robe. "There has been a breach of the portal there."

Finn frowned. "You seem rather unworried."

"It was contained. The knight did his duty."

"I see," Finn said, smiling. "Then what has stolen me from my warm bed?"

In his many years serving the Church, Cormac had never met a more bold and coldly calculating man than Finn Arne. He was the best trained of hundreds of Swiss Guards who protected the Pope. He had a predisposition to moral flexibility, making him a useful tool. His appetite for young women every night took him, however, down an unholy path Cormac had a hard time overlooking. Finn knew this but made no apology for it.

Cormac knew the captain's warm bed had a warmer female body still in it.

"The attacked is the son of Ardall," Cormac replied instead.

The smile dropped from Finn's mouth.

"Do I have your attention now?" Cormac questioned, gratified at the captain's change.

Finn Arne sat straighter. "Does His Eminence know?"

"The Pope has other pressing matters to contend with. It is best he know nothing of this—at least, not until it is finished."

"And the others?" Finn Arne asked.

Cormac thought about the Vigilo. The other Cardinals were all devout and strong, entrusted with most Vatican secrets. The Pope led the Vigilo but the Vicar was its true leader. It oversaw the portals, prepared for any attempt by those on the other side to return from Annwn. The Church led the Yn Saith knights as best it could despite the machinations of the old wizard, but over the centuries the Vigilo had lost much of its power. Cormac breathed deep. Beyond this new situation there was an opportunity to gain a power the Church had had only once in its long past.

Including the other Cardinals could disrupt what chance Cormac had of gaining that power.

Finn Arne would know the truth, as would the Seer.

That would be it.

Cormac returned the man's icy stare. "You alone will know of this."

"The portal here is safe?"

"It is. Cardinal Seer Ramirez and Ennio Rossi protect it. If it were not safe, I would know."

"What is it you want me to do?"

"Bring young Ardall here," Cormac ordered. "This must be done discreetly and quickly."

"How did you learn of this? Certainly not from McAllister."

"From a spy in the employ of Archbishop Glenallen at my behest. I have had a certain bookstore in Seattle watched for some time now. Even if the old man avoids capture in one of his places of business, the Vigilo knows what transpires there," the Cardinal said. "I have spies in all places, Captain. Never forget that."

"Did the knight remove—"

"The boy's memory? No, he did not," Cormac grunted. "There is more going on here than what lies on the surface."

"What of McAllister, should I encounter him?"

Cormac fought the distaste in his mouth. Richard McAllister. He was one of the older knights, a man whose past haunted him. While Cormac knew that past to be a hard one, the knight had lost the capacity to rise above it, for the role he was asked to play. He was an infected wound the Church could not afford to turn gangrenous.

"He should pose no threat. Of the seven Yn Saith, he is the weakest. I doubt he has the constitution to challenge you or your men. Leave him be. His time of reckoning is coming."

"Then I will fly at once." Finn Arne pushed away from his chair.

"Sit *down*, Finn," Cormac commanded sharply.

The captain lowered back into his chair, his dead eye an agate in a harsh face.

"Be wary, Captain," the Cardinal said. "Don't run back to your *warm bed* too quickly. There are other forces along the Seattle waterfront you should be reminded of. The Kreche still lives and the old wizard is adept at calling on aid from all quarters."

"The Kreche . . ." Finn Arne scowled.

"It lives longer than most halfbreeds, nigh on ninety years now," Cormac reiterated. "It is not a factor to be taken lightly, Captain Arne, especially if Myrddin Emrys is pressed into a fight."

"I will be cautious, Your Grace."

"One more thing," the Cardinal said, leaning forward. "The Ardall boy may have a seed of some kind on his person. It will be unlike anything you have seen before. Search his home, search his person. Search anywhere you think it could be and bring it to me unchanged."

"You believe the old man has plans for the boy then."

Cormac nodded. "The wizard is mostly impotent now, but he can be . . . unorthodox."

"It will be as you ask, Your Grace."

"You have the Lord and the Church on your side," the Cardinal Vicar said. "Let no one stand in your way."

"I will not, your Eminence," Finn Arne promised.

"The jet will be ready when you arrive to the airstrip," Cormac said. "Assemble your team. The centuries-long secret of the Vigilo cannot be discovered by this boy. Be the Shield you were meant to be. Do not delay." The Cardinal paused. "And do not fail me."

Finn Arne rose, bowed, and left, fire in his lone eye.

Cormac watched him go. Finn would see the job done now that his focus was in the right place. It had been years since the Kreche had last been observed in the city of Seattle, just as it had been years since the Heliwr strode the world. If the boy had been given the seed—if the old man had surfaced to gain his new champion—then Cormac and those of the Vigilo had to be prepared to counter the wizard and be ready to take advantage of it.

But why had a fey creature from Annwn gone after the scion of Ardall?

There was some element Cormac missed.

He shook his head. With religious zealotry feverish in the Middle East and throughout the world, Cormac would do what was necessary to destroy it and other evils.

To gain the power of the Heliwr would tip the scales in favor of the Church.

And give Cormac a direct path to the papacy.

Assured Finn Arne was gone, Cormac changed into his official robes and ventured into the bowels of the papal apartments. The light of overhead lamps dimmed with every floor he left. Down he went, each descended staircase a gripe to hips and knees, until he entered tunnels devoid of any light source and had to flip on a flashlight. Chill seeped from the stone, followed by damp and mold, strengthening until he had to breathe through his mouth. The bones of the city's birth grew around him, decayed from millennia of dripping water and misuse.

Navigating the slick floor, Cormac made his way toward the catacombs of St. Peters Basilica.

Other passages met his approach, disappearing into darkness, but he ignored them. Cormac had used the tunnels for decades and knew where each led—a world forgotten by all but the academic. Now only rats lorded over the kingdom the Cardinal Vicar walked through. He hunkered within his robes for warmth. There was still a part of him that hated the indignity of traveling in such a way. Secrets were necessary, but thieves preying upon tourists above had it better. If the visit were unimportant, he'd have gone back to bed.

Instead, he traveled to discover if all *was* well with the portal.

The catacombs littered almost the entirety of the Vatican's underpinnings, a 108-acre foundation of rotten stone, labyrinthine ways, and ancient tombs lost to dust. During the time of Jesus Christ, the Roman emperors built a rounded area surrounded by tiers of seats for equestrian events; it was in this circus where Saint Peter had been martyred, crucified, buried, and where the Basilica now stood. With the foundation of the Catholic Church rooted in Vatican Hill, the city grew and erected walls around the sacred grounds.

But not solely built to keep invaders out, the Cardinal reflected.

Leaving the close tunnel behind, Cormac entered a large cavern, the walls worn stone free of markings or ornamentation. In the middle of the room an ancient well surrounded by waist-high stone circled a fathomless black hole, its bucket and thick rope newer than its wooden crank. Three other passages left the room, disappearing into darkness.

The only sound was Cormac's breathing and the rustle of his robes.

St. Peter's Basilica was directly overhead.

A chill passed through his body.

Emanating from the passage on his left was a movement of icy air like the brush of clammy fingers against skin. In the depths of the tunnel a hundred yards away, an underground branch of the Tiber River ran. There in the subterranean depths, he knew a dark veil shimmered on the river's bank, silver streaks of light flickering like a strobe light through bits of fog.

He probed the darkened tunnel, hoping to hear nothing.

"It is at peace, Cormac," a voice like aged paper said.

The Cardinal spun, reaching for the knife in the folds of his clothing.

An old man stood at the entrance of another passage, his back crooked and bowed by excessive age beneath a crimson robe, tufts of white hair keeping his ears warm and not much else. There was no expression in his dark-skinned, leathery demeanor; eyes as pale as curdled milk gave no hint to what they no longer saw.

"It is worthwhile to check from time to time, old friend," Cormac grumbled.

"It is," Cardinal Seer Donato Javier Ramirez agreed. "And nice to be visited from such an honorable guest, even one who is so ready to wield a knife." He turned his head upward and grinned. "Not only that, but to beat the sun in its rising as well. Interesting."

"You know too much in these depths for an old blind priest."

"I know much," Donato said. "It is a lonely life, but life is a rarity here. It draws me."

"It is a life well suited for the Lord's work, my old teacher," Cormac said, grasping his shrunken friend's frail hands. "You look well, Donato."

"I am," the Cardinal Seer said, squeezing firmly back. "And the portal is well, I assure yeh, Cardinal Vicar."

"Nothing from the other side?"

"The same as the day I first saw it," Cardinal Ramirez said. "But I see much, yeh understand. A problem has arisen if yeh are here. One of the other portals?"

"Seattle."

"Ahh. McAllister. Is he alive?"

"He is. And the portal is safe," Cormac answered. "There have been, however, some . . . interesting events."

"And yeh want to know if Annwn mirrors that knowledge?"

"Yes."

"Let us go then. No time to dilly-dally. Birds and worms, yeh understand?" Cardinal Ramirez cackled.

The blind man led the Cardinal Vicar through rising passages, the air growing drier with each step. The walls evolved from rough-hewn stone to delicately carved friezes; embedded holes bore sarcophagi, and wooden caskets housed undisturbed remains. Some of the world's most renowned men were buried in the catacombs, interred forever in the bowels of St. Peter's.

The Cardinal Seer did not deviate through the domain of the dead.

They eventually came to a door with elaborate scrollwork, bands of rune-encrusted iron wrapping its thick timbers. The Seer whispered a word accompanied by a tender touch and the door swung open.

Cormac stepped into warmth.

A fire blazed from a hearth in the corner of the room, casting its glow over two plush chairs and a bed pushed up against the wall. Shelves containing books of various sizes and colors lined the other walls. A pedestal sat centered in the middle of the room, holding a Bible as old as any Cormac had seen.

"Come in, come in. Make yehself comfortable."

"A humble man with a humble lifestyle. I envy you sometimes, Donato."

"I am well cared for, and I enjoy the peace here in a way those who live above me could never comprehend. When a man becomes my age, all he wishes is a warm meal, a soft bed, and well-read books."

"You still have so many of them?" The Vicar looked around. "But you're—"

"Blind? I know that, Cormac," Donato said with amusement. "Rossi reads to me when he isn't out carousing a young man's life."

Donato had been one of Cormac's earliest teachers, a man whose faith outshone his extensive scholarship. Despite his advanced age, the Cardinal Seer served the Church in a way only a handful of people had over the centuries, ultimately keeping the world safe from an unimaginable threat. The Cardinal Vicar had been one of the older man's first projects—having come into Cormac's life at its darkest hour—and it now appeared Ennio Rossi, the young knight of Rome's portal, had become the Seer's new crusade.

"Where is the knight?" Cormac asked.

"Eh, not quite sure. I have not heard him return, although with the many girlfriends he has, I doubt he had a hard time finding a place to sleep."

The Cardinal Seer moved to where black velvet draped a circular object hanging on the wall beside the bed. Reaching up with shriveled hands, Donato removed the shroud to reveal a round mirror with a wide silver frame that shone with an ethereal inner glow. Celtic runes of an ancient sect danced in the firelight; the glass of the mirror glimmered like ice. Cormac shivered. He had the impression of something dark looking back at him.

"Care to join me?" Donato asked over his shoulder. "It has been some time since yeh've used the Fionúir Mirror."

"No, to do so always makes me ill," Cormac said.

The Seer chuckled. "I'll sweep the surrounding countryside of Caer Llion. I doubt I will see anything. Philip is a weasel when it comes to privacy."

Cormac stood apart, watching. With only the snapping of the fire's embers echoing in the room, the Seer stared with blind eyes into the mirror, beyond his own image. He breathed slower and his face slackened, becoming like a statue. The white film over his eyes faded and disappeared altogether to reveal eyes so brown they were almost black.

Cormac shuddered. It was always a shock to observe it happen.

Several minutes went by. Nothing happened.

Then the depths of the mirror began to swirl, starting slowly but speeding to a pace that knotted Cormac's stomach. The silver tint of the glass rippled through the colors of the rainbow, faster and faster, until they bled together into a blinding light like the sun. Cormac was forced to shield his eyes. Just as quickly, the light deadened to opaque like slushy snow. Cormac relaxed, black dots dancing in his eyes. For reasons he never understood, the loamy odor of the forest after a hard rain filled the chamber.

Memories of his childhood in Ireland swirled through him, leaving nostalgia even as the mirror's effects disappeared.

Shaking a bit, the Cardinal Seer let out a deep, tired breath.

"The Fionúir sees much," Donato said, his eyes scanning the mirror, viewing features Cormac could not. "Looks peaceful. Caer Llion is as it has been for centuries—shrouded in mystery. The black mist surrounding the castle is as impenetrable as always. The curse tablets blind me even as I am blind here."

"Philip wants us to remain that way."

The Seer sighed. "Vanity, I suppose."

"Could be," Cormac responded. "Or we are not meant to see his activities."

"He rarely ventures outside the castle walls. I've only caught him thrice. Now that he controls most of Annwn, there is no need for him to do so. The battles are few and far between." The older man paused, musing. "Still, amazing he has been alive as long as he has. The Lord surely works in mysterious ways."

Cormac looked at the ancient Bible. "The answer for his longevity is what scares me."

Still bathed in the pale gray light, the Seer nodded. "Indeed." He leaned a bit closer to the mirror. "The rest of the countryside appears as it has for me and my predecessors—the forests are thick and healthy and the water of the rivers clean in the lowlands. The mountainous regions of the Carn Cavall and Snowdon, however, are a different tale; with her magic, the witch wears down the upper forests and all who live within them. The fey suffer. Those who remain free struggle to remain so."

"What of the countryside where the Seattle portal exits?"

The Seer took a few moments and frowned.

"Nothing. Dryvyd Forest is empty."

"Continue to keep a close watch this week. The events in Seattle warrant it, I think."

"Will yeh share with me what has transpired?"

"I cannot," Cormac said sadly. "Not even with you, old friend."

The gray light emanating from the Fionúir Mirror went blank as Donato pulled away, the shimmering glass reflecting the room once more. Eyes returning to milky blindness, the Cardinal Seer swayed on his feet for a moment before steadying. "The Lord wishes to call me soon," he said, rubbing his shrunken chest with a bony hand. He replaced the black cloth over the mirror. "It is time to find my replacement. My end comes, Cormac."

"Not too soon, I hope."

Donato allowed Cormac to guide him to the bed. "I will remain as strong as the Lord will allow me. Yeh know that."

"I do," Cormac said.

"Now leave me," the Seer said curtly, sinking into the bed. "The effects of the mirror will wear off in time. Yeh have duties to perform. The sun is rising, and that bodes well on the day."

Cormac covered his old mentor. With a warm last look, he left the Cardinal Seer to his soft bed and warm chamber.

Soft snores quickly followed him out the door.

Donato was right; the Seer was getting old. But he had fire left inside, and Cormac hoped it would see him through at least a few more years.

Rather than return to his residence, Cormac traveled upward through the catacombs of the Basilica, slipping through a secret passageway into the Sacred Grottos with its populace of dead Popes and dignified personages. He would begin his day early. By the time he reached the nave, others were already about, most administrative workers or priests, the day bustling with activity even as the sun rose. Soon Rome and St. Peter's would be flooded with visitors, and Cormac would be busy with his daily duties.

As leader of the Vigilo, it was another day of protecting the world from Annwn.

At least Captain Arne was on his way to Seattle.

A set of Swiss Guards saluted him as he passed into the vestibule, their traditional garb of blue and red stripes a blemish amidst the beautiful sculptures and paintings. He nodded to the two men politely, barely seeing them.

How had the son of Ardall gotten involved in the affairs of the Vigilo? How did the world of Annwn fit in with it?

And could the Cardinal Vicar use it to his advantage?

Cormac would ensure answers were swift in coming.

Chapter 6

"Father, don't make me do this!"

Lord Gerallt Rhys of Mochdrev Reach ignored his daughter's plea, which just infuriated Deirdre all the more. Rather than fight the implacable emotional wall her father had erected, she ended her protestations, knowing them futile. The two ascended the wide set of outdoor stairs leading from the keep to Merthyr Garden, the identical towers on either side sentinels to their approach. Lord Gerallt huffed loudly, barely able to overcome the long staircase or even continue the conversation. Deirdre wished it was not so. Her father was a proud man, as enraged as a cornered dragon when on the practice field, but over the years he had become portly, unfit for extended activity.

That included speaking when walking to the garden.

If she didn't love him so much, Deirdre would have resented him for it. After all, a ruler had to have the strength and stamina to keep his people safe.

Which should have included his daughter.

After what seemed eons to Deirdre, they gained the hilltop where it leveled off into Merthyr Garden. A lone pathway lined with roses cut through the well-kept lawn. Trees of apple, cherry, and pear stood proudly groomed while the sweetness of ripening fruit filled the air. On the outskirts, rows of herbs and vegetables yielded the food used by many of the Reach's citizens.

The place was sacred to Deirdre. The Merthyr Garden also happened to be the resting place for Lady Lorelei Rhys.

Lord Gerallt didn't stop. He continued up the gentle rise until the pathway ended. There, away from the flora of the garden and open to the sky, the Rosemere greeted them, the wide pool contained by short marble blocks, the waters allowed to flow freely down to the castle below by two troughs. It was not the focal point of the hill, though. From the middle of the Rosemere, a thick, thorny vine grew, twining around a soaring, ancient snag where rose blossoms larger than all others splashed crimson.

Nothing stirred where the ashes of her mother had been sown.

With his breath caught, Lord Gerallt stared at the Rosemere for a long time.

"Does she . . . still love me?"

It nearly broke Deirdre's heart to hear the sorrow in his voice. The anger she carried melted away.

"She does," she lied. "Although even that fades now."

Lord Gerallt looked about to weep, his gaze still fixed where the remains of his wife lay bequeathed. Deirdre felt his pain. Finally, he turned to his daughter and, with an encouraging smile that rang false, gripped her thin shoulders gently.

"You must see him," he said quietly.

"Father, you know what he plans fo—"

"Dearest, please understand," Lord Gerallt cut in. "The situation is perilous. Mochdrev Reach is on the edge of two kingdoms, in shadow, between the hammer of Caer Llion and the anvil of the Carn Cavall. Lord John Lewis Hugo merely wishes an audience today. It may mean nothing."

"He's not a lord at all," Deirdre said darkly.

"No, he isn't. He is an outworlder," he replied. "But he is also wickedly smart and absolutely ruthless."

"My wishes mean nothing then?"

"Ruling is a hardship unto itself, Deirdre. Sometimes it is harder to do what is best. You will loathe me for saying this, but *sometimes* that includes marrying into situations you may not like for the betterment of all."

"I would rather fight and die," she spat, her anger stoked anew.

Lord Gerallt frowned. "And you can speak for those innocents here, at Mochdrev Reach?"

"You rule them."

"I do. I also must protect them from harm."

"But not your daughter, apparently."

Frustration reddened Lord Gerallt's face. "You don't mean that."

Deirdre looked away and said nothing.

"It would be but a thought for that witch, the Cailleach, to extend her power here and reduce these crops to ash. Not only the Tuatha de Dannan in the Carn Cavall would suffer then. And know this: Philip Plantagenet would steal you away anyway. The Reach would lie in ruins like so many other principalities, and Caer Llion would rule our people. Only the war with the Tuatha de Dannan keeps Philip's eyes from our direction. If you challenge that and bring attention to the Reach, he will use your refusal as a reason to put a garrison of his Red Crosses here. Everything you love would be gone. Do you not see that, Deirdre?"

"You would be a king before a father?" Deirdre asked pointedly.

"A good king must be," he said. "No matter how much it pains him to say it."

Despite the panic growing inside her, the hurt that Deirdre caused her father stabbed at her heart. This was not his doing. It didn't matter though. She saw no way out of the situation that did not involve ruining either her life or those living in Mochdrev Reach.

"Regardless, Lord Hugo may not be seeking what rumors have brought here," Lord Gerallt continued. "Out of respect for you, he asked to see you where you wish. I understand why you chose the Rosemere. This place . . . it has power for you. You came here as a little girl; you seek guidance here still. If there is a place in Mochdrev Reach that may protect you, this is it. Hopefully the respect he has shown bodes well. Or . . ."

"Or what, Father?"

"I would rather not think on it."

Deirdre nodded, sadly understanding. So much depended on her. She knew it. She was Lord Gerallt's oldest child. At twenty-three years old and unwilling to embrace the duties other women of the Reach preferred, she was unmarried—not because she wanted to be alone but because she had not met the right man. She preferred to spend her time in study, on the practice field with men twice her age, or tracking in the south plains.

It was a good life, one of her devising. Now that life was being drastically altered without her leave.

Just like when her mother died.

At that moment, a man dressed in black robes bearing the silver lion crest of Caer Llion strode into Merthyr Garden, two Templar Knights in white trailing him. Deirdre had not yet met John Lewis Hugo, but she knew him instantly. First advisor to Philip Plantagenet, the outworlder walked with a commanding arrogance that set Deirdre's teeth on edge. The right side of his face was a ruined black mask, burned traumatically, melted like wax. People said it had happened while fighting one of the most powerful fey lords, when he and his High King had first entered Annwn centuries earlier.

Deirdre knew she hated him immediately.

With a word to his Red Crosses to remain behind, John Lewis Hugo approached like he had already won a great prize.

"Lord Gerallt, your garden is beautiful," John Lewis Hugo greeted, smiling as best he could, the charred right side of his face making it difficult. "I trust you have had sufficient time to speak to your daughter?"

"I have, your lordship."

"Thank you for the welcome. Your household is not lacking when it comes to pleasantries." John Lewis Hugo bowed but he did so shallowly. He then turned his eye on Deirdre. "I would imagine that has a great deal to do with you, my lady. It has been far too long. You have grown into the beauty I knew you would."

"We've met, my lord?" Deirdre asked, confused.

"When you were quite young," John Lewis Hugo said. He turned to Lord Gerallt. "Please leave us. There is a great deal to discuss and I would speak to Lady Deirdre alone."

Lord Gerallt gave his daughter a quick warning look before leaving the garden, making his way back to the castle.

"You know the reason for my coming?" John Lewis Hugo asked.

"I do."

John Lewis Hugo turned his gaze upon the Rosemere, hands behind his back. She didn't like the way he looked at the resting place of her mother, a mixture of interest and irritation. It was a long time before he spoke.

"I understand you communicate with your mother here," he said finally.

"I come to be near her sometimes, yes."

"Then you don't speak to her as we are speaking now?"

Deirdre tried to keep calm. Philip and his advisor had invaded Annwn with one intention: destroy the Tuatha de Dannan with sword and flame, and bring their one god to fill the void. To display interest in fey, magic, or anything associated with the Celtic religions of old would be a death penalty. That included speaking to witches long dead.

"Pay no mind," he said simply, noticing her apprehension. "The High King may wish to see his father's crusade fulfilled and his Templar Knights spread to all corners of Annwn, but I am far more pragmatic. How you choose to spend your time in worship is your affair. If that includes speaking to your mother here in this magical pool, so be it."

Deirdre knew she could not trust him. Like a snake, he was capable of striking without a moment's notice.

"Mochdrev Reach is a great city, an important castle," John Lewis Hugo said, his eyes—one blue and the other milky white but alive—staring up at the tall towers. "Once, the Reach did not exist—this was just a lone hill with a single oak at its pinnacle lording over these lands. A battle found its way to the plains south of here, as they have everywhere in Annwn, elves against humans. These elves fought valiantly but were continuously pushed through the plains to these hills. Here they stood, through trickery. To create a diversion and save their people, two elven brothers lured the human army up a southern draw while their brethren fled. The brothers fought side by side at the top of this very hill, unyielding. They slew hundreds, alone, buying the time their nation needed, before a sea of cowardly arrows cut them down.

"It is said the hillside wept at their courage and sacrifice. This spring is the result of that day, their blood the origin of the ancient rose bush."

"I know the history of my own people," Deirdre said.

"You know your people killed those brothers then," John Lewis Hugo said, turning toward her with a coldness she had not seen in another before. "Outright. And settled these hills to form the Reach?" He paused, the darkness suddenly gone. "We share a great deal in common, my lady. We both have fought the fey. We hail from the same shores. True, your ancestors were the first to Annwn, and settled here long before the High King and I arrived centuries ago. You are part of a proud history here in Annwn, and a member of a prouder family. It is the High King's wish to meld our two peoples into one, uniting against the common enemy."

There it was. Deirdre didn't know what to say. John Lewis Hugo had worked in the marriage proposal so smoothly she hadn't seen it coming.

"You mean marriage," she said. "To drag us into war."

John Lewis Hugo stood stoic. "You must consider that. Although I sincerely doubt the High King would bring his might against fellow kinsmen."

"I simply do not understand why anyone must war with another."

"It is in the very heart of man to wage war, Lady Deirdre," John Lewis Hugo said. "It is unchangeable. While I do not care for the deities those of Annwn pray to, I do care about the overall outcome of Annwn's future. That future has Caer Llion as the capital of the whole continent, with the High King's Lord at its head."

"He isn't my Lord," she pointed out.

"Indeed," John Lewis Hugo said. "Your people fled the Misty Isles before the Christian God drove the gods of old from those shores. Still, it is time for the High King to marry, to have a family, to produce an heir. It is a great honor that he looks upon you with favor—and it would be folly for Mochdrev Reach to ignore him."

The veiled threat shot dread directly into Deirdre's heart.

"There are many more worthy women," she countered. "Women who would be better matches for Philip Plantagenet."

John Lewis Hugo smiled. "Do not be so quick to dismiss yourself, Lady Deirdre. There is a strength that shines within you like the summer sun. Redheads are powerful creatures, always have been. They command respect from men and women alike. It has ever been so with the Celtic people. Even the Tuatha de Dannan respect a redheaded human. That makes you unique." The charred face came closer to her own. "Desirable even. To some."

With his hot breath on her cheek, madness filled Deirdre. The High King's advisor did not stop there. John Lewis Hugo traced a long, cool finger down the side of her cheek, his touch alien. The desire to flee, to fight, to do anything that removed the inappropriate caress overcame Deirdre, but she was rooted in place, unable to move. Panic set in. Deep in his eyes, madness flickered. He did not want her, not in a sexual way. He enjoyed making her fear; he enjoyed watching that fear manifest and seeing how she reacted to it. Deirdre understood immediately that John Lewis Hugo was far darker and more evil than anyone she had ever encountered.

Just when she thought she would break the spell and lash out, the High King's advisor withdrew.

"Indeed, you *are* powerful," he said smoothly as if nothing had happened. "In one month you will present yourself to the court at Caer Llion. Bring whatever retinue you deem fit for a queen of Annwn. I am pleased we understand one another and I hope to serve you further. I wish you a good day, Lady Deirdre."

At that, John Lewis Hugo turned on his heels and left Merthyr Garden, the two Templar Knights following him back to the castle keep and likely returning to Caer Llion.

Trembling with wrath, Deirdre watched them go. It was as she had feared. Philip Plantagenet wished for a bride, and for reasons she could not fathom, he had chosen her. It would not happen. Not if she had her way. Deirdre had never met the High King, but if he was anything like John Lewis Hugo, she wanted no part of him.

The fire she had banked for her father's benefit roared back to life, lending her strength. Deirdre needed advice from someone she could trust.

She needed ages of wisdom.

Deirdre stepped to the edge of the Rosemere, eyeing the ancient rose bush, and began to hum. It was a rich melody, one of the oldest, a call for the dead. She anchored herself to Annwn, drawing on its life as well as that within her. She grew weak, the life force she possessed being slowly drained to conduct the magic, but she stood resolute as she had so many times before.

Her request did not take long to be answered. The Merthyr Garden fell away. So too did the azure of the sky and the crimson of the rose blooms, the world reduced to shades of gray.

Instead the water of the Rosemere flickered and swirled, sluggish at first but picking up speed as it circled the dead tree at its center.

Then the world sunk in on itself, absorbing the light of the day and inversing it until a shape as dark as midnight hovered on the surface of the water. It stood proud as it rose into the air, a true form coalescing into a woman draped in folds of a black cloak, floating as though in a breeze. A cowl tried to hold red locks of long hair from a white chiseled countenance, but strands of it flitted wildly across her mien. It was a beautiful face, one Deirdre knew well. As she breathed in the odor of rotting mulch and darkness, the gray eyes of the shade peered at her.

—Child—

The voice was inside her head, spectral, the sweetness Deirdre remembered replaced by dryness. Even now, after so long, a part of her yearned to step forward into the pool and embrace the woman, but she held her ground, knowing the danger.

"I am here, Mother," she said.

—You have the stink of corruption on your flesh—

Deirdre didn't know what her mother meant, then remembered John Lewis Hugo touching her cheek—the slithering carress as it crept over her skin—and felt revulsion all over again.

"Yes, I do."

—You have been kept alive to enact great harm—

The shade's emotionless voice penetrated deep into Deirdre.

"What do you mean, Mother?"

—What would you know of me, Child—

Deirdre paused, unsure how to proceed. In death, there were events hidden from her mother, both past and future. Never had she pronounced such a dire prediction. The dead also rarely spoke linearly—a question could lead to a wholly different avenue of discussion—the riddles maddening to unravel.

"Who wants me alive? What harm?" Deirdre pleaded anyway. "Mother, do you mean Philip Plantagenet? John Lewis Hugo? Who?"

—A lord of shadows is in the world once more, stirring evil—

"A lord? I don't understand!"

—I know not, Child. It is not for me to know. Or you—

Deirdre frowned, thinking.

"What am I to do about this marriage proposal?" she asked instead, hoping for the help she had come for.

—You will love, Child. It will be the love of your life—

She almost laughed. "With Philip Plantagenet?"

—The lives of the Outworlder King and my Child are intertwined like vines, to be cut at the harvest—

"No . . . that cannot be, Mother!"

The Rosemere hissed at her vehemence. The dead did not like being angered once called. Deirdre stood her ground. They could not harm her, not unless she disengaged from the pool or stepped within its boundaries to enter their world.

Deirdre took a deep breath.

"I refuse to believe I will be with Plantagenet," she said. "That is not my destiny."

—A destiny is dark until the present sheds light on it—

"Mother, what am I to do?"

—Nothing you desire will come to be. Only what you fear will come to pass—

"You are saying I cannot prevent what comes?"

—Look here. Death—

In her mind's eye, she saw a vision. Smoke blew across a battlefield littered with bodies of the dead and dying. The scene possessed no sound, but Deirdre imagined wailing on the air. Bloodied twisted creatures milled among bodies of men and Tuatha de Dannan alike, their limbs unnaturally angled by savage intention. She was in the battle, being pulled away from a fire that was being swallowed by darkness. Then an unknown man cradled her, but his attention was drawn to the sky where a brilliant fire burned the heavens.

—Death—

The vision changed.

Darkness surrounded her, suffocating her, until she realized she was in the depths of a great mountain honeycombed with labyrinthine passageways. She was not alone, though. A creature stalked her, its baleful red eyes fixed on her but also not fixed on her, its body as insubstantial as smoke but deadlier than any beast Deirdre had encountered or read about. She ran but it chased, impossibly fast, until the very stone walls collapsed and true night suffocated her scream.

—Death—

It changed again.

In warrens beneath a domed castle filled with art more ornate than any she had ever seen, caskets in walls housed the dead. The dank smell of ages mixed with the sweet odor of nearby water, where magic coated the air. Two old men wearing priestly robes wielded swords to defend all they knew. Whether they survived the Templar Knights attempting to kill them or if they failed, she knew it did not matter; the other world burned, and it spread into Annwn, consuming Mochdrev Reach, her people, and all she loved.

Unbidden tears stung Deirdre's eyes.

The vision blackened to nothing. Deirdre opened her eyes and looked at her mother as she peered back. Her gray orbs seemed to be mirrors into Deirdre's soul.

"What does this all mean?" she asked, trembling.

—My time has come. Follow your heart. No matter your choice, Child—

"No, Mother. Don't go."

Deirdre wanted to reach out. The apparition instead slipped back into the Rosemere, her figure disintegrating like ash in water. The pool stopped churning. The smell of decaying life dissipated. As the day brightened about her, the buzzing of bees and the songs of birds in the Merthyr Garden returned with stunning clarity.

With sunshine warming her, Deirdre stood staring where the shade of her mother had vanished. It happened just that quickly. She already missed her. She also knew little from the meeting. The riddles her mother spoke rarely came to fruition the way Deirdre expected, even if there was a bit of truth in them. More questions swirled inside her than when she had called the shade. With whom would Deirdre fall in love? How did the false king play into the future of her life? And how would the visions she had been shown come—or not come—to pass?

She had no answers.

The one thing she did know was that the life she knew was drastically changing, and there was nothing she could do about it.

"I thought you would be talking to her *forever!*"

Deirdre spun.

Sitting on the soft blossom petals of a nearby rose bush, Snedeker stared at her, stick arms crossed, a frown tugging at his wood and moss features, his gossamer wings irritably fluttering.

"You should not be here!" Deirdre hissed, angry all over again. "I told you to stay out of sight until the sun set. If John Lewis Hugo caught you here—"

"Yes, yes, your father would feed me to the cat," Snedeker opined. "What he doesn't know is I'd kill that cat with three quic—"

"And kill the rest of us!"

"Boghoggery, settle down, Red!" Snedeker grumped, launching from the rose blossom and flying toward her. "I won't *actually* kill the cat."

"Wait right there," Deirdre said, observing her fairy friend closer. "You are entirely too happy. And your little pack looks to be a burden. What do you have?"

Guilt crossed the fairy's wooden features.

"Nothing!"

"You lie," she said. "I can always tell when you lie."

"Are you sure you aren't a witch?"

"Out with it!"

Annoyance crossing his face, Snedeker pulled a ruby the size of a thumbnail from the sack on his back.

"Where did you get that?!"

"From the coach that brought that pompous burned ass! It was encrusted with them and other jewels." He hefted the ruby. "This one was mostly loose anyway, Red. Mostly. Isn't it beautiful, how the sun . . ."

Deirdre ignored the rest of what the fairy said. It was the only way she kept from throttling him. If the High King knew a member of the Tuatha de Dannan was within the Reach, it would spell certain doom for them all. She might be bringing war to her father's kingdom, but at least it would be on her terms and not that of a thieving fairy.

"You must put it back. Now."

"I think not," the fairy said quickly. "They are leaving. And besides, I have merely borrowed it."

"Knowing you, you've borrowed it until its owners are long dead and dust."

"Just so."

Deirdre sighed. "The damage is done. Give it to a family with many children in town. Don't let them see you. By giving it away, I hope you learn a lesson."

The fairy didn't budge, hovering in midair.

"Snedeker . . ."

"All right, all right. Swampmutton."

As the fairy flew away, his shoulders a bit slumped, Deirdre looked up at the mountains that grew at Mochdrev Reach's northern border and thought about what the shade of her mother had said. The line of jagged peaks known as the Snowdon burst from the older, rounded hills of the Carn Cavall, not unlike the emotions that swirled within her. Her mother had been a powerful witch before she died; she knew much of what was to come. The vision of the Tuatha de Dannan dead on the battlefield could mean only one thing—the fey had chosen to fight Caer Llion. And the man Deirdre would fall in love with? It couldn't be Philip Plantagenet. But who? Another outworlder? The man holding her in the vision? And more importantly: when would this come to pass?

It no longer mattered, she thought. And it no longer mattered what the High King of Annwn, his advisor, or even her father wished. Deirdre knew she would rather die than succumb to a boot heel, particularly one from Caer Llion.

Because the Tuatha de Dannan felt the same.

Deirdre turned back to the Rosemere. Its waters were at peace but she was not. Those who knew her knew that when her mind was made up, nothing would change it. Stubborn like an ox bull, her father often said. He was right. No one was going to tell her what to do, especially a man who had proclaimed himself High King long ago and would use that power to steal Deirdre away from all she knew and loved.

She would not let it happen—come what may for Mochdrev Reach and those who lived within its walls. She had to stand and fight, no matter the consequences.

No matter where that stand would take her.

Deirdre left to find her father.

Lord Gerallt would be the first to know.

Chapter 7

With a cascade thundering behind him, Richard sat on the edge of the Waterfall Garden Park pool in contemplative reflection, waiting for the tourists and vagabonds to leave.

It would not be long now.

Mist from the falls swirled at his back, icy and persistent, but he barely felt it. The events of the previous night played over and over in his mind, lead chains weighing on him. The fairies from the portal had attacked Merle's assistant, cajoling a cu sith into dastardly service. If Richard had not been there, Bran would have been killed. It had been the obvious culmination of an orchestrated plan, one set into motion specifically against the boy for reasons the knight could not fathom.

Richard had intervened and in the process had exposed his secret.

Now the boy knew about Arondight.

Why had the attack come against this new bookseller of Old World Tales? Had Richard made the right choice in not removing his memory?

The knight exhaled angrily. He only had an answer for the

latter concern. It was necessary, of course. Bran retaining his memory meant the only ally Richard had in convincing the boy that Merle was a danger and not to be trusted.

Nearby the portal throbbed, a chilly reminder he was right.

The knight pulled his coat close. He knew one thing.

Bran was lucky to be alive.

As the cold wind captured vagrant leaves and sent them spinning outside the iron-barred walls of the park, a man wearing a black overcoat with collar held tight and a broad-rimmed hat entered the secluded Waterfall Garden and waited in the shadows. Richard ground his boot into the concrete, annoyed. He knew the man, hated him. Richard also knew the Churchman had found him for a reason and that reason went beyond coincidence.

Once the last straggler left the park, the man approached, his thick-fingered hands folded over a paunch that rarely missed a meal.

"Archbishop Louis Glenallen, find another soul to torment," Richard said darkly.

Righteousness peered at the knight. "How unfortunate you yet live, McAllister."

"Why are you here?"

"I know of the attack," the Churchman said. "I know you failed. Again."

"Here to gauge my faith, huh?" Richard questioned. "Want to offer me some absolution, some penance, in your hallowed box of confession?"

"Not at all," Archbishop Glenallen replied. "I know, just as you do, that a lifetime of confession and Hail Marys could never erase the pain that erodes *your* soul. No, I'm not here to offer you salvation. I want to know how the attack happened, and why you didn't do your job?"

"Your Church no longer holds power over the Yn Saith."

"Ah yes," the archbishop snorted. "The covenant the sorcerer made with the Seven. A more foolish man this world has never known. The truth is, the Church does what he, and you apparently, can no longer do—protect the world from evil."

"Your arrogance and ignorance is startling."

"Is it, now? There was once a young man," Archbishop Glenallen began. "He carried right in his heart, accepted Arondight—the great sword forged by Govannon and later discovered by Lancelot of the Lake—and vouched with blood the safety of a city, of an entire world. This young man had a soul that was old. But he was idealistic and desired to have all that the world offered. Pride became his enemy. Going against the advice of his elders, against the wisdom of ages wrought, he married. He thought he could have it all—the duty that God had bestowed *as well as* the earthly treasures of the heart.

"Some might call that arrogant, McAllister. Some might say that man's presumption is a grave ignorance of and above itself."

"That man was a fool," Richard said coldly. "And no longer exists."

"You are right. He is lost." The archbishop shook his head. "God only forgives those who repent their wrath, their sins."

Richard said nothing. There was nothing *to* say.

"Nevertheless," the archbishop continued. "There is no reason why we shouldn't work together as needed now. Our roles are the same; we merely go about it differently. I maintain a large diocese with thousands of souls, but I am also responsible to the Vigilo for the portal, just as you are. I have no ulterior motive, no reason to lie to you. There is far too much evil in the hearts of men, but think how evil would spread if God-fearing people realized they shared the world with myth and fairy tale. That mankind was not alone and creatures not mentioned in the Bible existed. The Church and its knights *can* work together, as long as there is need. Right now, I believe there is such a need; your actions have made it so, I think."

"You chastise me, bring up painful memories, and then you ask for my help?" Richard snapped with disgust. "Do you know how fork-tongued you are?"

Archbishop Glenallen darkened. "As usual, you have *no* idea to whom you are speaking. I know a boy was attacked. And not only that, but you did not remove his memory of it. I want to know the why of it."

Richard cursed silently.

"Yes, that's right. I know fairies called upon the cu sith you failed in stopping several months ago," the archbishop said. "Why did they attack the boy though? Who is he?"

"I don't know," Richard admitted. He stood and jammed his hands in his pockets. "He was walking in Pioneer Square feeding his homeless friends. He is safe. That's all I know. The creatures are dead. I missed my chance to alter the boy's memories. What else is there to know?"

"The question is how did you know he was in danger?"

The knight darkened.

"Say nothing more," Archbishop Glenallen said. "I know you were following him."

"Spies, eh? I suppose you have already notified your superiors."

"I have."

Richard wanted to beat the man within an inch of his life. With the Church conniving, it would complicate his own efforts to discover why Merle had chosen Bran and for what end.

"Does that disappoint you, *knight*?" the fat man asked.

"Only you do, Glenallen."

"Hmm," Archbishop Glenallen mumbled. "And what of the wizard? Does he have any ideas about this?"

"I have not spoken to him of it," Richard said. "Or with the others. I have not put as much stock in the attack as you have, apparently."

"You would not have followed him if you did not."

"I have no allegiance to the Church, but don't believe for one second that it means I am in league with Myrddin Emrys. The man is a liar, a cheat, and has brought me nothing but pain."

"You are his puppet."

"To say I hate him would be a vast understatement," Richard pointed out.

"And yet the boy returned to Old World Tales. Clearly he does not feel the same way," the archbishop said, smiling without humor. "That is problematic, don't you think, McAllister?"

"Leave me in peace, Glenallen," Richard sighed. "I tire of you."

"Whenever Annwn reaches into this world, there is a reason behind it," Archbishop Glenallen continued. "The Church demands that you fulfill your duty to its utmost. It's why God chose you. Mankind deserves to be kept safe."

"Even from Church charlatans?" Richard chided. "The blood on Church hands reddens even your own." The archbishop immediately turned a deep, explosive shade, but the knight held up his hand. "What? Are you going to have me killed if I don't do what I am told? When will the Church realize it no longer has authority over the portals? Over the Seven? Over me?"

The imposing man stepped close to Richard, fire in his eyes.

"What happens when a man not only forsakes his Church but that of God as well, McAllister?" He leaned in closer. "What if it happens to a knight of the Vigilo? How long do you think such a knight has to live? The Church has no need to dispose of you; the fey coming through the portal and your lack of faith will do it as assuredly as it did your own wife."

The point drove into Richard like a stake. Fury came crashing over him, urgent in its need. It didn't matter if killing the archbishop would reduce the knight to everything he hated about the Church—Richard had much to repent for, and what was one more thing?—and Louis Glenallen was a stain on the very tapestry the knight defended every day of his life. Glenallen would not be missed in the larger scheme of the world, and Richard would be purged from his duties by death.

Arondight was a will away from fierily materializing.

The archbishop saw his danger and took several steps backward. "Regardless of what transpired last night, your faithlessness could get us all killed," Archbishop Glenallen snarled, but fear had overtaken his beady eyes. "Fulfill your role, and make it not so."

Before Richard could reply, the Churchman fled.

Louis Glenallen vanished into the streets, undoubtedly returning to his safe haven of St. James Cathedral. The white stone twin towers of the Church's Seattle bastion would not hold the answers the knight sought. They would have to come from elsewhere.

Richard began removing his shoes and socks.

He knew where to begin looking.

Finally with no one around, Richard placed his naked feet into the Waterfall Garden pool and closed his eyes. He shivered involuntarily, the icy water stabbing him like hundreds of needles. It was always difficult in the colder months. As the eddying cold numbed his toes, the knight focused on the water—its feel, its fluidity, and its ability to transform all things. It was the molecule of life and change, and it reveled in its freedom to roam. Richard joined with it, the water cool on his soul. For a moment he was released from his guilt, his inner turmoil, his inadequacy, and Richard realized sadly that he had always felt this free twelve years earlier.

Traveling with the water, the pounding of the waterfall ceased. The world darkened.

He concentrated on Arondight—not to call forth the fabled sword, but to be drawn to it.

The disorientation ended suddenly with birdsong, the sweet scent of growing grass, and the warmth of the sun on his face.

Richard opened his eyes to Annwn.

The decadence of Seattle and its claustrophobic buildings disappeared, replaced by a small isle in the middle of an expansive lake bordered by verdant green hills. In the distance, the jagged peaks of the Snowdon loomed. Richard sat in an emerald carpet, the grass and clover tickling his exposed feet, a dream made real. Rhododendrons, lilacs, pennyroyal, and other bushes grew wild and free amidst moss-covered rocks. The sweet smell of virgin nature coupled with air not of the sea intoxicated the knight, and he looked out over the day in silent thanks, the rippling water of the lake glimmering like sapphires under the sun.

The memory of autumn fading, Richard sat up and glanced around.

At the apex of the isle the remnants of a fortress rose against the sky, its stone crumbling from age and neglect. Much of the inner courtyard and keep had long since fallen into itself, leaving the walls and towers to stand alone. Richard knew not who had built the castle, but it had existed for centuries. Along the circumference of the shore a barricade of crooked briars grew, the vines thick like tree trunks. Thorns as large as axe heads protruded from them, deadly and sharp, glistening with a greenish venom he was told would kill on contact. If anyone could pass the Aughisky—the loch fey beast warding the isle—the wall would end any access.

The only other prominent feature of the island grew near the knight—an oak tree as large as the castle with leaves as golden as the dawn.

Richard gained his feet and walked up the hill.

The oak ruled the whole of the isle like a lord. It was ancient and knotted with branches reaching in all directions, the trunk massive and its roots buried deep. Finches and other birds darted among the foliage and ferns beneath, singing their song to the day, while insects lazily drifted on the air.

Despite knowing the tree was as deadly as the wall of thorns, Richard wanted nothing more than to lie down in its serene shadows and sleep forever.

Circling the tree, seven bluestone blocks erupted from the earth like rib bones, each chiseled with druidic symbols. On the one closest him, Arondight glittered, the sword resting point-down on the diagonal face, its runes winking at Richard as if in greeting. The other blocks also bore weapons as unique as the one Merle had given Richard at his knighthood—a battleaxe, war hammer, heavy gauntlets, dagger, spear, and diamond-shaped mace.

The earth beneath his bare feet thrummed with power as he neared the great tree. At his approach, the roots and branches tensed, ready to protect the relics on the rune-written blocks.

"Achlesydd," Richard soothed, calling the tree by name.

The oak relaxed, recognizing him as a Knight of the Yn Saith.

"What's on your mind, Rick?"

Richard turned. A sandy-haired man with finely chiseled cheekbones and an average build stood nearby, his feet as bare as Richard's own, his blue eyes inquisitive. He wore denim jeans and a coat that offered protection from elements not present in Annwn.

"Alastair," Richard greeted. "It's been many months. You look well."

A smile brought life to Alastair Finley. "Life is good. Quiet.

The family grows and I've gotten quite a lot of research done the last few months. How are you?"

"I am here," Richard said simply. "The family is well then?"

"Yeah, all is good," Alastair replied, looking away. "The kids grow like weeds. Mark actually likes school and Maddy is able to stand now."

The knight of the Betws-y-coed fairy glen in Wales lived a peaceful life with wife and children, his portal one of the oldest and relatively inactive due to its odd entrance placement in Annwn. He was a good man, fair in all things. In another lifetime the two knights would likely have been close friends, their scholarly background a common bond. But Alastair enjoyed a life the other knights chose not to embrace and one Richard had lost, leaving an unbridgeable gulf between them.

A ghostly shimmer formed a few feet away, solidifying into a short, heavyset Italian man who hugged his barrel chest closely as if trying to stay warm.

"Damnable snow and ice," he bellowed. "I *hate* Chicago in the fall and winter."

"Sal, you hate everything," Alastair said.

"You're tellin' me," Sal grumbled. "What the *hell* did I have to traipse outside in this weather for?"

The other two men ignored Sal.

Soon other forms coalesced in the afternoon sunshine. In all, six men and one woman stood on the isle near the grandiose oak—the summoning bringing them from diverse countries, different cultures, and unique backgrounds.

They were the Knights of the Yn Saith.

"Thank you all for coming," Richard said. "I know during this time of year it is a test of will to answer a calling."

"We know you would not do so if it were not necessary, Richard," James St. Albans said, his British accent thick. "No need to apologize."

"I find this meeting a little odd. The Paris portal has been quiet," Arnaud Lovel said. Fat pushed at the boundaries of the Parisian's clothing. "I've not had reason to leave my home in many months."

"That's apparent," Sal grunted.

Arnaud ignored the insult. Richard shared all the details of the previous night—the cait sith's entry, the escape of the fairies, the cu sith and its attack on Bran, the visit by Archbishop Glenallen, and how Rome was aware of everything that had transpired.

"The cait sith mentioned the fairies being the end of the Word," Richard finished.

"A Pope can die," Danica Roderick said, her sleek blonde hair almost white in the sunlight. "But it does not end the Word. Or the Church."

"It would have to be something else," Richard agreed.

"Whatever it is, it isn't affecting the rest of us," James said, his long-fingered hand stroking his short goatee. "Like Arnaud said. The gateway in London has been peaceful for at least a year."

"The same in Vienna, Danica? Rome, Ennio? Sal?"

Everyone nodded agreement.

Richard frowned. Ever since his knighthood, creatures of varying sizes, shapes, intellects, and purposes had come through, an unbroken stream of dissent. It seemed he was the only knight having to deal with it.

"The calm before the storm," Richard murmured. "Testing me."

"Huh?" Sal asked.

"Lulling us into false security."

"Smokin' something, more the like, Rick," Sal grunted.

"It is our role to keep this world safe, Sal," Richard growled, suddenly angry. "It requires looking at all possibilities. Or perhaps you aren't capable of doing that, eh?"

"Look," the Chicago knight snapped. "If you had stopped the cu sith from coming through in the first place, none of this would be happening!"

"Sal!" Danica shouted.

"No. He's right," Richard said. "I am the weak link among us, no matter if I like it or agree with it."

"That's right," Sal rumbled.

The other knights glared at Sal. He stared back unperturbed.

"If the Lord of Annwn moves against one of the portals, it

makes sense for it to be against the weakest link," James said. "No offense, Richard."

"Not only that," Arnaud added. "But how does this boy figure in?"

"He was attacked. That much is clear," James said. "The question is who in Annwn wants him dead? Wants Richard possibly dead? And why?"

"Without the Heliwr, finding answers is difficult," Danica noted.

"Only one of us may know more," Alistair said, glancing at Ennio Rossi, the youngest of the knights.

"Well, pup? Got anything to add?" Sal asked.

"You've been quiet, Ennio," Danica prodded.

Tall and handsome, Ennio shrank inwardly like a mouse confronted by cats.

"I know you have friends in the Vatican, Ennio," Richard assured. "And I am sure even a few are good people. But Church leaders are like all in established hierarchies—they look for advantage and use it to gain more power. At *our* expense. You will not be betraying anyone by sharing what you know."

"The Church has taken a keen interest in what happened," Ennio said finally. The other knights nodded encouragement. "I know the Vigilo is aware of what took place in Seattle. The Cardinal Seer said as much when he warned me to watch the gateway with extra attention."

"The Cardinal Seer," Sal said. "If he knows, then the Cardinal Vicar knows . . . possibly even the Pope. O'Connor and the Seer are as thick as thieves."

"The Vicar is a fair man," Ennio blurted.

"No, Ennio," Alastair said. "The Cardinal Vicar sees the position of Pontiff near his grasp and seeks any advantage to gain it. If he knows more about what is going on, he's going to play the cards the best way to ensure he benefits from it. Have no doubt about that. It is important for us to know what he knows to better gauge our response."

Ennio was quiet, unmoved.

"Come on!" Sal insisted "We don't have all day."

"The Cardinal Vicar knows," Ennio said simply.

"Go on," Richard pressed.

"Cardinal O'Conner entered the catacombs early yesterday morning," Ennio added. "He spoke with the Cardinal Seer."

"That is interesting," James murmured. "A man who oversees the entire diocese of Rome with very little time *making* the time to walk amidst the dank caverns and bone-ridden catacombs of antiquity. Must have been quite a reason for him to do that."

"He rarely visits the portal or the Seer," Ennio conceded.

"He needed the Seer's guidance," Arnaud offered.

"Well?" Sal growled at Ennio.

"The Seer was greatly tired when I visited," Ennio replied, clearly annoyed by the burly Chicago knight. "Donato napped for some time, but when he awoke he shared what transpired. The Vicar made him use the mirror."

"He wanted to spy on something specific in Annwn then," Richard said.

"They looked at Caer Llion as well as the woods around it."

"The Vicar's spooked," Sal said. "Must think Philip is up to something."

"And since our portals haven't been attacked, this *must* be tied to Richard and the boy," Alastair pointed out. "I agree the attack from Annwn cannot be happenstance. The interest of the Vicar might not be either."

"The boy is the key to the puzzle," James said.

"He is," Danica agreed.

"The Church knows of him. Glenallen confessed as much," Richard said. "Since they spied on me, it is probable the Vigilo knows Merle has a new apprentice. The boy is in danger. Simply because Merle can avoid capture by the Church doesn't mean the boy can do it as well."

"Richard, do you know who this kid is?" Sal asked. "Why has Merle taken him in?"

"You know Merle," Richard said. "Could be anything."

"Could he be near to knighting a new Heliwr?" Danica questioned. "Or perhaps he has seen one of our deaths and found a replacement? Anything is possible with his extended sight."

"It has been more than ten years since the Heliwr strode the world," James said. "*Could* Merle be championing another, Richard? I think we all agree it is more than time."

"If he does act to fill the role of the Unfettered Knight, he does it without my counsel."

"You should ask him, Rick," Alastair said.

"You know him as well as I do," Richard said. "He acts when it suits him."

"I can tell you one thing I've learned in all of my studies," James said, pushing his glasses up his nose. "It would be to our benefit that the next Heliwr share our values and not be controlled by the Vatican. Decades ago one such Heliwr walked the world, and he enacted all sorts of mischief for the Church. Assassinations. Political pressure. Theft of important secret information from many countries. In our current political climate, a Heliwr controlled by the Church could destabilize the Middle East further. Imagine, an assassin removing Islamic leaders with the ease of magic. It would be another crusade. It would ultimately lead the world to all-out war, more than likely."

"One of us should send the Vicar to his crypt," Sal muttered.

"He will be exposed for his greed if he is indeed attempting to gain control of the Heliwr, Sal," Arnaud said. "Instead, we need to focus on this boy."

"Bran is just a kid," Richard answered. "Merle *is* unpredictable though. He might have found a new Heliwr."

"Undoubtedly the old codger has wheels within wheels turning," Sal rumbled. "He always has."

"Ennio," Richard said. "We know not what is going on here. Keep aware. St. Peter's is the heart of Catholic tenure and although a Pope's death would not be damaging to the world, perhaps those in Annwn have a plan that we simply cannot see yet."

The Rome knight nodded but said nothing.

"If the rest of you come up with any other ideas or solutions, we'll reconvene here," Richard continued, hands in pockets. "Be strong. Thanks for coming."

The other knights began to fade from the sunshine.

Richard sighed, the answers he had sought still beyond his reach. He breathed in the peace of the beautiful Annwn day, hoping it would settle the disquiet growing at his center.

When he returned to Seattle, he felt no different.

Chapter 8

The night dark and dank about him, his dreams filled with the darkest creatures of the subconscious, Richard sensed movement of foreign air and erupted from troubled sleep to grab the wrist of his transgressor.

"Let go of me, jerkoff!" a voice yelped.

Richard did not hesitate. Thick blankets thrown off, he gained his feet like a cat and slammed his assailant against the building of the alley before realizing he recognized the voice.

It was the boy.

Bran pinned and of no threat, Richard swept the darkness. Moonlight glimmered like frost beyond the alley where he made his makeshift bed, but it failed to illuminate beyond a rough outline. No sound penetrated the gloom; it was the middle of the night and the city slumbered. Memories of the previous night still thick, Richard penetrated the shadows where danger could lurk, not taking anything for granted.

It took only a moment. No other entity existed in the alley.

The boy was alone.

Richard shook Bran. "What are you doing here?!" he seethed.

Bran ignored the vehemence and stared back with cold eyes.

"Merle . . ."

"Merle *what*, whelp?"

"Merle sent me to find you," Bran said, pain at the edge of his words.

His adrenaline flowing away, Richard let the boy go. Bran slid down the wall but quickly straightened, adjusting his coat and regaining his composure.

"I told you not to go out at night," Richard admonished. Bran just stared back with a mixture of awe and distrust. When the boy didn't answer, Richard grabbed the front of his coat anew. "Why does Merle want to see me?"

"I want to know what happened the other night."

"What does Merle want?" the knight repeated, ignoring the request.

"Look, I'm not an idiot," Bran said. "I've been around. Been taking care of myself a long time. Never have I seen creatures like we saw the other night. Never have I seen a man with a flaming sword running around a city like it was the damn medieval ages."

"You should go to a Renaissance fair then," Richard said.

"I'm serious. Who are you?"

"You obviously didn't heed my advice and leave Old World Tales."

"I talked to Merle, yes," Bran admitted. "He convinced me to stay, although he didn't share much. He is more full of shit than that crazy Tee Goodkind down by the wharf. You know, the guy who believes he isn't homele—"

"I warned you," Richard interrupted angrily. "Get away from that old man as quickly as you can. You have no idea how he will twist your life. Now leave me to bed. I no longer care what he wishes of me—or you for that matter."

"Elizabeth," Bran said simply.

Richard hoped he'd heard wrong but knew he hadn't.

"What did you say?" he hissed.

"He told me to just say the name *Elizabeth*," Bran stammered. "Said . . . said you would come, if I said that name."

Anger flooded him. Richard tightened his grip on the coat and pushed him into the brick wall. It was all he could to do not beat sense into the boy.

"What kind of games are you playing? Who the hell do you think you *are?!*" he raged.

Unfamiliar fear crept into Bran's eyes. Realizing what he did, Richard flung Bran aside and to the wet ground like a rag doll.

"I know," he said. "You are only the messenger. This is a discussion best had with its owner."

Before the boy could reply, Richard was already striding out of the alley. It took him less than a minute to cover the dead two blocks to Old World Tales. No one was about; no cars sped on the Viaduct above or on the streets of the Bricks. It was a silent world devoid of life. But when he turned the last corner, the lights of the bookstore blazed like fiery windows into hell.

Richard did not deviate. He burst through the front door with burning conviction.

The bookstore owner sat calmly in one of his plush chairs, legs crossed, his pipe smoking into the air above him. He eyed the knight with cool discernment. Over his shoulder, Arrow Jack sat perched and awake, the beady eyes of the merlin like a knife stabbing the knight.

"I am going to ask you this one time," Richard snarled, pointing a finger at the old man like a sword. "Why the hell did you send for me!?"

"Annwn is on the rise," Merle stated.

The old man's serene manner only fueled Richard's anger.

"What the fuck does that have to do with Elizabeth!?" he roared.

"Everything. Or maybe nothing."

"Riddles," he spat. He turned to leave and in his fury, almost bowled Bran over. The boy didn't move.

"Get out of my way," Richard snapped venomously.

"Bran, you have played chess, yes?" Merle questioned.

"I used to play when I was a kid, yeah," Bran said, looking uncertainly at the knight but still not getting out of his way. "My father taught me when I was about six."

"Explain to Richard what happens at the start of a game."

Richard had had enough. "Merle, don't sit there an—"

"Tell him, Bran," Merle cut in.

"Uhh, usually the pawns are moved forward."

"Precisely," the bookseller said. "Why?"

"They begin the game to allow other pieces into play."

"A player moves a pawn; his foe counters with a move of his own," Merle said, eyeing Richard. "The same is true in Annwn and this world. Pawns are moving, pieces being pushed into place with victory as the goal. All I know is those pawns must be countered. No matter what you may think, Richard, I do not entirely see the forces that move to imbalance the world, only a suggestion of them in the air, on the earth, and at the edge of my awareness." He paused. "That suggestion moved me to have Bran find you tonight and bring you here."

"You still have not answered my question," the knight said.

"I will get to it," Merle said. "First, I must discover how much Bran has learned during his reading this past month."

"I knew it," Richard scowled. "There is *no* reason to include him in this."

"There is," the old man disagreed.

"I am right here, ya know," Bran said, although Richard detected a bit of fear in the boy's voice. "I can make my own choices. And if this has anything to do with what happened the other night and I can learn just what the hell went down out there in the Bricks, I want to know."

"Very perceptive of you, Bran," Merle said. "We certainly mean you no harm."

"If you believe that, boy, then you are not as bright as I thought you," Richard said.

"Hush, Richard," Merle said, eyes flashing. *"Now."*

"I will not!" the knight raged.

"Look, I don't know who you think you are," Bran said to Richard. "But I have a right to know why that enormous dog thing came after me."

"You are in no position to know what is best for you in this."

"I will be the judge of that."

"Fine," Richard said, angry. "When it bites you in the ass, don't say I didn't warn you."

"I meant what I said, Bran," the bookseller asserted once more. "We mean you no harm. But you must hear what I have to say, now, before it is too late."

"Has this to do with the other night?" Bran asked.

Merle nodded. "I asked you to read about pre-civilized Britain. Have you done so?"

"I've read a bit. A lot since the other night, in fact."

"Then you know it was ruled by Celtic tribes before Rome added them to its Empire."

"Right," Bran said. "Julius Caesar conquered lower England."

"This is a mistake, Merle," Richard interrupted.

"Richard!" Merle growled.

The knight grew quiet. He hoped once Bran had heard what the old bookseller had to say, it would scare him sufficiently to ignore whatever request Merle had up his sleeve.

Then he would find out why Merle had brought up Elizabeth.

"Julius Caesar. Just so," Merle resumed. "And what religion did he encounter there?"

"The Celts were pagans, I think," Bran answered. "Believed in many gods and goddesses. Kind of like Rome."

"Very true," Merle said. "Christianity eventually grew in Rome and spread through the empire. When that happened, the religion the Celts practiced all but disappeared overnight."

"How does this tie in with what happened to me?"

"What you experienced the other night was real," Merle answered. "Celtic machinations with you at their heart. You were attacked by fey creatures this world has not known, at least in a real way, for millennia."

"That can't be true," Bran said. "It's folklore."

"Indeed," Richard said, not sure if he wanted to laugh at or chastise the boy. "Didn't believe your own eyes, eh?"

"All folklore has a basis of truth," Merle said, looking at Bran with an earnestness the knight knew to be all too dangerous. "The gods and goddesses Julius Caesar encountered and fought existed—and still exist. He went there looking for riches and resources to expand the empire. In his first effort, he encountered far more than he bargained for. The Celts, with the fey Tuatha de Dannan, repelled the Roman general. The next summer he brought several battalions of his heartiest fighters, and that was the beginning of the end for the Celts and their religion."

"But you say their gods, these fey, still exist?" Bran questioned.

"They disappeared," Richard said.

"Not exactly," Merle corrected. "They retreated from Roman Christian advance over the next three centuries, withdrawing deeper and deeper into the wilds of what would become Wales, Ireland, and Scotland—and, when they had nowhere left to run, from this world entirely."

"This is all pretty hard to believe, guys," Bran said shaking his head. "First I was attacked by a fey creature. And now you are telling me that there is a place outside this world where they exist still? Like, really exist? I've seen some crazy people on the streets, Merle, but right now you are officially the craziest, and you don't even live there."

"Is what I tell you so hard to believe?" Merle asked. "What's important is that you were attacked. *That* was real enough. It was also for a reason, one we must discover."

"How can you know it was for a reason?" Bran asked. "I'm no one."

"Someone does not believe that, Bran."

"Who?"

"If you've done enough reading, you'll know magic heavily influenced the ancients. This world has relegated magic to unreal blasphemy, a novelty for sleight-of-hand magicians and Hollywood. As Julius Caesar and those after him discovered, magic does exist, albeit lesser now with the turn of technology, and it existed when the Celts ruled the breadth of the Isles. Part of their power relied on artifacts imbued with abilities—weapons, mirrors, brushes . . . you get the idea. One of these, a mirror or something like it, with extraordinary power, is owned by someone or some-*thing* in Annwn—and that entity wants you dead."

"Annwn?" Bran said incredulously. "Annwn is the Celtic name for Avalon."

"You are more well-read than I had anticipated," Merle said.

"So Avalon? *The* Avalon?" Bran asked. "The place King Arthur was taken to recover from his wounds after battling Mordred?"

"The same," Merle said. "It's where most of the fey traveled to flee persecution."

"Bullshit," Bran said. The boy peered closer at Merle. "Who are you, really? You're obviously not a bookstore owner."

"No games," Richard broke in. "Just tell him."

"Actually, I *am* a bookstore owner," Merle said. "My birth name is Myrddin Emrys. I was born on the shores of northern Wales and have since been counselor and guide to those who would listen." He paused. "Some have called me Mithranlyn, Maerlyn, and He Who Cannot Die. You'd know me better as Merlin of the Lake, I'd wager."

Bran looked from Merle to Richard and back again. "You actually believe this."

"Believe it, boy," Richard said. "And as I said, I warned you."

"It would make you centuries and centuries old!"

"Fifteen of them, to be exact," Merle said, a sad smile on his bearded face. "Long years."

"Not possible," Bran murmured.

"Oh, it's possible. I've had to live it," Merle countered, drawing on his pipe and emitting a volley of smoke. "Don't *ever* let anyone tell you immortality is a good thing. It is a fate I wish on no other."

"How did it . . . ?"

"Happen?" Richard finished. "You must not have gotten far in that reading."

"Richard, please. You are acting like Sal," Merle reprimanded. "My father was an incubus who seduced my mother, a human. A unique parentage, to be sure. I live a past I have witnessed and studied for centuries, but through baptism at my birth I was saved from the evils of my demon blood. I happen to see certain aspects of the future. It also has made me extremely long-lived."

"A demon?" Bran asked.

"Yes, a real demon," Merle said seriously.

"And you help guide the world?"

"I try. Others say I meddle," Merle said, eyeing Richard. "Everyone has their opinion."

"And you do magic?"

"Once I did, but no more. It has become too . . . costly . . . to do so."

"So there is no way for you to prove it then," Bran said, shaking his head. He looked at the knight. "What does Richard have to do with this?"

"Call Arondight," Merle directed the knight.

Richard sighed but was happy to prove to Bran the reality in which the boy found himself. He put his right hand out with palm toward the floor, closed his eyes for a moment, and took a deep breath. He made his call. Without a word or a sound, the sword made of gleaming steal and silver etched with marvelous runes appeared in his hand, its point resting on the floor. The runes glowed azure with inner flames. Bran stared at him in disbelief. The knight gripped the blade and stared hard at the boy, twisting the sword so Bran could see the beautifully crafted weapon clearly.

"How did you . . . ?" Bran asked, bewildered.

"This is Richard McAllister," Merle began. "The sword he holds is Arondight, the weapon Lancelot of Camelot wielded once upon a time and which has been passed to worthy men through the ages. Richard is one of seven knights who protect the portals between this world and Annwn. It is his role to keep this world safe from the other and vice versa."

"The other night, when I was attacked, I saw a burst of blue fire," Bran said, looking at Richard. "It came from you then?"

"From Arondight," Richard corrected.

The sword disappeared like smoke.

"It comes and goes that easily?" Bran questioned.

"The knights have been given certain attributes to carry out their duty," Merle said. "Richard can call Arondight at will, as well as enact a few other forms of magic."

"And the dog that tried to kill me? It came through a portal?"

Merle nodded. "One such portal gave those Celtic gods and goddesses—along with many of their followers—the chance to flee Rome's new Christian rule. The Celtic *mythology* didn't disappear. It merely moved. The cu sith and the fairies that controlled it are part of that world—and they were after you. At the peril of those around you, they will continue trying to kill you unless you find out why."

"How can you know that?" Bran asked. "Do you have one of these mirrors or whatever?"

"Fairies are tricky things," Richard muttered, seeing an opportunity. "They have no allegiance. But I am convinced they were after you. That is why you should flee this bookstore, the city, and maybe the country, right now. Having failed it is certain they will try again."

"You say certain." Bran turned to Merle. "What do you think?"

"I think you are important in what is to come," the old man said. "It is that reason for the attempt on your life. And no matter how Richard desires to save you from some imagined fate, I agree it will happen again."

"Why am I important?" Bran asked, frowning.

"I see much," Merle said. "It is but a promise of a shadow, but I sense it about you."

"Wait," Richard said. "Who is the boy to you, Merle? I have no doubt you are playing games, as usual, but what makes him special that Annwn would attempt to kill him? That you would recruit him?"

Merle chewed on his pipe stem, thinking.

"Well?" the knight pressed. "Who is he?"

"He is Bran Ardall," Merle said simply.

Richard couldn't believe what Merle had just said.

"What are you *playing* at?" the knight hissed.

Merle never took his blue eyes from Bran. "To protect yourself, you will have to do what is necessary. It will not be easy."

"You think they will come again?"

"Eventually, yes. It is unavoidable," Merle responded. "Tonight. Tomorrow. A year from now. Every once in a while, one of them gets past the knights. When that happens, you won't have Richard to protect you again, I'd wager. Might not happen tomorrow or the next day, but it *will* happen."

Arrow Jack screeched loudly. Merle hushed the bird.

Richard watched the boy. Bran was scared. He had been attacked without provocation. He had seen two different fey creatures that ought not to exist. If he believed the owner of Old World Tales to be the Merlin of story and fable, sorcerer, advisor to King Arthur, and immortal, Richard knew Bran was more than likely considering checking himself into an asylum.

Richard had been in the same place many years past.

And when Bran discovered who his father was, he would balk completely.

"Time is short," Merle advised. "Others will want to find you—that much I've also seen. You must come with us. Now."

"I'm not going anywhere," Richard asserted.

"You are," the old man said. "To Annwn. To protect young Ardall."

"You tamped the wrong leaf into that pipe, I think," Richard said. "I am not the Heliwr."

"To return to my chess metaphor, Annwn is moving its pieces into position for an event that is sending ripples through time," Merle said. "Even now, I feel it. It must be countered or both worlds will die. Of that there is no doubt."

"More doom and gloom, eh?" Richard grunted.

"I have never been wrong," Merle said. "To prevent what comes, I have seen that both of you must travel into Annwn and end what will assuredly come."

"And if I don't go?" Bran asked.

"You will be dead within the month, I think," Merle said. "I see many possibilities, but that one remains constant in the multiple alternate paths. The Lord of Annwn is tenacious."

"You now think Plantagenet attacked the boy?" Richard questioned. "You are sure?"

"It fits," Merle said. "I am not wholly certain—that should make you happy, Richard—but there is some aspect of it that is . . .

unclear and yet swirls about him. I sense Plantagenet in this, but also not."

"Real helpful, as usual," Richard said.

"And easy for you to say when I have no idea of knowing if it is true or not," Bran said, his features darkening in uncertainty.

"I've seen greater men die for less, Bran Ardall," Merle said.

"Your father was one," Richard said, seeing another opening.

Bran frowned. Merle gave Richard a dark look.

"You knew my father?" the boy pressed.

"I did," Richard said. "For several years. A good man."

"You as well, Merle?"

The bookseller took a deep breath. "I did. He was as Richard described—a good man. A better knight."

"He was a knight?" Bran asked. "Like Richard?"

"Yes and no," Merle answered. "Charles Ardall was unique. Needed. The role he fulfilled for the world was as important as the one Richard carries, but was different."

"You recruited him?"

"I did," Merle said. "Like Richard. Like Sal. Like the others."

Bran stood like a statue, looking at the chess game on the table but not seeing it. No sound filled the room. On one side, Richard waited, hoping the boy had figured out he was just one more pawn in a very old game; on the other side sat Merle, continuing to smoke his pipe, patience written in the very wrinkles of his face. The knight and the old man locked eyes for a moment, both aware of the conflict between them, before Merle returned his gaze to Bran and puffed another plume into the air.

"If you knew him, what would he have done in this situation?"

"You can't be thinking about doing this, boy," Richard said.

"Charles *was* in this same situation," Merle said without hesitation. "He chose to do what is right. Two worlds are on the brink of war. If this world discovers Annwn, war destroys both."

Turmoil seeped from Bran. Richard knew the boy had likely read enough Celtic mythology to know there were beings and creatures that could easily destroy him if they got through one of the portals. It was not a difficult risk calculation. The knight also knew Bran to be a tough kid, unable to back down from a fight.

Richard cursed Merle for how he had played this game.

Bran turned to the wizard. "You knew all of this when you spoke to me that first time out front, didn't you? Knew me and what you wanted of me?"

"I did, to a point," the bookseller admitted.

"And if I do nothing, fairy creatures will kill me?"

"They will."

"Why me?"

"That I do not fully know," Merle said. "It could be retribution for a past recrimination against your father. It could have to do with your working with me. I do know this: It will take a combined effort by you and Richard to discover what is going on and to put an end to it."

"And I am to leave all that I know?" Bran thought out loud.

"No. It will be here for you afterward," Merle said.

"It feels like I don't have a choice."

"You always have a choice," the wizard said. "Choice governs the entire universe, and choice will see it to its end."

"Bran, think it through," Richard argued, trying to hide his anger. "Do not trust this man. Not ever. Myrddin Emrys never tells anyone the whole truth. He knows more than he lets on and it can have dire consequences. He has ruined numerous lives in his pursuit to control the events of this world. I am one of them. You should not do this."

Long moments passed.

"And what is it I am to do?" Bran asked. "Confront this lord?"

"I have known this day would come for a long time, Bran," Merle said. "The Lord of Annwn craves more than is his right. He must be stopped. He has some design on this world and I do not know what it is. I do know this—you leaving this bookstore with us is the only way to protect the races of two worlds. It's the only way to—"

"It is the only way for me to be safe," Bran finished.

Merle nodded.

"Do we go to kill him then? Is that your intent?"

Merle looked to Richard. The knight was impassive like stone.

"I see," Bran answered for them. "You ask me to be a murderer."

"If you do not go, Richard will fail," Merle countered. "And you will die here. Of that, I have seen all too clearly."

"Dying—that is the lack of choice I am talking about."

"I am not going," Richard said flatly. "That ends it."

"You have already chosen to, Richard," Merle said.

"The hell I have!"

"Elizabeth would want you to go," the old man said. "And trust me. You want to go as well. I have seen her death tied to these events; I have seen her death marking the beginning of a course in the world that will lead to answers for you. It is the reason I ask that you go and not one of the others."

"I don't believe you."

"It is what it is, Richard," Merle said, certainty in his eyes. "And all I know is, I am afraid. She is a puzzle piece in this. I wish I was wrong and could say differently. I know the pain you carry better than you realize. I think by going you will understand it better—what transpired between you and Elizabeth, and possibly even find a bit of solace." He paused. "And you must leave this night, to make the difference two worlds need."

Bran looked to Richard. The knight stared back hard. He felt trapped once more. Years earlier the old wizard had convinced him to join the Yn Saith as a graduate student. It had led to a life of darkness, sorrow, and regret. The anger from Merle bringing up the death of Elizabeth had evolved to unsettled curiosity, though—as Merle undoubtedly knew it would—and the knight could not quell the swell of it. Answers he had been at a loss for years could be his. But that knowledge would come at a price, as it always did with trusting Merle.

Duty to do what was right collided with his self-loathing and hatred of the bookseller. There was only one choice the knight could make though, and he was not happy about it.

Richard turned to Bran.

"When can you be ready to leave, boy?"

Chapter 9

The cold night enveloped Bran when he stepped from Old World Tales.

He could still turn back. It would not be a hard thing; he owed no one anything. Merle had a sense of urgency Bran did not question, but there had to be another avenue he could go by that did not involve entering Annwn. Life on the streets was exceedingly real, and Bran had confronted his fear numerous times there, but what he felt now bordered on insanity. Sadly, no alternate option presented itself. The part of Bran that questioned his decision wanted to retreat back to his warm bed and pull the covers over his head.

It was a large step to believe Annwn existed.

A larger one to step into it.

Wearing a warm coat, Bran hiked his backpack higher on his shoulder. He had to go, he realized. The opportunity to discover who had tried to kill him and what had truly happened to his father gripped him in a way he had never experienced. Questions long-carried would not be denied. They were embers blown into flame, and each step he took down the street was one closer to answers.

Richard led Bran and Merle on a direct path, barely contained annoyance in every aspect of his bearing.

"Do I call you Merle or something else?" Bran asked.

"I have gone by Merle for so long, to call me anything else would be wrong."

Richard snorted. "Are you sure about the boy in all of this, old man?"

"I am, Richard," Merle replied. "You will see."

"Like you *saw* with me?" the knight said darkly.

Merle ignored the rebuke; Richard continued on. Bran wondered about their dynamic. It was apparent the two shared a stressful history, one in which the knight blamed the wizard for a terrible past event. Richard clearly did not trust Merle.

Should Bran? What had he gotten into?

After traversing two blocks, Richard brought them to a halt across the street from the triangular park fronting the Underground Tour. The downtown skyscrapers above rose stark against the half moon and star field, the city like a graveyard. It left him on edge. He had no idea what to expect. Every shadow was capable of hiding an attacker.

He had to be ready for anything.

"How did my father die? Really?" Bran asked Merle.

"In Ireland, as you already know, I believe," the bookstore owner answered. "Your father was killed by an explosion. Your mother was lost at the same time. I never discovered who did it; for some reason it has been hidden from my sight. Another will acts against my own."

Bran breathed in cold air, afraid to ask. "Did he die doing his duty? Being this Heliwr?"

"He did," the bookseller said with obvious regret.

"Merle," Richard growled. "If I go, who protects the portal?"

"I have made arrangements," Merle said. "It will be safe. I move chess pieces into defensive positions as well as anyone."

Richard looked away.

A different aspect bothered Bran. "How did you know I was—"

"Special?" Merle interrupted. "I've seen it before, Bran. It was how you carried yourself. When you accept who you are, the world will open up for you in ways I can't explain. You will have to experience it for yourself."

"Now you sound like a new-age pagan," Bran said.

"I am who I am, Bran. No more, no less."

"You can't be thinking of making this boy the new Heliwr," the knight accused.

"Never has a knighthood passed from father to son, Richard," Merle said, eyes scanning the night. "You know this."

Bran kept up with the other two men. They were walking across the street, their footfalls echoing, the knight bringing up the rear, when Merle jerked to a halt. He scanned the gloom, eyes probing. Across the street, the park triangle opened up, its tall totem pole a beacon of muted colorful paint. Nothing moved. It was a dead world.

"What?" Bran whispered.

"Richard. Arondight," Merle ordered.

The knight didn't question. Concentration filled his face.

Seconds passed. Nothing happened.

Merle raised a questioning eyebrow.

A grimace tightening his face, Richard fought a pain Bran could not see until the sword flared to sudden life in his hand, the silver hilt and steel of the blade catching the moon's glow and accentuating it in the dark.

As if drawn by the weapon, a man wearing a sable coat and matching uniform emerged from behind the pergola into the light of the lamps, an ink stain given life. Coming to a stop at the street curb, he waited as if he had expected their coming. Both hands buried in pockets that bulged with suggestion, he gave Richard a snide grin despite the knight and the azure flame of Arondight moving protectively in front of Merle and Bran.

One eye in the middle-aged man's chiseled face lay dead. The other held fiery purpose.

"Finn Arne," Merle hailed. "You are a long way from home."

"Indeed," the other replied in a worn German accent. "First time to Seattle. But it appears you beat me here."

"What do you want?" Merle asked icily.

"I suspect you know," Fine Arne said, looking at Bran. "You've done half my work, it appears."

"This young man has no business with you or your betters, Captain."

"Betters? Cute, wizard," Finn Arne replied. "That's not what I hear. The boy has been requested to appear in Rome. He *will* be coming with me."

"No," Richard growled. "He won't."

"Why Rome?" Bran asked, looking at the newcomer.

"Stay silent, young sir," Merle whispered, gripping his shoulder.

"The Cardinal Vicar of the Diocese of Rome wishes to see you, Bran Ardall," Finn Arne said in a bored voice. "It has been ordained by the Catholic Church."

"I know you are under orders, Captain," Merle intoned, stepping forward. "And I know you take those orders as gospel. As well you should. In this situation, however, letting the young man pass and carry out his future will protect the Church more surely than a visit to Rome."

"Hand the boy over, wizard," Finn sneered. "Or we will take him at consequence."

"Try it, Arne," Richard countered.

"You might believe you have authority here, McAllister, but you'd be wrong," the man snarled. "And from what I know, I doubt you can maintain that sword long enough to put up much of a fight anyway."

"That's what the last dead fey thought," Richard threatened.

"This is your choice then, Myrddin Emrys?" Finn Arne asked. "To make this difficult?"

"Life is difficult. No reason for it not to be so now," Merle said, pushing up coat sleeves to free his hands and forearms. "In this matter, your Vigilo leaders are very wrong."

"You posture fake power," Finn Arne countered flatly. "Your time is over."

The wizard said nothing.

"Very well. I tried civility," Finn Arne said, pulling two handguns and aiming at the knight. Other men wearing similar uniforms coalesced from alleys and behind corners on cue, all pointing weapons at the three men. "The hard way then, Myrddin Emrys."

"Looks that way," Merle said.

The men closed ranks, silent and well practiced. The impulse to flee swept over Bran. Adrenaline coursing through his veins, he realized with certainty that he had nowhere to go. The soldiers moved to corner them, a wide semi-circle tightening its trap.

Unlike the knight and wizard, Bran was helpless.

He wondered anew at his choice to enter Annwn.

"Lose the sword, McAllister," Finn menaced. "Now."

Richard brought Arondight up and cleaved the air with its blade, blue fire erupting along its runes and lancing out in a broad arc. Flames incinerated the air. The ring of magic swept up Finn Arne and those close to him, sending them flying. The other soldiers did not wait. Even as their leader landed with a curse, the dozen untouched fighters unleashed gunfire at Richard, the reports shattering the night. Richard brought his fire up again, a wall of protection; even as Bran ducked, the bullets never struck, turned aside by Arondight.

"Run!" Richard roared

"Run, Bran!" Merle pushed.

As the knight maintained the impenetrable circle of fire, Bran stumbled after Richard, half dragged by the bookseller as they crossed the street toward the Pioneer Park triangle. The cacophony of gunfire echoed all around them, the smell of gunpowder heavy and pungent on the chill air. Bran looked everywhere, hoping for the police. No one came. Finn Arne had regained his feet and, while roaring commands, fired his handguns with deafening accuracy as the bullets fought to reach untouchable marks.

Free of the trap set by Finn Arne, Merle peeled away from Richard and pulled Bran with him behind the safety of the ancient pergola, its iron and surrounding maple trees shielding them.

"Now listen to me, Bran," Merle demanded. "When you and Richard—"

"Do not move," a thick Italian voice ordered from behind.

As the two men turned to confront their assailant, black feathers and talons landed upon the soldier's face, screeching venom. It was Arrow Jack. Like a tornado of hate, the merlin tore at the exposed flesh of cheeks, forehead, and eyes, shredding all in bloody anguish. The soldier dropped his guns and ran, arms flailing above his head, while the bold bird winged away to find more prey.

"Now, when you two enter the portal—"

"Wait." Panic seized Bran. "You aren't coming into Annwn?!"

"I cannot," Merle said, grasping Bran's shoulders with steel. "I am needed here. There are balances to be maintained, futures to be watched from afar. You both will go, accompanied by my Arrow Jack."

"But I have questions—"

"No time," Merle cut Bran short. "You will make your way. Stay true and the path you take will be the right one. Listen to your heart. Listen to Richard. He has gained much experience through life's trials."

"I don't think—"

"It is as I've foreseen," Merle finished. "You will be strong like your father."

As Bran pulled away, confusion warring with the anger of being deceived, gunfire erupted into the pergola. Bran quelled a scream. Richard charged across the street, bellowing his rage at the fighters, Arondight a flaming shield. The light of the sword grew dimmer, though, as the warriors, under the direction of Arne, struggled to tighten another noose. Richard fought to stay between his two charges and their foes, but Bran could tell the knight was growing tired.

He either did not have control of Arondight, or its power was finite.

"This is your last chance to turn back, to ignore your destiny, to make your father proud even in death," Merle shouted at Bran. "It is a choice you must make."

Richard stood over them suddenly, a pillar of wild magic. He knocked another burst of gunfire from the air and sent another arc of fire at the soldiers, Arondight as fierce as its owner.

"All right," Bran agreed.

"We must go. Now!" Richard roared.

"Take this," Merle shouted over the din. He shoved a tiny, square wooden box at Bran, its top carved with a glimmering Celtic knot. "Use it only when you feel you *want* protection."

"What about you?" Bran screamed, shoving the box into a jeans pocket.

"I'm not impotent," Merle said and winked. "Now go!"

Richard did not wait. He hauled Bran across Yesler Way and back over First Avenue. Merle stayed with them, also exposed to the wrath of Finn Arne, their only safety behind the knight's fiery shield. When the three men came to a new alley opening, Merle nodded at Bran before darting into the protected darkness. Bran watched him go, worried for the old man but more worried about his own predicament.

"The stairway down, at the corner," Richard pointed out.

Arondight vanished then, the protective fire gone.

Darkness swallowed the street. Before the soldiers could take advantage, Richard grabbed Bran, threw him into the alley, and pressed him against the brick of the building. Bran hit the wall hard. They were cut off from their destination as Finn Arne and his men moved to capture them, the captain the only man Bran could see.

"Damn it!" Richard exclaimed.

"McAllister!" Finn Arne yelled with eager mockery. "The old man may have the ability to disappear. You do not. Give the lad up. There is nowhere for you to go. Your wizard has left you, as has the ability he knighted you with."

"You do not command me," Richard bellowed. "Or the boy."

"No?" the captain said, leveling both handguns at the knight. "Those who hold the weapons make the rules. Or didn't you know that?"

Bran huddled behind the knight. The alley was like pitch, the shadowy outlines of dumpsters and a far-off van their only possible protection. They were pinned—certainly not able to gain the stairs Richard had pointed at.

Then a quiver ran through the bricks at his back.

"I don't want to have to kill a knight!" Finn Arne shouted, clearly frustrated.

"You won't have to," Richard snapped.

In a blur of massive movement that blocked out even the weak starlight and made Bran flinch involuntarily, a creature as large as an elevator dropped between the knight and the captain from the rooftops above, thundering the street upon its landing. Screams of fear and curses mixed with the strobe flashes of renewed gunfire. Snarling with demonic ferocity, Finn Arne leveled his own gunfire at the two-legged beast, its blunted face and thick body mere yards away. Bran couldn't believe what he saw. With lank oily hair falling from a balding pate and around sharply pointed ears, the obsidian hulk raged and, with one huge fist the size of a cinder block, struck Finn Arne in the chest.

The captain flew across the street, as though a crushed gnat. When he landed on the steel bench, his backbone and ribs snapped sickeningly in the night—the strike a killing blow.

In response, the fighters advanced despite the lack of effect their weapons had on the powerful beast. The massive protector remained fixed in his spot, shielding his face and chest with his arms, blocking the alley and its occupants from harm.

"I got this, Rick," it rumbled. "Get your glow rod workin' and get outta here."

"No, I won't leave you to them, Kreche!" Richard shouted.

Dozens of bullets struck the muscled mass of Kreche with deadened thwacks, each adding to its pain. Bran didn't know what creature the newcomer was or how it could withstand such an assault, but he knew it was only a matter of time before it was overwhelmed.

"Can't do this forever," Kreche grimaced.

The being's need bolstered Richard somehow. Where a downtrodden and lost man had just stood, a righteous knight replaced him once more.

Arondight exploded into existence.

"Go," Kreche hissed.

On the heels of the knight, Bran stepped out of the alley, the fire of Arondight protecting them once more. Ten men bore down on them, their weapons automatic ferocity. The soldiers were not going to quit, even with their leader gone.

As he stepped clear, Bran saw the bleeding holes littering the beast's deeply muscled chest and arms. It breathed heavily, its strong jaw clenched. Black ichor bled down a noseless flat face where a bullet had grazed its brow between nub horns. Bran didn't know how the behemoth still stood, but he no longer took it for granted.

"Thank you," Bran said, gazing into its black beady eyes.

"Make it count, scion of Ardall," it grunted. "Farewell."

Richard sent his fire hurtling toward most of the men before running from cover with Bran, trying to make it to the staircase. Once again, Arondight held off their attackers. Bullets ricocheted off of the brick buildings around them but could not hit their mark. The knight kept them safe, at least for the moment.

Bran looked backward as they ran, and was taken aback.

In the yellow lamplight, Finn Arne had returned, barking orders at those men still on their feet, as if nothing had happened to him.

Bran and Richard gained the stairway cut into the sidewalk, inky blackness below, as the sound of closing police sirens chased after them. His feet barely hitting the narrow stairs, Bran plunged downward. Richard came after, Arondight lighting their way. With Finn Arne screaming above, Richard slammed into the door at the base of the staircase. It buckled under his weight and they were through.

The world below embraced him with dank coolness.

"How did that captain survive that punch?!"

"He's unique," Richard answered hotly, moving through the tunnel's gloom as quickly as he could. "I'll explain later."

"What about that thing?"

"The Kreche can take care of himself," the knight snorted. "Nothing can withstand him, nothing in this world anyway. Those Church soldiers will flee or die for it."

The underground opened up to Bran, a world lost to another age—broken stone and brick in dusty piles, ancient corroded steel beams, glass and old faded signs in the corners. The light bulbs above dark, Arondight offered the only illumination. Disorienting shadows flitted about them like elusive companions. Bran moved among them through the passageways..

Arrow Jack shot past Bran, sending electricity coursing through him. The bird flew ahead, having escaped the mayhem.

"Why would the Church want me?"

"Lapdogs of the Church," Richard corrected. "Who knows why they want anything."

"You mean—"

"Yes," Richard grated. "I don't know. All I know is the Cardinal Vicar wants you as badly as the Lord of Annwn apparently."

"I don't understand!"

"Well, I don't get it either!" Richard thundered.

"Where is this portal?"

"We'll find it sooner if you shut up," Richard shot back.

They moved down the dead corridors, the walls close. Several twists and corners later, they stood before a glassless window that looked into what appeared to be an old bank. Richard left the corridor and moved into the shell of the building; the ancient vault door hung off its hinges and dust coated everything. Trash from the turn of the century filled all corners; ancient spider webs hung from the beams, caked in grime. Richard ignored it all and moved deeper into darkness.

The world Bran knew disappeared with every step.

In the middle of the concrete floor a hole opened, stairs leading into a depthless gaping maw waiting to swallow them. Holding Arondight high like a torch, Richard made his way down carefully, unperturbed by the rotten odors emanating from the hole. Into what appeared to be a basement of Old Seattle, Bran followed, the air a chill ghost on his skin.

They entered an empty square room made of jagged, worn red brick, uncluttered by the refuse that had marked the floors above.

None of that mattered to him.

In the center of the wall in front of him, the bricks had fallen away to reveal a hole in the earthy clay, shimmering with fog.

Arondight could not penetrate its depths. Emerald ivy grew around the opening, its vines pushing the brick free, nature destroying what man had built. Bran had been expecting something more grandiose—more magical—a gate bearing carved Celtic runes or a tunnel leading into the earth. The portal was instead a swirling void.

Then a breeze as soft as goose down nudged his cheeks, filled with the mingled smells of dewy grass, growing trees, and intoxicating flowers.

"How can this exist here?" Bran breathed, dumbfounded.

"A sorcerer named Tathal Ennis created it, meant to hide it for his own personal gain. He was attempting to import items from Annwn and sell them to the highest bidder in Europe. The Church discovered the portal after Seattle's Great Fire and hunted him down, but with no luck. Once a portal is opened it cannot be closed, and clever spells in the room above help keep people from venturing here."

Bran looked back to the portal. He didn't know what to say.

"Don't panic," Richard ordered. "There is more for you to know once we are on the other side. Keep moving forward once you step in."

"What's it like?"

"You'll see," the knight said before murmuring. "So will I."

Arrow Jack flew in ahead of the two men. Bran took a deep breath.

As Merle had said, there was no turning back.

With Richard in the lead, Bran entered the portal.

Chapter 10

"I have returned from Mochdrev Reach, my king."

Philip Plantagenet ignored the entrance of John Lewis Hugo and stared out the uppermost window of Idyll Tower, watching dawn come alive as the Harp of Tiertu attempted to soothe his stress. It didn't help. He had seen thousands of sunrises grace Annwn, each one carving the peaks of the distant Carn Cavall Mountains from the night sky and burning away the gray fog from the Forest of Dean east of Caer Llion, but no sunrise during his centuries living in the land of the Tuatha de Dannan had brought such high stress—and such promise.

He rubbed the reddish stubble along his jaw, his eyes gritty from lack of sleep. It was a critical time and much demanded his attention.

"Welcome back, old friend," Philip greeted finally, silencing the self-playing fey harp with a thought and turning to his long-time advisor. "I trust your trip was uneventful?"

"It was, thankfully," John said, half of his face a hideous mask Philip had never grown accustomed to viewing. "Meeting with Lord Gerallt and his daughter went as planned. As I knew it would. The lord gave his blessing in private. Lady Deirdre is ordered to court in one month and will bring her retinue. And my king . . . she is a beautiful woman, strong of spirit and body. She will produce you a fine heir, one worthy of two worlds. You both will unite two peoples."

"I am still not entirely sure it is the right time for me to marry, to have children," Philip thought out loud, crossing his arms. "There is much work left. My father ordered the destruction of the Tuatha de Dannan and the annexation of Annwn. That has not yet happened. Does your use of the cauldron truly portend the time is now? Are you sure she is the right woman?"

"I am," John said. "Marrying the daughter of Mochdrev Reach will unify the peoples from Britain. With the additional might, you will crush the Tuatha de Dannan and fulfill King Henry's crusade. Is that not the trust you have been charged?"

It was, of course. Philip turned back to the sunrise. There was still a part of him that resented leaving his war unfinished, putting individual happiness before completing his father's commandment. A man had his duty first; what came after was his alone. Over the eight centuries of his war, many women had enjoyed the pleasure of his sheets, all of them broomed from his royal suite just as quickly. None had produced children. John blamed it on use of the relic: such a potent magic rendering Philip impotent. Stoppage of its use—or so John believed—would lead to the heirs his long family line required.

Philip did not question his advisor. But his purpose in Annwn was yet to be finished, and it remained a festering wound to his honor.

"What did Gerallt's daughter say?" he asked finally.

"She is angry, as is usually the case with arranged marriages," John said. "Yet she knows her obligation to Caer Llion, and it will lend her the strength to do what is right."

Philip wondered. If he did marry Lord Gerallt's daughter, Mochdrev Reach would become a powerful new asset to his empire. The breadth of Annwn he had already conquered was vast but the populace sparse, particularly in the south. The men and women of the Reach were the descendents of the first humans to enter Annwn, coming to the sacred isle with the fey long before Philip had been born. He knew his history. He also knew countries could not be conquered without consolidation of force, and that meant bringing the Reach into his army and plan. John was right. The best way to do so was through marriage.

"My king," John said, hands folded before him. "Gwawl, son of Clud, requests an audience. He can wait if it pleases you."

"Are the preparations complete for Annwn's newest visitors?"

"They are," his advisor answered. "Master Goronwy and his hounds will lead a large company of Templars to the portal. The Cailleach has agreed to go for her normal price, of course. It should be enough."

"The hag should be more than a match for the knight," Philip said. "You are sure the boy and knight will enter Annwn?"

John did not answer but instead stepped to the middle of the room where the Cauldron of Pwyll sat upon its granite pedestal, the water in its silver mouth flat like ice. The rest of the study was much as it had been for most of Philip's life—a refuge for the High King of Annwn. The room held many of the possessions he brought with him from London, but it had also become a journal of his time in the Sacred Isle. On one wall, opposite the world map of his birth, a map of Annwn hung, its breadth exposed for easy viewing. Shelves lined the other walls, filled with tomes from the library at Oxford, his own personal writings, and the combined knowledge of the dead rebel druids from the university at Caer Dathal. Rugs, ornate chairs, an oak desk buffed to a deep gloss, and acquired magical artifacts filled out the room.

"You look tired," Philip said.

"The cauldron . . . taxes me, my king," John said, touching the silver lip of the wide bowl. Philip observed the ruined mess that was the left side of John's face, as it had been for centuries. The unpolluted childhood friend of Philip had vanished long before, the sad consequence of imprisoning one of the most fearful and powerful fey lords. "I am but a shadow of my other's former self," John admitted.

"You have given much. It is not in vain, I assure you."

"Thank you," John said. "What of the Lord of Arberth?"

"I care not about Gwawl," Philip said, disinterested. "He is as demanding as he is ugly. Why has he come, especially at this early hour?"

"He would not say, my king."

Philip gazed at the burgeoning morning. He had far more urgent items of interest to cater to. The demon wizard had acted as the witch had estimated. While Philip hated using fey creatures to lure the unsuspecting knight and boy, it was a necessary evil. Plans he and John had orchestrated were nearing completion—and it was time to reap the reward.

"Let him wait," Philip commanded. "The day I have wanted for centuries has *finally* come, and it deserves my attention fully."

"Yes it does, my king. Our efforts now begun, however, cannot be stopped. Separating a knight from his portal is a battle won, but I worry if the boy gets free, it could cost us the war."

"I know your apprehension. Action has ever been the doctrine of my father's vision, and its time is now, John, after all of these centuries. Whether the boy lives or dies, it will be to our benefit. Are you not confident in the portents of the witch? In your own auguries?"

"I am, but Myrddin Emrys is . . . wily. He could have pulled wool over my eyes."

"The wizard is wily, indeed," Philip agreed. "Like playing gwyddbwyll against the worthiest of opponents. And for your sake I hope you can see through that wool. If what you have seen is true, I have the advantage. The Heliwr is nigh to gracing two worlds again after almost a decade, and as he does so I will rule him."

"The Templar Knights are assembled in the northern courtyard, my king," John reminded.

"The cauldron then, one more time."

Without word, John placed both hands upon the cauldron's rim and stared into it, furrowed concentration twisting his face. A ghostly film stole across both of his eyes, even as the depths of the bowl stirred with a brackish glow that illuminated John with wicked intent.

"What do you see?" Philip questioned impatiently.

John remained bent over the water. "I see a merlin, flying against the azure sky, its wings darkening the land beneath with shadows. Those shadows fall over Caer Llion."

"Is it Myrddin Emrys?"

"Difficult to know, my king," John replied, squinting into the light. "But I do not believe so. It feels not like the wizard. More... free. Less intelligent." John paused. "I now see a seed sprouting from soil as black as midnight, growing into a warped tree of daggers and deep roots. It stands alone, powerful, unfettered—but sad, the forest encircling it unwilling to encroach upon its presence. Red eyes from the dark. Red eyes."

"The hawthorn tree. Am I anywhere near it?"

"No, my king."

Philip darkened. It was not what he had hoped.

"Night, as terrible as the dawn," John continued. "It falls over the enormous dome in Rome where a raven sits upon a cross, lording over all from the gloom."

"A merlin. Now a raven," Philip mused. "Do you at least *know* the raven's significance?"

"I do not," John replied. "The raven is an animal of great power. A defiler."

"The Church is that defiler, needing direction," Philip said. "Where is our prey now? The knight and the boy should be our focus."

John clutched the sides of the bowl with white-knuckled hands, beads of sweat springing to life upon his brow. "They will emerge within Dryvyd Wood when the sun rises and will be far from the safety of the portal by midday, my king. The Shield and the men of the Church who challenged them have not followed. A halfbreed intervened and caused great damage to them."

"Good. Good. Come back to me now, John."

The cauldron glow faded, leaving the advisor's mismatched eyes clear but circled by dark exhaustion.

"When the time comes, will you have the strength to blind the Vatican?" Philip asked.

"It will not pose a challenge," John answered, straightening.

"I hope not."

"I could never dishonor your father and brothers that way."

Philip looked back out the window, the sun rising from its bed to paint the world in color. Those of his immediate family were dead long centuries past, their remains lost to antiquity, their desires dust with the exception of Philip. King Henry II of England had been a man of vision and power—one who sacrificed his family for gain. As a boy living in the trades quarter of London, Philip had not known his unique parentage. It was not until he had been brought before his true father and begun his secret education with Master Wace of Bayeux that he left his apprenticeship and embraced a greater calling, his existence as an outsider made clear.

The mantle Philip carried had finally ripened to fruition.

"I want *you* to lead the Cailleach, the Houndmaster, and the Templar Knights," Philip ordered. "I want the boy brought directly to the dungeons to begin his new life."

"What of the knight with him? He is a grave threat."

"He will be broken like the boy—and made an asset."

"He could also undo your plans, my king."

"If what you say is true, this knight is near broken anyway," Philip countered. "He is the weakest of the Yn Saith."

"He is," John said, looking away. "But I still feel—"

"Your true feelings are known."

"The knight is not necessary," John finished. "Kill him and concentrate on the boy."

"I do not care for your tone, John," Philip said darkly. "Use of the cauldron has warped your logic. Imagine the power our army would acquire with the Heliwr *and* a knight of the Yn Saith at its head. Imagine the authority we would hold over the Church and its governments. The ability to end the Tuatha de Dannan and shape both worlds in the Godly image intended." Philip paused. "One thing I have learned these great many years, my friend, is usurped power is power acquired. I mean to have it rather than lose it."

"I have to concede attaining the services of Arondight would be a great boon to your efforts," John said. "But the risk remains severe."

"The sword of Lancelot is a prize beyond any I now possess," Philip remarked. "Give the knight to Duthan Loikfh. The Fomorian is the best at what he does."

"And the boy, my king?"

"He may not be as hard to persuade as you think, John," Philip said. "If what you've seen it true, he is a wanderer, lost, looking for direction. He has never had the finery we have had for so long. He may join us willingly if given those things his life has lacked as a street pauper."

"Indeed," John said. "I also still worry of the Tuatha de Dannan."

"What of them? I control Annwn."

"Right now, my king," John pointed out. "But the fey have yet to be defeated."

"They are fractured, weak," Philip said. "The strength of the Templar Knights has grown as that of the Tuatha de Dannan has diminished. If not for the Carn Cavall Mountains, Snowdon, and the Nharth who shield them both, the war would be long been over."

"Master Wace would preach caution. The Seelie Court—"

"The various courts are broken, leaderless," Philip countered. "But you are wise to fear the possibility. Caer Llion will not be left unguarded. Have faith in that, John."

"I do, my king. Our work is nearly finished."

"Not finished, John," Philip said, already thinking ahead. "Only just begun."

John nodded stoically.

"Be sure the Cailleach is given payment," Philip said. "She will need fresh breeding materials for the army. No reason to anger her as before."

"A lowborn child from town will be given upon our return," John assured.

"Leave now," Philip commanded. "And I've changed my mind. Take Gwawl with you. He would do well to witness our new strength, and what we do to our enemies—a little reminder for his rebellious nature. Include Evinnysan; Fodor, son of Ervyll; and Sanddev, along with some of the pets from the dungeons. Take the boy and the knight alive. I want their reeducation to begin in earnest and in health."

John nodded but lingered.

Philip stared at him hard. "Something else?"

"If the boy escapes, we will have to release the bodach to hunt him—to kill him. He and the knight cannot be left to their own devices. And releasing such a powerful tool weakens our burgeoning strength, no matter how slight."

"See that it does not come to that," Philip asserted.

"Your will is my will, my king." John bowed low and left.

Alone once more, Philip breathed in the warming morning air and gazed over the land. He was happy John had left. The marriage his advisor hoped for, while practical, did not interest him this day. Instead he thought of the trap.

John had little cause to worry. The Cailleach would be a hardship the knight would not overcome. She was highly intelligent and too powerful, even for one bearing Arondight.

The High King turned back to his table and the unrolled floor plans of the Vatican and its catacombs he had attained two centuries earlier. The ghost of a memory surfaced unheeded: his father, grown old from family machinations, standing in an altogether different crypt near a tiny royal sarcophagus. The buried boy—Philip's older brother, William—had been murdered during infancy by evil banished from Britain centuries before. Sorrow trailed down the face of Henry II, moved to tears by a long-held angry grief. That day he proposed a life to Philip different from any other. With several heirs in front of Philip, Henry II decided to make a weapon out of a son who would never have vast amounts of wealth or significant title. The King of England offered him a new world, but one only a *man* with courage, conviction, and the Lord's grace could attain.

Philip lost the dwindling remnants of his boyhood that day. He had been thirteen.

The classic and military education Master Wace gave Philip granted him the tools to enact what was needed—a wealthy world awaiting conquest, ripe with possibility.

THE DARK THORN

The sounds of the new day caught up with the sun, the town below his window and the castle around him coming to life.

Philip smiled. After centuries of fighting, Annwn was his.

The world of his birth would not be far behind.

Chapter 11

When Richard stepped into the portal, the world of smell and touch disappeared.

He could see Bran behind him, but the boy appeared translucent, concealed by blankets of mist. Arrow Jack was nowhere to be seen. Neither Richard nor the boy spoke, both fixated on the path before them, their footsteps silent as they fell on vertigo-inducing nothingness. Richard forced himself to put one foot in front of the other, hoping he had not made a mistake in coming. With the decayed odor of Old Seattle and the adrenaline from the gunfight fading, he fled from a past filled with pain into an uncertain future.

All the while, the mysterious words of Merle haunted him.

The gray lightened, a point as blinding as the sun growing in front of the two travelers, until Richard had to shield his eyes. As the illumination grew, the feeling of being pinched—of being reduced in physical size by a force more commanding than gravity—squeezed the air from his lungs. Just as he was in danger of passing out, a blast of light surrounded both men, and the shock sent Richard to his knees.

He opened his eyes.

The void and the crushing grip were gone.

In its place, warmth and a verdant meadow spread around him, the dewy emerald grass sprinkled with clover and small purple flowers under a sun rising to the east.

Behind him, a shimmer like heat rising over cooked pavement rippled in the air.

Bran lay near him, shaking off what they had just experienced.

"Is this . . . ?" the boy asked.

"Annwn," Richard answered, standing. "The ancient land of the Tuatha de Dannan."

Richard had never been to Annwn beyond visiting the Isle of the great tree Achlesydd along with the other Yn Saith. Sky like he had only seen in the Rocky Mountains lorded overhead, clear and clean. Insects buzzed, a persistent hum amidst the twill of birdsong. Despite it only being morning, Richard knew the afternoon and early evening would be hot. The only blight surrounded the meadow like a wall: a forest grown unruly repelled the sunshine, its limbs twisted as if in pain, its depths dark like runny pitch.

Richard felt akin to it, like an ink stain on clean cloth.

"You okay?" he asked Bran.

"I am," the boy replied, also standing and smacking blades of grass off his knees.

Richard grunted and looked around, getting his bearings. He had never seen the majesty of the massive range in the distance from this vantage; its jagged snow-encrusted peaks burst from the remnants of what looked to be an ancient era of previous mountain building.

"Hope we aren't going into those mountains," Bran said.

"They are the Carn Cavall, the newer spires, Snowdon," Richard said. "Hard country, wild and still free. With any luck we will not be going there."

"Will the Church men follow us?"

"Not if I know the Kreche," the knight snickered. "They won't get *near* the portal."

"Finn Arne took a punch from the Kreche that should have killed him," Bran said. "How is it he is okay?"

"You know I possess Arondight," Richard said. Bran nodded. "The Captain of the Vatican's Swiss Guard possesses Prydwen, the Shield of Arthur. It keeps him from harm, no matter the damage done."

"He is invincible?"

"Yes," Richard said. "Mostly."

"But I didn't see a shield."

"Trust me, it is there," Richard huffed. "Can we get going now?"

Not waiting for an answer, Richard set off into the forest parallel to the Carn Cavall, his strides long with purpose. Bran hurried after. The plants and sounds were the same, the feel of the grass beneath his feet familiar, the world appearing no different than their own although summer now replaced fall. But something was off, a feeling of illness that traveled from his boots into the core of his being.

Before he could think more on it, the shadowy forest enveloped them, the airy lightness of the day blocked like a thunderhead in front of the sun. Wrongness surrounded them, dank and stale, the trees sapped of life. No animals or insects stirred. The forest was a dead zone.

"What a dismal place," Bran observed.

"Dryvyd Wood was designed this way."

"Designed?"

"Well, designed probably isn't the right word," Richard said. "Allowed to grow terrible is closer to the truth. Don't stray from me and *do not* touch the trees, at least not until I tell you it is all right. They are none too friendly."

Bran looked around with wary apprehension. "Where are we going?"

"The capital fortress of Caer Llion in the southeastern part of the island," Richard said.

"Where are we now?"

"In the middle southern reaches of Annwn, I believe."

"So you've been here before?"

"Never."

"What's at Caer Llion? This Philip guy?"

"Philip Plantagenet, despot of the Tuatha de Dannan," Richard muttered. "Caer Llion is the capital of his empire. It is there we will find him."

"And we go to kill him?" Bran questioned.

"Perhaps," Richard said. "He makes Hitler look like a joy. Merle believes our coming to Annwn will remove Philip. If he is truly the man behind the attack on you, I come here to find answers and destroy whatever looking glass he uses to view our world. We will start with him."

"Why hasn't anyone tried to stop him before now?"

"By the time the Third Crusade wrapped up in the Middle East, Philip had already conquered most of Annwn," Richard said, weaving through the trees with care. "He has grown strong over the centuries, somehow living far longer than his natural span. That's another mystery I intend to unravel. At any rate, his vast army and Caer Llion protect him. Stealth is about the only tactic and weapon we have going for us, unfortunately."

"The Third Crusade. But that would make him . . ."

"Exactly," Richard affirmed. "Old."

"How can that be?"

"We don't know. Merle suspects Philip possesses a relic of some kind."

"A relic?"

"A longevity talisman, something from the old world probably," Richard replied as he glanced at the forest canopy. "A necklace or ring or something."

Arrow Jack landed on a wobbly tree branch, his dark feathers blending into the black leaves. The bird took off again, his wingspan a scythe through the blue of the sky.

"Why did the bird come?" Bran asked.

"He is our scout. He'll keep an eye ahead for trouble."

They hiked through the forest, the rolling land easy to navigate, Richard avoiding every overhanging limb, every exposed root. Bran mimicked him. The sun swept overhead in a golden arc, but the cool shadows of Dryvyd Wood infiltrated the knight's clothing and left him chilled. It had been a long time since the knight had ventured from the Bricks, and suddenly being thrust into nature made him uneasy. Arrow Jack winged from tree to tree, a companion vanishing and returning at whim. No animals appeared, no sounds intruded. The forest was a burial ground.

The feeling that Richard had made the wrong choice grew with every step.

The sun crossed midday, beginning its slow decent, when they came to a stream sliding like a silver snake through exposed gnarled roots, gurgling as it rode over rounded rocks.

They were fortunate to have come on a stream so quickly.

Richard removed his boots and socks, and stepped into the slow-moving stream. "Stay where you are, Bran, on the bank."

The boy halted. "What are you doing?"

"Searching for something."

"For what?"

"Just wait," Richard snapped.

Bran darkened. The knight didn't care.

Richard closed his eyes, focusing on a memory from a lifetime ago, trying to remember the spell Merle had taught him. The necessary words materialized as if he had used them that day. As he reiterated a series of five Welsh words backed with a hum, he passed his hand over the stream in slow circular motions, his palm open and face down, calling. Warmth spread from his use of the ancient magic but he barely felt it. Instead he foraged along the bed of the stream with his mind, seeking the one specially shaped rock he hoped existed.

Several feet away a white glow formed in the running depths.

"There it is," the knight whispered.

He burned with concentration, new sweat pricking his skin as he tightened his use of the magic. The light broadened, pushing its way out of the water, the brook giving way to the power Richard employed.

"Get back, Bran."

Before he could see if the boy heeded him, a small rock erupted from the stream, its expulsion sending water cascading in all directions. It flew through the air as it was beckoned, the stone coming to hover below his hand, a sphere tumbling with rapidity. The knight closed his fist over the stone, its smoothness like ice, a near perfect band of gray rock still wet from eons of submersion.

"What's that?" Bran questioned.

"A fairy ring," Richard replied, holding it up in the sunshine.

"Looks like a rock with a hole in it."

"A hole for your finger," Richard said, annoyed anew. "This little stone will protect you from certain appetites Mankind has among the fey."

"And those would be?"

"Remember the cu sith?" Richard asked.

"How could I forget?"

"Fairies controlled it," the knight said, tossing the ring to Bran who caught it. "Some creatures here in Annwn have power over others—power to control humans. That ring, born of wild nature, will protect you."

Frowning, Bran slid the circle over his right hand middle finger.

Arrow Jack screeched from a limb high in one of the trees across the brook, the sound quick and earnest even in the deadened air of the Dryvyd Wood.

"What did he say?" Bran asked.

"I. Don't. Know," Richard answered angrily. "He's your bird. You deal with him."

"My bird?"

"Yes, *your* bird. Every Heliwr has a guide. I think Arrow Jack will be yours when the time comes."

"Merle said knighthoods don't *get* passed from father to son."

"And he lies," the knight said. "Don't forget it."

Richard replaced his socks and boots and without a look back jumped over the dry stones of the brook. Bran followed. The trees thinned and lost their threatening feel almost immediately, the misshapen limbs and trunks of Dryvyd Wood less twisted, its foliage greener and more vibrant. Richard exhaled from holding his breath; he was pleased they were through the unnatural forest. Birdsong reentered the world. The oppressiveness of the crooked forest vanished entirely.

"Something has been bothering me," Bran said. "Why didn't the Church captain kill you? He had his chance, both guns pointed at you. It would have been easy."

"He couldn't," Richard said with distaste. "He was attempting to wound me—or at least lead me away from you. The Vigilo would never condone the death of a knight, no matter how grave the need or the grievance."

"The Vigilo?"

"That's a long story."

"Seems we have the time."

Richard exhaled sharply. "The history of the knights. Where to start." He organized his thoughts, hating the sudden role of teacher. "After His crucifixion, Jesus Christ came to His remaining disciples and instructed them to make followers of all nations. Arguably the most important apostle, Peter traveled throughout that ancient world and to Rome where he founded the Catholic Church. At that time Rome was pagan, so Peter spent years sermonizing to and baptizing thousands of people, converting them to Christianity. Those early Christians were persecuted and hunted for the next three hundred years, until Emperor Constantine legalized and legitimized Christianity in the Roman Empire."

"I know most of that," Bran said.

"What you don't know is Peter was a sly old bastard. Before his death, he founded a secret group within the fledgling Church, and it was this tiny society of trusted men that was given the duty to protect the tenets of Christianity and its daily gain at all costs."

"And this group, the Vigilo, commands the Church?" Bran questioned. "I find that really hard to believe, to be honest. Conspiracies swirl in our world. Why have I not heard of this?"

"Not really that hard to believe," Richard snorted. "Vigilo means 'watchful' or 'vigilant' in Latin. To be a watcher is to not be directly involved. Some of its members are high-ranking Cardinals in the Vatican who maintain anonymity with absolute discretion. Others are hidden from even me, their identities secret. They don't influence doctrine. Instead they protect it and the power they have accrued—at any cost."

"How do you and the knights fit in all of this?"

"Over the centuries that followed Peter's own crucifixion, the Vigilo worked hard to ensure Christian persecution was as limited as it could be. But the group was mostly religious scholars and strategic planners; they had no strength of arms to carry out their desires. The Vigilo needed brawn. They got it with the Order of Virtus—a precursor to the knights of the Middle Ages— hundreds of soldiers spread over the continent and later, the world. With them in place as a stabilizing force, the Vigilo began working in earnest to erode pagan influences in the Empire to secure Peter's direction."

"The Celtic gods," Bran said. "And the Vigilo rid the world of them?"

"In part," Richard replied. "The Vigilo asserted itself in the Isles like everywhere else, influencing with machinations, paying off clan leaders to pressure their people to embrace Roman culture. Greed is a powerful motivator. Eventually the Celts pushed their own gods and goddesses away into the wilds of what would become Wales and Ireland; all the while the Christianity of the Vigilo filled the void left behind. It didn't all happen at once; it took several centuries. But during that time, as the Order of Virtus secretly spread across the Isles bribing people and killing any fey creature they crossed, they found the first portal."

"And placed men to guard it," Bran said. Richard nodded. "But if you are part of the Vigilo, why didn't you give me to Finn Arne? I thought Merle was responsible for your role as a knight, which means he'd be a part of this secret organization as well."

"In a way, Merle is. But he freed the Order of Virtus from the authority of the Vigilo by giving us power of our own—power that separates us from the Church and the strength it now possesses. For many centuries Vigilo soldiers were the scourge of Europe and the Middle East. Behind the scenes, they began most of the Crusades and many of the other wars that plagued the world. But with one of his last acts of magic, Merle gave the portal guards each a relic of great power and therefore autonomous will, to balance the growing power of the Church and the Vigilo. He knew if the Vigilo had its way, it would destroy Annwn and all who resided there, it would erase what the Church thought of as blasphemous. I control the entrance to a portal, and nothing passes without my leave. It is in that way the portal is not controlled by any one group."

"That is why you might not kill the Lord of Annwn," Bran added.

Richard shrugged. "True enough. I am my own man."

"And you are still a part of the Order of Virtus?"

"The Order disintegrated long ago," Richard said. "Only seven of us remain at any given time. It is all that is needed—one for each portal. We are now the Yn Saith, the Seven."

"If all of that is true, how did Philip enter Annwn? No knight stopped him?"

"Remember how I said the Vigilo has started many of the religious wars?"

Bran nodded.

"The irony is that they are partially responsible for our foray into Annwn. In the twelfth century, Henry II, the father of Richard the Lionheart and John Lackland, raised Philip in secret. The King of England decided to make an assassin of his fifth born. With the aid of the Vigilo, Henry set into motion a crusade against Annwn, using Philip as a weapon. With an army behind his son, Henry sent them through, condoned by the Vigilo. It was after that act of warfare that Merle gave the first Yn Saith power, to prevent such acts from happening again."

"This is all too much," Bran said in disbelief. "These things happened centuries ago."

"Believe it, boy. It's all true," Richard said. "But one thing you need to remember. Do not trust Merle. Often his intention is good but rarely for those he finagles in these charades. When he says he has a mere shadow of a doubt about your future, what he really means is he has seen the path you will walk and it suits his wishes just fine, while affecting your life forever."

Richard watched Bran chew on that statement. The sooner the boy began questioning every aspect of coming to Annwn, the better.

"What happened to his magic?" Bran asked finally.

"He is demon spawn, baptized by the Church at his birth and pulled away from the evil impulses of his father. He does age, albeit slowly, and the older he gets, the less control he has over his power. He has now become so old he can no longer control his magic—it is wild and unpredictable, his weakening human form unable to fully contain the demon magic if used. He could lose control; he could destroy the world."

"Well, how can he keep things from us?" Bran questioned, a bit angry.

"How the hell should I know? Do I *look* like Merle?" Richard asked angrily, temper flaring. "Let's get one thing straight. He may like you. I don't. You are a kid and one who might get me killed here. So just . . . stop asking me questions."

Richard stormed ahead before Bran could reply. Even though he had gone along with Merle's wish, a part of Richard rebelled against the boy. Demons. Magicians. Fey creatures and Church conspiracy. The world he had spent years protecting now at his back. While he knew a great deal about Annwn, it could kill him if it discovered his presence.

He was not the Heliwr with authority here.

And all the while he had to survive with a boy who barely shaved.

Before the knight took a dozen steps, Arrow Jack screeched loudly in the trees above just as a series of deep resonating coughs thundered in the distance. The sound was unmistakable.

The braying of hounds on hunt.

"Damnit," Richard muttered, eyes combing the forest.

"What is it?"

"We are caught." Anger replaced shock in the knight. "They knew we were coming."

"Who?!"

"Who do you think!?" Richard exploded, already turning around. "While I was gabbing with you, our entrance into this world was discovered!"

The barking grew louder.

"What can we do?" Bran asked hurriedly.

"I don't know! Go back, find some kind of protection."

"The portal is hours away! There is no protection for us back there!"

"Oh?" Richard shouted. "We'll see about that."

Richard flew, his long limbs carrying him forward back the way they had come. Bran kept up. The knight could not believe his luck. They were already hunted.

But by whom?

Through the holes in the forest canopy where the rolling hills rose toward mountains, the sickened areas of Dryvyd Wood became visible again, a throbbing stain of decay with a powerful disdain for life.

Richard ran straight toward the heart of it.

Chapter 12

With Bran a shadow on his heels, Richard fled through Dryvyd Wood's dark confines as if chased by death itself, with one thought ricocheting through his mind.

Escape.

The harsh deep braying of the hounds penetrated him like splinters, the sound closer with every running step. Richard kept his anger focused on flight. No matter how many directions taken or hills crossed, the hounds were an indelible presence, unshakeable in their hunt. The brook where he called the fairy ring had long-since been crossed, the ill-twisted trees that protected the portal surrounding them once more. Through the canopy the Carn Cavall and Snowdon grew in the far distance, the mountain heights an unattainable safe haven the knight now wished more than anything to be within reach.

"Where are we going?" Bran breathed hard.

"I'll know it when I see it."

"The stream back there maybe?" Bran suggested. "Hide our passing?"

"A movie cliché, nothing more," Richard said. "These hounds

are far too well-trained to be thrown off our scent so easily."

The pursuit echoed everywhere, no longer just behind, the barks on top of them. Richard slowed to a quick walk, eyes casting about for the right spot.

"What are you looking for?"

"There," Richard pointed out, moving up the gradual slope where anorexic trees grew in stagnated competition with one another. There wasn't much space between them. In their midst, a tiny outcropping of granite broke free from the forest, a serrated throne within the malformed, dark wood.

"This is your plan?" Bran asked increduously.

"Stay close behind me," the knight ordered. "And remember what I said about the trees."

Bran flinched where he was almost touching one.

"Exactly," Richard said simply as he backed them against the thrust of rock.

Minutes passed, each one an eon as the inevitable approached. It didn't take long. The first hound burst into view, as large as the cu sith but sleeker and faster, like an Irish wolfhound. Dirtied white wheaten fur coated its frame as the canine barked low to the ground until it sighted Richard and Bran, red ears flattened against its box-like head. Others quickly joined it. Twelve dogs circled them, each threateningly cutting off escape.

Richard stood in front of Bran, muscles taut for the fight. He called Arondight and it materialized into his hand without difficulty, the runes along its silvery blade throbbing azure.

The dogs growled lower in response but did not flinch, digging in.

Minutes passed in stalemate.

Then a hound more powerfully built and larger than the others emerged from the path of their flight. Upon its back rode a short, stocky man with a matted copper beard and matching wild hair.

The hounds moved aside, their eyes still fixed on their quarry.

With both hands gripping the thick fur of his mount, the rider grinned maliciously, his hunt over. Only when the houndmaster drew close did the knight see he was not alone; behind him rode an ancient woman, her cheeks gaunt and wrinkled, her stringy gray hair falling over blue-tinged skin as if dunked in ice. Death hung upon her, permanent and unyielding, but in her watery orbs a fire of terrible life burned with murderous malice.

"Now be still, my pretties," the short man cajoled, his green eyes never deviating from Richard. "Tell ya when, tell ya when, ah will."

The beasts whined, their desire obvious.

"Be still yourself, Goronwy," the ancient woman growled, her gaze shifting from Bran to Richard as she slid off the lowered hound, rags hanging from her bones as if in afterthought. "Let me off this flea-bitten beast."

"We have no quarrel with you," Richard snarled.

Stormy eyes fixed on the knight. "Nah, not with me. With someone else. Come with me now, like a good lil' one."

"Never," Richard replied, his ire raising flames along Arondight.

"You know me, yes?" she prodded.

"I do. The Cailleach," Richard answered. He looked around. "Odd summer day today, isn't it, witch?"

"Yar, knight," Goronwy said beside the ugly woman. "Powerful, she is. Don't give my dogs reason to be let loose."

"Bring those dogs closer and they will be whining, houndmaster," Richard taunted.

"Oh, they will, in time," the witch cackled. "They love flesh and—"

Richard didn't give her a chance to finish. He flicked the tip of Arondight in the direction of Goronwy and sent a ball of azure flame shooting forward, a whoosh of burning air. The mount of the houndmaster shied away, eyes wild, as he cowered, fear twisting his warding limbs.

Before it could incinerate its intended victim, the flaming ball broke course, pushed aside by a powerful gust of wind to disintegrate harmlessly into one of the malformed trees.

"Knight of nothing," the Cailleach cackled, her hands coated in ice.

"What does your master want?" Richard asked.

"You," she said. "Both."

"Not a chance."

"In my world now, portal pup," the Cailleach sneered. "The High King paid well."

"Paying you in how many lives to be his *bitch*?" Richard spat. "What else have you destroyed, other than the seasons?"

"I do that for free. Eternal summer. For his war," she said, then flicked her tongue at him with lurid suggestion. "Though I do miss my winter curves. Care to touch?"

"Your dreams have nothing to do with this."

"Your loss."

"Will be your life," Richard replied.

"Ah see. A lot o' fight in ya," the crone mocked. She turned to Goronwy. "Make sure they don't escape, but keep those mutts out of dis."

The witch didn't wait. She attacked with a wail, a whirlwind of frigid air rushing toward Richard. The knight expected it. He jammed Arondight into the ground, its runes flaring like the sun. The world fell away while his fear turned into adrenaline. The gale shook the limbs of Dryvyd Wood and ice shot through earth, coating the world in silvered glass. But the wind lost its tenacity as it met the sword and the power Richard wielded. Gritting his teeth and hoping Bran was smart enough not to flee, the knight kept his focus on the hag, an indomitable spirit against her wintry wrath.

The icy power of the witch could not reach them.

The Cailleach growled frustration and ended the blast.

The clearing coated in ice and frost, Richard pulled Arondight free of the ground to face his adversary anew.

"That it?" Richard asked, sweat prickling his skin.

The question had the desired effect. Face contorting in rage, the hag wove her glowing white hands in the air—until a thunder shook the wood and cut her off.

Appearing from the east, two dozen warriors reined-in horses to surround the ring of dogs, the men dressed in black with breastplates bearing the silver insignia of a hawk below faces chiseled in hardship. Quick on their heels, a second group arrived, the white-cloaked riders wearing chrome greaves, canonical helmets, and hauberks beneath white mantles stamped with a crimson cross. All of the warriors were heavily armed, some with broadswords or axes, others with bows and quivers of arrows. The warhorses stamped impatiently, waiting on their masters.

Richard felt the day grow dark.

Their chance of escape had vanished.

The warriors bearing the cross were Templar Knights.

"Hag!" a man in black roared, his engraved breastplate of a higher quality than those around him. "Step away!"

"Lord of *Assbirth*," the Cailleach snapped. "These are more crafty than you know."

"No one speaks to the Lord of Arberth thus, witch," a mounted blonde man said, his finely chiseled features flushed with rage. "Lord Gwawl is one of the finest men beneath the banner of the High King. He should have you skinned alive."

"He is under the king in some way, true," the Cailleach screeched. "Shut the hole above your chin, Sanddev, or ah'll do it for you. Yeh be too purty to be here anyhow."

Men about Lord Gwawl snickered. Sanddev glared at them.

"Let us pass freely and I will let you live!" Richard yelled for all to hear.

"Let *us* live?" Lord Gwawl barked a laugh, the Cailleach forgotten. "Look around you. Apparently the Seven have grown daft over the years."

More laughter echoed. Richard tensed, prepared for the worst.

"Talk is wasted. The hunt is over. Let us take them—now," a man beside Sanddev said, his raven hair braided and hawkish eyes fierce for confrontation.

"Evinnysan has the right of it," Sandevv agreed.

The Cailleach grinned gleefully. The houndmaster whistled shrilly into the air, calling his hounds back. The ringing song of warriors freeing weapons echoed in the dark forest.

"Enough!" thundered a voice.

From behind the wall of lathered horses, another man rode forward. Both warrior groups parted. Richard knew the man, had learned a great deal about John Lewis Hugo from Merle during training. Wearing fine sable clothing beneath a shirt of chain mail, the rider glared at those around him, half his face a ruined mask. Despite the destroyed flesh, both eyes glared with equal ferocity at the knight, the contempt palpable. He carried no weapons but to either side of his horse lumbered two Fomorians, brutish giants Richard knew once existed in the old world.

Richard barely gave Philip Plantagenet's second-in-command pause. An inky blackness rippled in the shadowy background of the forest behind him, absorbing the light as it came, the stale odor of unwashed bodies permeating Dryvyd Wood. Human faces, twisted and deformed, appeared from the darkened mass, attached to short spindly limbs and crooked bodies. Down on all fours, tortured frenzy glimmered from beady black eyes. Others had snouts like wolves, eyes burning with bloodlust and fangs slavering. They came mewling low like eager cats awaiting a meal, muscles twitching for release.

The horses balked at the beasts, panic threatening to overwhelm them. Helplessness cascaded over Richard. There were too many creatures, too many men holding weapons. Even two Fomorian giants. It was over.

"Knight!" John Lewis Hugo shouted. "Stand down!"

"I will not!"

John Lewis Hugo grinned, the burned side of his face inflexible. "What fun would that be, eh? Quit this. I have no wish to harm you."

"That's why you bring those abominations of nature."

"I believe the High King requested you be *unspoiled*, is how he put it," John Lewis Hugo said. "The demon wolves are here to protect you from those who would do you harm, nothing more."

"Philip Plantagenet should have died in his cradle as history recounts!"

"But that was not the Word's will, now was it?" John Lewis Hugo countered. "Instead of spending your life enabling the hypocrisy of the Church and that senile wizard, you should embrace a larger cause to set things right."

"John Lewis Hugo," Richard said carefully, curbing his anger. "Do not forget who you are. You are a good man. Let that twisted creature that has been imprisoned inside of you free and do the right thing here."

"So shortsighted. You know not of what you speak."

"You are as wrong as those creatures behind you."

A frown shrouded John Lewis Hugo's face as he turned to the witch.

"Have the demon wolves take them cleanly," he said.

The Cailleach made a curt hand movement.

As if a dam had broken, the creatures bound around their master and the Fomorians, coming straight for Richard. The knight did not panic; he sent his fire into the nearest of the creatures, setting it ablaze and the trees around it. More demon wolves were cut down by azure bursts, their hissing and screams madness in the air. More came on, a torrent of claws and glee, the destruction of their brethren only emboldening them further, a curtain already falling upon the knight. Richard knew he could not stop them all. With his power threatening to overwhelm him like a flood, leaving him a useless husk, the knight focused on his enemy and conserved what he could.

Dryvyd Wood fell away as did Bran's yelling.

A beast broke through his defenses to slash at his exposed side, its claws burying deep.

With a howl of fury and pain, Richard split the creature in two. Black blood showered the air, the demon wolf's cleaved halves hitting the ground.

More beasts gathered beyond the carcass-ridden ground, waiting to attack.

"Lord Gwawl!" John Lewis Hugo commanded.

The beasts came again. This time Gwawl commanded Sanddev to lead his warriors alongside the onslaught of blackened razor-sharp teeth and claws. Concealing his grin at the opportunity given him, Richard swiped the air with Arondight anew, the flames leaping off the blade in thick spurts that shot at the legs of the attackers. The beasts and horses leapt aside.

It was what Richard wanted. The knight sent his power between them, driving them to alter the path of their attack—to slam against the tree trunks, limbs, and roots of Dryvyd Wood.

The forest exploded.

The trees, so packed together, came alive, snatching whatever intrusion awakened them. The demon wolves came on; the horses screamed in terror. Limbs shot out like lightning to wrap about the struggling twisted limbs and legs they encountered, squeezing with intensity born of wood and sap. The warriors struggled to get free, hacking at the limbs in horror, but for each one cut free several more took its place. Panic ensued. The roots greedily bore their captives into the black soil, men, horses, and demon wolves stuffed beneath the ground—some already dead, most suffocating as dirt choked their screams away.

One of the last caught, Sanddev slid into his grave, screaming incoherently for aid.

He disappeared in moments.

John Lewis Hugo and Gwawl yelled orders at the remaining panicked men. The demon wolves milled about, unsure what to do.

"Keep bringing your pets to me!" Richard shouted. "They die!"

"Like Elizabeth McAllister?" John Lewis Hugo returned at a distance, his voice oily. "Without a *real* man to protect her."

"What did you say?" the knight hissed ferociously.

"Your dead wife!" John Lewis Hugo yelled. "Or have you forgotten her already?"

Disbelief and anger filled Richard. The past he so wished he could forget came to the fore. He stepped ahead, leaving Bran against the granite outcropping, his rage pushing him to destroy the dozens of enemies between the two men.

Arondight winked out of existence.

Richard fought to reclaim the blade but it was too late. Maddened by the pain inflicted upon them and driven into motion by the disappearance of Arondight, the beasts flew forward in a frenzied rush, bounding between the animated trees to come straight at the knight. Richard charged forward, his anger overwhelming his faith and sense, until ice from the Cailleach pelted him backward.

He brought his arms up to ward off the frozen assault of the witch—just as the hideous things swarmed him.

Richard spun like a top and crashed into Bran before righting himself, dozens of shredded holes in his clothing and mewling bodies upon his back.

The knight locked eyes with Bran.

Revenge left as the knight knew he had to protect the boy. Arondight answered his call again, flames chasing its length. With a heave of desperation, the knight threw off his assailants, blasting the demon wolves still on him and around him, pushing them back. Fire hurtled from the sword in a concentrated arc, setting fire to wolves, horses, and the Templar Knights who fought to enter the fray.

A sudden hole of possible freedom opened.

"Run!" Richard screamed.

Bran whirled to flee. He vaulted over the charred bodies of blasted men and animals, given an advantage by the consuming chaos. He was through the gap in a moment, tearing across the hillside with Richard a step behind, the angry shouts of pursuit quickened.

"Where?" Bran cried.

"Anywhere," the knight shouted. "Just keep running, no matter what."

Dryvyd Wood passed in a blur. Guttural growls chased them. Richard ran all out, ignoring his wounds and not looking back, keeping away from the trees. Terror gave him powerful strides, enough heart to take him back to the portal.

Before he knew it, claws clamped over his legs.

Cradling Arondight, Richard went down into the forest mulch.

As the knight blasted the demon wolf off of him, Bran was there, his face ashen. Grabbing Richard's bloody arm and torso, the boy hauled the man to his feet and forced him to stumble away. Richard felt his adrenaline fading to haziness. Behind them demon wolves and Templars tore toward them, mere yards away.

"Go!" Richard roared, pushing Bran.

It was too late. In moments, Templar Knights circled the

companions. The remaining demon wolves slinked across the ground, madness distorting the once human and wolf faces, but they did not attack.

Weakness stealing over him, Richard fought the darkness. It was inevitable. The fight would be over soon.

No longer able to will it into being, Arondight vanished.

"Richard!" Bran screamed.

Richard tried to stand but couldn't.

"It is over, McAllister," John Lewis Hugo condemned from the safety of his steed.

Breathing hard and weakened by loss of blood, Richard watched Bran pull a brown wooden box from his pant pocket. The knight thought he should know what the box signified but understanding had fled him like his wits. It didn't matter anyway. Before Bran could do anything with it, the beasts swarmed them, the demon wolves' eyes shining as they gripped him and Bran in bands of iron.

The black angular bodies bore Richard down like a wave.

Chapter 13

The new day brought Bran cramped muscles, the odor of fresh horse dung, and a headache as strong as the leather bonds handcuffing him.

He stirred from false sleep, the nightlong pain racking his body heralding the morning. Around him the camp awakened, warriors rising to gather their bedrolls and possessions, preparing to leave. Bran took small note of the activity, the misery of being shackled to a pole for the night foremost in his thoughts. Other than his pack and coat being taken from him, Bran had not been touched; John Lewis Hugo had ordered his men to ignore the two prisoners under penalty of death.

Now with the golden aura of the rising sun spreading through the forest, Bran wondered anew what he had gotten himself into.

He looked over at Richard. The knight lay nearby where the giant had dropped him, similarly bound but unconscious, his bloody clothing hiding the wounds beneath. Richard breathed shallow, and it was harder for Bran to discern than the night before.

Trying to relieve a throbbing ache near his groin, Bran shifted his weight around on the pole. It didn't help. Ever since the demon wolves had swarmed him, the pain had intensified.

Worried he was wounded, Bran looked down.

As before, there was nothing amiss.

"Awake, are we."

Bran twisted to see John Lewis Hugo staring down at him.

"You know," the leader said. "None of this would be necessary if I felt you would listen to truth and not flee. Your knight lies there. Dying. Broken. Why? Because centuries of lies precede this moment."

Bran ignored him as he had the previous night.

"Still stubborn, I see," John Lewis Hugo observed. "It is common in your world, from what I understand. The knight and his wizard in particular. Fools. Made a fool out of you also, did they not? They fail to tell you all. Does that not anger you?"

Bran turned away. The man echoed Richard's warnings.

"That's right," John Lewis Hugo continued. "I see you know of what I speak. Myrddin Emrys hides much. There are factions everywhere, each trying to gain the advantage. The wizard represents one such group and he meddles, twists lies to truths to achieve an agenda. What does the wizard know of this world?"

"He says your king is a tyrant," Bran said finally.

"And Myrddin is so wise, having not visited Annwn in centuries?"

Bran didn't know what to say. Merle had coerced Bran to enter Annwn and yet had not come, his intentions riddled with mystery. Merle had also left Bran with a knight incapable of maintaining his power. It raised questions he did not have the answers for.

"I know you feel gratitude toward Myrddin Emrys," John Lewis Hugo said. "It is only natural given your situation."

"What the hell does that mean?"

"Everything," John Lewis Hugo said. "Those who are lost can be found. Those who desire a path have it offered. There are those who ensure the sheep are shepherded by sheer will. Philip Plantagenet is one such shepherd. You are too if we have surmised rightly, if you are given the chance of course. The High King extends his welcome to you and offers a place at his side. No more sleeping out in the open; no more worrying about when your next meal will take place."

Bran flushed angrily. "You have been spying on me."

"We leave nothing to chance, Bran Ardall."

"If that is true, then why try to kill me?"

"Is that what the knight and his master told you?" John Lewis Hugo clucked. "Do not be so quick to trust McAllister. He has failed a great many times in his life. Care he does not fail you."

"I'm here because a cu sith attacked me," Bran said. "I wanted answers."

"I know not of what you speak," the deformed man said. "If you were attacked at some point, I surely do not know from what quarter. We have watched you but nothing more. You were not harmed yesterday even by the demon wolves. Think on it. How can that be, if I wished you dead?"

"If this isn't about me, then let me go."

"I could," John Lewis Hugo answered. "But my king commands your presence, and I do not trust you to not flee out of ignorance. You therefore are an enigma, but one the High King believes can serve a purpose."

"And what would that be?" Bran asked darkly.

"That is for him to explain," John Lewis Hugo answered before rising and leaving.

As the scarred man barked further orders, Bran looked to Richard. The knight lay unmoved, broken, the physical damage minor compared to that within. John Lewis Hugo had used Richard's painful past to an advantage. At one time, Richard had a wife. She had been killed. That death was tied to the knight in some way. Bran did not know more than that. Yet Richard distrusted Merle just as John Lewis Hugo and his king did. Could Bran be on the wrong side of things? Or did the severely scarred advisor weave lies to suit his agenda?

Like his cramped muscles, the questions would not leave him.

The group broke camp. After the giants picked up the poles bearing the fettered prisoners, John Lewis Hugo traveled east through the new morning. The Templar Knights and remaining men led by Lord Gwawl surrounded Bran and Richard, their eyes hard and proud. The houndmaster scouted far ahead with his canines while the Cailleach remained behind to maintain control over the demon wolves that brought up the rear.

The ache from being carried like a slung pig grew worse as the day progressed, the swaying motion tightening his bonds to agony. The dawn stretched to mid-morning as the forest thinned, the larger oak and maple trees giving way to beech and alder. Through breaks in the woodland, Bran caught glimpses of rolling verdant hills broken with white eruptions of granite, the stone like shattered bones through emerald skin. Atop one of the higher hillocks, the ruins of what had once been a great castle stood, its walls, towers, and buildings crumbled beneath the onslaught of time. It looked like one of the paintings Merle had in his bookstore, a remnant from an age long past.

Bran wondered why John Lewis Hugo led them within the shadows of the forest when it would have been easier and quicker traveling out on the plain.

He found his gaze focused on the mounted Evinnysan.

"Boy, do not look at me so," Evinnysan growled, his green eyes flashing hatred. "Or I'll shove this here sword up your cave."

The men around him laughed, mean glee in their eyes.

Richard moaned then, his eyelids fluttering.

"Give him aid!" Bran pleaded.

"Why ever would I want to do something that helpful?" John Lewis Hugo replied. "You should be thankful the High King has not thrown you in with the knight's lot."

Lord Gwawl frowned. "Was the knight meant to not be—?"

"Harmed?" John Lewis Hugo finished. "No, no he wasn't. But not everything goes to plan. I will explain this to the king. None of you will be culpable." He stared at each man around him. "But the boy must go to Caer Llion—unharmed."

Bran turned from the mocking stare of Lord Gwawl.

"My Lord," Gwawl continued. "The wolf things you brought . . ."

"Ahh yes, the demon wolves," John Lewis Hugo intoned. "They are terrifying, a small part of a much larger force. If you are worried about your men fearing or spreading rumors, let them. It might make them sharper than they were yesterday."

"I think—"

"*That* is your problem right there, Gwawl," John Lewis Hugo said angrily. "You think too much."

"You sent my men to die in that cursed forest," Gwawl countered, before spitting on the ground. "While the Red Crosses of Caer Llion watched from safety."

"Be careful of whom you offend, Lord."

Lord Gwawl fell quiet but crimson anger spread over his face.

"The wolves will speed *your* king's vision," John Lewis Hugo added. "They can infiltrate into the harsh conditions in the Carn Cavall and will travel far from this world. That is all you need know. I suppose what you are *really* worried about is, yes, they will keep you and your fellow lords in their place."

"Unnatural beasts," Evinnysan spat.

"You don't *have* to like them, Evinnysan," John Lewis Hugo replied with rancor. "*You* just have to do what you are told."

A howl erupted behind them, silencing the lords like a death stroke. As quickly as it had come it was silenced. John Lewis Hugo gave his companions a dark look and, kicking his horse into action, rode back the way they had come. The warriors around Bran did not keep their misgivings silent.

"That one was killed fast. Perhaps they are not so difficult to kill."

"Unnatural to bring such creatures into the world."

"Who does the king think he is, creating those beasts?"

"They are fierce. Should send them into Snowdon against the Morrigan."

"What else are they breeding beneath Caer Llion?"

Each opinion varied, the warriors chattered on as they entered a darker patch of Dryvyd Wood; the dappled sunshine vanished. The mystery of Annwn, with its foreign setting, frightening creatures, and hardened men, heightened Bran's anxiety. He had no weapon, no ability to protect himself. He had not understood the danger of Annwn. He had hoped for answers, even adventure. He had been an ass. The growing realization he could die in a foreign world at any moment now stung like shards of steel.

Bran might not see Seattle again.

Those he knew in the Bricks would never know his fate.

The pain at his groin intensifying suddenly, he pushed the thoughts away angrily. Thinking that way about death did him no good. He sighed and shifted his weight, trying to alleviate some of the bound pain. He would confront what came with the same hard reality he had faced on the streets and relent to nothing.

That's when, from a brambly bush nearby, Bran saw emerald eyes staring at him.

He blinked, the ache in his body replaced by surprise. The eyes followed him from an oval face coated in colors of the forest, inquisitive and alert as they watched the captive and those around him. The rest of her was hidden from view, but curly red hair framed a young face. On a branch next to her a fairy sat, its body composed of sticks and moss fused together, a natural camouflage.

Bran was so astonished by the two he almost cried out.

The woman shook her head—and just as quickly vanished.

A screech in the trees above caught his attention. Arrow Jack jabbered down at Bran, the feathers of the merlin ruffled. Several warriors shot annoyed cursory glances upward and made warding signs of evil. Richard had mentioned the bird would be their guide. That had not worked out well. Arrow Jack continued his screaming though as if warning the world of impending doom.

Bran kept his eyes open, looking for the girl.

She did not appear.

"Who you looking for?" Evinnysan mocked. "I see nobody."

The man next to Evinnysan laughed—just as an arrow sprouted from his chest.

Dazed, the warrior slid out of his saddle, a dead sack gurgling to the ground. Lord Gwawl, Evinnysan, and the men around them shouted in shock as they drew weapons, the ring of steel thick. They had little time to react. The forest erupted as men and women wearing leather charged from the thick brush and trees, attacking the mounted men with swords and axes. Steel upon steel rang, and the sounds of men grunting, screaming, and dying filled the air.

Fear gripped Bran even as the world tilted crazily. The giant carrying him collapsed, struck down. Bran landed hard, his head slamming into the damp forest floor, the world spinning in and out of darkness. Through the haze he saw the giant that carried Richard drop as well, two massive crossbow bolts shot through its neck at awkward angles, the wounds pumping black blood into the day.

Before Bran could attempt to free himself, calloused fingers tugged at his ropes.

"Be still, lad, don't make the knots tighter," the voice chided.

Bran turned to face a small man the size of a barrel, eyes as black as coal fixed on his freedom. Bran took in his rescuer. Wavy black hair streaked with gray matched his beard; the brown leather of his tunic was belted tight and displayed half a dozen knives and a coiled whip. He looked armed for war and fully capable of carrying it out.

"Who are you?" Bran finally stammered.

"Does it matter?"

In seconds his rescuer cut the bonds imprisoning Bran's hands and, moments later, those of his feet as well. Nearby two other smallish men bearing a resemblance to the other freed Richard, the knight a bloody rag doll. Around them two separate groups attacked, slicing in like swords thrust at the same time to divide Bran and Richard from the warriors of John Lewis Hugo at the front and the demon wolves at their back. All the while arrows flew from hidden bowmen in the forest, the shafts striking with unerring precision those warriors who got too close to Bran, the knight, and the three little men who aided them.

Adrenaline pumping life back into his numb limbs, Bran gained his feet only to be dragged away from the conflict, Richard carried right behind him.

"Get them!" John Lewis Hugo screamed from the melee.

The Templar Knights redoubled their efforts, hacking into their foes, but the lithe men and women of the forest were steadfast, a wall of will.

The raging battle faded behind Bran.

About a hundred yards away, he burst from thick foliage into the outer fringe of the expansive plain, the brush limited and trees sporadic. Fierce women on bareback horses confronted him, their various weapons drawn and glinting in the sunshine, most wearing sleeveless jerkins the color of dried mud and short green riding pants. The few men were similarly prepared for war, while nearby an ancient man with white hair above pointed ears stood weaponless, his face wrinkled like a prune.

Several dozen horses waited, mounts for those who fought.

In their midst, a centaur towered over the rest and stared down at Bran. Eyes as blue as ocean depths burned with authoritarian conviction. She held a long ash bow with a knocked arrow. The horse end of the creature was pristine white and powerfully built; the woman half sat naked and proud where she began just below the belly button, her arms and shoulders toned, long blonde braids hanging over pert tanned breasts.

"Got 'em, Aife, my dear," the tiny man said.

"Where is the Queen, Kegan?" the centaur questioned.

"Perhaps the halfbreeds were more difficult to dispatch."

"If true, our time has come," Aife grunted. "Belenus, look to the knight."

The stooped old man knelt at the side of Richard, his fingers probing the knight's limp body with precise movements of gnarled fingers. Richard moaned, his body moving weakly as if warding off the attack that had already wounded him. Belenus ignored the protestations of his patient, his concentration absolute.

"Belenus . . . ?" Aife pressed.

"He is badly wounded, Huntress," the healer answered. "The quicker we return to Arendig Fawr, the better chance he will have to live."

"Conall. Kearney. Give the knight to me," the centaur ordered.

"Wait!" Bran protested. "Who are you? What are you doing?"

"We are those who save your life, human," Aife said icily.

The gnomish men who had freed Richard lifted him as Aife rode up. A shimmer coalesced around her, rippling like waves in crystal water. When it cleared the centaur had vanished. Instead Aife stood upon naked human legs while behind the white horse she had been a part had regained its head, pawing the earth and shaking its mane.

Aife knelt and lifted Richard free, closing her eyes.

The same flickering of light occurred again, and once more woman and horse were joined, the knight cradled to her chest.

"Horse the boy now," Aife commanded. "We must cross the Tywi River with all possible speed."

"What of Morrigan?" Kegan asked.

"She is able, Horsemaster," Aife retorted before galloping northward.

"Know how to ride?" Kegan asked Bran.

"No," Bran stammered.

"Nothing like learning on the fly, says I."

"I'll take him," a feminine voice said.

Bran turned to behold the redhead he had seen earlier breaking from the trees of Dryvyd Wood. She moved with grace, each step quick and certain, her loose-fitting dark green clothing splattered with blackish blood like the sword she held. The woman barely gave him a glance, her eyes round and green as she passed to meet a chocolate mare that whinnied at her approach.

"Willowyn," she greeted.

The fairy darted from the forest then to hover among them all. "Ashrot, Deirdre! Outworlder or no outworlder. Let's go, let's go!"

"Ride hard, Lady of Mochdrev Reach," Kegan said as she mounted.

"Like the wind," Deirdre said.

Kegan made a makeshift stirrup with his linked hands. "Up you go, lad."

"I don't—"

"Now!"

Bran stepped into it and Kegan boosted him up with more strength Bran thought the Horsemaster could possess. He settled in behind the woman, still unsure. The fairy followed, giving Bran what he thought to be a dirty look before flying ahead.

"You had better not let go," Kegan said with a wink. He turned to the redhead. "Aife is already making for the river and the city. We will follow anon."

"Ready?" Deirdre questioned over her shoulder.

Bran gripped her hips loosely. "Where are you taking me?"

"Away."

Before Bran could ask more, the quivering muscles beneath him leapt into motion, hooves pounding the soft ground. Bran threw his arms around the rider's waist from sheer fear.

As they entered the plain's rolling expanse, a horn blew behind them, its blast deep and penetrating.

The sound of the fight faded quickly.

Willowyn carried her two riders northward, her gait powerful and even. The fairy was nowhere to be seen. Bran's extremities came back to life in painful alarm as he held tight. Even as the realization of his freedom stole over him, he wondered if he had merely left one ill only to embrace another.

Willowyn galloped on.

And the Carn Cavall loomed, a hazy smear of promise on the horizon.

Chapter 14

Cormac stared hard at Finn Arne, nearly at a loss for words. The captain gazed back across the desk like a statue, his report finished.

The events in Seattle had not gone as Cormac had hoped. Not at all. The Ardall boy had escaped, aided by McAllister and the wizard, able to flee into the portal with help from that monstrous halfbreed that lived along the pier. The company of Swiss Guard Finn had taken with him lay broken, several of them severely burned, others sustaining broken ribs, legs, or arms. It had taken a great deal of persuasion to set them free from authorities. Finn bore no wounds, the Shield of Arthur bequeathed by the Vigilo protecting him from harm.

Cormac wanted to throttle Finn Arne, shield or no shield.

The Cardinal Vicar fought to maintain his composure. But he saw what failure had done to the captain. It infuriated Finn Arne that McAllister had bested him.

Cormac would use that vengeance to gain advantage.

Donato Javier Ramirez, the Cardinal Seer, sat in a ridged high-backed wood chair, his presence almost invisible. Cormac needed his long-time friend in the room more than ever.

"I am more than disappointed, Captain," Cormac said finally.

"Understandably, Your Eminence."

Cormac chose his words carefully. "Do you wish to make atonement for your failure?"

"More than anything."

Long moments passed. "I will call on you this evening. Leave us."

Finn Arne vanished from the room, leaving the two Cardinals in privacy. Alone with his mentor, Cormac dropped his guard and let the stress he felt out.

"My old friend, this is intolerable!"

"Patience," the Cardinal Seer said. "Remember the Lord's will."

Cormac nodded absentmindedly, frowning into space.

"Cormac Pell O'Connor," Donato prodded. The Cardinal Vicar looked up. "Got yer attention, I see. Yeh have always been an academic and political student. I've seen ambition drive yeh to yer current position. But let me remind yeh of one thing, the most certain thing I have learned in my long life. God has a plan beyond any that yeh may have. To rebel against it for yer own desires is evil's purpose."

"I wonder if I will feel the same once I enter the twilight of my own life," Cormac sighed.

"Twilight, my boy? Twilight can come at any time, regardless of age."

"I suppose you are right," Cormac said, not truly believing it. "The others should be gathered by now. Shall we proceed and relate what trouble I've started?"

Donato barked a weak laugh and rose on legs grown far too spindly. Holding the withered arm of his oldest friend, Cormac guided Donato out of the room and down the polished hallways of the Vatican, the weight of ages pressing in around them. The two men had walked these same steps countless times, but he knew few such walks remained. Donato only had a few years left. Cormac didn't want to think on it, but he knew it was coming.

And after would be a darker world.

After navigating the Papal Apartment passages, the men passed two Swiss Guards and, closing an oak door behind them, entered the personal audience chamber of Pope Clement XV.

Cormac knew he would have to play his best game.

"Greetings Cardinal Ramirez, Cardinal O'Connor," Pope Clement XV welcomed in heavily accented German. "I trust this meeting is as important as its urgency hints at."

Cormac helped Donato sit at the room's circular table before finding his own seat. Seven other Cardinals, each from various parts of the world, filled polished oak chairs of their own and nodded to the Cardinal Vicar—some out of amity, others obligatory respect. No windows or vents were set in the walls; it was a private room for meetings of clandestine import. Three chandeliers cast light, the paintings of past pontiffs dead centuries past mingling with life-size statues carved of Saint Peter, Saint James, and the Virgin Mary. Above it all and hanging from a large cross mounted on the back wall, Jesus peered down on the gathered in twisted agony, the wood glowing with a waxy ethereal sheen.

The Cardinals, all of whom were men over fifty and part of the Vigilo, were dressed in similar loose-fitting crimson robes. Pope Clement XV, who wore a simple white robe with gold stitching, sat in the largest and most ornate chair at the table.

"We have what could become a dire situation, Your Holiness," Cormac began.

"What has transpired?"

Cormac related all he knew about Bran Ardall, what had transpired in Seattle, where the boy had gone and with whom, and what the appearance of the son of the last Heliwr could mean.

When he had finished, a pall of tension filled the room.

"You failed then, in more ways than one," Clement said darkly.

"Unfortunately, yes," Cormac said. "The Ardall boy is in Annwn."

"And you chose *not* to inform me of this *before* you lost him?"

The Cardinal Vicar met the hard stare. "At the time, Your Holiness, we barely knew what was transpiring. Archbishop Glenallen in Seattle saw to the knight, but we were unsure about the boy. No Heliwr in the history of the Church has been born of the previous owner of the title. And with the developments in the Middle East and the wars taking precedence there, I didn't want to draw your attention away from what you are trying to achieve with the extremists."

"I see," Clement said with distaste. "I will address that line of thought later. Continue."

"The boy is in Annwn, as I said," Cormac resumed. "The Cardinal Seer observed that the High King of Annwn sent a group to capture him. I think the attack on the boy in Seattle was to somehow draw him to Annwn so he could be detained."

"Could not the attack be retribution for some grievance by Charles Ardall long since passed?" Cardinal Villenza argued, his pate balding and jowls heavy.

"It could," Cormac admitted. "But Philip Plantagenet *knew* to send his Templar Knights to the portal at a specific time—and John Lewis Hugo kept the boy alive once captured. No, the anticipation of the boy coming through the portal is the key. And if someone wanted him gone, why go to such lengths to keep him alive?"

"Templar Knights," Cardinal Tucci spat. "Those the Church failed to kill are a disgrace."

"The wizard was also a part of this," Cormac reminded.

"If Myrddin Emrys has taken interest in the son of Ardall, it stands to reason the child is of importance, possibly to us as well," the Pope said.

The Cardinals murmured interest among one another. The Cardinal Vicar remained noncommittal, his own desires kept private. To control the Heliwr was to have unlimited power. If Bran Ardall had been chosen to become the next Unfettered Knight, the boy would be vulnerable to persuasion. The wizard undoubtedly knew this and had already poisoned that prospect. The Vigilo would have to find a way to gain the champion and once again regain an authority to shape the world.

"Another problem to consider," Cormac added. "The events in Annwn are unsettling, true, but the implications could bring that battle into the Vatican—into this world. If Philip were to pollute and gain the Heliwr, it could be disastrous. It could destroy us."

"Is the knight in place not capable of protecting the portal?" Clement asked.

"Ennio Rossi," Cardinal Villenza said. "As we saw with Bruno Ricci two decades ago, even a knight can be bested."

"McAllister," Clement snorted. "Even a knight can *betray*."

"What Cardinal Villenza suggests is we prepare the Vatican for the worst," Cormac continued. "The walls that surround the Basilica and the Papal Grounds were built not only to protect the work established by Saint Peter but to contain those on the other side of the gateway. The catacombs lend time to counter any threat that could force its way through the portal and into the Basilica. I believe we should address our defenses."

"Is there really a threat though?" the Pope countered. "Cardinal Seer?"

Donato leaned forward in his chair, his milky eyes serene. "There is, my Cardinal brethren. Last eve, as I looked into Annwn, terrible things I saw. Philip and his legion of Templar Knights have grown strong and as yeh know, both hate the Catholic Church. Most of Annwn has fallen. But that is not all. Twisted things helped overcome the Ardall boy's knight protector—some kind of human melding with feral animal. Never before I have seen halfbreed beings such as these, nor have my predecessors documented their existence. The Morrigan saw them destroyed with her arts, but if more exist they could pose a problem."

"The boy is no longer in Philip's control then?" the Pope questioned.

"No, both he and the knight were saved by the Morrigan," the Seer said. "They make way toward the Carn Cavall as we sit here."

"*What* is McAllister *doing* there?" Cardinal Villenza asked.

Silence again filled the room. No one knew.

"And you still cannot view Caer Llion, Seer?" Clement asked.

"Not at all, Yer Holiness," Donato answered. "The curse tablets set into its walls and very foundations prevent my sight. I am as blind to Caer Llion as I am to these walls."

"These creatures came from the castle?"

"I have combed the land. They are nowhere else. Created in Caer Llion, I say."

"This could be nothing to us," Cardinal Tucci said.

"History has taught much in this instance," Cormac interrupted. "Men like Philip—the men of his family—are not satiated with the power they accrue. He will never stop, of that you can be sure. He may have these halfbreeds to war with his rebellious fey left in the mountains. But in time, he will turn his gaze this way."

"Then we have two problems," Clement summarized. "There is the boy to consider, and what rises from Caer Llion."

"If these halfbreeds are part of a larger scheme, we must be ready," Cormac agreed.

"Suggestions, Cardinal Vicar?" Clement asked.

"Fortify our defenses here. Order the portal Archbishops to prepare their knights. And keep an eye on Annwn. If the worst comes, the Vatican must be ready to evacuate everyone who resides, works, or visits. The Swiss Guard will be pivotal for that role."

"Make it happen," the Pope ordered. "All of it. The job of the Vigilo is to protect the Word of God and ensure its expansion. If those of this world realized there was another world with many of the fey they have thought mere mythology, pagan influence would ruin thousands of years of doctrine and belief. That cannot be allowed to happen. Give the knights what they need. We must be steadfast to prevent Annwn from ever returning to our shores." He paused. "And if battle comes it will be one we are prepared for. Understood?"

The Cardinals nodded in unison.

"If you hear of anything else, notify me immediately—unconditionally," the Pope ordered. "Now, excuse Cardinal O'Connor, Cardinal Ramirez, and myself."

The sound of their robes a long whisper, the Cardinals left.

"I asked the others to leave; this will not concern them," Clement said darkly. "It has always been my stance to leave Annwn to its own devices as long as it did not attempt a return. That threat has become palpable, in my mind at least. Do you agree?" Both Cormac and Donato nodded. "I am pleased you both agree and I am sure you will do what is right—do what is necessary."

"I have been thinking the same, Your Holiness," Cormac said.

"Cormac, you and Donato have been friends a long time,"

Clement said, staring hard at the Cardinal Vicar. "What is said to one the other hears. You both have been steadfast and strong in my support. But you anger me, Cormac. As the leader of the Catholic Church, I demand to know what is going on at all times. The events in Iran, Iraq, and the East Bank do hold much of my attention, and much of my duty is pomp, but it is also my role and none other to oversee the entirety of our faith, and that includes protecting Rome." He paused. "There are many secrets the Vigilo are not privy to yet that I am aware of, knowledge that can benefit situations the Church finds itself in. Don't forget that."

"It will not happen again, Your Holiness," Cormac replied, biting his tongue.

"Now, I know the knight below is inexperienced," the Pope stated. "Is that a worry?"

"He is quite capable," Donato answered. "Young and strong."

"Ennio Rossi will aid us in what must be done," Cormac added. "Of that, I promise you."

"Good. Good," Clement said, rising. "Do what must be done. That is all."

"Holy Father," Cormac said, bowing in farewell.

As Cormac helped Donato from the room, the hot gaze of the Pope pressed into his back like a knife. The Cardinal Vicar grinned. Despite having done his duty by informing the Pope of Ardall, the Heliwr could yet still be within his grasp.

He hoped Ennio Rossi would be receptive to what Cormac had in mind for Finn Arne.

"It is time we spoke to Ennio," Donato breathed.

"It is indeed, my old friend," Cormac agreed. "And find where Annwn is hiding Bran Ardall."

"This must be done, Ennio," Donato urged.

The young knight sat on the edge of the Seer's bed, his eyes betraying distrust. Cormac stood nearby, more and more irritated with each passing second. The wavy-haired knight shot glances at the Cardinal Vicar, skepticism captured in his uncomfortable posture. Donato tried to curtail such feelings, his papery hands squeezing those of the young man with emphasis.

"Yeh know I would not ask yeh of this if it were not of great import."

Ennio nodded. "I know, Cardinal Ramirez."

Impatience crept into Cormac. Ennio Rossi was a strong knight but youth made him unpredictable. He was unable to see the gray from the black and white of Myrddin Emrys. The Cardinal Vicar and Seer would have to make a strong case for Ennio to follow their plan.

Trying to hide his contempt, Cormac gazed to the far wall where the black shroud hid the Fionúir Mirror, a stain in an otherwise warm room.

It waited for Cormac like a ghost, a cold promise.

He turned to the knight. "If all things were equal, Ennio, there *would* be no need."

"It goes against all I have been taught," the Italian responded. "I trust you both, whereas the others would never agree to what you are asking. I believe, however, this passes boundaries that should not be crossed."

"It *is* an odd situation," Donato agreed. "Cardinal O'Connor and I cannot even explain the last time a person from this world entered Annwn not by accident. Myrddin Emrys stresses the need for the two worlds to remain separate, just as the Church does. But this is a situation that *could* lead to a much larger war—a war of cataclysmic proportions for all involved. Trust me, son, this is something we must stop at all costs."

"Who exactly are you sending in?" Ennio asked.

"You will meet them. Good God-fearing men, no worries," Cormac assured.

Ennio nodded, the lack of enthusiasm written on his face. Cormac didn't blame him. For centuries ever since Myrddin Emrys had given the knights their power, there had been a tenuous relationship between the Church and those who guarded the portals. But the boy was not allowing his betters to aid in his decision-making.

Cormac grew angrier at the thought. Although the knight could best him easily with the Arthurian-bestowed knife Carnwennan, the desire to grab Ennio by the shirt and shake him until teeth rattled persisted.

"It will be done then," Ennio said. He did not look happy about it.

"It is the right choice," Donato assured.

"Are you ready, Seer?" Cormac asked before Ennio could change his mind.

The frail man took a deep breath, weighing his decision.

"Donato?" Cormac pressed.

"Yeh will be coming with me this time, I warrant?"

"I will. I have to."

"Let us find Bran Ardall then," Donato said wearily. "Before yer distaste for using the mirror or my part to play in it ruins our convictions."

They approached the mirror together, Ennio watching from the bed. Donato was slow, but his milky eyes were wide open and ready for what must be done. Cormac had few close people in his life, but the relationship he had with Donato gave him an insight into the Cardinal Seer others might miss. Donato was tired. If he began to falter, Cormac would be there for the Seer, certain reprimand or not, to try the next day instead.

"Stand next to me, Cormac," the Seer ordered as he pulled the black cloth free of the mirror and dropped it to the rug-littered floor. "I will guide us. Keep your thoughts firmly fixed on me to start. If you do, there should not be a problem."

"I remember."

The Seer took a deep breath. Cormac did the same.

Flames from the hearth swirled in the depths of the Fionúir Mirror as if it contained an inner fire of its own. In the reflection Cormac watched the milky eyes of his friend drain and become darkest brown. Light from the glass then washed over him, enveloping him, first gray and then lightening like a sun breaking through fog. The room vanished; the mirror disappeared. The Cardinal Vicar remained focused on his mentor, embracing the tingling sensation, and never deviating from Donato's command.

Suddenly free from his body, Cormac chased the soul of Donato into Annwn.

The light softened, and a mixture of earth colors infiltrated the swirling gray, darkening. Lines solidified. Shapes formed. Soon Cormac stared at a lush forest beneath crystal blue sky. No sounds came to him, no smells intruded. His other senses were gone.

—Dryvyd Wood—

The voice of Donato echoed in his head.

—Where was the Ardall boy captured?—

The view spun dizzyingly, sickening Cormac. As if they were birds on the wing, they flew between the branches of gnarled, malformed trees, into the heart of the forest, where the luminescence of the sky gave way beneath a thick canopy of blackened leaves.

Donato brought them to a halt amidst nightmare. Rotting and bloated carcasses of twisted creatures littered the torn up mulch of the forest floor, their faces frozen in angry death. The things were halfbreeds as the Cardinal Seer had said, a cross between something human and something animal. Fire had reduced them to charred flesh in places, their bones exposed to the air and blackened. Cormac knew how the creatures had met their deaths; the power of McAllister could not be ignored.

—The capture occurred here, Cormac—

The grisly scene suffocated the Cardinal Vicar. The ill-bred beasts presented a large problem for the Church. In the past, halfbreeds were very rare, the incompatibility of the fey and humanity making it difficult. Most died after conception or were stillborn. The few survivors, like the Kreche in Seattle, were usually hunted and destroyed. If Philip had found a way to breed these evil monstrosities and use them in his war, how many of them existed? Were they being bred in Caer Llion? What other abominations could the despot of Annwn be creating?

In a small way, Cormac admired Philip for destroying the pagan influence that took so much away from God. But he also knew Philip would never be content. Spying on Annwn in this manner gave the Church the knowledge it needed to decide how to protect itself.

The world spiraled again and Donato sped them through the forest to the outskirts of a vast plain. Dead men, horses, and more halfbreeds littered the ground, rotted and exposed.

—The Morrigan ambushed the Templar Knights here. With the boy and the knight, she fled northward across the plains and into the foothills of the mountains—

—Can you find the boy now?—

The view in his mind spun wildly as the mirror zoomed into the heights of the sky and flew northward. Cormac saw Snowdon breaking out of the ancient Carn Cavall like pikes out of lumpy shields. The remaining fey who rebelled against Philip roamed free in those environs, the Carn Cavall the last bastion of freedom in Annwn. He saw drained rivers entering lakes mostly dried, thick forests of pine, ash, and oak slowly dying, boulders and rocky cliffs.

At one time it had been a lush world, filled with teeming wildlife and vibrant health.

It had since been reduced to the longest of droughts.

—The seasons witch remains with Philip?—

—She took part in the battle for the boy, Cormac—

Donato sped them up toward Snowdon until a wall of gray prevented their view.

—This is where the boy was taken?—

—Or where they will be soon. The Carn Cavall is a large range, and the Nharth of the forest hide much from me with their magic. Philip as well, no doubt. All I know is the boy came this way and there are no other refuges for them to find solace—

Cormac pondered this.

On foot, it was a start for an experienced tracker.

—Show me Caer Llion—

The mountains vanished. The same sickening feeling overwhelmed Cormac as they moved southward at excessive speeds. The view slowly solidified into the massive battlements, towers and walls of a large castle lording over a town grown up around its foundations. Smoke rose from hundreds of chimneys until the steady breeze carried it away, the town an anthill of activity and expanding life. Beyond and to the south, the expanse of the ocean rolled into white cliffs where a variety of sea birds kited in the wind to dive for food.

The kingdom Philip had forged seemed oblivious to the boot heel of the tyrant. As long as the men and women embraced Philip, they were safe from persecution.

The Tuatha de Dannan could not make that statement. They fought the son of Henry II and had become the hunted.

—Caer Llion, Cormac—

—Go in closer—

—We will not be allowed—

Donato pushed forward anyway. Just when Cormac could make out significant details inside the open-air windows of the castle, a black mist swallowed his vision and grew thick like molasses, repelling the two men. Dizziness rolled over Cormac in waves, the need to retch food not in his stomach strong and urgent.

Donato pulled their vantage back quickly.

The feeling of being torn from the inside subsided to a dull ache.

—I forgot what that is like, Donato. Philip is there?—

—Most likely. He rarely leaves—

—What about his right hand?—

—John Lewis Hugo leaves often. Battles. Political intrigue. Pure sin—

Just as Cormac was about to ask after Philip's advisor, a spear entered his mind, shredding coherant thought.

He wanted to scream. Malignant darkness cut into the thoughts of the Cardinal Vicar while encircling his throat with thick-roped malice. The Cardinal tossed up what strength he had but could not stop it, his mind choked by an unseen force. The migraine grew as if someone poured flaming gasoline on it. Never had the mirror inflicted this kind of pain in the past. His mind being torn apart, Cormac could feel Donato struggling too. He realized they were being attacked, an unfamiliar mind strangling both Cardinals, the glee from their assailant thick and repugnant. It was an evil Cormac had never encountered before, crushing in its wickedness, reveling in its power to destroy the men it had ensnared.

Donato!

Cormac tried to scream. Nothing happened.

Then the pain vanished, the noose pried loose by Donato with warm feelings of love born of family for Cormac. Years of using the mirror giving him a small advantage, the Cardinal Seer gave his once-student a mental shove away from the evil entity toward their world—away from the harm that accosted them.

Cormac tumbled free of the mirror.

Time slowed, darkness absolute.

When he became aware again, Cormac panted real air, trying to regain control over his muscles. He pushed his body up off of the cold stone of the floor and, opening his eyes, looked to Donato.

Fear twisting his features, Ennio crouched over the Seer.

Donato did not breathe.

Cormac fought his weakness and crawled to the side of Donato. His irises, which had been white in life, were obsidian orbs staring at the ceiling, the leathery skin of his face shrunken against gaunt cheeks. Nothing stirred about the man—no rise and fall of his bony chest, no movement in his limbs.

The Cardinal Seer was dead.

Cormac held the empty shell of Donato Javier Ramirez. Tears swept away his vision. He choked back the urge to scream. Something in Annwn had done this. As a last gift, the Cardinal Seer spent the last of his life to throw Cormac out of the mirror and away from harm, embracing his own death so Cormac may live.

Dark emotions rolled through Cormac and two certainties shook him.

The Vatican was now blind to what transpired in Annwn. And Cormac had lost his longest and oldest friend.

"What happened?" Ennio mewed.

"You will do this thing I ask of you, Ennio," Cormac murmured, ignoring the knight.

Ennio swallowed hard. "I will, Cardinal Vicar."

Cormac nodded and clutched the dead Seer close. That night, he would call Finn Arne to his chamber and prepare him to become the instrument he needed. It would be easy. The captain burned for a chance to confront McAllister again. Once the son of Ardall was his, the Church would regain the Heliwr—with Cormac as his superior. When that happened, the person responsible for killing his oldest friend would suffer unlike anyone in the history of the world.

Sorrow rolled down his cheeks.

Donato was dead.

And as when he learned of his murdered family, Cormac wept vengeance.

Chapter 15

Slowly gaining the Carn Cavall, Deirdre rode upon Willowyn with Bran at her back when the faces in the mist quizzically materialized, just as she knew they would.

"Deirdre . . . ?" Bran said uncertainly.

"It is all right, Bran, they mean you no harm. They are merely curious."

"What are they?"

"The Nharth," Deirdre said. The Morrigan, Kegan, and the other fey members in their group ignored them. "The Nharth are friends. Even in the hottest days, they cloak the strongholds of the Tuatha de Dannan, a magical wall to keep the prying eyes of Caer Llion and elsewhere out. When they gather in one place, this fog forms."

Bran looked closer, now as curious as the Nharth. Deirdre just shook her head. The outworlder still sat behind her but his death grip about her waist had lessened, his safety finally realized. It had come to Deirdre long before, but in its place a pervasive sadness grew. Whereas the plains of Mochdrev Reach were vibrant, the forest now around her died slowly. Fir trees once thick and green were dusty and browned, the evil power of the Cailleach more pronounced. Fog swirled in and out of the branches and the path they were on, hiding most of the ill effects, the colors washed out, brushed over with gray paint. Few animals stirred around them. The heat of the day grew despite the fog, unnatural. Streams reduced to a trickle as they ran toward the plains and the Rhedewyr—all angles and powerful grace—drank from them at rest stops while their riders stretched legs and kept an eye on possible pursuit.

Deirdre took a deep breath, free of Caer Llion and John Lewis Hugo—at least for the moment. She and her father had come to the Tuatha de Dannan city of Arendig Fawr two days earlier to discover what options lay before them. She had insisted on going; Lord Gerallt had agreed as long as he had final say in matters. The Morrigan had been gracious, offering what meager aid she could to those who would defy Philip Plantagenet.

Lord Gerallt and Deirdre had been arguing about their course of action when the two outworlders had entered Annwn.

The whispers from the Nharth began when Deirdre and Bran could no longer see a dozen feet away. The voices were not heard as much felt, a touch of breath on skin, a kiss of ghost lips on the nape of the neck. More faces came into view to disappear just as quickly. Deirdre sat her mount, still unused to the foreign appraisal. The Nharth came in all shapes and sizes, some with horns, single eyes, or almost-human features. More appeared in the misty shadows like smoke given substance, curious glances mingling with animosity. Hundreds visited but all vanished, the beings as insubstantial as the fog around them.

"They are like ghosts," Bran said. "Creepy."

"The Nharth are merely different," she said. "As I said, nothing to worry about."

"Where are you taking me? And where is Richard?"

"Arendig Fawr," she said, looking at Bran. "The Queen's capital. The knight is there right now, with healers. John Lewis Hugo and those halfbreeds hurt him deeply. I don't know how or why he—or you for that matter—are still alive."

As the Nharth slowly dissipated into nothingness once more, Deirdre watched Bran rub his wrists where he had been bound.

Crimson welts cut deep into them. He said nothing. Deirdre at least respected the boy, no matter where he came from. The outworlder had taken almost as severe a whipping as his companion. Bruises darkened his skin where scrapes and cuts did not, many of them probably lasting for weeks. Like the knight, he would also have to see a healer.

"Ye seem to be faring better, lad," Kegan said, his own horse a step beside Willowyn.

"I am, thanks to being free."

"Hungry?"

Before he could reply, Kegan tossed him a green apple from his sack and handed him a knife. Deirdre hid her amusement at how voracious Bran began cutting into the fruit.

"Gonna cut his thumb off for sure," Snedeker snickered from the air.

"Quiet, you," Deirdre chided.

"It will take days to heal those bruises, I think," Kegan said, pointing at Bran's wounds and ignoring the fairy. "The Dark One wanted ye badly, it seems. Thankfully the Morrigan kept ye from him at all costs."

Deirdre caught the Queen of the Tuatha de Dannan looking their way. She was a tall woman, armored in blood-spattered onyx plate that appeared lighter than it probably was, her limbs lithe, raven black hair pulled back from white cheekbones. Deirdre had only met her twice now. More concerned by their safety, the Morrigan had not yet spoken to Bran. She was a soul made of steel, the wisdom of ages in her unlined face. Power radiated from her being and even from a distance it made Deirdre feel small and inconsequential.

"She took a great risk ye know," Kegan said, also noticing the attention.

"What do you mean?" Bran questioned.

"We are the hunted, lad. Have been for ages. The Dark One and his ilk have warred and spread from your world throughout this one, and the peace we desired so long ago—the peace we wanted to find upon fleeing your world—has become a wisp of smoke. Now they control all but these mountains and even the weather. We strike, we plunder, we survive, and we disappear to do it again. Saving ye and the knight exposed us. We will have to watch paths for months now, even more than already done."

"Why would she care?" Bran asked, perplexed. "Richard and I are nothing to you."

"Why does anyone do what they do?" Deirdre noted, shrugging. "Because they feel it to be the right thing, of course. And usually advantageous."

"I read about a Morrigan once," Bran said. "In my world."

"From what I understand, we are a source of false tales in your world," Kegan laughed. "Time has erased us like a footprint in a stream. But I am real, am I not?"

"All *too* real," Bran replied.

Kegan grinned. "First time ye've ridden, eh?"

"It is. The pain in my ass grows worse every time I have to get back on."

"Then walk," Deirdre said, grinning.

"It will become easier," Kegan said, smiling at the redhead. "Imagine my sons and I. We have to climb the mane like a rope in order to mount the Rhedewyr."

"With my luck lately I'll fall off and break my neck," Bran said.

"Where there is a will, young Bran. Where there is a will," Kegan said. "Getting thrown is not the worst that could happen. My father told a tale of my grandfather's grandfather who, in his drunken dotage, fell off his horse and lost a leg. The hoof severed it right off." Kegan made a quick slicing motion. "Stay on and ye will not have that problem."

"Can I ask you a question, Kegan?" Bran asked.

"Always, lad."

"What are you exactly?"

The Horsemaster looked quizzically at Deirdre and burst with a loud guffaw.

"I am what I am," Kegan chuckled. "I imagine ye want to know I am a clurichaun."

Bran frowned. "Is that like a leprechaun?"

"No, no, nothing of the sort!" Kegan said indignantly. "No, I actually *work* for my bed and meals, lad. Lazy imps the leprechauns, the lot o' them."

Willowyn brought Deirdre and Bran to the Morrigan, who had decided to wait on her own steed at the side of the trail, her piercing blue eyes never deviating from them. Deirdre knew Bran felt the power of the Queen too; the outworlder shrank a bit as they grew closer.

"Kegan, ride ahead," the Morrigan said simply, her lips thin.

"My Queen," the Horsemaster said with a nod, leaving.

"Are you well?" she asked both Deirdre and Bran.

"Better," Deirdre responded for both of them. "Thank you."

"I apologize for not speaking with you sooner," the Queen said, looking only at Bran. "There were . . . matters of safety and the wounded to consider. It is important we cover our passage fully and I oversee it personally. To make a mistake would be dire indeed." She then noted Bran's wounds. "You have been injured but you are strong—more so than you probably think. Like the Lady of Mochdrev Reach here. It takes such people to survive, what you have and what is to come. Has your ride been comfortable?"

"It doesn't matter, as long as I am not tied up," Bran said.

"Very true," the Morrigan agreed. "No one likes to be under the yoke, do they, Deirdre?"

"Aye, Queen."

"You are taking me to Arendig Fawr?" Bran asked.

"Worry not that you have exchanged one captor for another. You are as free as the birds in the trees and can leave at any time, with our helpful guidance of course," she stressed. "We are indeed going to Arendig Fawr. Those of the Tuatha de Dannan who will not live beneath foreign rule are spread out over these mountains in conclaves to not give our foe the chance at a single death strike. It is in this way we assure our way of life. Arendig Fawr is the center of our people, for the moment at least."

"And where did the other outworlder go?" Deirdre asked.

"Assuredly Aife has already made it to Arendig Fawr and McAllister is being treated as I speak to you."

"So you know him?" Bran asked, clearly shocked.

"Never met him," the Queen admitted. "But the Yn Saith are known to us."

"Then why save us? If anything, we have endangered you all."

The mien of the Morrigan darkened. "Innocents shall not suffer under Philip, no matter who they are. And the vaunted High King of Annwn has interest in you that goes beyond mere curiosity. If he wanted you dead, you would be. He captured you for a reason and it could not have boded well for his enemies. That means the fey living in these mountains. That means me."

"I see," Bran said, looking uncertainly at Deirdre. "I was told by John Lewis Hugo the king wanted to share his side of things and then let me go."

"Wanted to talk to you while shackled to that Fomorian, no doubt," the Morrigan scoffed. "Sent the Houndmaster and the Cailleach, two of his most powerful, after you? Aye, sounds like to me Philip had a lot to speak on."

"How did you find us?" Bran asked.

"We have spies who watch those who leave Caer Llion," the Morrigan answered. "Knew John Lewis Hugo leaving meant importance. But Arrow Jack also warned us. The merlin is quite resourceful. Even now he is helping to watch our back trail to ensure we are not being followed."

"You understand him?"

"One must listen to hear," the Morrigan said.

"Sounds familiar," Bran said. "Merle said that to me once."

"Myrddin Emrys," the Morrigan sighed. "A wiser man you will not meet. You do well to listen. He has aided the Tuatha de Dannan over the ages. It is hard finding allies in this war but he has ever been one."

Deirdre looked to the Queen but didn't say anything. The redhead had spoken to the Morrigan at length about Mochdrev Reach joining the cause of the Tuatha de Dannan. It had caused a rift with her father but it was necessary. The Queen had offered protection for a time but there was more to discuss after saving the outworders. At least the Morrigan was open to adding allies, especially human ones, and that gave Deirdre hope.

"I overheard many of the men around Lord Gwawl say they don't agree with Philip," Bran offered. "They all hate the demon wolves. Perhaps you have more allies than you know?"

"Gwawl," the Queen growled. "Always a snake, that one. He sides with power rather than honor, what is right. It is hard to see those we once called friends side with an enemy who wishes our destruction."

"Mochdrev Reach is an ally of the Tuatha de Dannan," Deirdre finally spoke up with a certainty that surprised even her.

"That remains to be seen, Lady Deirdre. Your sire has yet to make that clear," the Morrigan said. She turned back to Bran. "The last true ally we had came from your world—the last Heliwr."

"The *last* Heliwr?"

"The Unfettered Knight," the Morrigan said. "The last being Charles Ardall."

"My father," Bran echoed. "You knew him? Knew I was his son?"

"Aye. Arrow Jack said as much," the Queen said. "Charles Ardall visited these same mountains several times in the past."

Deirdre had not heard anything about Bran's parentage. The knowledge surprised her. It seemed the appearance of the knight and Bran could not therefore be happenstance. She didn't know why they were in Annwn, but if the knight survived his wounds there was a chance they would consider joining the Seelie Court against Caer Llion.

And help sway Lord Gerallt to join Arendig Fawr.

"You favor your father a great deal," the Morrigan said. "In many ways."

"I didn't know him well. He died when I was young."

"He was strong and kind, a rare man who never made a mockery of the world, the kind who leaves it a better place than when he entered it. I know very few I can say that about, but he was one of them."

"Why did he come here?"

"Why does any Heliwr come into Annwn? To make amends."

"I don't know what that means, to be a Heliwr," Bran confessed.

"I see. The wizard is playing the game close to his heart," the Morrigan said. "The Heliwr is the Unfettered Knight—not chained to govern any portal between the two worlds. Whenever a crossing occurs from either world, the Heliwr is responsible for setting it right again if one of the Yn Saith fail."

"Well, who is the Heliwr now?" Deirdre asked.

"There is not one."

"So my father . . . hunted people down, then?" Bran asked. "Like a bounty hunter?"

"Aye, and when other mischief transpired," the Queen replied. "But now is not the time to speak of such things. Deirdre has no wish to hear a history lesson, methinks. We can make Arendig Fawr before nightfall. There is much we must discuss in the presence of McAllister and the remnants of the Seelie Court. You are safe for now. Relax and enjoy the ride."

The Morrigan trotted away but turned back suddenly. "These demon wolves you speak of. Did it sound like there were more of them?"

"I don't know. Maybe."

"I see," the Queen said.

With the Morrigan leading, the group continued through the rugged terrain of the Carn Cavall. Deirdre guided Willowyn as a quiet Bran finished his apple. She wondered about the outworlders again. The visions her shade mother had shared included her tie to some outworlder. Could Bran be the one her mother had spoken about? Could Richard McAllister? She did not know. The two had come into Annwn for unknown reasons. Were those reasons linked to her life? Could her mother be that clairvoyant? Whatever the case, events had gone tragically awry for them. Was John Lewis Hugo tracking them? Was Richard dying? What would Bran do if the knight did die? The Morrigan seemed fairly certain the knight would recover. If he did, Deirdre wondered how the outworlders would shape her future.

The afternoon wore on as the sun arced the sky. The land died the farther they traveled. One moment broad meadows filled with long browning grasses and lazy insects surrounded her; the next she passed under what once had been enormous waterfalls, now dried to a small trickle. Fewer and fewer forest animals watched them, emaciated and furtive. No birdsong lent music to the day. The peaks of Snowdon loomed, only its uppermost crags still covered in glacier.

As Snedeker sat on her shoulder and Deirdre thought about how she would convince her father to join those in the Seelie Court, Bran touched her arm from behind.

"So, how did you get involved in all of this?" he asked.

"Not the shortest of stories," Deirdre answered, wondering how much she should tell him. "I live in a city called Mochdrev Reach, out in the plains south of the Carn Cavall. My ancestors aided the Tuatha de Dannan when they fled the persecution of the Misty Isles, choosing to settle apart from the fey. When Philip Plantagenet arrived with his Templar Knights, the Reach kept apart from both groups, autonomous.

"That separation is coming to an end," she continued. "Philip Plantagenet has taken over much of Annwn and now wants to marry the Reach with his city of Caer Llion. It would bring the two separate groups of humans together, undoubtedly as a single force to fight the Tuatha de Dannan here, in the Carn Cavall."

"By marry you mean . . . Philip marrying *you*?"

"As you can imagine, I'm not too keen on the idea," Deirdre said.

"You shouldn't be," Bran said, frowning.

Still staring at the outworlder, Snedeker grunted darkly on her shoulder.

"I would rather choose love than have it forced on me," she said. "My father, the lord of Mochdrev Reach, is at Arendig Fawr right now to discover with the Morrigan if there is anything that can be done, if we should join with the fey and defy Plantagenet or if we should be absorbed by Caer Llion to keep our people out of harm's way."

"Tough choices," Bran said. "I would imagine you are hoping to not be married to the High King, although war can't be much better." Deirdre gritted her teeth at the thought of the forced marriage. "On the streets where I have lived most of my life, the main lesson I have learned is to knock the bully down. Knock the bully down, and they leave you alone."

"It's a bit different when thousands of your people are in danger if you want to knock the bully down," Deirdre said, suddenly taking up her father's argument.

"Better than you wedded to a tyrant though, right?" Bran asked.

"You are sweet to say so. And yes, that's how I feel."

"I would fight to keep you from that cracknettle, Red," the fairy sniffed. "He will never lay his hands on you if I have my way."

"Thank you, Snedeker," Deirdre said, hiding a grin from the earnest fairy.

"And you are friends with a fairy?" Bran asked. "That seems a bit odd."

"Mind your own business, hotsquirt," Snedeker shot back, his wings shaking irritably while pointing a twiggy finger at Bran. "I seem to recall a certain fairy helping with your freedom!"

"Okay, okay, don't get all pissy with me," Bran said. "Jeez."

The fairy crossed his wooden arms, watching Bran darkly.

"Yes, Snedeker and I are friends, even if he *is* a bit temperamental at times," Deirdre said, giving the fairy a reproachful look. "Have been friends now for years. He is prone to thievery, but he has always been there when I needed him."

"Cat's right, I have!" Snedeker glowered.

"Well, I hope something can be done," Bran said. "About Philip, I mean."

Deirdre fell silent. She hoped that as well.

The company continued into the mountains, the sun waning to the west. Other trails met their own, disappearing into the forests in varying directions. Deirdre took a deep breath. She didn't know what she had gotten herself into with Caer Llion but she was happy to be as far away from there as possible. Snedeker remained on her shoulder, watching Bran closely with a look of disgust on his mossy face. Deirdre found it odd the fairy was taking such an interest in Bran, but Snedeker had always been a bit odd.

As she thought more on Bran, the mists and trees thinned to reveal Arendig Fawr.

The city grew at the base of a sheer rock wall that thrust into the purpling evening sky, its heights lost in obscurity, its size, construction, and collection of fey awesome. In its shadow, fey intermingled with one another—ogres, leprechauns, cu sith, Fomorians, brownies, cait sith, fairies from different clans, and countless unknown others. All roamed free, most giving Deirdre and Bran quick glances of curiosity, entering and leaving large huts grown from living trees, vines, and flowers that blended with the forest. Through the foliage and hundreds of buildings, Deirdre could just make out the giant set of stone doors standing open and leading to the Cadarn, tiny gnarled trees growing from the rock face above the black maw. Somewhere to the north the roar of a waterfall thundered.

Bran looked as surprised as Deirdre had felt two days earlier upon arriving.

"Arendig Fawr," Deirdre introduced.

"I've never seen anything like it," Bran said.

"It's the home of the Queen," she said. "The city goes deep into the mountain and far above in the trees. Most of the conclaves are protected by natural formations in these mountains, like this. The Snowdon is filled with secrets, ones of which Caer Llion has no knowledge. Thousands live here, thousands who depend on the Morrigan to keep them safe."

"There are so many here, so many fairy folk."

"Tuatha de Dannan, Bran. Fey. Calling them fairy folk is a slight."

"That's right!" Snedeker said.

"What you see here is what Caer Llion would see destroyed—all of it," Deirdre said, ignoring the fairy. "The buildings. The people. The very way of life the fey live. He has tried for centuries—and failed."

"Maybe Philip can be stopped then," Bran said mysteriously.

With Snedeker taking to the air, Deirdre slid off of Willowyn and did not answer. She hoped the lord of Caer Llion could be stopped too. The warriors who had rescued Richard and Bran faded into the populace. Belenus hurried off toward the gaping hole at the base of the cliff, leaving his stallion in the care of Connal and Kearney. The clurichauns guided the other Rhedewyr away like prattling mothers.

"Kegan, time is required to prepare quarters for our guest," the Morrigan commanded, dismounting her own steed.

"With haste, my Queen," Kegan said, bowing.

"Not too much, I hope."

"Wait," Bran shouted after the departing leader. "I want to see Richard."

"In good time," the Morrigan said.

Deirdre nodded to Bran. "You are truly safe now."

"Thank you," he said, dismounting.

"No. Thank Willowyn," she said with a smile as she patted the Rhedewyr. "I must care for her. I am sure we will see one another soon."

Bran stood there awkwardly, hands in pockets, just staring at Deirdre. He said nothing. She felt heat rise into her cheeks and grew uncomfortable under his gaze.

"Come, lad," Kegan said, lightly grabbing Bran's elbow. "Let us find a meal, ye and I, before ye fall in love."

Deirdre watched the outworlder blush as well. Bran flashed her a smile; she returned it, though she didn't like how it felt. She watched as Kegan guided Bran to a series of huts nearby where fires offered tantalizing aromas of what they cooked.

When they were gone, Deirdre turned to Snedeker, who also watched Bran disappear.

"What is wrong with you?" she asked pointedly.

"Nothing! Nothing!"

"You have been interested in that boy since we saved him," she said. "Could barely take your eyes off of him. Why?"

"No reason," the fairy said, wriggling in the air. "Never seen an outworlder is all."

"Other than John Lewis Hugo?" Deirdre said. When Snedeker didn't respond and just kept staring after Bran, she sighed. "I don't know what you are up to but I don't like it."

"There is something magical about him."

"Well, keep an eye on him if it makes you happy," Deirdre

growled in warning. "Just leave him be. He already doesn't like you, I can tell."

"I am an acquired taste, Red, you know that," Snedeker snorted.

Deirdre strode away from the fairy, muttering below her breath. She had better things to do than argue with Snedeker. Leaving Willowyn momentarily with the guards at the entrance to the Cadarn, she traveled into the mountain toward the healing quarters, her eyes adjusting to the sudden gloom. She made her way upward, the stone steps worn from centuries of use, the walls chiseled smooth and carved with faintly glowing runes by great artisans. She would visit the knight and, if he looked to survive, gauge how best to proceed with her father.

Once gaining the healing quarters, she was directed to a lone room where the knight had been moved.

She was not prepared for what she saw.

The knight lay on a bed, naked, his clothing cut away and revealing the damage the demon wolves had done. It left a lump in her throat. Purpling bruises covered most of his body as if he had been pummeled by Fomorians, and tiny gashes of varying sizes littered his skin, a heady balm preventing them from bleeding. Two larger rents along his ribcage were bandaged, but they were already crimson. A waxy sheen of sweat coated his skin. He appeared to be dead if not for his shallow breathing and the attention he still received from the healers.

Belenus and his ancient aid looked up. The Morrigan stood at the back of the room, still wearing her armor and deep in thought.

"How is he?" Deirdre asked.

"McAllister may yet live," Belenus said, his wizened face reflective. "Aerten has worked hard but the morning will tell. We have put him in a healing sleep. He has been gravely injured, and the halfbreeds that attacked him possess a venom that even now courses through his body. We have countered it the best we can with the life magic of the Tuatha de Dannan. He will heal quickly if it is meant to be, but that remains to be seen. It would help if he was whole of spirit, but we sense a deeper pain in his being that cannot be healed and which might become his undoing."

"What do you mean?" the Queen asked.

"He has a wounded spirit," Aerten said, shrugging. "It slowly kills him anyway."

"I see," the Morrigan said. "If his condition changes notify me."

Belenus nodded as the Queen left the room.

Deirdre sat on the bed next to the knight. She had not gotten a good look at him during the battle, but what she saw intrigued her. He was a handsome man, she thought. The wavy black hair and pale skin. The length of his body and muscle tone. The chiseled cheekbones and strong jawline. Belenus was right though. There was even in slumber a darkness that pervaded his soul, one even she could sense. She found herself reaching out and brushing his clammy cheek with a gentle touch. His eyelids fluttered but did not open.

She sat there a few moments, staring at the knight, willing him to live.

Then she sat a few moments longer.

Chapter 16

The void burned the man, its flames caustic memories, and he was lost.

The things he once remembered as arms throbbed pain, unresponsive and leaden. Dark fire licked his soul, unceasing. He was powerless to prevent it. Pairs of crimson eyes blinked at him, watching him, cruelty and demonic malevolence in their depths. More memories. Nothing made sense, the torture driving paranoia along his nerves like lightning.

He didn't know who he was. He didn't care.

He reviled himself, but he knew not why. He pushed the memories away. It didn't matter. Within his being, angry hornets buzzed, filling him with hate. Heat bloomed inside, and he knew the demon eyes danced with glee, slavering their wickedness in all-consuming madness. Part of their essence entered him and he cried out. He knew he was sickened by the past. It no longer bothered him. It made up who he had become. Worms slipped through his dreams, eating their way out, and the place his heart had been was empty, the disease having started there.

He failed to remember why it began. Wailing punctuated the void, sorrow so raw it crushed him deeper into despair. He had cried that way once.

Then a song of growing things dulled the chaos, until a foreign sound intruded upon his suffering, out of place in his dismal world.

It was the sound of a fairy manically screaming.

Memories flooded back as if a dam broken. The fey. Seattle. Old World Tales. Merle. The sword Arondight. Elizabeth. Louis Glenallen. Annwn. John Lewis Hugo. Bran and Arrow Jack. The flood of demon wolves as it broke like a tidal wave upon him, rending claws and evil teeth ripping at his exposed flesh.

He broke the surface of clarity.

He was Richard McAllister, Knight of the Yn Saith.

He lived. And he hated himself for it.

Richard opened his eyes, blinking wildly to clear his sleep away, disoriented from the nightmares. It was night, the circular window across from him allowing moonlight to infiltrate the room. He lay in a soft bed, the covers pulled up to his chest. A hint of lavender mixed with earthy herbs he could not identify clung about him. He tried to take a deep breath but couldn't; he then realized bandages bound his chest tightly.

"Let go of me, you prattstick!" the fairy yelled.

Richard found the reason for his awakening. Bran lay on a bed of his own, his fingers gripping the stick-like figure of a fairy. The fey creature struggled in the fast grip like an overly large dragonfly caught in a trap. Bran held on despite the fairy's fit. For the first time, Richard wondered where he was, how long he had been asleep, and what had transpired since the attack at Dryvyd Wood.

"What were you doing, Snedeker?" Bran hissed.

"Nothing, tosser!" the fairy growled, squirming. "Release me!"

"It was up to no good, boy," Richard muttered.

Bran sat up, clearly surprised. He maintained his hold on the fairy. "You're awake. How do you feel?"

"I'll live," Richard said, wincing from a flurry of pain as he sat up. "If barely."

"You should lay back down. Rest."

"Mother hen now too, eh?" Richard glowered. "Mind your business."

The fairy had stopped fighting, realizing the struggle was futile or hoping the boy would grow lax for an escape. Bran held the creature up so Richard could see it.

"What was this thing doing?" the boy asked.

"Why ask me? Ask it."

With his free hand, Bran pulled free the box he had tried to use in Dryvyd Wood before the demon wolves fell upon them. It was the size of a jeweler's box. In the glow of the moon, an image of a silver knot on its wooden lid shimmered in the dark. Richard knew exactly what it was and what it heralded.

He cursed Merle all the more.

At the appearance of the box, Snedeker fought harder. "Get that thing away from me!" the fairy screamed. "I do not want it!"

"Have you opened it, boy?" Richard asked.

"No, I haven't," Bran replied. "Merle said to use it when I wanted protection."

"Use what though? Do you even know?"

"I guess I just assumed—"

"Never assume," Richard cut Bran off. "Not here. Ever."

"No one does this to an Oakwell fairy!" Snedeker screamed. "When I am free, I will destroy you both with a word from the Lady of the Lake and the authority she has besto—"

"Shut up, fairy," the knight growled. "Before I pull your wings off and really give you something to cry about."

Snedeker quieted but continued to rail against his prison.

"I told you, Bran," Richard admonished. "Don't trust Merle."

"Do *you* know what is in the box?"

"I do. And you should throw it away right now."

Bran sat still, pondering what Richard said. The knight looked about the room. The walls seemed to be cut from the very rock of a mountain, but they were carved with elegant care, the lines simple and smooth. The furniture was built likewise and covered with colored silk. It was most certainly a conclave of the Tuatha de Dannan. The knight probed his body then, determining how much damage had been done. He seemed whole. The demon wolves had inflicted grave wounds on him, but he was still intact.

"Where are we?" Richard asked finally.

"Arendig Fawr, as of two days ago."

"How?"

"The Morrigan and her fey saved us from John Lewis Hugo while you were passed out," Bran explained, still looking at the box.

"Oh, just *open it* already," Richard said. "It won't harm you. Not yet, anyway."

Bran gave Richard a quick look before doing as he suggested. Pressed into a lush bed of red silk, an acorn-like seed rested, tiny veins of silver streaking the wood. Even in the pale light Richard could see it. It was a beautiful object, but one the knight knew to be very dangerous. After a few moments, the silver of the seed pulsed with a ghost light like a slow heartbeat, one that did not make a sound.

"What is it?" Bran questioned, mesmerized.

"A very special seed," Richard said. "And I bet that little bastard was trying to steal it."

"I want nothing to do with that thing, tosserpig," Snedeker spat. "Why in the fires of the Erlking would I want a stupid seed like that one? When I am free, you both will suff—"

"Why were you after this?!" Bran asked anew, shaking the fairy again.

"I just wanted to see it!" the fey screamed. "Not steal it!"

"Why did you want to see it?" the boy asked. "Tell me! Or so help me I'll feed you to the closest dog I can find."

"I will kill any flea-bitten mongrel you send at me, including you!"

Bran shook the fairy with more vehemence. Richard withheld a smile. The boy was as tough and vindictive as the streets could make him.

"It called to me!" the fairy whined at last.

"Called to you? When? Now?"

"Back in Dryvyd Wood, when you were trussed up with the Fomorian!" the fairy revealed finally. "It pulsed magic like none I have ever felt. I just wanted a peek, a peek I say!"

Bran frowned. "What does it mean, Richard?"

"Fairy, I never want to see you again," Richard rumbled, ignoring the question. "If I do, the only thing flying will be your ash upon the wind. Got it?"

"I understand, fair knight!"

Richard nodded to Bran. The boy released Snedeker.

The fairy flew out the window like a dart and vanished into the night.

"Damnable fairies. What other trouble have you gotten yourself into?" Richard griped.

"What is this seed?" Bran asked instead.

Richard took as deep a breath he could. Long moments passed. A part of him just wanted to go back to sleep, but he knew the question to be too important to not answer. Grunting pain as he swung his legs out of bed, he gave Bran his darkest look.

"I had hoped it wouldn't come to this, that we could discover what Philip was up to and return to Seattle without Merle's omens coming true in any form," Richard said. When the boy didn't respond, the knight continued. "The seed in the box is called the Paladr."

"The Paladr?"

"Remember how the Yn Saith received their power? Merle gave the knights their power to have the authority to make difficult decisions without interference from the Catholic Church and its own desires?"

"Merle's last great act of magic, you said," Bran said.

"That's right. It did not *only* involve the knights of the portals. He foresaw a need for a lone knight, one not tied to the portals, one who would roam free to do things the portal knights could not. For seven hundred years, he fulfilled that role. But nearly losing control of his power imbuing the knights with their new authority in the twelfth century made him realize he could not do what was necessary any longer."

"The Heliwr," Bran stated. "My father was the last, right?"

"He was. And a good Heliwr he made too."

"And what of the Paladr?"

"Do you know of Joseph of Arimathea?" Richard asked.

"I saw his name mentioned in a book at Merle's store," Bran said. "The leather one with the rose on its front. I didn't read much of it though. Had just started."

"Merle setting your future in motion, without your leave I might add," Richard spat, his anger making him dizzy. "No matter. Joseph of Arimathea is the man who gave up his tomb for the burial of Jesus Christ after His crucifixion. He was also given the Holy Grail, the cup used by Christ at the Last Supper that later caught His blood when the Roman soldier Longinus, who meant to discover if Christ still lived, stabbed His side with a spear. Joseph and his family left the Middle East, carrying the Grail to begin Christianity in Britain. To accomplish this, God gave him a staff that helped carry him across all of those miles. Once he arrived in Britain, he drove the staff into the ground and it grew into a black hawthorn near where Glastonbury Abbey would later be built.

"The Paladr is a seed from that tree."

"What is it for?" Bran probed. "Why would Merle give it to me?"

"I will get to that. You should be asking me to finish the story," Richard retorted. "The hawthorn that grew is a powerful tree, and for generations Joseph's family watched over it, kept it safe, and cared for it. Merle knew the power the tree possessed, and when time came for the old man to relinquish his duty to someone else, he came to Glastonbury Abbey. Joseph's family or the hawthorn—no one except Merle knows for sure—gave the old man a lone seed. The seed bequeaths the power of the Heliwr to the person—if they are worthy.

Bran gazed back into the box.

"The Dark Thorn is the promise of the Paladr, the staff carried by Joseph of Arimathea as he hunted a new beginning," Richard murmured. "And all the power and responsibility the Dark Thorn gives the Heliwr. If you want it, that is."

Fear crept over Bran as Richard hoped it would.

"Merle believes I am the next Heliwr?"

"To accept the Dark Thorn is to become the Heliwr, yes," Richard said darkly. "The Heliwr is the Unfettered Knight, able to roam both Annwn and our world, to hunt down those who occasionally get past the portal knights, to set right what evil fey and evil men desire of Annwn, to help keep the two worlds separate."

"I thought Merle said knighthood was never passed from father to son?" Bran said, his hand shaking a bit.

"The old man lied, as usual."

"How does the Paladr become this magical staff?"

"That I do not know," Richard admitted. "Your father was already the Heliwr by the time I accepted Arondight from Merle. I know the seed offers itself to the right person in some way but other than that . . ."

"And if I refuse the Paladr?" Bran asked.

"It has happened before," Richard said, shrugging. "The world will go on without a Heliwr, as it has done for more than a decade."

Bran gave the seed a final glance before closing the box. Richard did not envy the boy and his place in this mess. The knight had long ago made his decision to accept Arondight, and it had led to nothing but pain and hardship. Bran was now being told that he might have to make a similar decision, with nary more information than Richard had possessed. All Bran had to do was look at the knight; he lay scarred and destroyed of spirit, evidence of what it meant to take on the mantle of knighthood in service to the higher good.

"I'm no knight, no one special," Bran said.

"If you believe that then don't accept it."

The lonely sound of an owl hooted outside, a reminder that a world existed beyond the walls of their room, one where danger lurked everywhere.

"Why do you hate me?" Bran asked, the question stunning the knight.

"I do not wish this on you, not after how my life has gone," Richard said, the darkness of the room coalescing around him. "Merle was adamant I bring you, leaving no choice. But you are right. I don't care much for you. We have virtually nothing in common. You don't respect me or understand why I choose to live in the Bricks. You would do anything to escape them, even if that means working for Merle, a man who uses you."

"You have more to offer than living on the streets," Bran said angrily. "As do I!"

"Not everyone is the same, you little bastard," Richard grated. "Even still, I would never wish knighthood on you. I've been used and so will you be if you accept."

Bran shoved the box back into his jeans pocket.

"I think you need your rest," the boy said neutrally.

"I do," Richard sliced the tension aside. "Since we are in Arendig Fawr, I hope to speak to the Morrigan in the morning. It will be then we will find our course of action in all of this."

"I see," Bran said coldly.

"And be happy that damnable fairy is now gone," Richard said. "And keep the Paladr safe. No reason for it to fall into another's hands, especially those of a fairy."

Bran looked out the window where the moonlight played among occasional ephemeral clouds passing under the stars. Richard eased back to his bed. He marveled that the boy had the courage to stand up to him.

Merle had chosen a strong soul. That was true enough.

But the knight hoped their discussion would give Bran pause before accepting the Paladr and making a huge mistake.

He closed his eyes. Sleep came swiftly.

A FAINT KNOCK on the door awoke Richard.

He watched a gnarled old woman carrying two baskets filled with bandages, salves, and pungent aromatic herbs enter. She nodded a silent greeting, the golden light of morning coloring her long white hair, before she sat at his side and began unwrapping his dressings. Despite being in pain, he felt better than hours before. When his abdomen and chest were exposed, however, it gave him pause. The wounds inflicted by the demon wolves were terrible to look upon, harsh slashes in his rib cage muscles and bruising everywhere. The gashes were already healing, pink skin raised around the scabs; the terrible bruising alternated from purple to green to yellow. Richard had never been so damaged as a knight. If not for the administrations of the fey, he undoubtedly would have been much worse off.

The woman cleaned the wounds and began rewrapping them when Richard heard boots come to a stop at the doorway.

"Morning, Kegan," Bran said, yawning as he rose.

"Let us go, lad," a clurichaun invited from the doorway. "Let Aerten do her work. The Cadarn and the world outside its stone walls awaits"

"I will go with you as well," Richard said.

The short, bearded man stopped. "Do you think that wise, knight, given your injuries?"

"The air will do me good."

The clurichaun grunted. Richard waited for Aerten to finish her work and then pushed himself gingerly off the bed. The old woman ignored him and vanished out the door. Realizing his clothes were gone—the better since they were undoubtedly bloodstained—Richard put on a new white shirt, green pants, and black boots placed on a chair nearby.

They fit well, and soon the three of them left.

The corridors of the Cadarn were cool but dry, filled with fey creatures and a few humans. It was carved from the mountain and more permanent than the grown buildings of trees, vines, and flowers Richard knew the fey usually preferred. Orbs lit his path, highlighting masterful alien artistry in every arch, each step, and all chiseled statues. Silk flowed like rainbows hung intermittently on walls and from the ceilings, beautiful banners of various forest scenes hanging against the black granite of the mountain. Passageways arched to new levels shrouded in mystery while other hallways burrowed deep into the world, the odor of water laced with minerals heavy on the air.

Richard took his time as he followed the clurichaun and Bran down a spiraling staircase. The knight was weak, weaker than he thought when he had sat up in bed, but he had never been the type to lounge while healing. There was too much to do, now more than ever. He just hoped he would continue to heal and be able to carry out what he knew would be soon coming.

"Clurichaun, what of the Morrigan?" Richard asked. "I must speak with her."

"My name is Kegan O'Farn," the other replied. "Not clurichaun. To answer your inquiry, the Queen has called for a gathering of the Seelie Court. It has not done so in two centuries. She is quite busy. Ye and Bran Ardall will need to show solidarity with the Court if today is to have any meaning beyond words, that much I can tell ye."

"What is this Seelie Court, Richard?" Bran asked.

Richard gave a snort. "Feel free to answer him, *Kegan O'Farn.*"

"The Seelie Court is composed of the lords from all fey belonging to the light," Kegan said, ignoring Richard's mockery. "As for why it is important, the Tuatha de Dannan are a reckoning force but are spread over the Carn Cavall and beyond—some out of necessity, a few from condemnation. Arendig Fawr is the capital, it is the reason ye see so many different fey about ye, but the other conclaves are more race concentrated."

"The fairies live with the fairies," Bran suggested. "The leprechauns with other leprechauns..."

"Correct ye are," Kegan said, smiling, as he guided Bran and Richard through the giant doors of the Cadarn into the late morning sunshine. "The lords of these conclaves rarely discuss matters. It takes a grave reason, like the war with Philip, to make it happen. The Morrigan feels she has a good reason to call the Court today."

"That reason has to do with us?" Richard asked.

"I know not, although it is interesting ye are able to leave your post, McAllister. Ye are not the Heliwr," Kegan stated, looking at Richard darkly. "But your appearance brings hope."

"Hope for what?" the knight questioned.

"That is for the Morrigan to say. Whatever she wishes to discuss with the lords, it will be a difficult task."

"Why?" Bran prodded.

"They rarely all agree—and several will not appear as commanded," Richard interrupted, shielding his eyes from the hot sun. "When is the Court convening, Kegan?"

"The gathering is not until late afternoon at the earliest," the clurichaun said. "It will take time for last night's request missives to arrive and longer for them to be answered. While we wait, I meant to show Bran some of Arendig Fawr."

Bran looked to Richard.

"Might as well," the knight said. "A walk should do us both good."

After receiving a sour green apple and a loaf of warm wheat bread smothered in butter from Kegan for his breakfast, Richard walked Arendig Fawr. The city was a lot larger than he had originally thought, encompassing much of the mountainside. The Cadarn fulfilled the role of a palace, the city populace living around it. As he walked near buildings constructed of nature, Richard observed bakers, butchers, spinners, tailors and shoemakers. Carts filled with vegetables and fruit made their way to the city market, and other than the occasional leprechaun sitting idly by with bottle in hand, everyone worked at perfecting whatever trade they employed.

But to the careful eyes of the knight, there was an underlying darkness—a pervasive sadness—that haunted each set of exotic eyes he looked into, every smile sent his way that was far too brief.

Richard knew what that sorrow meant.

It was the look of life being swallowed by war.

The sun passed its zenith and Kegan led his charges to the far northern side of Arendig Fawr, outside the city. The forest, mostly large fir and pine trees, gave way to a flat oval meadow encircled by a smattering of oak and lesser brush—and filled by hundreds of horses.

"The Awenau," Kegan shared. "The gathering place of the Rhedewyr."

The great animals cropped at the browning grass, their muscles rippling beneath coats shimmering like sun-drenched water. Some turned toward them, marked interest in their round eyes, while the foals and yearlings frolicked, lost in their own worlds of delight. A few humans tended the Awenau while two young clurichauns bearing a striking resemblance to Kegan worked together on the same horse, one humming while he dug clean the inside of a hoof, the other grumbling as he pulled the horse's mouth wide to look at its teeth. Several other fey aided the horses, but Richard could tell the important work was done by the short clurichauns.

"The Rhedewyr aren't fenced in?" Bran asked.

Kegan barked a laugh. "There is no need. They depend on us as we depend on them."

"Horses in our world would never be allowed to roam free like this," Richard explained to the clurichaun.

"Horses in your world aren't that smart," Kegan argued. "The Rhedewyr come and go at their own volition. They know when they are needed. My sons and I, along with a few others, tend them as required—a relationship that benefits both the riders and the cared for." He smiled. "And look who wants to greet ye."

Richard observed one of the Rhedewyr cantering toward Bran, a tall chestnut mare with a flowing black mane and tail. The horse pranced to a slow trot as it grew near and stopped to nuzzle Bran with affection.

"You see, lad," Kegan said. "Smart."

"Willowyn," Bran breathed, smiling. The boy looked around as if seeking someone but disappointment quickly filled his face.

"I am surprised at the amount of humans among the Tuatha de Dannan," Richard said.

"All are ancestors of the Misty Isles," the clurichaun sniffed. "Philip brought thousands of men and women and hundreds of those Templar Knights with him. Over the centuries not all of their children embraced the rule of the Usurper. Those who cannot tolerate him come to us—out of a change or safety or any number of other reasons."

"How can you know they aren't spies sent by Philip?"

"There *is* no way, knight," Kegan acknowledged. "Other than the Nharth. Those in the mountain fog know much about a person."

Richard watched the Rhedewyr, thinking. They would be an integral part of what was to come. He would have to speak to the Morrigan about them. There were things he and Bran would need if what he thought came to pass.

It would require sacrifice.

It would not come easily.

Hoping he would be strong enough for the gathering Seelie Court, Richard finished his breakfast and tried to enjoy the innocence of the Awenau.

He knew that innocence would not last.

Chapter 17

Richard watched the lords of the Seelie Court take seats around the Cylch Table.

The Sarn Throne stood empty next to him, the Morrigan yet to arrive. Dozens of orbs chased away the shadows from the uppermost chamber of the Cadarn, the soft light illuminating colorful banners of the fey nations that hung from the rock ceiling. The cool air bore a hint of crushed lilac and earthy minerals. Foot-wide waterfalls trickled down hewn rock at four different places, the water vanishing below. Despite the care that had gone into creating such a beautiful room from solid rock—and the elegant curve of powerful runes carved into the walls to keep the concerns of Seelie Court secret—Richard failed to find any solace.

The memories John Lewis Hugo had invoked lingered.

And angered him.

Since walking Arendig Fawr and feeling stronger, Richard turned his thoughts to his capture. The advisor for Philip Plantagenet knew intimate chinks in the knight's armor, had used them to compromise the faith Richard used to maintain Arondight. How John Lewis Hugo knew of Elizabeth the knight did not know, but it had neutralized his escape from the demon wolves.

Even now, Richard was unsure if he could call Arondight.

He closed his eyes briefly, and saw the dead vision of her.

Stares from the summoned lords prickled him back to reality. He met each with stern authority, hiding the turmoil within. He would not show weakness.

The lords were as different as the lands they warded, governed by petty bickering and centuries-long squabbles. Lord Eigion of the Merrow, his skin near translucent and neck gills pulsing faintly, continually fought Lord n'Hagr of the Buggane to keep the coastal ogre-like people of Caer Harlech from destroying the fish populations of the sea. Unapologetic for her nakedness, Horsemaster Aife stared hard at Lugh of the Long Hand—the defender of Arendig Fawr and bearer of the magical spear Areadbhar—for the occasional ill treatment of the Rhedewyr. Beside Lugh sat Mastersmith Govannon, his meaty hands folded on the table, an outcast living in the outskirts of the city. On the other side slumped Caswallawn, barely cognizant in his perpetual drunken stupor, as Lord Finnbhennach glowered over all, his broad frame mammoth even seated, his bullish horns gleaming where they erupted from black skin.

A bearded human and a woman sharing his fiery red hair and fierce eyes stood near the wall of the room. The Tuatha de Dannan gave them distrustful stares as well.

Six thrones, including the guest seat for Bran, remained empty—lords who had been killed, lords who had joined Philip.

And lords who chose to ignore the Morrigan.

Richard shifted in his seat, which sent a fresh burst of agony through his middle. The wounds were healing. Richard knew he still suffered internal bruising though. His healers assured him that too would fade with time, but Richard knew he had no time to give.

In calling the Seelie Court, the Morrigan had other intentions.

The Queen deemed Bran important to the meeting, inviting him to sit in with the Court. No matter how much Richard hated involving the boy, he could not ignore the wishes of the Morrigan anymore than he could order the Pope. That afternoon, he had learned more about the battle at Dryvyd Wood and his rescue as well as what else the boy had done while in Arendig Fawr. It was obvious the Queen of the Seelie Court saw something in Bran Richard did not.

Merle had as well. Giving the Paladr to Bran had begun indoctrination into a role the boy would not understand—until it was too late.

Richard remembered the day he had accepted Arondight . . .

Springtime had finally arrived in Seattle. Richard sat on a bench in the Quad at the University of Washington in his first year of graduate studies, his shaggy hair midnight black and pale forearms absorbing the first sunshine of the year. Ancient cherry trees bloomed around him, breezes sending a pink petal storm upon the air, while gargoyles—weathered from decades of sitting on the oldest buildings of the school—stared down at him, some wearing gas masks marking the turbulent time of their creation. The day infused winter-heavy hearts with the giddy possibility of summer, and Richard was no different.

Sitting with legs crossed, he absorbed *The Once and Future King*.

"Interesting choice, nose in a book on this beautiful day."

Richard dipped the novel and shielded his eyes to view an old man, his beard white and skin tanned to the depths of its wrinkles. Both hands in khaki pockets and his white collared shirt gleaming, he had a scholarly appeal, an empty pipe hanging from his mouth like an afterthought.

Richard liked him instantly.

"Is my book the interesting choice or choosing to read outside?" Richard asked.

"Both, I think."

"It beats grading papers, that's for sure."

"May I?" the older man questioned, indicating the empty side of the bench.

Richard nodded and scooted over a bit.

"T.H. White," the man observed as he sat, removing his pipe and holding it like a cherished thing. "A very good writer. Took many liberties with the lives of Arthur and Lancelot and the rest, though I suppose he had his reasons. Many other writers have done the same—Bede, Gildas, Nennius, Geoffrey of Monmoth,

Wace, de Troyes, Mallory. Even Tennyson, Twain and Bradley. All have it right; all have it wrong."

"I've read most of them, as part of my undergrad work," Richard said, turning the book over and looking at the cover. "This is an infinitely easier read but just as engaging—maybe more so with its relevance to World War II."

"So you prefer the easier trod path then?"

"Sometimes," Richard admitted. "When it makes sense."

"Did you graduate in four years?"

Richard peered closer at the old man. Icy blue eyes stared back, unflinching.

"Look, I don't mean to be rude but who are you?"

"Four years? Five years? Longer?"

"Five," Richard replied, perplexed but intrigued. "I was biochem for a while but my heart wasn't in lab work. I finished with an English Literature degree."

"Then you *do not* take the easier path when it matters?"

"No, I suppose I don't. I could have graduated on time with a degree I would not have been happy with—and saved money and time just to do something I would have hated. I could have started a life, made money, had a family, and become prey of the system." Richard paused, suddenly wondering why he was telling this stranger anything about his life. "Anyway, *The Once and Future King* is not as simple as it may appear; it's a literary commentary on how mankind fails to bring about a government that does not take advantage of its people."

"Ultimate power corrupts ultimately," the man said. "No matter if it is totalitarian or socialist or democracies run by hierarchal laws—'might *by* right' or 'might *for* right' or 'right *for* right.'"

"Right," Richard said, grinning. "You've read it then. Any merit in it? That mankind will never be truly free of tyranny unless it abolishes *all* government?"

"I believe quite strongly in what White had to say," the bearded man said. "Sadly there are those in humanity who will never be satiated, who are moved by evil—from the vagabond to the leader of a country and all between. Mankind is flawed. No form of government can account for that. It offers belief in a utopia that is unattainable. Gotten to Lancelot's portrayal yet?"

"Just," Richard said. "He is . . . a very imperfect character. Nothing like the romantic ideal boys aspire to be and girls hope to marry. Desperate to prove himself. Angry and ugly to boot."

"Yes, he was imperfect," the white-haired man said, tamping fragrant tobacco into his pipe. "Of course, just another fabrication to suit the writer. Lancelot was anything but ugly. Interesting idea though. I enjoy subtexts very much."

"Are you a professor here at the University?" Richard asked, closing the book.

"No, no, but that would be an honor, too," the old man chuckled. "I sell ancient and rare books. Why don't you come down to my bookstore tomorrow in Pioneer Square. It's on First, near Yesler. There are a few items there I think you might be interested in."

"I'll try," Richard said, knowing he would not go.

"Good day then, sir," the man said, lighting his pipe. "Be sure to enjoy it. A nice day like today should be treasured, particularly in Seattle. See you tomorrow."

The bookseller left, retreating beneath a rain of broken pink blossoms.

Richard shook his head and reopened the book.

The conversation with the old man lingered with Richard that night. The next day he bussed to the bookstore and made a choice that had changed his life forever.

That choice had now led him to Annwn.

Movement in the Cadarn tunnel caught his eye. Bran materialized from the darkness and entered the chamber, Kegan at his side and Arrow Jack an obsidian blur flying to the back of the empty seat next to Richard. He returned the earnest stare of Bran. Distrust from the argument stressed the air between them. Richard offered the empty guest seat next to him. Bran took it as the clurichaun sat next to Horsemaster Aife.

The Morrigan entered the room then, red silk swirling from her black gown, her pale angular face stern, exotic eyes hard as obsidian. The lords rose, all eyes on the Queen. Two fairies hovered above each of her bare shoulders, awaiting any orders she may give. She was tall, thin, and regal, each movement graceful as she gained the Sarn Throne, her stare fixed upon her supplicants around the table as the fairies first organized the wayward trails of crimson silk and then settled on the throne much like Arrow Jack had on the chair now occupied by Bran.

The odd menagerie of lords bowed to the Queen before returning to their seats.

The chamber doors closed with a silent whoosh of air.

"Greetings to you, Lords of the Seelie Court," the Morrigan said, her voice firm and controlled. "I know some have traveled great distances in a short amount of time. It is not without purpose. You have been gathered to help address recent events that do not bode well for your peoples and the future of Annwn."

"We are honored to return to Arendig Fawr, Queen," n'Hagr baritoned, two canine teeth overlapping his upper lip like yellow daggers. "It has been too long."

"As the four empty thrones note, some of our brethren have perished, embraced Philip's rule, or neglected to answer my calling," the Queen said. "Of the last, Lord Fafnir has sent no word and Lord Latobius declined the invitation out of care for an ill child."

"Sick dragon, eh?" Lugh muttered. "Unappreciative traitor."

"Lord Latobius has all to lose and nothing to gain," Eigion argued.

"Latobius has not been a part of the Seelie Court for centuries," Lugh countered, staring hard at the lithe merman. "He knows not what is given him so freely. The Nharth watch the trails; the blood of the Long Hand reject attack. Tal Ebolyon is kept safe by others. What does he give in return? Nothing. Let him rot. Lord Fafnir as well."

"The Tuatha de Dannan *are* fractured," Govannon said simply.

"What you all say is true," the Morrigan interrupted. "But even the Snowdon will be unable to defend the upper conclaves of the coblynau and dragons—just as Arendig Fawr and those you lord over are safe. War is coming for us all. If we are to have any chance at surviving and ending the reign of the Usurper, we need them."

"Need them for what?" Caswallawn slurred. "For centuries, no aid. Nothing. Did they help protect my lands, my people?" The drunk slammed his fist down on the table. "No! I agree with Lugh—traitors, both of them."

"Lord Caswallawn, your rancor is on your breath," the Queen quipped angrily. "Still your tongue. You dishonor my guests."

Caswallawn fell silent under her icy gaze.

"Why have you gathered us, Queen?" Lord Finnbhennach asked.

"There are events transpiring none of us can ignore. That *I* cannot ignore," the Morrigan replied, touching each person in the room with her eyes. "We have been at war now for eight centuries, longer if you consider our last days in the Misty Isles. Slowly we have lost our place in Annwn and every day we retreat further—retreat from what we are. Philip Plantagenet controls more than just land; he controls our very lives.

"Mastersmith Govannon is right," she continued. "The Court is fractured, weakened. Every sunrise our enemy grows stronger and we remain unchanged, unable to form a cohesive battle against Caer Llion. In time, far sooner than later, our Court will be ferreted out, and when that happens, each of our peoples will die in succession." She paused, her features cold and certain. "Unless we of the Seelie Court unite—and attack."

"Under the Rhyfel Banner," Lord Eigion said.

"Finally," Caswallawn mumbled, sitting straighter.

"Pardon me, Queen, but is that not an impossibility?" the human man appealed, scratching his red beard. "I know I lack the experience the rest of you possess—being human without an immortal life has that disadvantage—but the Seelie Court has been undone for millennia. By your own admission we lack the might of Lords Fafnir and Latobius. Not to mention that of Lord Gwawl and others who flocked to Philip. How can the Seelie Court raise a banner of war without them?"

"The threat of Caer Llion grows, Lord Gerallt," the Morrigan addressed the room. "You know this as well as I. Philip and John Lewis Hugo move new pieces upon the gwyddebwyll board, pieces never before seen. Lords once friends are gathering at Caer Llion, their might added to the Templar Knights for purposes not entirely clear. Lord Gerallt has the right of it though; this will not be the Seelie Court of old. Too many seats here are empty. We will therefore leverage the new pieces delivered to *us*, with hope of renewing the Seelie Court and countering the dark elements set in motion against us."

"Queen, why did we not do this a decade ago? A century ago?" n'Hagr rumbled.

"Lord Finnbhennach," the Morrigan gestured. "If you please."

The horned man grabbed a canvas sack from behind his seat and withdrew a limp carcass as black as pitch. The dead creature was that of a lynx, tawny muscle beneath shiny fur—but all resemblance to the cat ended there. Where four paws should have been, large talons like those of a bird sprouted; instead of a whiskered feline face it had the head of an eagle, its beak sharp even in death. With a long wingspan of sable feathers dangling freely from its upper shoulder blades, Lord Finnbhennach tossed the halfbreed on the Cylch Table with disgust.

"Lords, take a long look," the Morrigan requested.

"What is it?" Aife asked.

Lugh leaned forward. "Some aberration of nature?"

"Worse," Richard said, breaking his silence. "Far worse."

The table turned to the knight. He stared back, unperturbed by the attention.

"You have the right of it, Knight Richard McAllister," the Queen said. "It is a new fey halfbreed, a cross between cliff eagles and highland cait sith."

"Like small griffins?" Lord Gerallt said.

"Aye, griffins," Lord Finnbhennach agreed. "With some dark art, Caer Llion has bred these foul creatures. Like rutting cats, they multiply at an astonishing rate. In the skies they are like swallows, blotting out even the noonday sky, deadly. I lost an entire herd of my best cattle to these." The lord pounded the table with a massive fist in emphasis. "*My best cattle!* Meat and milk for some of you here. Nothing but strewn skeletons, picked clean."

"I do not see the link between the halfbreed and Caer Llion," Lord Eigion said, gesturing mildly with a webbed hand. "We know nothing at all."

"We know Philip is involved," Richard countered.

"How, knight?" the merrow asked.

Richard looked to the Morrigan who nodded back. "When Bran Ardall and I came through the portal into Dryvyd Wood, we were met by unwelcome company. The Usurper sent his advisor, witch, and houndmaster to capture us, but he also sent some kind of halfbreeds—part wolves, part human. You know how difficult it is for these types of creatures to mate naturally and survive—only a handful have ever done it. If Philip has managed to produce these demon wolves, this griffin is more than likely his as well."

"I killed more than three dozen demon wolves freeing our guests," the Queen admitted. "They did not die easily. They are unlike anything I have seen."

"Then we should attack them now, end this threat," Caswallawn maintained.

"There is more, Lord Caswallawn," the Morrigan said.

"There is," Lord Finnbhennach continued. "The Usurper is drawing all possible resources to Caer Llion—grain, fruit, weapons, men, other supplies. My scouts watch day and night, and every day there is more to fear."

"The High King requested a marriage alliance with Mochdrev Reach, where my daughter Deirdre and I hail," Lord Gerallt said. "Plantagenet is indeed drawing what might he can to Caer Llion. I can only assume it is to move against you all here."

"Lord Gerallt and Lady Deirdre are here offering their support if we rally our own," the Morrigan said, nodding to them. "There is goodness in human hearts yet."

"Philip is planning something large," Deirdre confirmed.

"What that something is, Lady Deirdre, we do not know," the Morrigan added. "But if the lord of Caer Llion intends to escalate the assault on the Tuatha de Dannan, our survival might depend on gathering what remains of the Seelie Court and countering him as soon as possible."

"Lord Fafnir and Lord Latobius will not support that," Lugh said.

"Without their might, we risk annihilation," the Queen agreed.

"If they did not heed the summons . . . ?"

"They will," the Morrigan said. "Sitting to my left is Richard McAllister, knight of the Dryvyd Wood gateway and friend to the Seelie Court. With him is Bran Ardall, the scion of Charles Ardall, the last Heliwr. They entered Annwn with the intent to discover who tried to kill young Ardall in his native city by an assassin cu sith, only to become prisoners of John Lewis Hugo. There is more to this than I can see, events that do not mesh with what we know to be true; our visitors are intertwined in this madness as we are and have just as much to lose.

"As already observed, both Lord Fafnir and Lord Latobius have chosen to disregard the summons I sent them," the Morrigan continued. "It will take an actual visit from a source both of the wayward lords respect to realize the error of their dismissal; it will take a strong voice to persuade Lord Latobius and especially Lord Fafnir of our mutual enemy—to convince them to leave their mountaintop dens and mobilize for war."

"Who will go then?" Govannon questioned. "If not you, my Queen."

"I have chosen McAllister to do what I could not."

The Lords of the Seelie Court looked at each other and at Richard. No one spoke.

"Will you do this thing I ask of you, knight?" the Queen asked.

Richard met her stern gaze. He had known the Morrigan planned to use him in some way, the request he attend the meeting nonnegotiable. What the Queen of the Tuatha de Dannan advocated made sense; Knights of the Seven held noble status among the Seelie Court and would be given opportunities others would not. No matter how much he wished to walk away from the madness, a part of his heart beat to maintain his knighthood and duty. He may have never met the lords in question—only read about them in ancient books Merle kept safe—but what he knew put him in a strong position. At the very least, the coblynau of Caer Glain would respect Arondight for its past.

If he succeeded, the prospect of gaining a favor from the Queen could not be ignored.

"I will do as you command, Queen."

"And young Ardall?" she said, looking at the boy. "What of you?"

Richard beheld Bran. Uncertainty deadened the eyes of the boy. It was a choice Bran had to make on his own, one the knight would not influence.

"Home is not an option, is it?" Bran asked Richard.

"It is if you wish to put yourself at risk," Richard replied quietly. "I may not want you intertwined with what lies in that box, but what Merle said in Seattle is true. Whoever wants you dead will try until it is done."

Bran stared at the dead griffin on the table before looking to the daughter of Lord Gerallt. Richard did not like the look. The boy truly had gotten himself into more trouble than he'd be able to handle if he had become infatuated with the lady of Mochdrev Reach.

When Richard glanced at her, he was surprised to find Deirdre had eyes only for him.

"I go where Richard goes," Bran said simply.

"I have every faith Richard and Ardall will return the two Lords of Snowdon to Arendig Fawr along with all the might of the coblynau and dragons," the Morrigan submitted. "The Seelie Court will be strong once more. Lugh will accompany the knight and his charge on their journey, choosing six warriors from the Long Hand for protection and answering any battle preparation questions Lord Fafnir or Lord Latobius may have. Kegan and one of his sons will share responsibility for the Rhedewyr mounts needed for the trip."

"See to it, Lord Lugh, the Rhedewyr are not ridden to their deaths," Aife said with threatening scorn. "Sacrifice them to gain Tal Ebolyon like you did last year at Caer Vyrridin, and I will not be pleased."

"I will ride them as I deem fit," Lugh said coldly. "You command me not."

"If it means regaining my kingdom all the quicker, then let nothing stand in our way—including how we ride the Rhedewyr,"

Caswallawn growled. "They will live. This is war!"

"Revenge clouds your judgment, *Lord* Caswallawn, as does Govannon's ale," Aife said, flushing with ire.

Caswallawn stood, as did Lugh, lightning in their eyes.

"All Horsemaster Aife requests is to ride the Rhedewyr with care," n'Hagr growled.

"What do you know of restraint when you fish the ocean dead, n'Hagr," Lord Eigion spat, his gills flaring pink in anger.

The room erupted into chaos. Each lord other than Govannon and Kegan were screaming at one another, pointing fingers, gesturing wildly. Richard looked to the Queen for guidance but she sat impervious on her throne, watching the bickering with cold eyes. Beyond her taut, pale features sadness emanated, centuries of worry weighing down the long-lived fey woman.

It became obvious it would take more than the Snowdon lords to unite the Seelie Court.

"Listen to yourselves!" Bran thundered.

The chamber emptied of noise, all eyes turned to the boy.

"You face death and you yell at one another?!" Bran roared, eyes flashing.

"Speak not of what you do not know, *lad*," Caswallawn said, loathing twisting his soured cheeks. "Son of Ardall or not, you know nothing of us, of our trials. I lost my kingdom, my *people*, and all that I am to one such as you. For centuries I have waited for the opportunity to strike back at the outworlders. Now is the time, and sacrifices must be made!"

"Easy for you to say, someone who has nothing to sacrifice!" Aife shouted.

"I know petty bickering when I hear it," Bran shot back. "I may not know you but that much I know."

"Then you know *nothing*," Caswallawn snarled.

"I'm surprised you know *anything*, other than the bottom of a beer keg."

The room went deathly still. Tension tightened about everyone like a noose. Richard placed a steadying hand on Bran's forearm while shielding him from any possible harm.

"Insolent *fool!*" Caswallawn hissed. "How dare—"

"Sit *down*, Caswallawn," the Morrigan roared, her fairies fluttering behind.

"Bran Ardall is right," Richard said, his hard eyes warning Caswallawn away. "None of you have the right to demand anything from one another. What you face is far more dire than the seeds of these arguments." Richard turned to Aife. "Horsemaster, the clurichaun and I will ensure the Rhedewyr are kept sound. Of that I promise."

"You are going to pin all of our hopes on these *outworlders?*" Cawallawn spat.

"There will be much to sacrifice," the Morrigan interceded. "From all of you. For you, Caswallawn, I demand patience. Not all outworlders are thieves of lives like Philip, just as not all drunks are wise."

Color drained from Caswallawn and he sat down.

"And what of the other knights?" Govannon asked. "Are they able to help?"

Richard pursed his lips. "They cannot. I will speak to them once we finish here, to warn them of what is coming. They fulfill the role handed them, guarding the portals with their lives. To leave their post and come here would leave the portals undefended."

"But you are here," Lord Gerallt pointed out.

"The portal is guarded, by one more than a match for anything to come through it," Richard said. "Bran Ardall can attest to that."

"And of Myrddin Emrys?" Lord Eigion inquired.

"He is weak," Caswallawn scoffed. "Powerless."

"Of that, Caswallawn is correct," Richard agreed. "The wizard is as he has been for centuries—unable to perform even the smallest aspect of his craft. If he attempted magic, he very well could lose control unleashing dire consequences for the world. He cannot help in this."

Silence pervaded the chamber. The uneasy truce between the lords lingered.

"It is settled," the Morrigan said, rising from the Sarn Throne with elegant resolve. "On the morrow, Lord Lugh will lead Richard

McAllister into the Snowdon, to speak with Caer Glain and Tal Ebolyon. With the sun you will leave Arendig Fawr and return the Seelie Court to its former prominence. Caer Llion will feel the might of our resolve once more. Please gather what might remains in each of you; McAllister will not fail us, and the need to move quickly once he returns will be tantamount."

The lords of the Seelie Court stood and bowed, an act Richard found more perfunctory than meaningful. The Queen stepped from her dais and strode through the opening double doors of the chamber, her fairy companions following on the air behind her. Lord Finnbhennach threw the dead griffin back into its bag, and with a polite nod of gleaming white bull horns to Richard, also left the room, his tall, heavily muscled frame only covered by a kilt. The other lords and the clurichaun followed, some casting approving glances at Richard and Bran, others ignoring them entirely. After a few minutes, Richard was alone with Bran and Arrow Jack.

"That was a brave thing you did," Richard said.

"Not so sure about that," Bran said. "Why did you keep using my last name?"

Richard stood, feeling tired. "The name Ardall holds much weight here. Your father is still greatly respected. Some of these lords, and in particular those we go to meet, will view you as an acquisition of power, one that can tip the scales in their favor against Philip. They see an Ardall and have hope."

"But I'm not anyone. I'm not the Heliwr."

"They have a perception, no matter the truth," Richard said. "I hope it will be enough."

"You used me then."

"I'd say the Morrigan used you by your invitation," Richard mused. "I am averting a larger threat, hoping to avert a larger war with a smaller one. If the Tuatha will unite to attack Philip, perhaps that will alter any possibility of Philip attacking through the portals, if that's even his intent."

"You are getting us involved in a way that might kill us."

"Life changes our direction sometimes," Richard breathed. "You could die walking down the stairs of the Cadarn. The future is not a sure thing—not in love or dreams or promises. Never forget that."

Bran did not look convinced.

"Trust me," Richard said. "I accepted the wishes of the Morrigan for a reason. It serves us and in the end will protect us in another problem we face."

"What do you mean?"

"We will talk in the morning," Richard answered. "I am tired."

Bran muttered something unintelligible under his breath but didn't give Richard another look. He walked through the chamber doors into the environs of the Cadarn, Arrow Jack flying after.

The tunnel swallowed them both, leaving the knight alone.

He sighed. The boy echoed a growing fear in the knight. Richard risked their lives even as he questioned his ability to control Arondight. Journeying into the reaches of Snowdon aided the Seelie Court but also diverted him from facing his inadequacy to call the power of his fabled blade as well as his uncertainty of knowing how to break into Caer Llion. He hoped the trip into the mountains would give time to overcome both problems.

Richard peered up at the numerous fey banners hanging from the ceiling, the orbs lighting their every color.

And never felt such sure darkness.

Chapter 18

The foggy morning clung to Arendig Fawr like a hoarded blanket.

Richard stood outside of the Cadarn with Bran, the grogginess of early waking leaving him grouchy. Kegan had woken them but not returned, still visiting the Morrigan inside the mountain. Nearby, six black-haired warriors of the Long Hand ignored him as they prepared their Rhedewyr for the journey, the dark elvish hellyll lithe and powerful in white and gold armor, their slanted dark eyes stern above chiseled high cheekbones. The city slept, cradled in gray gloom, only a few risers mingling between the darkened buildings and peering at the gathering warriors with wary glances.

Arrow Jack sat perched on a tree growing from the rock cliff, watching all.

From the Awenau path, Deirdre led her mount and two other Rhedewyr out of the forest shadows, her fiery hair hidden by the cowl of an ashen cloak. While her steed held its head high, the accompanying horses plodded like decrepit old men.

"Are you coming?" Bran asked her.

"Good morn," Deirdre said. "I am. And so is Willowyn, of

course."

"I know you wish to aid us, Lady," Richard said. "But I do not remember the Queen asking you to be a part of our journey into the Snowdon."

Deirdre stared hard at Richard, her green eyes flashing even as they punctured his soul. "My father, Lord Gerallt, wishes it," she said. "If my people are to go to war with the Tuatha de Dannan against Caer Llion, I will express his wishes to Caer Glain and Tal Ebolyon. Mochdrev Reach *will be* represented."

Richard sighed. She gave him a final pert smile before turning to Bran.

"This is Westryl," she introduced. "Your Rhedewyr."

"Mine?"

"You did not think we would be riding double again, did you?"

The boy flushed. Richard didn't like the look he gave the girl. If Bran spent more time fawning over the redhead than focusing on survival, he may not make it back home.

"I guess I hadn't considered it," Bran said.

"Westryl is a bit spirited," she said, flashing a smile and patting the horse. "But so are you, standing up to Caswallawn the way you did. Westryl will keep you safe just as I would."

"I think I'll manage." Bran cupped the nose of Westryl, who stared at him with deep, sorrowful eyes. "Why so sad, Westryl?"

"Westryl lost his rider a few days ago, as did Lyrian here," Deirdre said, introducing Richard to the second mount. "Both are Orphaned and having a hard time of it."

"Their riders died rescuing us, Bran," Richard added.

"They did," Deirdre continued sadly. "Seven became orphaned in Dryvyd Wood alone, as Kearney explained to me. The Orphaned are a sad aspect of being at war with Caer Llion. They bond with a single rider and carry him or her until their end. When a rider dies, the Rhedewyr become stripped of identity and, wallowing in loss, usually die within two moons. Sometimes they bond with another, but more likely die from heartbreak."

Richard patted Lyrian. The power in the massive Rhedewyr reverberated through the magnificent animal. The knight felt bad his freedom had come at such a high cost.

"You fit in better now," Deirdre said, noting Bran's new clothing.

The boy shifted uncomfortably, the new shirt, tunic, pants, and boots Kegan had supplied fitting loose beneath his cloak. If the lord of Caer Llion meant to recapture them, it would be more difficult if they blended in with the surrounding fey.

Out of the foggy woodland, Lugh materialized, leading two dozen more hellyll into the clearing. The defender of Arendig Fawr spoke low as he gestured south toward the plains and Dryvyd Wood, his warriors listening intently. The group separated into three equally sized groups then and faded into the ether, leaving their leader to walk toward Richard alone. He carried Areadbhar, his spear, its long-bladed burnished steel tip glowing like enflamed silver.

"What's going on?" Richard asked.

"The Nharth have warned the Morrigan of an intruder," Lugh said, standing solid alongside his spear. "I have dispatched the Long Hand to investigate."

"What could it be?"

"It is probably a wayward Nordman or a lost banshee, but caution warrants care, especially after your rescue and journey to Arendig Fawr. Whatever it is, it will either be guided back to the plains or killed outright."

Richard nodded to the dark elf as Kegan and his son Connal emerged from the Cadarn. The Morrigan, Lord Eigion, and Horsemaster Aife followed to stop at the open doorway, speaking in low tones.

"We are prepared to leave now, Knight McAllister," Kegan said, hiking up a large bag on his back. "Best to leave before others wake."

"We must make one stop first," Richard said.

"Where are we going?" Bran asked.

"You'll see."

The knight and the boy traveled west out of Arendig Fawr, beyond the outlying homes of its denizens. Birds chirped, heralding the new day, while the fog began to burn off. It would be another hot day. Kegan, Deirdre, Lugh, and the hellyll warriors were left behind to complete the preparations. Soon they would be on their way to the dungeons of Caer Glain and Lord Fafnir, and there was much left to do.

"We go to Mastersmith Govannon," the knight replied finally. "You cannot go into the heights of the Snowdon weaponless. From what I learned while speaking with the Morrigan, the Mastersmith will have something for you. He always does."

Eagerness lit Bran's face. Richard hoped the Queen wasn't making a mistake.

After ten minutes of walking, smoke tickled his nose. They moved out of the forest into a meadow where the only stone building Richard had seen in Arendig Fawr sat backed up against the cliff, the structure made of finely cut gray-black stone blocks in the shape of a castle turret that seemed to absorb the sunlight. A massive chimney sprouted from its side where pungent smoke exhaled, and at its back, rivulets of water ran down the rock wall directly into the building's interior.

Fiery light flickered through narrow windows, angry eyes watching.

"What is that stench?" Bran asked.

"Smithing is not a clean art," Richard said. "The reason Govannon is way out here, on the outskirts of Arendig Fawr."

Richard entered the building, Bran a step behind. The thick odor of hard work and fermented sweet beer swallowed them. Eyes adjusting to the gloom, the knight saw he was in a large armory filled to bursting. Weapons hung from walls and crammed entire corners—swords of all shapes and sizes, battle and pole-arm axes, spears of varying lengths and design. A table showcased hundreds of daggers and longer knives while beneath shields—some round, others as tall as a man—were stacked neatly. Various pieces of armor dangled from the ceiling and littered any available space, vacant steel clothing waiting to be filled.

There was enough smithy work to outfit an army.

In another corner a distillery sat, surrounded by closed barrels.

From the fire-soaked shadows of the rear, the forceful pounding of a hammer meeting steel and anvil pierced his ears, steady and rhythmic. It seemed to infiltrate the world and all within it.

"Govannon!" Richard yelled. "Mastersmith!"

The fall of the hammer ended, it's last strike ringing throughout the room.

"*Chyneuwch!*" a deep voice rumbled from the darkness.

Faint marble-sized orbs of milky light came into being, hovering just below the ceiling, growing stronger until they illuminated the entire armory and highlighted the swirling rune work on each artfully crafted item.

"Well met, Richard McAllister of the Yn Saith, well met," the burly shadow welcomed as he navigated the mess of his making. "And the scion of Ardall. Greetings to you as well this morn."

As the man came into the light, Richard got a good look at the fey smith in his natural environment. He was the largest man the knight had seen. Wiping grime-stained hands on a towel at his waist, the Mastersmith had massive shoulders and arms to apply his trade, balanced out by a huge paunch and thick, tree trunk-like legs. Blue eyes glittered beneath craggy eyebrows, his skin flushed with heat, black hair pulled back beyond a thickly bearded face.

"How fare you, Govannon?" Richard asked.

"The fire is neverending, my friend," Govannon said with a grin. "It calls and demands like the Dryads of old. What do I owe this visit?"

"My companion. He requires a weapon."

"I see."

"You are quite talented," Bran said, looking around.

"Like many things in life, what calls to a person is what is meant," Govannon replied. "I don't command talent as much as it commands me."

"I can't believe all of this exists," Bran admitted. "It's like I'm in a dream."

"No dream, of course," the smithy bellowed a laugh, winking at Richard. "I remember when I first arrived here in Annwn, I too could hardly believe it. Belief can be a tricky thing. Do you know there are men and women here—people who were born here and know no different—who don't believe in *your* world?"

"People tend to not believe what they can't see," Richard stated.

"Good your sense of wonder is strong then."

"A hidden world is one thing though," Bran said. "Dragons, goblins, fairies, elves, leprechauns, witches—these are tales where we come from."

"Oh, they are real, Bran Ardall," Govannon said. "Dragons are in the heights of Snowdon. Goblins exist but are rarely seen during the day. Witches of varying skill are on street corners in every major city. So are leprechauns." He paused. "As for elves, another story. Few exist. The dark hellyll remain but their elven brothers and sisters left Annwn centuries ago with their sylvan counterparts. Who knows if they yet live. Now we work hard without them, to maintain the wonder of the world. One day, it will need us again, with or without the elves, in Annwn or in the Old World."

"That's a bold endeavor," Richard said. "Mankind . . . it destroys what it doesn't understand."

"Aye. 'Tis the reason I drink as much as I do," Govannon laughed.

"Philip Plantagenet is not drink-worthy," Richard muttered.

"Not of my ale, anyway."

As the mood grew somber, falling armor from the rear of the shop sent adrenaline rushing through Richard like lightning, Arondight an electric call on his fingertips. The Mastersmith put a restraining hand up and shook his head. Almost in response, a shadow stirred where Govannon had been working, wobbly, tall, and thin.

"Smith!" it slurred loudly. "Beer!"

"Help yourself, Caswallawn," Govannon ordered. "I will not do it for you."

The drunk lord from the Seelie Court stumbled into view. Bleary bloodshot eyes stared at Richard and Bran from a middle-aged face thick with stubble and wear, a sour frown deepening an already pinched mouth. An empty wood mug swung from a lax hand.

The light of the orbs shifted about Caswallawn—and his left arm and leg disappeared.

Richard blinked, unsure of what he wasn't seeing.

Before he could say anything, the drunk-soaked eyes of the

lord focused on him and his features twisted in a snarl.

"Your company worsens, Mastersmith," Caswallawn spoke vehemently.

"It was not much to begin with," Bran replied, smirking.

"Outlander filth," the lord spat before filling his mug from one of the barrels nearby and wobbly returning to the building's rear.

"Ignore him. I do," Govannon said. "Caswallawn was the lord of Gwynedd, a province in northern Annwn, before Philip razed it to the ground, murdered his family, stole his land, and began using it to launch campaigns against us here in the mountains. He hates Philip and the world he came from. That much you saw yesterday. He is not the only one who hates your world, mind you. Now he is no better than a leprechaun, never leaving Arendig Fawr and unable to put his past to rest."

"He hates us by association?" Bran asked. "That hardly seems fair."

"Fair has nothing to do with it, Bran Ardall," Govannon pointed out. "I allow him his petty drinking, here, far away from Arendig Fawr—far away from the Morrigan. She is a hard woman and does not take too kindly to his form of debauchery."

"What is happening to his body?" Richard asked.

Confusion crossed Govannon's face until he grinned. "Oh. That. He possesses Gwenn, an invisibility cloak, one of only two known to still exist. The ability to create such cloth has been lost to the ages. Gwenn is all he has left, and it is the only reason the Morrigan tolerates his behavior, I think." The smith took a step back. "Now, care to look around and see what might appeal to you, young Ardall?"

Bran walked through several rows of glimmering artifacts.

"See anything you like?" Govannon asked after Bran had walked the entirety of the room.

"To be honest, nothing. It is all wonderful work but nothing catches my eye."

"That is odd," Govannon said, frowning.

"What do you mean?" Richard asked.

The Mastersmith shrugged. "My creations always call to their eventual bearer, and everyone who visits leaves with something—even if it is only gauntlets, boots, or a ladle for soup. It is a magic of mine, to find what is necessary for those who need it."

"Maybe it is because I am from the Old World."

"No, that is not it. How do you think Richard McAllister received Arondight?"

"You gave that to him?" Bran questioned.

"Indirectly," Govannon said. "I crafted Arondight. It has been passed for centuries to those who would protect the world and its people with honor and vision. It always finds a master. The knight Richard McAllister is merely the newest to use it toward its intended end." He stepped to Bran. "Do not fear me."

Bran stood still as Govannon gripped his forearm, his thick fingers like cords of steel, and closed his eyes for a moment before they reopened just as quickly.

"You are right. There is nothing for you here."

"What does that mean?" Richard asked, puzzled.

"I do not know," Govannon said. He looked Bran up and down as if gauging him. "It is like he is already armed. Perhaps it is a weapon I have yet to create. Interesting."

"Can he not take something to protect himself at least?"

"He cannot," Govannon said. "Every item here is meant for someone. They just have not visited me yet."

Richard nodded politely to the Mastersmith. He had a sneaking suspicion the inability of Bran choosing a weapon had nothing to do with Govannon having not created the correct item.

Not at all.

"Thank you for your time, Master Govannon," Richard said. "I hope we meet next time under better circumstances."

"You too, Knight McAllister. Come back when you return from Caer Glain and Tal Ebolyon. Perhaps I will have something for young Ardall then."

"Thank you," Bran said.

Govannon smiled. "My door is always open."

Richard watched the broad-shouldered smith return to his work and fade into the shadows where Caswallawn drank alone.

As the cool mountain air met Richard again, the whoosh of bellows pumping with authority chased after.

The hate in the eyes of Caswallawn went with him.

WITH TWO LONG Hand scouts leading the way, Richard, Bran, and the others left the safe haven of Arendig Fawr for the heights above.

The sun peeked through the fog, burning it away and coloring the world once more. Arrow Jack flew ahead, a fleeting shadow in the murk. Lyrian carried the knight forward, trudging after the hellyll warriors, rocking comfortably back and forth like a ship in calm seas. Bran rode Westryl next to Deirdre's Willowyn. Lugh, his angular face stern and eyes taking in every nuance of the day, rode his massive black battle roan, its scarred flanks testament to its battles. Kegan and Connal came last.

In minutes the group traveled a steep trail overlooking Arendig Fawr, the fey city growing tinier as they climbed.

It soon vanished altogether.

Deirdre dropped back, bringing her Rhedewyr next to Lyrian. Bran watched her go, his mien darkening when he saw where she stopped.

Richard refrained from throttling the boy for his jealousy.

"How do you feel, Knight McAllister?" the redhead asked, her eyes shining emerald as they boldly sought his own. "The wounds Caer Llion delivered you were quite grievous. I cannot believe you are already upon your feet, let alone riding."

"I heal," he said simply. "It is enough."

"My father is pleased you agreed to the Queen's charge. He believes it bodes well on the destruction of Caer Llion. So do I."

"I think your father puts too much faith in me."

"You are a knight. I have faith in you as well."

"I also think your father sent you because you are delusional and he needed a break from the madness."

She laughed, clear and pleasant. "That may be, Knight McAllister."

"My name is Rick. I'm not much on formality."

"Rick," she said, testing it with a smile.

"Where is your fairy?"

"Oh, him," Deirdre said, darkening a bit. "Snedeker told me what transpired the other night. I thought it best he not travel with us. No reason for you to worry. He is truly harmless. And as a loyal friend, I would rather his ashes not become part of the winds, or whatever it was you said to him."

Richard grunted. Deirdre grinned and didn't look away. The knight began to feel uncomfortable under her scrutiny. She was beautiful, the light smattering of freckles around her nose accentuating the smoothness of her pale skin. Her eyes shared a vast intelligence, and she sat her Rhedewyr with practiced, lithe sensuality and grace. Beneath her physical loveliness, a power resided, a power Richard could not define but one that gave her maturity beyond her years.

If he were a different man in another life, he would have been attracted to her.

Those days were long behind him though.

The day passed uneventfully as the sunshine finally cut through the fog to reveal the blue sky. Birdsong and wildlife returned despite the burnt aspect of the forest, the power of the Cailleach everywhere. The trees loosened their hold on the mountain slopes as they climbed, and more small waterfalls tumbled to a much larger river that could be periodically seen slicing through the expanding valley below. Richard had not realized how far they had ascended to reach Arendig Fawr; he could almost reach out and touch the peaks of the Snowdon above, where patches of glacial snow fought the witch's unnatural summer. In those upper reaches, the coblynau and dragons waited.

After a quick stop to take lunch and water the horses, the group continued on. The afternoon waned toward evening and still they climbed, the peaks purpling as the sun vanished in the golden, cloudless west. Exposed granite outcroppings shattered the mountainsides and long-needled blue pine grew around them, their odor sweet on the faint breeze even as they thinned from the altitude. The view became expansive, dizzying in its scope, as Richard viewed broken peaks all around them, the faint ribbon of the river still meandering far below and cutting off the forest they had ridden through from the other side of the vast valley.

As shadows lengthened toward evening and the rhythm of Lyrian drowsily lulled the knight, a splitting avian scream ripped through the stillness.

Arrow Jack.

The bird sat in a tree at the turn in the trail, wings flapping madly.

Screams of surprise from Richard's companions quickly followed as a shadowy wraith fell from the side of the mountain above, blotting out the sky like a thundercloud before landing in the midst of the company, separating Lugh and Richard from the rest of the group.

The shadowy creature turned burning eyes on Bran.

"Bodach!" Lugh roared. "Unseelie!"

"Get away, Bran!" Richard shouted.

Richard kept his seat as Lyrian reared in panic, whinnying loudly. Bran was not so lucky. He tumbled off Westryl and hit the packed dirt hard. Richard fought to get passed Lugh, who took up much of the path, but he couldn't get there.

Bran would die quickly.

Thankfully Westryl lashed out with his hooves at the beast, the horse keeping between the creature and Bran. Prevented from its quarry, the creature turned its flaming gaze on Richard, its stare terrifying with maddened intelligence. Magic filled his soul and Arondight entered his hand without problem, the sword casting azure light about the trail and highlighting their attacker. It had the shape of hyena but was much larger, six legs ending in clawed paws trampling the earth. A long snout lined with teeth snapped at Lyrian and the Long Hand that charged it. As the creature spun, striking at the warriors, Richard realized he could see through it as if it were made of smoke. But from within its outline bones, chunks of elvish armor, and even weapons glimmered in what daylight was left, as if it had absorbed all remnants of earlier prey.

Revulsion swept through Richard.

It was an Unseelie creature, one that had eaten the hellyll Lugh had sent out that morning.

Bran scrambled back toward the clurichauns even as Lugh charged his battle mount forward, the horse forcing his way past the beast to defend Westryl. Areadbhar a lightning bolt of silver, Lugh jabbed at their attacker, snarling battle madness.

The bodach shied away from the spear, quicker than Lugh, hissing hatred. Caught between the hellyll leader and the slashing swords of the Long Hand, the bodach ignored the manic horses and pounced onto the two closest hellyll like a cat. The warriors sent their weapons into the creature but to no effect; they might as well have been fighting air. They screamed as its claws punctured their armor and flesh beneath, ripping through steel and bone alike.

In seconds their lifeless, ravaged bodies hit the trail.

Bolstered through his pain by adrenaline, Richard spurred Lyrian into the melee; he held Arondight high, blue fire angrily running its length. The bodach shrunk from him as it dodged his first lunge, its crimson eyes narrowed. He thrust again, sending the fiery steel toward the broad chest of the beast as Lugh, enraged, thrust his spear at its hindquarters. The bodach dodged Arondight but did not gain safety from the triangular point of the spear; Areadbhar penetrated the smoky innards of the creature's thigh.

Bright golden fire coalesced there—so bright that Richard shielded his eyes. An inhuman howl of pain punctuated the trailside as the bodach wrenched away.

"Release, Lugh!" Richard roared.

"Hai, Grayth!" the lord yelled at his mount, ignoring the knight.

As Lugh tried to joust the beast over the edge of the trail, the bodach danced away from Richard. It gripped the shaft of the spear with two forefeet and, pulling it free, lifted Lugh clear of his Rhedewyr and sent him hurtling through the air to crash against the bare granite of the mountainside.

Lugh crumpled to the trail like an empty sack.

The bodach wasted no time. It scuttled toward the dazed lord like a spider. Before it could reach Lugh, Willowyn barreled into its side, slamming it away, as Deirdre slashed with her sword, the steel a blur, her hair as wild as her actions.

"Ayrith! Ayrith!" the redhead screamed.

The bodach buckled before the surprise assault, gathering itself in a dark mass, looking for an angle to attack her.

"Get out of the way, Deirdre!" Richard bellowed.

Too late, the bodach swiped at Willowyn, its claws like daggers. The Rhedewyr screamed in pain and stumbled backward, the side of her neck slashed to bleeding flesh. Deirdre somehow kept her seat, her sword flailing in impotence as she held on.

Eyes raging fire, the bodach bunched to strike at Deirdre.

"No! Richard!" Bran roared, completely unable to help.

Finally given a clear path, Richard sent azure fire hurtling at the Unseelie beast. The power radiated from his being, to do what was right in the face of grave evil. The fire struck the beast and sent it pinwheeling through the air. With the blue flames licking its smoky outline, it moved like a tiger toward Richard, fixated on its last remaining enemy with true power at his command.

The knight sent his magic into the creature again, to slow it, but the bodach was ready this time, leaping aside with ease.

It came on.

Realizing he was too far away for a killing blow, Richard charged Lyrian. He pummeled the creature with bursts of his will, keeping it pinned away from the others, unwilling to let it gain another advantage. The bodach fought the fire, the charred odor of burning garbage thick on the air. Richard was aware of Kegan and Connal pulling Bran away from the fight as the remaining hellyll helped the knight corner the creature against the rock bluff, trying to find openings, jabbing with their swords.

With their aid, Richard pressed forward, inching closer to the creature to strike.

Before he got close enough to deliver a killing stroke, the thing leapt backward from the fire suddenly and, scrambling up the jagged granite, disappeared into the night with bits of flickering flame still burning its body.

"Where did it go?" Bran breathed.

No one replied. All eyes probed the Snowdon, searching.

Connal calmed the horses while Kegan looked at the wounds Willowyn had sustained. Lugh fought to rise, his movements drunken. No sounds other than the snorting Rhedewyr and the heavy breathing of the Long Hand surrounded them.

Long moments passed. Nothing happened.

"Is it gone?" Kegan hissed.

Richard gripped Arondight tightly. "I don't think so."

The shadow dropped again—this time down the trail behind the clurichauns.

As the others rushed to aid them, Kegan jumped in front of his son, a long silver knife freed and a whip in his other hand. The bodach pounced. Even striking it with the whip, the monster flung Kegan aside like he was a puppet.

Ignoring Connal, the bodach came at Bran again.

The bodach struck the boy from behind, sending him to the ground. Warding himself from the creature with his arms raised, Bran roared defiance. It did not matter. The beast rose up, eyes flaming and a snout filled with teeth leering over him.

"Finalleeee," the bodach snarled venomously.

It reared up, its claws extended and glinting. It was happening all too quickly. Richard could do nothing but watch. The digesting dead in the opaque body were clear to the knight, stark in relief and reality.

Bran would become a part of it; Richard had failed.

Just as the claws fell, a blur of silver screamed in front of the creature's face.

The bodach swatted with both forelegs at the apparition but could not connect. With a flurry of flashing wings and chittering screams, it kept between the creature and Bran, blinding it from its prey.

"Snedeker!" Deirdre cried in surprise.

Gossamer wings a blur, zipping around so quickly Richard could barely distinguish it, the fairy flung dust at the bodach. The silver grit landed on the creature's face and the fiery eyes dimmed. The beast shook its head back and forth, trying to dislodge whatever had been thrown upon it, snarls of anger now replaced by snorting and hissing.

"Run, you doltish idiot, run!" the fairy shouted at Bran.

As Bran gained his feet, one massive ghost paw swatted the unaware fairy.

Snedeker disappeared into the night like an insignificant insect.

It was enough. As the bodach bunched to attack Bran, Connal was there, the clurichaun swinging his war hammer broadly, his face livid. He gave no ground. The head of the hammer passed through the bodach as if it were smoke, the creature laughing with dark glee. It ignored the ineffective attack. In one swift motion it lifted Connal from the trail. The hammer dropped from his fingers and he yelled out in pain as the shadowy beast squeezed.

The flaming eyes sparked—and then tore the clurichaun apart at the waist.

"No!" Kegan roared.

The halves of Connal flew apart in a crimson mist, the clurichaun dead before he hit the ground.

Inhuman laughter ricocheted off the cliff.

Ignoring his growing weakness, Richard drove Lyrian straight toward the bodach. Not expecting the attack, the Unseelie creature had nowhere to go. Blue flames lit the night as Richard brought Arondight down in a raging arc. The bodach tried to evade it but was too slow; the sword cleaved one of its legs. The howl of the beast deafened the air. As it shrunk into an inky mass, it retreated toward the only area it could—the cliff edge and the open air beyond.

With as much will as he could muster, Richard sent his power into its chest. Fire exploded, a torrent of magic. The bodach fought for a moment, still cradling its lost leg, before the flames sent it flying off the cliff into the black abyss below.

All went still.

Arondight dissolving, Richard nearly blacked out atop Lyrian; he managed to remain horsed, if barely. Silence fell over the Snowdon. Deirdre aided Lugh. The remaining warriors of the Long Hand helped her as well and looked after their dead.

Kegan cradled the remains of Connal, weeping audibly.

"What was that thing?" Bran breathed.

"Part shadow, a death machine given life," Richard mustered, wiping his sweaty brow and gulping the mountain air. "It is a pure hunter, one of the Unseelie Court. Given a scent, it will never stop . . . never stop until its prey is dead."

"Whose scent did it have?"

"Yours, of course," Richard snapped.

"Why me? How?"

"It could have been anything." Richard shook his head. "Your coat. Some scrap of torn clothing. There are few bodachs left, those who exist are imprisoned and only released as assassins. Someone wants you dead—badly."

"Did you kill it?"

"No," Richard said, dismounting and barely keeping his feet. "But it will be gone for a few days."

"How can that be? It can't be more than a few hours behind us."

"It landed on the other side of the river," Richard said, pointing over the edge toward the ravine. "Bodachs can't tolerate water. It will have to find some kind of bridge or fallen tree to cross for it to begin its pursuit again. That should take several days, unless . . ."

"Unless what?"

"Unless we are very unlucky."

The knight turned to Kegan. The clurichaun sat with what remained of Connal in his arms, the tears cascading down into his beard. Richard didn't know what to say.

Such grief had left him long ago.

"We will bury him here, my son. My son, my son," he repeated in a whisper as he rocked back and forth.

With Snedeker returning, Willowyn, Lyrian, and the rest of the Rhedewyr surrounded Kegan and Connal. All of the horses lowered their heads, eyes closed.

Richard watched the homage to the horse caretakers.

It would be a long night of sorrow.

Chapter 19

The first ghostly murmur dragged Bran from troubled sleep.

He raised his head up, fully alert, and listened to the night. The group had moved off the trail into a sparse copse of fir trees where they couldn't be seen by possible mountain travelers. The insects had long since ended their song and the stars occasionally fought through the foggy film of the Nharth that had snuck in as true night fell. Whatever animals that were still living in the Snowdon ignored the travelers. The sleeping lumps surrounding the dying fire did not move, and the hellyll Bran knew to be on watch was not evident. Arrow Jack sat perched, unmoving, above, and Snedeker slept nearby on an island of moss, his wings fluttering with every breath he took.

Nothing stirred. The camp was as silent as if the world had frozen and he alone could observe it.

The sound that had woken him was not clear.

With disappointment, Bran looked to the bedroll where Kegan should have been sleeping.

It was empty.

Bran laid back and stared up into the tree limbs, unsettled.

The death of Connal was imprinted on his memory. Blame burned inside him like a fever. The clurichaun had tried to keep Bran safe—and had sacrificed his life for it.

There was no chance of removing the guilt.

While somewhere in the darkness, the bodach followed.

The whisper came again, more obvious now that he was awake, a tickling in the recesses of his mind. It was foreign but not intrusive, an offer rather than a command.

With sudden insight, Bran pulled the box containing the Paladr from his pocket, the silver knot scrollwork on its lid glimmering in the palm of his hand.

He ran his thumb over the lid of the box, about to open it.

"Think on this, boy. Don't be rash."

Bran stilled his hand. Richard stared at him from his bedroll, the knight lying on his side with eyes glittering in the midnight.

"What do you mean?"

"You have awakened the Paladr."

"I don't think so."

Richard looked off into the darkness, half of his face lost to shadow. "It is aware, offering itself. Whenever you are in danger, it responds to the one who carries it. It did so in Dryvyd Wood and it is doing so now. I can feel its magic even from here."

"I haven't felt this before," Bran countered.

"No, but I bet you were thinking about Connal just now."

"How did you know that?"

"What happened when you were confronted in Dryvyd Wood? When you were attacked by the bodach tonight?"

"The Paladr became hot in my pocket, like my hip was on fire."

"It responds to your need when you are in danger," Richard answered. "It is offering the protection and power of the Heliwr."

"Did you know?" Bran asked. "Know what Merle meant by protection, I mean?"

"I guessed. I know the old man far better than he gives me credit for," Richard said. "And I'm telling you to think it over. For all the reasons we've discussed and thousands more."

Bran looked back into his hand, lost in thought. Merle had

thrust the box there during the fight in Seattle with the command to use it only when Bran *wanted* protection. He had thought it a talisman of some sort, used and eventually discarded. Instead, if what Richard said was true, using the Paladr would come with a lifetime of servitude as the Heliwr. Richard had cautioned Bran to not trust Merle. In so doing though, the knight advocated Bran turn away from the one thing that offered protection—and the ability to never let happen again the sacrifice Connal, the two hellyll, and the other Tuatha de Dannan in Dryvyd Wood had made on his behalf.

"What happened to you?" Bran asked. "How did you give up responsibility over your own life, over the faith in yourself to summon Arondight?"

"Why are you even interested?"

Bran withheld his acidic reply. An owl hooted a lonely cry nearby. Long moments passed. Like many of the damaged people he had met on the street, Bran knew the knight would eventually share his story.

"I had a wife once," Richard began finally, haltingly. "She was . . . my world. And she was taken from me."

"And?" Bran prompted.

"Elizabeth," Richard went on, his voice barely a whisper. "Elizabeth Welles. We met after I left my graduate studies at the University of Washington, met one night as she passed the bookstore. She loved books. She had a smile that could level me. Loved to joke. She saw the brighter side of living life. When we met we both just knew. We were married and I moved out of the bookstore apartment to share one with her in Pioneer Square.

"I was already a knight when we met, watching over the Seattle portal and keeping the worst of Annwn from coming into our city. Back then I was only several years older than you are now, cocksure of myself but unsure of my place in the world. She came into my life and it forever changed. She gave me more meaning than anyone ever had before her and since."

A wildcat growled ferociously nearby, interrupting the tale, followed by a frightened squeal cut short by whatever prey the cat had killed.

"Did she know you were a knight?"

"Leaving in the middle of the night with no explanation leads any spouse to become suspicious," Richard said tightly. "I can still remember the night I told her—about Annwn, the fey of both Courts, King Arthur, and how I possessed a power few in history had ever known and fewer yet had carried. She laughed when I told her the identity of Merle—laughed until I called Arondight. She spent the next several months reading all she could about Celtic mythology, the history of Europe and the Vatican—as well as my place in all of it. The questions were endless for days and days."

"If I told anyone about this, I think they'd have me committed," Bran said.

"When Merle first told me, I considered it myself."

"And John Lewis Hugo knew of her, used her against you."

"He knew all of it. Somehow," Richard said, darkening. "As Merle suspected in Seattle, Philip has one of the relic mirrors. It's the only explanation."

"How did she die?"

"A korrigan, a shapeshifter and illusionist of sorts, came through the portal," Richard said quietly. "I did not stop it in time."

Bran nodded. The knight appeared haunted, an inner hatred—a manic self-loathing—having entered his eyes.

"When she died, you changed."

"I did," Richard agreed. "My role led to her death. Yes, I had power, power to prevent it. But sometimes that is not enough. I was young and foolish and believed that power gave me right to live and enjoy life as I saw fit." Richard paused. "I tell you this now not to share my pain—nothing else pains me more than speaking of Elizabeth—but to prevent your *own* pain. I do not wish on you what I've gone through. You still have a choice."

"So do you," Bran replied.

Richard laughed darkly. "No. This is all I am now."

"I don't think so."

"Once I lorded over the portal because I enjoyed how special it made me feel in the much larger scheme of the world," Richard added. "I was humbled in the worst way, by a God I know exists and yet does not care for me. Now I stand guard against Annwn, hoping to prevent other people from having to experience the pain I've lived with for years and years now."

"God has nothing to do with this," Bran asserted.

"Doesn't He?" Richard growled back.

Long minutes passed. Both men stared into the night.

"The bodach," Bran said finally. "It won't stop."

"It won't," the knight said. "Once set upon prey, it will never give up."

"And what if you aren't there to protect me?" Bran asked. "Or Deirdre? Or Lugh?"

"If we rejoin the Seelie Court and it helps pull down the very stones of Caer Llion, your safety will not be an issue," Richard said. "You will be free of harm."

"Free until something else comes after me."

The dying fire snapped, sending a coal shooting like a star into the night.

"That could happen to anyone," Richard said. "You still have a choice."

"And was Kegan's son given a choice?"

"People die, Bran," Richard said coldly. "The world is not all light and airy. Connal's death is sad. But it does not make it your fault."

Bran squeezed the Paladr box. "If I had the means to stop it, then I *am* at fault."

"Bran, don't be ridicu—"

"No!" Bran hissed, a fountain of repressed rage bursting forth. "Kegan holds silent vigil tonight over Connal's grave because his son fought to protect *me*—to protect a stranger not even from his world! And he's not the only one. How many died saving us from John Lewis Hugo and his minions?" Bran burned with conviction. "Saving me? And *you?*"

Richard stared hard at Bran. Seconds turned into minutes.

"You know, I've seen the way you look at her," the knight said.

Bran knew exactly what Richard meant. Deirdre slept nearby. Bran could see her red hair and the easy fall of her chest. From the time he had first seen her in Dryvyd Wood, to riding with his hands about her waist, to staring at her across the table at the Seelie Court meeting, Bran was falling for her. He had never felt like this. Sadly, it was obvious she favored the knight for a reason Bran could not fathom. The way she looked at Richard when he wasn't aware could not be denied. It couldn't be how he treated her. The death of his wife had destroyed him. It had to be something else, something Bran was not.

"Becoming a knight won't help you woo her," Richard said, as if reading his thought.

"That is *not* the reason I do this!"

"Isn't it?"

"I won't let more blood spill at my account," Bran said, turning the conversation away from Deirdre and gripping the box like a lifeline. "She has nothing to do with it. Will you help me or not?"

"I will," Richard murmured. "If you are truly set on this."

"Merle knew," Bran whispered. "He knew it would come to this."

"No," Richard said stoically. "Merle knew the possibility could unfold. It is you and you alone who make this choice. You can turn away right now, leave it behind, forget it."

"Can Kegan forget his son?" Bran said bitterly. "Can I?"

"No. I suppose not."

"Unlike you, I want to be responsible for myself," Bran said. "Right now I am no better than you on the street, asking for a free ticket, hoping others will take care of me while they foot the bill. No longer."

"That's it, huh?"

"I *have* to own my part in all of this. It is the only way."

"There is more for you to hear," Richard growled low, the dying embers of the fire mirrored in his eyes. "What you plan goes beyond responsibility into martyrdom. Once, long ago, the Church existed to educate and build safe communities, where people watched out for their neighbor in a savage world. This is true of Christianity, Catholicism, Islam, Buddhism—all of them. For centuries Christians mingled with Muslims who traded with Buddhists, and peace was maintained through mutual respect.

"But somewhere along the way, the relationships people held

with other God-fearing people took on new, selfish undertones. Religion became something to fight over, despite the explicit instructions within doctrines to the contrary. Meaning and peace gave way to greed and fear. Hundreds of wars have been fought over it. The influence of religion is the main culprit for much of the death in our world. The Pope, his Cardinals, and even Archbishop Glenallen crave power and hope to see their Church expand and grow, just as Saint Peter ordered of them through the Vigilo. They are no better than Philip Plantagenet, extreme in their own beliefs."

"What is your poin—" Bran started.

"Let me finish," Richard said. "If you choose to take on the mantle of the Heliwr, you will have to walk a fine line between all of them—and maintain the balance between them and Annwn. The power you will possess will not be your power alone but that of two worlds—*needed* by two worlds. All will try to use you to their advantage, just like they tried with your father. Is that something you truly want? Can you even comprehend what I am saying?"

"I don't know," Bran admitted, his anger subsiding. "But I cannot keep relying on you. On others."

"You are bent on this then?"

"I am. You convinced me. How do I become the Heliwr?"

"As I told you back in the Cadarn, I have no idea."

Bran opened the box. The silver outline of the Paladr winked. He took it out and held it in his hand. The Paladr was warm, the edges of the acorn-like seed smooth against his palm. He hoped he was making the right choice.

The earlier whisper came again, a tickle of sentience.

Away. Upward.

"It wants me to go up into the mountains," Bran said, surprised by the voice.

Richard undid his blankets as if to rise. "I'll come with you."

"No," Bran said. "I will do this alone."

"I see," Richard said simply, lying back down.

"If I don't return by morning . . ."

"I will come looking for you, yes," Richard offered. He sighed. "Good luck, boy. I can no more tell you what to do than the Church should. I hope you know what you are doing."

Bran looked to where he knew the uppermost fringes of the mountains existed. He saw nothing. Fog swallowed the entirety of the Snowdon whole. It would be a long, dangerous climb in the middle of the night.

Bran fought his fear. It would do him no good.

WITH THE CAMP long at his back and letting the whisper of the Paladr guide him, Bran followed a small deer trail and climbed over the boulder-strewn mountain, in search of answers he had to have.

The seed in his hand burned the entire time.

The Snowdon reared above, a massive presence; the Nharth swirled around him, faces lost in the mist. Even though the darkness of night hid most of the world, Bran had no trouble making his way; some aspect of the Paladr guided him, outlined the world in shades of gray as if it knew the land and every obstacle, bend in the path, and low-hanging tree branch. It called him onward, through a forest grown wild with pine and fir, the power of the witch oddly absent, and the heady odor of healthy life blending with the mineral tang of trickling water all around him.

Bran breathed in the cool night air. It would have been oddly relaxing, if not for the circumstances.

He was a long way from home, from the life he had once led. Speaking to Richard and hearing how the knight had fallen to such dark depths did nothing to dissuade Bran from his choice. He wanted to make something of his life. The death of Connal had been the final straw breaking his burdened back.

He would die before becoming a man he despised.

"Where you think you are going, treesqueak?"

A whir of wings flew passed and Snedeker hovered in the air before Bran.

"To find my own way in this world."

"The woods at night can be quite dangerous, outworlder," the fairy said, looking darkly about him as if another bodach would appear at any moment. "You should not be here alone. You are lucky I found you."

"Fly back to camp," Bran ordered, mostly annoyed.

"You command me not, hotpie," Snedeker said, crossing his arms, the wood of his face stubborn. "I am more than a hundred years older than you. You would do well to listen to me. Do very well."

"Have it your way then," Bran said, moving a branch aside. "I can't stop you."

"Where are we going?"

"Now it's *we*?"

"Yes, we," Snedeker said.

"You are good at getting yourself into trouble, aren't you?"

The fairy appraised Bran indignantly. Bran stared hard back at the creature and realized he didn't know much about Snedeker other than the thievery he had attempted in the Cadarn.

"Did Deirdre send you after me?" Bran asked.

"Red doesn't control me either," Snedeker snorted. "Those who think they can quickly find I am less than agreeable."

"I was told fairies were not to be trusted."

"You keep poor company then."

"How did you become friends with Deirdre?" Bran asked, truly curious.

"I wooed a woman."

"Deirdre?"

Snedeker laughed, the twigs and moss of his body shaking. "You know nothing of fairies, do you, outworlder?"

"Of course I don't! Otherwise I wouldn't have asked."

"Settle down, meatsack. I will answer your question," Snedeker said, flying alongside Bran's head and peering into the forward darkness. "I am a fairy of the Oakwells, the most respected fairy clan in the eyes of the Lady. The summer is long and hot and has been burning for centuries. Food grows short at times. The Firewillows live closer than my clan to Rhuddlan Teivi where many humans live. I borrowed one of their maids—only one—who supplied their clan with milk, oh . . . two decades back, when Red was a young girl."

"You *borrowed* a maid?"

Snedeker flew in front of Bran only to turn with scolding face. "Yes. Borrowed."

"What happened then? The humans come after you?"

"No, the Firewillows did," Snedeker sputtered. "Even though they had plenty of milk, they would not share. Flaming slugs. They think they are the Lady's favorites. Think they were there at the beginning of the Misty Isles, as her beloveds. The Oakwells know the truth!"

"Sounds like you hate the Firewillows a lot," Bran said.

"They are sworn enemies," Snedeker said. "As are the other clans."

"So you left and ended up in Mochdrev Reach."

"To bring my light and intelligence to Red's life," the fairy said snarkily.

The trail leveled off where a thick forest pushed its way toward the cliff Bran had just climbed above. Massive fir trees with trunks as big around as an elephant thrust into the cool night air, reminding Bran of black and white pictures of the Pacific Northwest's Old Growth taken by early loggers in Seattle. No sound met his arrival; the forest slept with depthless surety. All around him the Nharth departed without provocation. The smell of dried needles and sap warmed sweet by the heat of day embraced Bran as he took the first few steps along the flat path, his way forward lost to the trees after several dozen feet.

In his hand, the Paladr goaded him gently to continue moving.

"Well, why did you attack that bodach?" Bran asked. "It seems a bit out of character from what you've told me so far."

"Shhhh!" the fairy whispered.

As the two passed the outer fringe of a lea, Snedeker stopped Bran with a silent warning gesture and pointed through the foliage. In the middle of the moonlit meadow and glowing like incandescent silver strolled a tall white doe, her neck long and elegant, her legs taut with nervous chiseled muscle. No impurity marring its beauty, the deer radiated innocence, the most beautiful animal Bran had ever seen.

But the fairy did not point at the doe.

From the far side of the lea, a tall shadow unnatural to the growth around it stood in the darkness, a statue in the midnight of the Snowdon. Unexpected thick bile rose up Bran's throat, and he wanted to vomit. Fighting the sick feeling that washed over him, the black outline of the entity solidified into a thin, tall man sitting upon a massive horse the color of damp ashes. The rider made no sound or movement. Branches grew out of the shadow's head until Bran realized they were multi-pointed horns bleached of color and very sharp. Every second that passed, the sense of wrongness about the creature and its mount intensified, forcing Bran to barely breathe, barely move, barely think.

The reality of what bothered Bran about the apparition struck him like lightning. It was not a man straddling a horse.

It was a centaur, like the woman Aife.

But unlike the Horsemaster of the Seelie Court, sick power radiated from the horned fey across the meadow, the venom of the being infiltrating Bran. Trembling involuntarily, it was all Bran could do to not become ill.

"Cernunnos," Snedeker whispered from Bran's shoulder.

"Who?" he hissed.

"The Erlking of the Unseelie Court," the fairy whimpered.

The centaur watched the doe graze the dewy grass, his eyes burning red like coals heated by bellows. The white deer seemed oblivious to what watched it, demurely feeding from the lea at its feet, its tiny tail flicking occasionally. A part of Bran wished to slink away—the nearby evil repellent to his heart—but he knelt, rooted in place, worry for the safety of the beautiful animal overcoming the instincts pounding in his blood to flee for his life.

With an achingly slow movement, Cernunnos pulled free a black bow as tall as a man; his other hand drew forth a feathered obsidian arrow. The head of the bolt flickered putrid green as he knocked it against the string. The Erlking of the Unseelie Court drew back the doe's death with a steady hand, fixing one baleful eye along the arrow.

"No!" Bran shouted without heed.

The glowing doe leapt ten feet in the air just as Cernunnos let go the string. The arrow shot like a bullet but harmlessly into the ground where the deer had been a moment before. The doe hit the lea bounding away, a blur of silver arcing through the night.

In less than two seconds she was gone.

The Erlking of the Unseelie Court, looking where the doe had vanished, strode slowly into the meadow beneath the moonlight, the horse chest rippling powerfully. He was taller than any Rhedewyr Bran had seen. Lank black hair fell over toned chest and arms, power radiating from him. The flaming eyes set within a narrow angular face never deviated from Bran. The dark weight of eons hung about the Erlking. At his feet a black stain of creatures skulked—tusked boars, slinking weasels, and other beasts of the night, all bearing red feral eyes that burned at Bran like the Erlking's own.

Snedeker shrank back, tugging on Bran's shirt, frightened.

It was all Bran could do to not to run.

—Human—

The scratching sound of the fey's voice hung like an anvil upon the night air.

—Do not fear me—

Bran hesitated but remained crouched low, illness permeating the air.

—Come to me, lad—

The repulsive sickness left Bran; in its place was a desire to stand and touch the being in the meadow. He stood, suddenly unafraid, aroused by something he could not define. The heart in his chest quickened; the blood in his veins raced. The smell of his own sweat and rotting oak leaves filled his nose, left him dizzy and confused. The world shrunk, reduced to only the two of them. He lost his memory and identity; the will he owned vanished.

In a flickering moment none of it mattered. Calm patience in the other replaced the fiery madness Bran thought he had seen, the peace he found in the burning eyes stretching millennia and would continue to do so.

He grew flushed as he did when riding with a redhead he couldn't remember. To join the centaur and creatures at its feet meant a lifetime of terrible desires fulfilled in the shadows, fear lost forever. He had to but join the Erlking and become one with darkness.

Something screamed in his ear but he did not care.

He was about to step into the clearing when his right hand began to burn, warm at first but growing in intensity until it engulfed his entire arm in a conflagration.

Looking down, a fairy ring about his finger shone with argent light, blinding in its pure radiance.

Memories returned at once.

Bran stopped but did not retreat, his courage bolstered.

—A fairy ring. Clever. There is no reason to fear me as the stink of the bodach is on you. You are already dead. The bodach will slay you before the Dark Thorn reenters the world—

Cernunnos laughed darkly then.

"It failed earlier tonight," Bran uttered willfully. "It will fail again. Next time, it will not be so lucky." Not knowing why, Bran raised the fist bearing the Paladr.

The crimson eyes of Cernunnos dimmed; the animals below him mewed lowly.

—The Seelie Court, my long lost brethren, is broken. You will join them—

With a dark look at the hand holding the Paladr and before Bran could gather courage enough to reply, Cernunnos shimmered and vanished. The beasts at his hooves lost their feral, manic appearance and faded from view in all directions. The sense of poisonous foreboding disappeared and true night resumed in the forest.

"What were you *doing?*" Snedeker chastised angrily.

"Where did he go?"

"Away, thank the Lady!"

"That was *the* Erlking of the Unseelie Court?" Bran asked.

"The Shadow King, yes," the fairy answered. "Safe we are. Those of the Unseelie Court lie in the space between sunlight and darkness. Rarely are the shadow seen. They *hate* humans, more than anything. Except perhaps my kind." Snedeker shivered again.

Following the jumping pull of the Paladr and trying to calm

his racing heart, Bran turned from the meadow and continued along the narrow trail through the trees, wary of even the stars peaking at him through holes in the forest canopy. Nothing was ever what it seemed in Annwn. The Erlking of the Unseelie Court knew of the confrontation with the bodach and, like the beast, wanted Bran dead.

One aspect of meeting Cernunnos remained fresh in his mind though.

The Erlking of the Unseelie Court had been afraid.

Afraid of the Paladr.

The trail steepened. Soon a brook bubbled along his right, the water a slow moving black ribbon. Mist not born of the Nharth twisted like vapor snakes, reaching for Bran while the air grew chillier. Above, the half disc of the silver moon highlighted the craggy white extremes of the Snowdon and pooled thick shadows around Bran. With every step he took, the sound of water falling against obstinate rock became clearer.

After what seemed like hours, Bran and Snedeker broke through the thick wood into an expansive opening beneath the stars, a carpet of thick grass spreading toward exposed rounded rock. The waterfall he had heard tumbled from a cliff face a short distance away to shake under his feet, the water a pane of glass before bouncing into the eddying pools of the brook. Copious ferns and moss grew along the rocky bank while fog stirred sluggishly above the water, the old trees surrounding the glen extending their limbs out over it as if to ward away the darkness. The waterfall captured the moonlight, diamonds twinkling and given the ability to fly.

Nothing else moved. All was serene, a magic suspended over the land, infusing Bran with every breath he took.

"Beautiful," he breathed.

Snedeker said nothing, mesmerized and hovering at his shoulder.

"What's wrong with you?"

With one shaking, leafy arm, Snedeker pointed at the falls.

The silver shimmer on the falling water detached and floated forward, the reflection of moonlight given substance and freedom. The lights floated near the water like large fireflies, hovering as if waiting on the two visitors.

"Lightbrands," Snedeker murmured in awe.

"What are they?"

"The fairy servants of the Lady," Snedeker whispered.

"What happened to your clan being favored first?"

Snedeker said nothing but instead dropped his head in respect. Five of the fairies separated from their brethren and floated upon the cool, wet air, their inner light brightening the shadowed shroud of the glen. Unlike Snedeker, who was made from bits of green leaves and peeled bark, the Lightbrands were smooth and naked, human-shaped figures glowing like celestial bodies freed from the stars. With wings fluttering like a blurred rainbow, they flew toward Bran unhindered.

"Where did they come from?" Bran hissed.

"Everywhere. From the water and light."

In moments, the fairies floated before his eyes in a line. Up close, they took on more human characteristics—high cheekbones, pointed ears, sharp chins and even toes. Three females and two males stared at Bran with blue eyes like oceans, white hair floating about their heads like silky halos. Wrinkled like a prune, the lead fairy came first, his long beard and wizened expression earnest.

Bran barely breathed. Snedeker sat prostrate on his shoulder, eyes averted in reverence.

The fairies began speaking then.

"Courageous young knight."

"Overcame fear for what was right."

"Protected the innocent."

"Despite possible harm to self."

"The Lady speaks."

The last words became a litany that slowly blended into a sustained hum as the fairies sped around Bran, flying in an unending circle. Snedeker twitched on his shoulder, curled up in a ball. The fairies flew faster and faster, a smudge of white arcing light like a halo, a dizzying pace Bran couldn't keep up with.

The hum fell away altogether, leaving a beautiful warm voice.

—Do you accept knighthood, Bran Ardall, line of Perceval?—

The voice was unlike those of the fairies, soft and lilting but ancient and very far away, as if the speaker were muffled. It bore the wearied tenor of eons and wisdom, unconditional love given but burdened by hardship and pain. It struck directly at his heart, consoling his guilt with forgiveness. The world blurred as tears sprang to his eyes. The question waited, an answer needed. The Lady wanted him to become the Heliwr. He wavered for only a moment before the memory of Connal dying and being cast aside like bloodied fodder mingled with the fear that he would never amount to anything beyond a street rat.

The warnings of Richard fell away. Bran chose his answer with conviction.

"I will," he said, and meant it with all his heart.

Just then, shadows detached from the gloom, slinking toward him, a menagerie of rabbits, ferrets, boars, and other animals, their eyes burning feral desire. The animal slaves of Cernunnos. Soon they had the glen surrounded.

Panic dampened the joy he felt being in the Lady's presence.

Azure light blossomed behind Bran.

"Looks like you were wrong about needing help," Richard said, moving to protect Bran's back, Arondight a fiery swath. "You do have a knack for trouble, don't you?"

Bran peered wildly around. Cernunnos did not appear. The beasts instead simply watched. It seemed the Erlking wanted to spy on what transpired but nothing more.

"I promise to keep them from you, whatever the cost," the knight said. "Do what you must."

Bran nodded and squeezed the Paladr tightly.

—Richard McAllister, my faithful knight, will you do what must be done to keep the office of Heliwr safe and see its duty carried out to fulfillment?—

Bran could feel Richard tensing behind him.

"I will, my Lady," Richard said finally.

—My paladins, it is done—

Heat blossomed in Bran's hand and then chest, dizzying and in a rush. When his head cleared, the Lightbrands whirling about him had slowed, become distinct creatures again. Once stopped, each bowed in midair, clearly exhausted, before flying back toward the waterfall and their waiting companions.

"Wait, I want answers!" Bran shouted, watching the Lightbrands disappear one by one like snuffed stars. "I don't know what to do! What do I do with this seed? What happened to my father? Did he go through this? What do you mean by Perceval?"

His questions echoed in the night.

"Wait!" he roared.

"They are gone," Richard said.

Bran wanted to chase after the fairies but suddenly found he could not move; his feet were anchored to the grass beneath him. Richard also began to struggle, similarly planted. Arondight vanished. Anger changed to dismay and then horror as Bran watched roots snake out of the ground and grip his boots; the tendrils did the same thing to Richard. They expanded until the two men were linked, the roots sprouting in various directions writhing up their legs as well as pushing deeper into the world every second that passed.

Bran tried to scream, but found his throat paralyzed.

Fighting his revulsion and losing, he became aware the heat in his chest pulsed also in the hand bearing the Paladr. He opened his fist. The seed winked silver at him as it invaded the skin of his palm, burrowing deep, vanishing into his body.

He tried to pry it free but the Paladr was inexorable.

A few moments later, it was gone inside him.

Snedeker yelled, frenzied, but Bran couldn't understand him.

The heat increased throughout his body, the change begun at his feet continuing. What had been his two legs fused into one; what had been his two arms split into many. Broad shiny green leaves sprouted from his elongating fingers and transformed into gnarled limbs, while sharp black thorns like small daggers erupted along what had been his forearms. Both Bran and Richard grew tall and broad, branching out into the night and into the ground, feeling the life force of the world and all it contained.

He could feel Richard fighting the transformation too, but the two were intertwined, the knight pulled into the magic that transformed Bran.

The glen disappeared as azure light suddenly flared around him, blinding Bran to the world. The heady darkness of rich earth was replaced by the feel of cold fire licking his body, entering his soul, as if he had been plunged into the deepest crystal-clear lake and the water had infiltrated his very pores.

Help me, he croaked. No one answered.

As despair born of uncertainty heightened, what had been his fingers suddenly grasped fiery blue steel, its strength resilient as it gave him inner strength, sharing with him a modicum of hope.

He gripped it tighter. It was solid and comforting.

It felt right.

It would always be there when he had need of it.

Comforting darkness cradled him, and he slept.

Chapter 20

Standing next to Pope Clement XV, Cormac clutched a Bible over his red and white vestment as if it were a lifeline, fighting the anger threatening to overwhelm him.

The problem was he didn't know if he wanted to be saved.

He wanted to laugh like a madman.

"To celebrate this solemn time, we are united in Christ, who died and too rose from the dead," the pontiff said, his voice echoing in the low-ceiled tomb. "Cardinal Donato Javier Ramirez has now passed over from death to life through the blessings that he received in his association with Christ."

Cormac barely heard a word, the wheels of reprisal spinning. The closed coffin of Donato rested to the side of a hole chiseled into the rock far beneath St. Peter's Basilica. Cormac could not take his eyes from it. The Bible favored by Donato lay on the casket, and baptismal water the Pope had sprinkled shined in the candlelight. The Vigilo were deep within Vatican Hill in a series of secret rooms few knew existed, below even the Sacred Grotto where more than ninety Popes and other distinguished dead lay interred. The funeral was the first Mass conducted in these depths during his Cardinalship and the proper forms were being witnessed.

The Pope conducted the private requiem, beginning with the Introit and orchestrating each rite with the respect Donato deserved.

Cormac hated that he couldn't keep his oldest friend safe.

After an opening reading by Cardinal Villenza, Clement cleared his throat to read from the New Testament.

"'Let no one keep defrauding you of your prize by delighting in self-abasement and the worship of angels, taking his stand on visions he has seen, inflated without cause by his fleshly mind, and not holding fast to the head, from whom the entire body, being supplied and held together by the joints and ligaments, grows with a growth which is from God,'" Clement orated, his deep voice echoing, before looking at the members of the Vigilo. "In this letter to the Colossians, Paul reminds us all to renounce other worldly gods, maintain our focus on the work of the Lord, and deny evil that which takes our heart from Him. Cardinal Ramirez knew this better than anyone. He led a long life with the basic but fundamental insight of not *only* looking to Christ for salvation but protecting His flock from Annwn and those who would remove the focus of our faith."

Clement began the Sanctus then. The Vigilo joined him like they had the previous prayers, their voices raised together.

The Cardinal Vicar welcomed the bit of solace the familiar chant gave.

With the appeal to God finished, Clement turned to Cormac. The Cardinal Vicar stepped forward and opened his Bible. The pages turned at once to the Gospel of Mark, bookmarked with the thick silken red ribbon. Tracing each familiar verse, Cormac stopped at the appropriate one, his voice shaky but growing in steadfast strength.

"The Passover Supper as told by Mark," Cormac started. "Jesus offered His disciples bread and, after blessing it, He gave it to them, saying, 'Take this, this is my body.' The Lord then took a cup of wine, thanked God, and shared His cup with the others. 'This is My blood of the covenant, which is poured out of many. Truly I say to you, I will never again drink of the fruit of the vine until that day when I drink it new in the kingdom of God.'" Cormac closed the Bible. "Donato is released to the glory of our Lord. He is now exalted and safe from sin, just as he kept us safe for the entirety of his days. Donato was a tireless man, given vast energy by the Lord no matter how many decades passed; he used his boundless wisdom to enrich our lives in the Lord and see the doctrine Saint Peter entrusted the Vigilo carried out as it was decreed."

Cormac swallowed hard. "In his duty, the Cardinal Seer was the type of rock the Lord charged Saint Peter with being—growing the flock and keeping it safe.

"Let us pray the Angus Dei."

When they were done with the Angus Dei, Cormac nodded to the pontiff.

Clement turned to face each Cardinal.

"Let us take Communion."

As the members of the Vigilo knelt to the cold stone, the Pope offered each a wheaten wafer and a lone sip of wine from a golden chalice as he repeated the tradition with his Cardinals. Cormac accepted the offering from Christ, but it was like wet ash in his mouth. The man responsible for the strength Cormac carried had been murdered, taken from the world by an insidious evil wishing the Church blind, the very role of Seer used against Donato through the Fionúir Mirror.

He had died saving Cormac.

God had a plan Donato had shared in the chamber before his death.

It was not the only time he had reiterated that belief...

Cormac had been twenty years old, a young priest in an ancient Church. Long gone from his native home of Ireland and finished helping his parents in the Middle East, Cormac had been studying and working in the Vatican for two years. The time was very different then, the ruin of the Second World War behind them, and Catholicism under Pope John XIII waning in popularity to a liberal cultural explosion in the world. But the Baroque and Renaissance beauty permeated St. Peter's Basilica as it had for centuries, and the arms of Bernini's colonnade permanently welcomed people into the bosom of the Catholic Church.

The Lord could be seen in every piece of artwork around Cormac until he absorbed the beauty and humility like a sponge.

Sitting on a bench in the nave of the Basilica and ignoring the wide-eyed tourists, Cormac read the *Historia Brittonum* for his studies. Sunshine from the dome fell over the massive bronze baldacchino while marble statues set into the walls watched from eternally frozen positions those who milled below.

The spot was one of his favorite places to read and think, despite the noise.

White robes swirled to a stop before Cormac.

Lowering the book, he glanced up.

"A word with you, young O'Connor," an older man said in lilted Spanish, his robes those of a Bishop, his coal-like eyes staring sadly at Cormac. "I was told I might find you here."

"I am at your service, Bishop . . . ?"

"Bishop Donato Javier Ramirez, of the Vatican Archives," he said as he handed Cormac a browned letter, already opened, from the folds of his robe.

"A missive for me?" Cormac asked, taking the letter.

"I am afraid so, my son."

Cormac frowned. Red inked Arabic markings voided multiple stamps on the envelope, his name and the Vatican address labeled in scrawled calligraphic script, the dry paper light as a feather in his hand. Cormac paused. He often received letters from his father and family in the Middle East, who worked hard to convert the Islamic peoples to Christianity, but what he held was not written in his father's hand.

One end was slit open, the actual letter cradled inside.

Cormac removed and unfolded the letter—and upon reading it had a mixture of disbelief, heart-stopping sorrow, and rage sweep through him like the angriest of storms.

The world blurred.

His heart hammered.

A paralyzed scream exploded in his head.

The letter notified His Eminence Pope John XIII in two short paragraphs that fanatical Shiite purists in the city of Kut had murdered Cormac's father, mother, and sister.

The foundation of Cormac crumbled.

"This cannot be . . ." he shook his head. "Cannot . . ."

The Bishop sat beside him and firmly gripped the young man's hands, praying to the Lord for guidance even as the first spark of furious ire lit inside Cormac.

"God has a plan, my son," Bishop Ramirez finished. "Always."

It took two weeks for the bodies of his family to be returned. The mass conducted in Ireland was a closed-casket affair; the whole village witnessed the ceremony and burial of his family. Cormac stood alone, aloof, his childhood home foreign and lost forever. As their coffins were slowly lowered into the peaty soil, the crisp wind of the Isles chilled cheeks to the numbness his heart already carried. He let them go, vowing to keep the pain of their deaths rooted in his being.

For years afterward, Donato mentored Cormac to view the Lord as the way to enact world change—that not all people different from the Church were evil but merely misguided.

After four decades, he remembered that day as if it were yesterday.

As he stood within the cold catacombs, he laid to rest one of his best friends and a second father, a man murdered by extreme hate just as his first had been.

It was hard for Cormac to see the plan God had put into play.

The final communion given, Clement stepped forward and baptized the coffin of the Cardinal Seer once more. He removed the Bible, left the cross in the center of the oak box, and stepped away. Cardinals Villenza and Tucci slowly lowered Donato into the chiseled hole until the coffin came to its final place of rest. For Cormac, it was hard to watch. Despite Donato carrying humility to the end, the Seer deserved a grand majestic Mass in the beautiful nave and halls above rather than a small funeral in the depths of the Basilica. But the role of Seer came with restrictions, and the world had to remain ignorant of Annwn and all of those who kept its existence secret.

"Until we also come to the Lord's doorstep," Clement said,

forming the cross over his heart. "The Catholic Church and the Vigilo say farewell to you, Cardinal Seer Donato Javier Ramirez."

The Vigilo also made the sign of the cross.

Cormac helped the others move a plain stone slab featuring a simple rose carved in relief with opened petals, his name, and the dates of his birth, service, and death. As the casket disappeared from view, tears burned. The boom of the stone fitting snuggly into place echoed like the final strike of a clock tower bell that would never ring again.

The Pope looked to Cormac.

The Cardinal Vicar stepped to the head of the tomb. "Lord, grant him eternal rest, and may perpetual light shine upon him within your vaunted love. Amen."

The Vigilo repeated the final prayer. With a sad nod, Clement left the room, his robes a whisper. The Cardinals also left, some sharing words of solace with Cormac, others stopping to squeeze his hands in faith and sharing of grief.

After they left, the catacomb room returned to cold silence.

Cormac knelt at the foot of the tomb and wept.

It was a long time before he left.

WITH A BRIGHT lantern held high and midnight having come and gone, Cormac entered the depths of the Vatican once more, this time leading Swiss Guard Captain Finn Arne and his team of soldiers.

After the burial of Donato, Cormac and the Vigilo had spent a somber dinner remembering the Cardinal Seer. Eventually discussion changed to Annwn and the evil festering there. The Fionúir Mirror had been covered by its shroud and would remain so without a Seer, the Church blind to Annwn—and Philip Plantagenet. Names of possible candidates for the role went long into the night. They settled on no one. It would be some time before they found a man sharing the convictions and doctrine of the Vigilo to take on the mantle of Cardinal Seer.

Unable to sleep and the murder of Donato galvanizing him,

Cormac enacted plans known to be heretical.

"If I may say, your Lordship, you seem quite tired. Is all well?"

"You may *not* say, Finn," Cormac warned. "You have more pressing matters to worry about than my feelings."

Finn Arne shrugged beside Cormac, a dark tool of fortune as they descended into the depths of Italy. Dressed entirely in black lightweight clothing and a number of pistols, knives, and semi-automatic rifles belted to his person, the Captain of the Swiss Guard watched Cormac with a dead eye alongside one burning with confidence. Two dozen armed soldiers of the Swiss Guard followed, allowed to pass through the Sacred Grotto where pontiffs of ages past were buried and into the secret catacombs beneath, armed like their captain. According to Finn, the guards were well trained and discretionary for the right price, the hardest men to have walked the Holy See.

"You have briefed your men of what they might encounter?"

"I have," Finn replied. "They are the best in the Guard. Several of them were in Seattle with me and have shared what they experienced with the others."

"Let's hope the best is enough," Cormac muttered. "And they all lack family?"

"Not so much a cousin among them, your Grace."

"Good. Good. I want you to find him, Finn. No excuses. Observe Caer Llion if you have the chance but do not return without Ardall."

"With the trackers and firepower assembled at my back, it will be done."

"Do not underestimate McAllister again," Cormac warned sternly. "He has almost as many tricks as the wizard." He paused. "There are also those you should turn from, fey creatures who possess far more power than any of you. Do not enter into contest like you did with the Kreche. Stealth will serve you better until you find Ardall. The longer you stay hidden from those who exist in Annwn, the better chance you will have of completing what I ask of you."

"As you have said already."

"You are sure you can track the boy?"

"With certainty. There are three men in this group who track." Finn patted the pack on his hip. "The map you've supplied will also guide us. When we gain the Carn Cavall, we will ferret him out and bring him to Rome."

Pleased, Cormac nodded. He had spent hours in the chamber of the Seer, pouring over archives of information to help better direct the captain once he arrived in Annwn. After Cormac notified the pontiff of Donato's murder, Clement had also bequeathed what knowledge he possessed as Pope. With that information and the journals of Donato to aid him, Cormac spent a sleepless night studying Annwn and, having witnessed the path McAllister and Ardall had taken after fleeing Dryvyd Wood, put Finn on the trail to gain what the Cardinal Vicar desired.

Even from the grave, Donato would help bring death to his killers. Through Finn, Cormac would control the Heliwr and use him to hunt those responsible for the murder of the Cardinal Seer.

"Kill the knight if you must," Cormac commanded. "Richard McAllister has become a serious liability. He has deviated from his role and in so doing has corrupted his purpose the Vigilo and the Catholic Church entrusted him."

"If all is equal, McAllister will pose no threat," Finn said, eagerness gleaming in his one good eye. "Not this time."

"Do not worry about Myrddin Emrys," Cormac acknowledged. "Without his power he is merely an old man and he cannot aid the boy. Destroy McAllister first. The boy will be yours after that. Bring him straight here, to me. No one else need know of this excursion."

"It will be done, your Lordship," Finn said. "I will not fail again."

Cormac leaned in closely. "Do this, and you will have whatever you wish."

Avarice twinkled in the depths of Finn's good eye.

The air grew chillier the deeper the men delved, every level producing older and older carved sarcophagi and tombs dating back centuries, their artwork eroded by age. After coming to a large four-door intersection, Cormac paused, bringing the group to a halt, emotion coursing through him. The right doorway led to the chamber Donato had once called home, the place of his death. Instead Cormac walked through the opposite doorway. Damper air rushed over his cheeks. He stole through the hundreds of yards of twisting corridors, leading many into a world only seen by a few, the sound of moving water growing stronger with every step he took.

Coming to a gaping black doorway, Cormac entered a new cavern. Wet minerals tinged the air. Four lanterns bolted into the low ceiling cast yellow light in a wide circle until snuffed by a cocoon of darkness, the illumination encapsulating a sandy bank where the movement of an underground branch of the Tiber River passed black as an oil slick. Near the shore, two rectangular stones erupted and were carved with hundreds of glowing white runes between which flashes of silver lightning arced within a shimmering void.

Ennio Rossi, his dark eyes haggard but back straight, waited by the portal, his hands thrust into his pants pockets.

Cormac gave the knight a cordial nod. "Captain Arne, Ennio Rossi here will see you and your men through to Annwn."

"Bearer of Prydwen," Ennio greeted Finn. "Shield of Mother Church."

"Knight of the Seven, it is with great honor we meet," Finn said, removing his eye from the portal. "My men are prepared for what is to come once through the portal. Expect our return soon."

Ennio deferred his gaze and stepped aside.

"Kneel, Swiss Guard of the Vatican," the Cardinal Vicar ordered.

Cormac blessed the group of soldiers for a safe return, but his thoughts were of Ennio. The knight remained hesitant to break the canon handed to him by the Church and Myrddin Emrys. No one was meant to pass either direction—not fairy creature, not man. Only the Heliwr had the ability to do so, and even the Unfettered Knight did so at great peril of spilling the long-held secret of the Vigilo. But the death of Donato had reinforced the need to enter Annwn, and without the Heliwr, Ennio knew he had no other choice.

When the prayer was finished, Cormac turned to Finn. "Remember what I told you," Cormac said, mostly so Ennio would hear. "Stealth is your weapon, not might of arms. Spy on Caer Llion, watch for any army being built. Return as quickly as you can."

Finn nodded, his face set stone, and entered the swirling portal. The men under his command followed their captain as well, disappearing as if through a veil of falling water. None turned back; none deviated. After seconds, Finn and his group of heavily armed warriors had disappeared from Rome.

The portal glimmered as it had for centuries, as if nothing had happened.

"Well done, Ennio Rossi," Cormac said, pleased.

"If the others find out . . ."

"They will not," Cormac assured. "The only one to possibly find out is Knight Richard McAllister and I promise, he will welcome the aid."

Ennio looked at the portal. "Why do you think Richard went into Annwn?"

"I don't know," Cormac lied. "Perhaps it is Myrddin Emr—"

"Merle has never sent a portal knight into Annwn."

"That you know of," Cormac corrected. "Without a Heliwr, anything is possible."

At the mention of the Heliwr, Ennio averted his eyes from the Cardinal Vicar and crossed his arms. Tension formed a rift between them. He knew Ennio did not tell him all that transpired in his role as knight, had not even told Donato everything. The Knights of the Yn Saith were close, able to communicate over the vast distances that separated them, and that bond and the knowledge that came from it remained an annoyance to the Church. If Ennio knew why McAllister had entered Annwn with Ardall, he wasn't sharing.

"Whatever transpires, Ennio, we must be vigilant."

"I will fulfill my responsibility," the knight answered.

"As the Cardinal Seer saw in his mirror, odd elements are swarming around Caer Llion. Evil grows there. Creatures not seen before are ravaging the countryside, and we fear Plantagenet is sending his machinations into this world. The loss of a portal knight is a grave concern to the Vigilo."

Ennio frowned. "Richard would never join—"

"He has had a hard life, my son," Cormac said, sowing doubt. "We know not his reason for entering Annwn and must be wary."

Ennio stayed silent, but Cormac saw his arrow had struck true.

"Be prepared for the worst if it comes to that," Cormac said. "The Guard has already been doubled in the chambers of the Basilica above. Hundreds more are near to calling. With you warding the portal, a large force at your back and the corridors upward so narrow, we should be able to contain any attempt by Plantagenet to enter Rome."

"When the Captain comes back through, I will notify you," Ennio said. "And if it comes to it, I can bring this cavern down around the portal so that no one can enter."

Cormac nodded politely, turned, and made his way up into the Basilica again and out through the façade into Italy's cold air. Plans he had set into motion were out of his hands now. The Pope wanted results; Cormac would give them.

And become favored for his next appointment.

Pontiff of the Catholic Church.

He sighed, suddenly tired. The loss of Donato drove him stronger than any papal authority, but he was still just a man. Myrddin Emrys could not be trusted, his knights lacking the conscience to do what was right. With Finn Arne acting as the Cardinal Vicar's extension, the Heliwr would be his and when that happened, Plantagenet would die along with those who had joined him in Annwn.

And any heretical enemies of the Church.

When Cormac crawled into bed, sleep came on swift wings.

Chapter 21

"My king, there is nothing I can do," John Lewis Hugo said, his voice low.

"Nothing you can do?!" Philip raged. "Nothing you can *do?!*"

John did not answer, his mask of ruined flesh impassive. Philip fought the urge to pin his oldest friend against the stairwell wall and beat him senseless. Caer Llion brooded like its king. Sunrise had not yet come, the corridors vacant of staff. It suited Philip. The spiraling staircase unfolded downward from his suites, the passage chilly and empty of servants. Whenever he ventured into the warrens beneath the castle he preferred no one to know. Gauging the progress of the witch, no matter how distasteful, had become of singular importance. The time to lead the crusade into the world of his birth was nigh upon him—the end of the war in Annwn his father had ordained and the beginning of his true calling.

Now his longtime friend and most powerful ally informed him that McAllister and Ardall were out of reach—out of reach!

"Answer me!" Philip commanded.

"My king, you know as well as I the cauldron has limits," the advisor said. "Once the knight and his charge fled into the lower reaches of the Snowdon and into the Nharth, they became and continue to be outside the range of my magical ability."

Philip mastered his frustration, if barely. The stairwell they descended opened into the expanse of the Great Hall where two Templar Knights snapped to attention from their post at the main entrance, the enormous banner of the Plantagenet House hanging above them, its roaring golden lion staring down with authority from a crimson field. Not capturing the knight and the boy rankled him. He wanted to add their power to his own. Philip had instead been forced to undo the magic chains binding the bodach for centuries and unleash the predatory Unseelie creature upon the boy.

The smoke-like beast had sniffed Ardall's coat and bounded from the castle like a sable bolt shot from a crossbow. The bodach was now within the Snowdon hunting. Or feasting on the dead.

It irked Philip that he didn't know which. John hadn't been able to view what transpired in the Snowdon and the Carn Cavall, leaving Philip in the dark.

Passing carved stone statues of stoic knights and ancient tapestries depicting victorious battles from his Annwn arrival, Philip and John traveled deeper into the castle and took a broad staircase down, its steps worn from ages of passing feet. Caer Llion had been built upon a large abutment of rock overlooking the sea, long before Philip was even born, and he had taken it as his main capital after invading Annwn. Over the centuries, he had fortified his new holding and conquered most of the island. By bribing the Cailleach to keep it eternally summer, the economy of the land grew as his people multiplied. With the growth of the great northern cities of Caer Dathal, Mur Castell, and Velen Rhyd in Gwynedd, Philip strengthened his rule and most of Annwn was quelled. His land, his rule.

With Philip watching the hall, John opened a secret passageway set behind a large wall-hung tapestry, its thickly woven fabric obscuring the entrance into the dungeons. Philip flinched as cool air mixed with the tang of human waste and unwashed bodies swept over him. He pushed down the bile rising in his throat; he hated going into the dungeons almost as much as he hated the fey and their ilk.

"What *have* you seen in the cauldron then?" Philip questioned.

The wall grinding to a close behind them, John mumbled a combination of words until a blue flame materialized in the air to light their way down the staircase. "Before the sun set last evening while you met with the lords, I traveled over the breadth of Annwn. The fey *are* moving. Thousands of Merrow have come ashore near Mynyw at Porth Cleis, armed and ready for spending long days on land. Up the coast, many of the buggane have left the ruins of Caer Harlech, heading toward the Snowdon. Both groups have entered the Nharth mists. There may be other fey joining them, but I cannot view the entirety of Annwn every moment."

"Mobilizing."

"Mobilizing," John agreed. "And there are others."

Philip frowned. "Others?"

"Lord Gerallt and his daughter have vanished. My spies know not where they have gone, but they are no longer in Mochdrev Reach. I believe they have betrayed Caer Llion," John said, gliding like a stain down the stairwell. "The Morrigan could be drawing these groups together for an offensive of some kind, one that would put our current plans at risk."

"You are certain of this? About Lord Gerallt joining the Tuatha?"

"It makes sense, my king," John said. "Mochdrev Reach has ever had ties to the Carn Cavall, playing both sides to remain at peace. Lord Gerallt offered his daughter, but apparently she is stronger than even I observed when I met her."

"You have been wrong another time, John," Philip said, angry all over again with his advisor. "And you wanted me to marry that traitorous whore? Redheaded bitch. I want Lord Gerallt *dead*. His daughter *dead*. The Reach made a Templar garrison!"

"The boy and the knight could be driving the resistance."

"If the bodach does what you say it will, there are no worries," Philip said.

"The bodach is formidable. But the power of the knight, combined with members of the Seelie Court, could withstand it." John paused. "I think we should reconsider our plans. I think it would behoove us to sweep the Snowdon clear before proceeding into the portal, my king. It is apparent the Seelie Court is not as weak as we had once thought."

Anger that had been smoldering reignited. In one swift motion Philip gripped his old friend by his black robe, fists wanting to fling the advisor down the staircase.

"You tell me all of this *now!*" Philip yelled.

Surprise on John's face became a dark cloud, his eyes hard like black agates of hatred. The friend Philip knew disappeared; in his place a terrifying creature stared back.

"Do not forget what I have become, my king."

Philip let John go but did not retreat beneath his hot gaze.

"My king," John said softly, his hate gone as quickly as it had come. "The choice will always be your own. I have done what I can to advise you with the knowledge I gained under Master Wace as well as that gleaned from the fey creature Arawn, whose being I trapped and consumed. War is uncertain. Once forces begin moving, the enemy counters. That is the nature of such endeavors. We must embrace all tangible probabilities, analyze them, to make the wisest course of action."

Philip stared hard at John. "We shall not deviate from my cause."

"Of course we will not, my king."

"We must leave behind a larger force than planned to maintain all that we have gained," Philip thought aloud. "Protect all that we have fought for."

"That would be wise," John said. "Master Wace would agree."

Philip backed away from his advisor and took a steadying breath. Rarely had they come to such angst-ridden moments in the past. He and John had always been close, despite the change made to rid Annwn of Arawn—a terrible and powerful fey lord. Other than the brief pleasures afforded him by a woman, Philip let no one but John near him. Together they had begun this conquest and together they would finish it.

"And the portal is secure?" he asked.

"It is," John said evenly. "The Templar Knights command every crag and trail. Nothing will prevent our entrance when the time is right."

"That is well," Philip commended. "I want to lead my army through the portal myself, without disruption. And I want you following right behind. I loathe Annwn. It is time we returned to the world of our birth—as conquerors."

"It will be so, my king."

"Is our way clear?" Philip questioned. "On the other side?"

"I cannot see within the Vatican," John answered. "But the catacombs beneath are empty of all but the dead and the knight."

"And what of him?"

"The whelp knows not what comes," John assured. "He is not even there half the time, carousing in inns and pubs with brew and women. Such a sinful world, ripe for our purposes. With the Cardinal Seer dead and the knight preoccupied by his flesh, when we enter the Vatican to reclaim your birthright, my pets will carve a way past the curse tablets and into the heart of the very Basilica itself. We will gain the Vault and the relics that lie within. With their power added to our own, we will crush the resistance here. Then the cleanse shall begin in that world as well."

"As it should, a long time in the coming," Philip acknowledged.

"What of the Morrigan, my king?"

"I want eyes patrolling the sky," Philip commanded. "Send the griffins into the Snowdon today at sunrise, reporting back in short intervals. They have bred like rabbits, and sacrificing a few will give a greater understanding of what the Morrigan is planning. Regardless of her design, it will be moot if Caer Llion is made aware in time."

"In whose keeping will you leaveCaer Llion?"

Philip had spent great amount of time considering that very point. The last few days had seen many meetings. Not all of the lords under his banner were trustworthy. With no heir due to the affects of the magic that kept him young, Philip did not have anyone to trust.

"Lord Evinnysan," Philip ventured.

"The wisest choice of the group I think."

"Not smart enough to take the throne, vicious enough to

protect my interests," Philip continued. "He will need to be watched."

"Much will need to be watched other than the Morrigan and Caer Llion," John said, turning down a new staircase where the air grew damp. "You should be made aware, my king, that a flock of griffins attacked a young dragon. It survived, if barely, winging back to its kin."

"And you worry that could motivate Tal Ebolyon?"

"Long has Latobius remained separate from the Seelie Court," John said. "Even if the dragon lord lends his power to the Morrigan, the griffins will protect the air. We have nothing to fear from that dying race. Their time passed with the shadow of the wind."

"Watch them anyway," Philip ordered, blocking the way. "Remember what Master Wace always taught during war seminar?"

"Overconfidence kills a leader."

Philip moved on. Master Wace of Bayeux. Centuries had passed since Philip and John had studied with their mentor in a tall tower rising just outside Oxford. The Master had given fourteen years of his life teaching tactics in warfare, philosophy from the far east and Greek antiquity, the history and politics of Europe and the Isles, and the intricacies of the Church and its followers. When Philip was young he had longed to be part of the family his father Henry II denied him, but growing into manhood under the tutelage of Master Wace had opened his eyes to the hypocrisy in the world— starting with his own kin. The bickering of his father and brother Richard over northern France, his father banishing Philip's mother to the Tower of London, the attempt by John to claim the crown while Richard fought in the Third Crusade—the sin of greed and jealousy drove wedges between his family members and the Word of the Church.

Philip promised he would never succumb to the sinful vicissitudes that had ruined his family and those he had seen in the poverty-stricken streets of London.

He repressed a snort.

The Seelie Court quarreled like his family.

Now, having lived longer than any of his father's descendents, he meant to finish what God and Henry II had ordained all those centuries earlier.

Bring religious order to the world—with the sword, if necessary.

The staircase ended and both men stepped into a vast empty cavern, their footfalls echoing off the foundation of the castle. Of the four available doorways, John selected the one on their right, away from the dungeons, his flame above lighting their way.

"Will the Cailleach be ready with the strap bags?" Philip asked.

"She will. Enough cattle hide has been acquired to make it so."

"It is almost time then."

"Lord Gwawl and the rest have sworn their allegiance," John said. "And given of their men and resources."

"Give them the bags then," Philip said. "Test them and ensure the water works. Explain what the bags are for. Do *not* tell them where they came from. I doubt any of them will turn on me after they realize the power I possess and control."

John nodded and continued onward.

"And if they do challenge me," Philip added. "They will be fed to the halfbreeds."

The staircase continued to wind down, but the stone of the walls changed from mortared blocks to slick rock, cut from the natural lay of the land. The corridors were ancient, having been there since the Celtic gods and goddesses had entered Annwn to escape their persecution from the Isles. Philip possessed it all now, to use as his whim dictated.

After what seemed an eternity walking in the clammy depths, they came to a locked door, one newly fashioned from thick oak and banded in unforgiving iron. A giant Fomorian stood guard, his broad shoulders filling up much of the hallway. He bowed, his eyes lost behind the visor of a helmet. A giant sword lay propped against the wall nearby.

"My king, the witch may not appreciate our visit to these depths," John said.

"I pay her price," Philip said. "She will do as I tell her or *she* will be fed to her creations."

John shrugged. He produced a key from the folds of his robe, and upon opening the door, he stepped by the Fomorian into the subterranean.

The Mhydew spread out as far as Philip could see, a lake as black as obsidian, its depths lost to the imagination and the air filled with the rancorous combination of minerals and feces. The blue flame rose high, revealing giant cones of rock clinging to the ceiling like dozens of teeth frozen in place. In the middle of the lake, a pyramid of organized stone jutted, and at its apex his ancient prize sat, catching dripping water from the ceiling that overflowed into the cache below. Flickering torches set into wall sconces faintly lit their area and that was all.

The Mhydew was a dark world of sharp points and cutting edges, shut away from the emerald lush grasses and hills of Annwn above. Every time Philip entered the immense cavern he felt small and insignificant.

He hated the feeling.

Along the shore, dozens of men and women bound to the rock by thick chains poured water from the lake into large leather flasks with stoppers and straps. With grime-covered skin, hair, and clothing, they looked like nothing human. Disgust rose up within Philip. They were those of his subjects who had broken the law, from murder to petty thievery to sodomy. For their transgressions they had been blinded by red-hot pokers, tongues cut from their mouths, and brought here to serve. Some died quickly, the fire to live extinguished as soon as they entered the Mhydew; some served the witch in other ways he no longer wanted to know about.

Either way, there were always others ready to fill the shackles; lawbreakers were all too easily found in Annwn.

One of them reached out and touched his foot then.

Philip drew the sword his father had given him but instead kicked violently out, slashing the blind woman along her cheek with the heel of his boot. Initially stunned and grunting with pain, she crawled to the lake and lapped at the water.

The wound healed immediately, a scar forming until even that disappeared beneath the dirty, blood-smeared face.

"They learn quickly," Philip observed.

"Even dogs can learn at a rapid rate, my king," John pointed out.

Philip supposed they could. "The witch watches them still?"

"Through some art of her own design, yes," John answered. "The fulfillment of your plan is upon us. The contraptions work splendidly."

Philip picked one of thousands from the cavern floor, observing it. It was almost as large as a horse stomach, several pieces of cowhide stitched tightly together. Two straps hung limply from the leather sack while a cork closed off a long reed tube.

"The army will be invincible," Philip breathed.

"It will indeed, my king."

"What of the last few regiments?"

"The last batches are growing. The griffins currently roost nearby the portal and the houndmaster curtails the bloodlust of the wolves with some staff fashioned by the witch. Even the death rate among the maulls has dropped considerably, and many are growing to destructive maturity. With your lords having gathered and the efforts of the witch coming to fruition, your army is on the cusp of completion."

Philip had waited a long time to hear John say those words.

Chilling screams of lust echoed from a staircase leading to the breeding pens in another cavern. The foul odor Philip had barely grown accustomed to wafted into the Mhydew from that dark exit.

"The Cailleach enjoys her work," John observed.

"Too much," Philip said with distaste.

"It is the only way," John assured. "Turning sin against the sinners has a certain poetic justice to it, do you not think?"

Philip didn't answer. He hated the abominations almost as much as he needed them.

"My king?"

"I want the witch at our side, John," Philip said. "I want her to be in full control of the army we have built."

"Whispers and rumors already swirl surrounding the half-breeds," John said. "My foray into Dryvyd Wood set the men under Lord Gwawl at unease. Rumors have spread. I think it wise to hide the creatures as long as possible."

"That is why the witch is so important," Philip said. "There will come a time when we will unleash the full army onto the world and those same men will be thanking it. Until then . . ."

"I will speak to the Cailleach now."

"Watch the plains. If Ardall and the knight appear, I want to know about it. And ensure the security of Caer Llion and our supply train. To be cut off from the castle while battling in the world of our birth would be unfortunate indeed." Philip paused, looking at the center of the lake. "See to it this room is more securely guarded as well. Place Templar Knights you trust implicitly. I want nothing to go awry, and our power here must not be disturbed *or* stolen as we transition from this world to that one. To lose the relic would be a great loss. Your head, in fact."

John nodded, seemingly unafraid of the threat.

"Make it happen," Philip said sternly. "Failure is not an option."

John bowed and vanished into the breeding caverns.

Philip watched his adviser leave. John had changed. When they had been young in that first century after imprisoning Arawn, John had been strong but sanguine, able to see the positive in any negative, able to take advantage of it. But over the years he had become darker, less than the friend Philip remembered. The hardship of ruling, no doubt. The earlier anger that had fed Philip now faded. He would speak to his old friend about it soon. John deserved any pleasure he desired; Philip would make sure his oldest advisor took advantage of their spoils.

The slaves on the shore continued their slow task.

Philip grinned.

He was going to succeed where his family had failed.

The kitchens of Caer Llion would be waking soon, their rising bread and simmering stews filling the needs of his people. He decided his own needs could wait. He would visit the Cathedral and pray for strength and victory before breaking his fast. He wanted to cleanse his soul. It was time the lords, after all of these centuries, discovered exactly what he planned, but he wished to do it with the filth of the Mhydew washed from him in all ways.

Philip raised the sword he had carried all of his adult days.

Exquisite care had gone into Hauteclere, the fabled blade of Olivier de Vienne, one of the peers of Charlemagne. It had been in the Plantagenet family for centuries. The crystal embedded in the hilt glimmered at him where it met the golden curving cross guard, the torchlight slicking the blade with blood.

Philip thought that appropriate.

Standing in the presence of the relic that had made his existence eight centuries after his birth possible, he was reminded of the appeal Saint Peter had made to the Gentiles—to bring them within the fold of the Church and teach them the grace of the Lord.

Philip would do the same to the heathens of two worlds.

And sit upon one throne forever.

Chapter 22

With sunshine warming his cheek and a hand shaking his shoulder, Richard broke the surface from an ocean of dreams into a birdsong-laden morning.

He opened bleary eyes.

"Knight McAllister," Kegan breathed, the clurichaun staring worriedly down on him. "You took some waking. I was about to get the others."

Richard blinked, sitting up. "Where are we?"

"From what I can tell, a glen of sorts. One with a waterfall."

Morning light streamed in through the eastern trees behind the clurichaun, blinding the knight with its intensity. Cool air mingled with the scent of dewy grass and churned dark earth. Muffled thunder came from the waterfall. For the first time Richard became aware of the tree above him. Branching out to all sides, the gnarled limbs of the hawthorn bore dark green leaves that absorbed the virgin morning light to shimmer with vitality. The trunk twisted from the black earth, sturdy and strong. Small pink flowers budded in the canopy; sharp thorns two inches long burgeoned like knives along every branch.

It was beautifully symmetrical except where a knob of healed wood existed, the branch having once grown there gone.

Bran lay nearby as well, also beginning to wake.

Richard took a deep breath, still unsure about what was going on. Then everything about the previous night came back to him in a sudden rush—tracking Bran through the forest; the Lightbrands and their beautiful dance; the ancient, lilting voice in his head asking if he was prepared to do what was needed; and his transformation into a tree that had also wrapped around Bran.

Richard bolted upright, scared he'd see bark for skin or tangled roots for feet.

All appeared right—two legs in pants, two feet in boots. He stared at his hands; no leaves sprouted, no thorns existed. He breathed a bit easier.

He felt normal.

"Ye are fine, McAllister," Kegan affirmed with a bushy questioning eyebrow.

"How did you find me?"

"The fairy there," Kegan pointed out.

Snedeker sat upon a large fern several dozen feet nearer the eddying pools of the brook, the frond bobbing under his minimal weight. Richard had forgiven the fairy due to his bravery when the bodach attacked, but he still did not trust the fey creature. With knees brought up and supporting his elbows, Snedeker stared at Richard as though he were a puzzle.

"Bran, how do you feel?" the knight asked.

The boy sat up, stood, stretched, and walked around the tree, frowning up into its limbs. Horror suddenly transformed his face.

"Yes, it happened. All of it," Richard growled. "I *told* you not to trust Merle."

"I turned into a tree!"

"Yes, you did. And you took me with you. Keeping you safe has become a dangerous bit of business, one I'm not happy about. Damnable magic," he said, wiping dirt from his clothing. "Where are the others, Kegan?"

"Waiting on us."

"What happened last night?" Bran asked wildly, looking from

the clurichaun to the knight and back again.

"Ye tell me," Kegan snuffled. "Ye were both laying here beneath this hawthorn when I arrived, snoring so loudly I didn't even need your merlin *or* fairy to find ye."

Arrow Jack screeched from his perch on one of the lower limbs, his eyes piercing.

"That tree wasn't here last night!" Bran said.

"Are ye sure you are okay, lad?"

"I'm serious."

"Serious like a heart attack, I suppose," Richard said. "Call the Dark Thorn, Bran."

"What do you mean?"

Richard wanted to smack the boy. He saw fear in Bran's eyes but excitement about what calling the staff could mean. He was the Heliwr now—it was what the boy wanted—and it was best to prepare him for any further attack the bodach or Philip made. Playing dumb would help no one and just infuriate Richard all the more.

"I'm sure it works like Arondight, Bran," the knight said. "Calm yourself. Close your eyes if you think it will help. Take time to reach out with your mind and soul toward a staff of dark wood, about your height, and *will it* into your hand."

Bran closed his eyes. He held out his hand as if he was going to grasp something. After a few moments where only the birds sang, a frown crossed his face.

He opened his eyes.

"Nothing."

"Hmm," Richard said. "For some calling a weapon is not easy. Think about it while we ride to Caer Glain this morning and when we stop for the night we will try again. We cannot spend all day training you. There are far greater events we must deal with and the first is Lord Fafnir and his coblynau."

"Aye, there are," Kegan said.

Now that he was more awake, Richard took note of Kegan. Sorrow suffused the caretaker of the Rhedewyr. Dark hollows hung beneath reddened eyes, but it was the overwhelming weight in his every movement that punctuated his pain. He had spent the night burying his son, holding vigil, and despite wanting to give the short man a few words of solace, Richard no longer knew how to broach such topics.

The knight knew no words would ever be enough.

As they returned to the others, Richard thought more keenly on the previous night. The boy was now the Heliwr, for better or worse. Merle was not to blame. It had been Bran's choice and he had to own it now. But something did not feel right about what had transpired in the glen. The Erlking's beasts had not attacked as Richard would have thought; they ringed the waterfall in a half circle, almost like they were curious. There was something else, though, that bothered him. At the moment when Bran had transformed into the hawthorn and taken the knight with him, Richard had felt out of place, as if he had lost a part of himself and later regained it.

None of it made sense.

Then again, when it came to magic, it rarely did.

"I know why ye came up here, lad," Kegan said behind them, as the path dipped down toward the trail where the others waited.

The words hung in the air between the clurichaun and Bran.

"I'm so sorry for your loss," Bran murmured sadly.

"I know ye are," Kegan said. "Connal was a fine son. He has become part of a broader fabric, one that serves other ends."

"Richard told you why I came up here?"

"No, but it is written on ye as plain as the day."

"Then you know why I had to come here, accept responsibility," Bran said.

"Connal was brave," Kegan said, shaking his head. "He was the type of clurichaun who never would have been able to live with himself if he had not tried to help ye. Of that ye can be sure. He died doing the right thing, protecting the Rhedewyr and others. It was not your fault." The darkness around his eyes intensified. "I admire how ye feel, I really do, lad, and there is no better way for ye to revere his sacrifice. Connal died honorably. But life takes winding paths into shadow at times and nothing can be done about it. It is enough for a father sick with grief to know, and ye owe him—and me—nothing."

"Life is no excuse, Kegan," Bran said. "I should have been able to protect myself, should have been able to help and stop what happened from happening."

"*Should* is not part of life," Richard argued over his shoulder. "It is what it is."

"Indeed," Kegan agreed.

Snedeker flew from tree limb to tree limb, never alighting for very long, oddly ignoring Bran, his face screwed up in thought. Richard did not know what the fairy was up to, but at least the fey creature could no longer try to steal the Paladr.

"Fairy, what happened last night?" Richard asked.

Long moments passed. Snedeker lightly touched down on a boulder in front of them and stopped to stare at Richard and Bran, looking so confused it was almost comical to the knight.

"Well, fairy?" Richard said.

"You became a tree, jackwagon," Snedeker answered, looking at both of them. "What do you *think* happened?"

"What happened *afterward*?"

"Nothing," the fairy said. "The tree just stood there beneath the stars. The Lightbrands were gone. The forest was silent. I hid from an owl that landed on you, but that was it."

"Well how did we become *ourselves* again?"

"How the brimquick should I know!" Snedeker replied with annoyance as they walked by his boulder. "When the sun rose I went in search of the clurichaun. Got back and you were there on the ground asleep, no longer part of the tree."

Richard grunted.

Apparently their ignorance would continue.

By the time they reached the others midmorning had come, the day warming but still dark from the previous day's deaths. Kegan left to prepare his belongings and those of his dead son for the continued journey, leaving Richard and Bran exposed to multiple sets of eyes peering at them with scrutiny. Deirdre changed a bandage on Willowyn in the middle of the clearing, curiosity filling her emerald eyes. Lugh frowned where he sat sharpening his blade, the side of his face bruised, while the four remaining hellyll were silent. All had bruises and cuts, clothing torn or armor dented by the bodach.

"I owe you all an explanation," Richard said after he had gathered his own things and mounted upon Lyrian. The rest of the company listened. "The bodach is more than likely still following us. Such Unseelie creatures are hard to kill. Once one gains a scent, either it or its prey dies." He paused. "Last night, Bran left the campsite to embrace the calling that had once been his father's own. He succeeded in enacting the magic. I went with him to ensure his safety. That is past now, and we must focus on the future."

"Is he the Heliwr then?" Deirdre asked.

"He is," the knight said. "But he is young and knows nothing of the craft. He will be as he was before, mostly helpless, at least until I can teach him a few things at our next stop of Caer Glain. We will hope Lord Fafnir at least respects the Heliwr by name, along with my blade."

Bran looked away, clearly angry.

Richard ignored him. "Are we ready to go?"

"Three of us are dead, Knight of the Yn Saith," Lugh said. "Two of my guards and Connal O'Farn. Is this quest not for naught? I have to wonder if the lords in question will adhere to the request of the Queen just because two knights tell them they must?"

The Captain of the Long Hand pinned Richard's own worry.

"Death cannot slow us, let alone stop us," he said simply. "They *will* join the Seelie Court. They must. It is up to us all to make that happen. Otherwise Annwn will be lost."

The others grudgingly nodded as they gained their own mounts.

The morning passed uneventfully. The horizon came into view as they climbed, the elevation thinning the trees of the mountainside. Lyrian took a slow but steady gait even as cliffs encroached on the group. The heights were dizzying, but Richard ignored them, focused on the task at hand. Evidence of melted glacial fingers existed at every turn, highlighting barren rock and soil. As the sun climbed into the sky, Lugh inexorably led the group farther into the wilds of the Snowdon, and Kegan, one horse heavy, watched the rear with Deirdre and Snedeker. No one spoke. The only sound was the clop of the Rhedewyr as they gained the heights. Richard found himself using the time to form the argument he would need to convince Lord Fafnir and Lord Latobius to join the Seelie Court once more.

"Who are the coblynau?" Bran asked Deirdre, who rode just behind him.

"Mountain dwellers, miners of wealth," she answered. "They are a bit taller than clurichauns and are broader through the chest and arms. Few have visited Mochdrev Reach in my lifetime or Arendig Fawr from what I understand. They tend to keep to themselves."

"They sound like dwarves to me."

"I do not know that word," Kegan said with a frown.

"A fairy tale creature, always mentioned with elves and orcs and trolls in our world," Bran said. "Why are the coblynau necessary? No offense, but men of short stature have a harder time reaching their enemies."

"We are good fighters, Bran," Kegan snickered, the darkness in his eyes leaving for a moment of mirth. He patted the knives belted at his side. "The coblynau are *excellent* fighters. With maces and axes, they can decimate enemies as a warm knife cuts through cream. Being in the dark depths, they work hard to bring the ores and jewels of the mountain depths to Annwn. Moving all that rock and equipment builds strong statures, no matter the size. They might not be able to run very fast, but put an armed line of them together and they are nigh unstoppable."

"Not to mention we need their iron," Richard interjected.

"Why is that?" Bran asked.

"Govannon requires it if we are to be equipped properly for war."

"I had always thought the fey hated iron or steel."

"Ha!" Lugh laughed. "We are *not* the Unseelie Court. Those of the shadows hate it."

Richard shook his head. The boy had a lot to learn about Annwn.

"No, we need the coblynau," Kegan continued. "The magic of the Mastersmith may be able to produce countless weapons and armor in quickened fashion, but he still needs mountain ore to outfit the army we will need to defeat Caer Llion."

"Why can't the coblynau see they are needed for this war?" Bran asked.

"Lord Fafnir," Kegan snorted. "He is very old—one of the eldest of the lords, set in his ways, a curmudgeon who thinks nothing outside his mountain. They trade when they have need but beyond that they *prefer* not to be seen."

"How will we even gain an audience with him?" Lugh asked, pressing his previous point. "If Lord Fafnir can defy the Queen, how?"

"A knight is a powerful ally," Kegan said. "The two knights both will intrigue Lord Fafnir. He has always been infatuated in the mysterious and unattainable. The perfect gem. The perfect gwyddbwyll game. The perfect meal. Bran and Richard are different and Lord Fafnir will be intrigued by that."

"Also," Richard added. "I possess Arondight."

"True," Kegan said. "Lord Fafnir owes fealty to the blade."

"I guess I just don't understand why this Fafnir believes he is safe," Bran said.

"Do *you* think an army can plod this trail?" Richard grunted. "That's why he is unwilling to get involved. He believes he is safe, no matter the size of the force against him. In a way, he protects his people because to send them from the Snowdon would lead to their deaths. But he is shortsighted. There will come a time when Caer Llion sends the Templar Knights and whatever else he has bred into these mountains. The warriors of Lord Fafnir will not be able to resist that kind of force. The last of the Tuatha de Dannan will be destroyed."

"Indeed," Kegan said.

"In our world, there are several leaders who shirk any responsibility when disputes arise," Bran offered. "They believe it wise to not take sides in war."

"Wisdom has nothing to do with position," Richard noted.

Noon became afternoon, the air lukewarm with a hint of fall that would never come. In the distance, glacial snowfields blinded the company, the remnants of a long-lost winter slowly shrinking into pockets of memory. The witch had done her job well.

Arrow Jack landed on a dwarf pine nearby and screeched.

"We are close to the entrance," Lugh notified Richard.

The trail took a sharp turn upward through a copse of disfigured, wind-blown pine and fir trees into a landscape strewn with boulders as large as houses. Nothing moved, the air stale. The clop of hooves on dry-packed earth echoed from all sides. They wove single-file into the heart of the mountains, the peaks of the Snowdon like crooked skyscrapers, the path become barely wide enough for the large Rhedewyr to pass. Richard remained alert for whatever was to come.

As the path leveled, they rode into a broad circle of grass dotted with clover. Ancient rhododendrons burst from the soil, forming a perimeter forest of their own, displaying dazzling clusters of flowers in all colors. At the back of the meadow, a glimmering granite rock face lay bare to the sky like a monolith, dwarfing the company from Arendig Fawr.

Staring darkly at them from the granite, a rectangular hole like a mouth yawned mystery, its depths lost to the sunny day.

Richard ignored the doorway, staring instead at the giant.

A man as tall as a Fomorian sat upon a shorter boulder next to the entrance, leaning against the rock shelf and snoring with enormous gulps of air.

Puzzled, Richard sat Lyrian unmoving, but Lugh, whose eyes could have pierced steel, brought Areadbhar to bear. The enormous man ignored the newcomers, sleeping the day away, his meaty arms folded over a barrel chest, the long stained and soiled coat he had wrapped about him a patchwork of rotting cloth poorly stitched and holes not yet given the treatment. A wealth of bushy yellow-red hair sprang from his head in matted clumps and a beard impaled by twigs and leaves clung to a jaw shaped like a brick. The sour stench of unwashed body emanated from him. He was a monstrous man with an evil, thieving look to him; even mounted on the high back of Lyrian, Richard felt dwarfed by the sleeper and feared what he might be capable of.

Richard dismounted and, leaving Lyrian to Kegan, walked

toward the opening, keeping one eye on the obvious guard.

"Do not enter."

Richard stopped, turning toward the giant. The rise and fall of the man's chest did not deviate, but the snoring had stopped.

"Llassar Llaes Gyngwyd," Lugh growled, gripping Areadbhar tighter.

Blue eyes slid open, bloodshot and yellowed.

"Lugh of de short spear."

"We wish you no harm, watchman," Richard greeted.

Llassar barked a laugh and leaned forward, his massive girth broadening in the sunshine. "Ah see whoeveh ye are, yeh've got a pet warrior wit ye."

Lugh darkened, his fair coloring burning. "Llassar, you—"

"Ah oughta kill ye dehr and now," Llassar said, eyes blazing.

"Areadbhar awaits," Lugh answered firmly. "What you did in Arendig Fawr has no place in this world. The Queen should have ended you right there and then."

"Fault lies with ye and yer hellyll," Llassar rumbled. "Ah only wanted a few days of meals and ale."

The warriors moved to the forefront of the group, alongside their leader. Lugh did not deviate. "And you got that. Then after getting drunk on Govannon's ale, brawled with your wife until several homes were destroyed and three people were severely hurt. You are welcome no more for good reason."

"And dey shoulda minded der own business!"

"Silence!" Richard roared. He looked back to the giant. "Your petty arguing has no place at this moment. Where is your wife?"

"Gone ahuntin'," Llassar said, snorting phlegm and spitting it in front of Lugh's horse. "Should be back nigh, ah'd wager."

"We seek audience with Lord Fafnir," Richard said.

"Be awaitin' a long time den. Fafnir has no wish to see ye."

"How can you be certain of that?" Richard asked. "Lord Fafnir should have been notified of a summons by letter days ago. Surely you saw to this request."

"Ye mean dis letter?"

The giant pulled the rotting husk of a bird from the interior of his jacket. On its leg, a wound piece of parchment dangled freely.

"That one, yes," Richard said. "We have come—"

"Fafnir wishes to be left alone," Llassar grunted. "Ah make sure dat happens."

"Left alone?"

"Aye," Llassar said, standing with a deftness that defied his size. He blotted out the sun; he towered over everyone. "Left alone." Silence captured the moment. Richard did not move. Battle infused the air, the tension thickening every moment.

"Kegan, please tie up the horses," Richard requested simply.

"Leaving me food, ye fool?" Llassar grinned. "Horse has a greasy taste ah favor."

"I was hoping to not do this."

"Do what, leader of dolts?" the big man snickered.

"This."

Richard murmured ancient words beneath his breath. With their cadence bearing lilting Welsh, warmth crept from Richard's chest as he tightened his control over them. He called on the grasses of the world. He called for a trap. He sent his energy into the ground through his feet, hoping it would be enough.

Llassar did not move, confusion heavy on his face.

As soon as words came, they vanished into a fading whisper.

"Let us go then," Richard ordered the group.

The rest were hesitant, but Richard strode forward, passing the enormous man as if he were a harmless tree. Llassar made a move to block the knight but instead fell to his knees when his feet refused to free themselves from the ground.

"My apologies, Llassar Llaes Gyngwyd," Richard said, waving the others forward.

"Wizard!" Llassar roared ineffectually. He fought to free himself from the grasses of the meadow that had entwined his boots.

"Kegan, see that the horses are watered," Richard commanded. "We will be gone from here by sunset, if I have my way. Deirdre, see that fairy stays here. No reason to tempt the ire of Fafnir."

"I have no desire to see that old wrinkled arse anyway," Snedeker said.

The clurichaun rounded up each horse as the rider dismounted.

"What if the bodach returns?" Kegan asked.

Richard frowned before eyeing Llassar. "Hope this ruffian is as strong as he looks."

"Rue de day, wizard!" Llassar shouted as the group filed passed the guardian. "Ah will not help ye, no mattah what beastie comes!"

Ignoring the vehemence sent his way, Richard strode toward the maw of the mountain and vanished into its warrens. Bran and the others followed. Darkness swallowed the portal knight instantly as the cooler confines of the mountain wrapped around him. He wondered how they would navigate the interior of the Snowdon, when soft white illumination spread along the wall and ground, growing with every foot placed on the rock. The tunnel broadened as it traveled, its flat floor dry but covered in a film of dust few footsteps had unsettled. Flecks like embedded jewels in the granite walls caught and refracted the light, dazzling in beauty. The air was clean, without taint or staleness. It was hard for Richard to fathom the dedication or ability it would take to carve the corridor from the living rock of the mountain.

After what he could only surmise as being near a quarter of a mile, flickering torches cast their yellow-orange glow ahead additional light for those who lived nearby.

"Someone is home," Deirdre whispered.

"Let's hope that someone is nice," Bran interjected.

"Stay close to me," Richard ordered, his deep voice echoing. "We are unwelcome guests, from appearances."

"Lord Fafnir would never think to attack this delegation," Lugh said.

"Still, things are not right here," Richard warned. "When and why did he begin to refuse communication with the Morrigan? Why set the brute Llassar at his gate? Remain vigilant."

The tunnel ended at a much larger, octagonal chamber with high ceilings supported by four large columns. Eight torches set high over long, jewel-encrusted mirrors illuminated eight stone chairs in the middle of the room, each lined with dark purple cushions and circling a fire pit filled with long-dead ash. Vases devoid of flowers sat on several tables, a thin layer of dust and gossamer cobwebs over all. With the exception of the maintained torches, it was a room unused for quite some time.

The footsteps of his companions echoed in the stillness.

"Beautiful room," Bran acknowledged.

"The Hannerch Hall," Lugh said. "For visiting lords from afar to refresh themselves before meeting the Lord of Caer Glain."

"Not much of that happening now," Richard observed. "Lugh, do you know the way to the court and throne room?"

"I believe the throne room is to the left, Knight McAllister."

Richard ventured into the dark passage. He suppressed a shiver. Being in the depths, closed in by shadows and rock, left his skin crawling. With the Cadarn, the sunshine of the day had been close at hand if he so chose; in the Seattle tunnels of the Underground Tour, the street had been right above his head through a narrow slab of sidewalk concrete. In the depths of the Snowdon, however, the mountain closed a fist about him. His skin prickling, he realized to be lost in the tunnels of Caer Glain would be a death sentence for all who did not have the passages memorized.

And he didn't.

"Halt. Now."

At the unfamiliar baritone voice, Richard spun just as the rock of the tunnel came alive.

Double spearheads, their tips glinting in the weak light, pointed at Bran's neck, bare inches from killing the boy. Richard froze; Bran surrendered his hands. Even as Deirdre, Lugh and the hellyll drew their blades, men short like Kegan but far thicker through the shoulders wormed their way out of hidden crevices in the walls, the holes invisible to those not looking for them.

"Put your weapons away," the apparent leader said. He had a grizzled appearance, a black bushy beard shot through with gray. Plates of armor sewn into chain mail covered his frame. "Or the human lad in the middle dies."

Four other guards stepped into the corridor, similarly armed.

"You, at the front. You trespass. Why?" the old guard questioned Richard, never taking his eyes off of Bran. "Answer truth or your companion dies."

"We mean to share counsel with Lord Fafnir, wise leader of Caer Glain," Richard said quickly. "We mean you and the coblynau no harm."

"That is for me to decide," the coblynau rumbled. "What is your business with Lord Fafnir? You are not dead *only* because of the Arendig Fawr armor your hellyll wear."

"We bring a request and news from the Queen."

"That may or may not be true," the guard said. "The Queen is rarely spoken of in these halls. It is a crime to do so now, punishable by death. Regardless, you are here uninvited and have entered our home without the consent of Lord Fafnir. Tell me what you will and I will decide its import and your fate."

"It is for Lord Fafnir alone," Richard continued.

"He has made it clear he is to not be disturbed."

"War is upon the world, coming to all heights of the Snowdon," Lugh interceded, his spear glimmering lethal gold. "To *your* people. To *my* people."

"We are impervious to war here. It has been ever so."

"No longer," Lugh argued.

The guard frowned deep into his beard. He gnashed his teeth and took a look at the rest of the company. His light blue eyes settled on Bran again before he turned to Richard for the first time, his spear still held rigidly at Bran's throat. The portal knight could see a war taking place within the guard, his duty conflicting with the common sense that so many in power did not have.

Richard hoped common sense would prevail.

"What is your name?" he asked.

"I am Master Guardsman Henrick."

"You have my word as a Knight of the Yn Saith," Richard said, approaching the two guards with mere feet between. "Of what I speak is true."

"The Seven?" The short man mulled it over. "Children's stories."

"Really?"

"The last knight to tread Caer Glain was named Mather Hobbes," Henrick said. "He wielded Witchbane, also known as

Arondight, and protected the colblynau from the witch—"

"Rosairh during the Shadow Rise several centuries ago," Richard finished, growing impatient. "That's why you can trust what I say. I am a knight and know the history." He smiled his most dark smile. "If you don't remove those blades from my companion's neck, you will see Arondight's wrath, and not much will be left of you, Master Guardsmen."

"You are in no position to threaten us, whoever you think you are," the coblynau said.

"You presume I care about my companion," the knight said. "Besides, it's not a threat. It's a promise. Arondight has never suffered fools well. Not while I've wielded it, anyway."

Henrick peered at Richard.

"If you possess Witchbane, reveal it."

"That is for your liege only," Richard said.

At this, Henrick grunted but removed his spearhead from Bran's throat. His companion did the same. Bran relaxed visibly.

"Now, when was the last time someone visited Caer Glain from the mountain below?" Richard asked.

"At least a decade. Maybe more."

"You know I speak truly then," the knight said. "We would not be here unless the direst of circumstances warranted it. And they do. For the entirety of Annwn, they do."

"Lord Fafnir will know of your arrival. More than that, I cannot say," Henrick said, stroking his beard. "I cannot remember a time when he welcomed visitors with anything but a kick out the front door." He paused. "Grace me with your name?"

"Richard McAllister."

"How did you get past Llassar, Richard McAllister?"

"He was . . . indisposed."

"I see," Henrick snorted. "I just hope Lord Fafnir does not force me to join you in death."

Richard stepped aside, allowing the Master Guardsman through. Henrick gave him and the others a cursory glance before striding down the hallway, the broad man mumbling darkly below his breath. The portal knight followed after Henrick, knowing he had won at least one battle in the war to reunite the Seelie Court.

Richard also knew there were more battles to come.

If he survived meeting Lord Fafnir.

The other coblynau guards closed ranks on the group from Arendig Fawr. Richard and the others were prisoners now, whether they liked it or not.

He hoped his bluster hadn't ended their quest.

Or their lives.

Chapter 23

Blackness cascaded before Richard, a vertical speeding ribbon of water, the sheets disappearing into the oblivion below like a deafening, runaway train. The origin of the waterfall was lost in the ceiling above, the light of the rock under their feet unable to infiltrate the gloom. Cold spray licked the world in wetness. The footing treacherous, Richard skirted the wall, as far from the yawning maw of the chasm as he could get.

"The Bydew," Hollick shouted in front of him, the young guard unworried, his blonde short beard beading with dampness.

"It is an amazing site," Richard yelled back.

The single file group passed the waterfall into a new series of dry corridors that steadily led into upper reaches. Smokeless torches lit the hallways every hundred feet. New corridors came and went, a vast array leading in all directions. Henrick did not once deviate, his path certain. More aware of them, the holes the guardsmen had been hiding in littered the walls of the honeycomb, able to hide an army if the need presented itself. Looking closer, Richard saw traps set in the ceiling, allowing rockslides to hinder the advance of any assault upon the mountain.

Caer Glain would be defended well during an attack.

Of that, Richard had no doubt.

After an indeterminate march, the passageway they trudged through opened into an enormous cavern where stationary bluish-white orbs cast their light over all from positions near jagged stalactites. Dozens of colorful silk tents, multi-poled constructions as large as any circus big top, pointed back at the serrated teeth of the ceiling, the stone floor beneath Richard's feet worn flat. The cavern was unexpected, a beautiful menagerie of warmth in the heart of cold rock. The knight had never seen anything like it.

Coblynau dressed in normal thick pants and flowing tunics of all shades scurried from dozens of passageways into the chambers beyond, most looking fearfully backward.

Richard brought his companions to a halt.

Three-dozen warriors waited, pole-axes, spears, and short swords drawn.

"Be still, knight," Henrick ordered Richard. "I will take care of this."

One of the new guards stepped forward ahead of the rest, a coblynau as stocky and thick as Henrick but younger and wearing armor as black as obsidian, his left cheek inflicted by a long gnarled scar that ran to his neck.

"Commander Masyn," the Master Guardsman greeted.

"Where do you go, Henrick?" Masyn asked disdainfully. "And who are these . . . visitors?"

"We must speak, Commander," Henrick answered. "In private."

Masyn frowned but nodded. The two coblynau spoke at length to the side, their words lost to distance. The longer the guards spoke, the more animated Masyn became, his scar darkening to purple. The conversation mounted to an angry buzz. Whatever was being said, Masyn disagreed with Henrick. All the while, Richard grew worried; he didn't think they would be able to fight their way free of Caer Glain if the need arose.

When Masyn and Henrick returned, they both bore scowls.

"Who is the knight here?" Masyn questioned.

"I am, Master Commander," Richard said. "I bear the Witchbane, Arondight."

"Show it to me then."

"I will not. It is for your liege lord to see."

"I do not agree with how you entered Caer Glain—with no invitation. It shows a clear lack of good intention."

"My deepest apologies," Richard assured.

Masyn grunted. "I must also inform you Lord Fafnir will not be pleased. He may kill you. All of you."

"The situation warrants that risk."

"Very well," Masyn snorted. "Follow me."

Surrounded by dozens of coblynau guards, Richard looked to Deirdre, who gave him an encouraging smile. The company was guided from the tent city marketplace, its stalls filled with produce, wares, and art. Warmer air met them in a new passage, the odor of cooking food and baking bread strengthening until they entered a series of kitchens with blazing hearths. Richard passed through more rooms, each catering to a discipline—tailoring, cobbling, carpentry, weaving spun silk into cloth, and others he had never seen before. Masyn progressed quickly through the bustling community, his anger evident.

The corridor finally ended, and Richard, Bran, and the others entered the throne room of Caer Glain.

It was a long rectangular area with massive granite pillars holding a ceiling lost to the underground midnight. It was hard for Richard to see most of it; the end of the hall he had come in lacked orbs or torches. Up the middle, the aisle was open, while to either side of it benches were pushed beneath rows of tables covered in dusty linen. Long banners of colored silk fell from the ceiling over statues lining both walls: distinguished coblynau warriors displaying weapons, kings sitting in dignity, and scholars bearing large tomes and wise faces. Each statue had a different massive jewel set into its stone, twinkling.

The only illumination in the hall came from orbs at the far end of the room where a multistep dais gave rise to a throne of ornate silver and quartz. It absorbed the light and shone like a star.

Upon the throne, Lord Fafnir glowered at everyone.

He was an ancient coblynau, bald with a long ratty beard

hanging from a face thick with wrinkles, black eyes burning from beneath bushy white eyebrows. Pale skin spotted with age like mold in milk hung in jowls below a round face while purple robes hid an emaciated frame. With a bony finger, he caressed the leather-wrapped handle of a black steel war hammer as though it was a prized cat.

Below the dais, six round oak tables stood, each bearing a checkered marble game board with two players seated across from one another.

"What is the meaning of this, Masyn?" Fafnir snarled, his teeth missing or rotted to yellow nubs. "Can you not see I am entertaining a tournament?"

"We have visitors, Lord Fafnir," Masyn answered, guiding Richard and the others forward. "Not of my making."

"Well, rid us of them," Fafnir said, waving dismissively as he watched one of the games. "I am busy."

"They were told this, my Lord, and refused to leave."

"Then kill them, Commander," Fafnir growled.

Masyn turned to Henrick and, with a raised eyebrow, began pulling his short sword free as the rest of his unit did the same.

"My Lord Fafnir!" Henrick roared.

All eyes turned to the Master Guardsman.

"Here is a Knight of the Yn Saith, on an errand of utmost importance for the people of Caer Glain," Henrick introduced, gesturing to Richard. "From the Morrigan, Queen of the Seelie Court herself."

Fafnir darkened. "Who addresses me thus as if I care?"

"Henrick, son of Harrick, Master Guardsman of Caer Glain."

"Commander, see this Guardsman is punished for insolence."

Before Henrick could respond or Masyn conduct his orders, Richard strode forth. "Lord Fafnir, I am Richard McAllister, Knight of the Yn Saith and emissary of the Queen. I must be allowed to speak. The courageous coblynau of Caer Glain deserve to hear the news I bear and risk their peril if they do not."

"What power does the Morrigan hold here, in *my* city?" Fafnir interrogated, gazing at the knight and still caressing the hammer at his hand. "She has meant nothing to these halls for ages."

"I represent her wishes in this matter, with her authority," Richard said sternly. "The Morrigan is still your Queen, whether you believe it or not is moot. Her judgment in this must be addressed and given its due."

Long moments passed.

"Do so then, if that will leave me to my games."

"King Philip of Caer Llion amasses an army of dark halfbreeds, nature twisted to a means that will see the world of the Seelie Court reduced to ash. Even as I speak, he mobilizes a force unseen before in Annwn—former lords, the Templar Knights now thousands strong, and demon-wolves, griffins, Fomorians, who knows what else. The final days of Annwn are upon you. Philip will not stop at Arendig Fawr; he will eventually be at your entrance, and even a brute like Llassar Llaes Gyngwyd will not stop him any more than Llassar stopped me. Your world will end then, this mountain your tomb. The Queen requests the army of Caer Glain join the Seelie Court to prevent this. Only by combining what forces of good remain will you have a chance."

"Caer Glain remains impartial and ever shall be so," Fafnir decreed.

"Even if the battle comes to *your* doorstep?" Richard pressed.

"I care not. Never has an army come to these halls and forever will that be true. The Snowdon is a fortress impregnable," Fafnir dismissed. "Despite that, wisdom has ever *not* been a part of the Seelie Court. They quarrel and hate. Forever has leadership lacked, under Arawn and under the Morrigan. Now you expect the coblynau to inherit eons of poor judgment, even while we are safe." He paused then waved them away again. "Take these people from my sight, Masyn."

"Are they still to be executed, Lord Fafnir?" Masyn asked.

"We will not go," Richard said loudly for all to hear, stilling Masyn with a hard look. "Wisdom calls you to action. If you do not join with the Seelie Court, Philip will see your head on the end of a spear!"

"I have heard enough *wisdom*," Fafnir croaked. "Guards!"

Richard stared dispassionately at Fafnir, the righteousness of his role as emissary to the Queen strengthening his resolve. The surrounding guards pointed their weapons at Bran and his friends. The room was in stasis with death lingering nearby.

Before the coblynau warriors moved, Richard reached across the ether and called Arondight.

Nothing happened.

Fear paralyzed him. There was something different, something he couldn't quite place at first. It wasn't that his faith had disappeared, not allowing him to call the blade. It was like the link he had with Arondight for years had suddenly vanished. It no longer existed. Feeling as though amputated, Richard thought back to the last time he had called the weapon, the night in the meadow when Bran had accepted the Dark Thorn. Arondight had disappeared when the magic of the Paladr had accidentally swept him up.

He paused. The magic hadn't swept him up.

It had reached out to him and pulled him in with purpose.

Understanding dawned. Anger hotter than any found in hell filled him. Grinding his teeth even at the thought, he reached into Annwn for what he knew existed there.

A polished black staff with a rounded cudgel-like knot for a head entered his hand immediately as if it had ever been there, runes along its top pulsing white ethereal light that pushed back against the darkness.

He had lost Arondight. In its place, he gripped the Dark Thorn.

The staff of the Heliwr.

"Merle," Richard hissed.

"It seems you possess tricks, human," Lord Fafnir cackled. "They do not impress me. Only a clever gwyddbwyll game and not much else does that these days. Guards, take them away!"

As the Arendig Fawr companions looked as shocked as Richard felt, he grabbed Bran and pushed him to the forefront.

"Bran, call Arondight!"

"I don't kno—"

"Do it or we are dead! Will it in your hand!"

Bran closed his eyes; concentration hardened his face.

In a second, the great sword bloomed sapphire, bathing the entire chamber in light that cast the torchlight aside like the rising sun did the stars. Bran held the fabled blade high before him, surprise filling his eyes.

"Witchbane," Fafnir said, awe in his papery voice.

"By the knights who have served Arondight, you and your people have been kept safe from those who coveted your mines, your jewels, your ores," Richard voiced firmly, taking advantage of the coblynau lord's awe. "In the days of the Misty Isles, twice this blade came to your aid and removed evil from your halls and killed witches whose craft depend on precious crystals. Honor this blade for it has saved you!" He paused. "Yet another time has come. The Cailleach sides with Philip and desires this mountain city her own—to bleed it dry like Rosairh the Eld tried so long ago. If you deny this blade and the shared histories you and it carry, you will die in a matter of moons."

"That is the course of action you ask of me?" Fafnir questioned, all awe gone, the ancient fey gripping his hammer. "To give my people's lives for a war that will never come here?" The coblynau became angrier. "The Seelie Court faltered long ago. How do two talismans like those you possess change anything?"

"It is not the sword but the knight," Deirdre interrupted loudly. "It is also this man standing before you with the Dark Thorn of the Heliwr. A more powerful knight the world has never known."

"You are pert and young—and empty," the old coblynau said as he appraised the redhead. "What do you know of war, woman?"

"I know what comes does so to destroy all," Deirdre said, unflinching beneath the hot gaze of Fafnir. "Not just the Merrow, not just the clurichauns or fairies. Not just my home of Mochdrev Reach. But all."

"She speaks truly, my Lord," Lugh added.

"And you think you make a difference, Richard McAllister?" Fafnir asked.

Richard let the fire running the length of the Dark Thorn die.

"I know I would die for your people," he said.

"Why?" Fafnir argued. "You hold no responsibility here."

"The greed in my world would see the resources of Annwn bled, your beloved Caer Glain stripped of riches and life," Richard said. "Even if you do not join the Seelie Court and go to war, once Philip finishes in Annwn he will take his army back into my world. It is the nature of such men to want more. When the powerful men of my world learn of Annwn, they will stop at nothing to possess it."

"And when that happens, all you know dies," Bran added.

Richard was suddenly very proud of the boy. Succinct and to the point.

The old coblynau sat unmoving. Long moments passed. The hall had gone quiet; tension returned once more.

"A game then," Fafnir said finally.

"My Lord?" Masyn questioned.

"The best decisions are made over games," Fafnir said, gesturing at the tables before his dais. "A game of gwyddbwyll will decide whether Caer Glain joins the Seelie Court or remains apart."

"This is more important than some ga—" Richard began.

"My grandson Faric against your own boy there, he who possesses Arondight," Fafnir said, pointing a crooked finger at Bran. "They are close to the same age, I wager."

All eyes turned on Bran.

"But I have never played," he stammered.

"That is . . . problematic," Fafnir said darkly. "Set up the board, Faric."

A coblynau with the same piercing gaze as the lord of Caer Glain except younger and fair-haired moved to one of the empty tables and began setting up game pieces, some in a diamond in the middle of the board and others in groups around the edges. When he was done, Faric bowed, looking directly at Bran, before sitting in one of two chairs.

Letting his rage at what Merle had done to him dissipate and focusing on the moment, Richard let the Dark Thorn fade away. He came to Bran, guiding him forward.

"Let the sword go, Bran."

The boy did so. Arondight vanished like smoke.

"What did you *do?*" Bran hissed.

"Ever play chess?"

"*I can't do this!*"

"You can and will," Richard assured. "Just as you stood up against Caswallawn, you will do what is right here. Have you played chess or not?"

"I told you in Seattle. I played with my father. Haven't in years."

"Gwyddbwyll is like chess. See the board?" Bran nodded as they stopped a dozen yards away. "A king starts in the middle of the square board. The eight pawns of the same color around him are guards, there to protect the king from the sixteen attacking soldiers around the perimeter. The guards, attackers, and even the king move like rooks, in straight lines. A piece is removed from the game only when two same-colored pieces sandwich an opposing piece. The point of the game is to move the king to one of the four borders without being surrounded on all four sides by the attackers and taken. For the king to be cornered without a move is a loss."

"Can I move one of my pieces between two of his pieces without being taken?"

"Yes, you can," Richard answered. "It is a simple and elegant game. But it does require strategy. So be careful."

Bran didn't seem convinced. Richard studied the game setup. It was a beautiful board, with shining silver and onyx squares alternating nine wide and deep. A king carved from amethyst stood in the middle, encircled by the pawn-like guards. In four groups along each border, attackers carved from black marble waited to ambush the king.

"Think ahead many moves," Richard advised.

"If it *is* like chess, I understand."

The knight nodded. Bran turned and sat in the small chair, barely fitting in it and towering over his opponent. Faric sat across from him, twisting the mustache of his beard as he appraised his opponent. He smiled politely. Bran did not.

"Let it begin then," Fafnir commanded, glee in his eyes.

"I am Faric, son of Fannon," the grandson of Lord Fafnir greeted.

"Bran Ardall."

Raising an eyebrow, Faric looked to his grandfather. Fafnir

frowned deeper but waved his grandson on. Faric selected a black marble attacker and slid it forward. Bran took a deep breath, gave Richard one last look, and moved a countering guard.

The game progressed slowly. Richard realized Lord Fafnir had trapped them already. The game was difficult even for the experienced. The coblynau who had been playing at other tables now watched the new game, whispering to one another with every move. Faric was quick to move, having obviously played the game many times in the past—certain and fearless. Richard observed every move made and tried to ascertain how it benefited Faric's play, as if he could will the information directly to Bran. The boy did take his time, looking at all angles, deciphering how one move could work in conjunction with other moved pieces. Just like chess, the killing attack in gwyddbwyll could come from any angle, any front. Seeing that attack before it was too late was the key.

The game played on, the throne hall silent, an hour gone. Bran had taken five pieces but had lost two. Most of the force brought to bear by Faric surrounded Bran, with attackers spread around the board staring directly at the endangered king. Richard found that he held his breath, knowing attacks could come from several fronts, leaving him frustrated that Bran might not see something until it was too late.

"Now it comes down to it, eh," Lord Fafnir crowed.

"Think it through, Bran. Think it through," the boy whispered to himself. "Take your time."

The pieces had gravitated toward one of the corners nearest Bran and he was close to reaching a border with his king. Six of his guards remained in a protective ring about the king. Faric blocked him from reaching the corner. Pieces on both sides would tumble like dominos in the next six or seven moves—the win or loss would happen fast.

Then Richard saw it, the opening for Bran. He hoped the boy did too. Bran reached to move a guard to block an attacker and break through to win—and then paused. Richard stopped breathing. So did the throne room. Bran withdrew his hand and stared at Faric. The coblynau ignored him, lost in the pieces, and then furtively glanced up at Bran.

Both understood. The game was over.

Grabbing the wrong piece, Bran moved one of his guards, cutting off the closest border and the win.

"What did you *do*?" Richard growled, exasperated. "Stupid!"

"Had the game won, ye did!" Faric said, shaking his head. Then made a move.

"I did win," Bran said.

"Ye did not!" Faric shot back, gesturing at the board. "It is a draw."

"That's right," Bran said with certainty. Richard saw what he meant. The king moved back and forth over two squares, unable to be captured by Faric in the safety of the quartz guards but also unable to reach one of the corners to actually win the game due to frozen attackers. The guards were also safe from Faric, leaving a stalemate.

Faric just sat there, looking puzzled.

"You knew," Fafnir criticized, his face wrinkled in his frown.

"No one wins in war," Bran said, standing up. "It's the same on the streets; it is the same everywhere, I would imagine. War is what you are going to have if you don't believe Richard McAllister and agree with the Queen's request, and it *will* be a war you will lose."

Lord Fafnir looked from the board back to Bran and back again. Richard could not believe what had just happened. The boy looked at him uncertainly before meeting the gaze of the coblynau lord. Bran had taken a grave risk. All in the chamber knew it and waited for the outcome. Richard hoped Bran knew what he was doing.

Otherwise he was going to beat him within an inch of his life.

"What say you, Lord Fafnir?" Richard asked.

"It is an odd situation in game play. Made more odd by your need," Fafnir admitted in his raspy voice. "This young man has shown more wisdom in playing a game than I or my forefathers have seen from that vaunted Seelie Court in previous centuries. He pulls a draw? On purpose? To make a point?" The ancient coblynau laughed. "He is rare, that one."

Richard did not answer. The hall was silent once more.

"Truly an Ardall?"

"He is. Son of Charles," Richard answered. "Philip has tried to kill him twice."

"Let him speak for himself," Fafnir commanded. "What has *he* seen?"

Bran hesitated before bowing. "Knight McAllister has said a war is coming to your home. He tells the truth. I have seen these evil creatures and those who drive them with my own eyes, unleashed by Philip. I met the Queen and other gathered lords, and they are prepared to fight—together. They need your aid and they need your resources. I cannot see how you will be safe if you alone stay here and do not join nor how they will be strong without your strength."

"I see," Fafnir said, pursing his already thin lips and gnashing his teeth. Long moments passed. No one said a word. "One course then, like your game. Both Faric and my other grandson Forrenhahl will join you and this war you believe will come. Caer Glain will supply the lords of the lowlands the ore they need. The fires will be stoked; iron will flow to Arendig Fawr."

Richard breathed easier and bowed.

"The warriors of Caer Glain will join the Seelie Court in Arendig Fawr within three days," Lord Fafnir promised as he stood unsteadily, even though the boney hand that gripped his war hammer was firm and strong. "May Ser Hendel protect us all."

"Thank you, Lord Fafnir," Richard said.

"Let us feast then," Fafnir replied and pointed at Bran. "And perhaps a game against Ardall there."

Chapter 24

Richard brooded as he walked behind his companions, his thoughts splintered with rage, the reality of what had been done to him threatening his composure.

Myrddin Emrys had tricked him—again.

Even thinking the words sent fresh ire through his blood. He was now the Heliwr. The Unfettered Knight. It was his duty and his alone to patrol the two worlds and keep them both separate. If the two worlds blurred when a fey creature crossed over or someone from his world broke into Annwn, it was now his responsibility to track them down, return them—or kill them. No longer chained to the portal in Seattle, he could venture where he wished as long as he had access to Annwn and its seven gateways.

The freedom gave him no solace. Richard had not been given a choice, and that betrayal gnawed at him like a splinter in his soul.

Merle had seen this. The wizard had known.

And he had not told Richard.

After the gwyddbwyll match between Bran and Lord Fafnir the previous evening, the leader of the coblynau had offered warm beds and meals. The group from Arendig Fawr took the offer with pleasure. The deaths of Connal and the two hellyll lay heavy on their hearts.

Not so with Richard. The duplicity that had knighted him Heliwr would not allow it. Deirdre had tried to prompt the knight into conversation. He had ignored the redhead as if she had played a part in the travesty. The way she looked at him made him angrier than he had a right to be, the pain from his past mingling with the present to form a self-loathing that boiled.

Before he had finished his meal, Richard left the throne room to wander the halls of Caer Glain and think on what had happened. No one stopped him. Coming to a small waterfall, and in the dark, alone, he thought back on the events that led to his melding to the Dark Thorn. Merle had told him knighthood would not pass from father to son. He had been right. Govannon could not give Bran a weapon. The boy now carried Arondight. The Lady in the glen asked if he would protect the office of Heliwr with his life. Richard had accepted. It was the reason Bran hadn't been able to call the Dark Thorn when they awoke under the hawthorn tree; it was the reason events had played out the way they had.

There was nothing Richard could do to change it.

And it pissed him off.

Merle had played his chess game and won a major battle in the war. Richard had been used as a pawn once more. So had Bran. When Richard had returned to his quarters, the boy had been there with questions more numerous than flies. Richard answered them, if barely. The boy's newfound authority was exciting to Bran; the new Seattle portal knight did not care how Merle had set him up. It made Richard want to rage against everything.

Even now, watching the boy as he strode ahead and his exuberance in learning all he could about the coblynau, Richard wanted nothing more than to drag him out of Annwn by the nape of his neck and be done with this business entirely.

"And which Ser is Merrick?" Bran asked Hollick.

The guard grimaced. "Ye really do *not* know the ways."

"No, not at all."

"Ser Merrick is the governing Ser of Pathways," the young coblynau said. "He keeps our way safe from the shadows of the

Unseelie and protects all those who walk alongside him."

"I'll never remember all of this," Bran said.

An overwhelming rush of hatred spread through Richard. Not for Bran, but for what the boy represented—a willing apprentice of Merle.

Along with Henrick, Hollick, and two coblynau guards named Charl and Gat, the Arendig Fawr delegation made their way through the bustle and out of Caer Glain. Fafnir kept good on his promise; hundreds of coblynau mobilized for war, and carts of iron ingots already made their way down the mountain for Govannon. The grandsons of Fafnir would also lead a contingent of coblynau warriors down the slopes to Arendig Fawr, giving their aid as best they could. While a part of Richard wished he and the others could stay a few days to recover from the attack of the bodach, he also knew time was of the essence.

The sooner he finished with Tal Ebolyon, the sooner he could confront Merle.

Thinking about how to convince Lord Latobius to rejoin the Seelie Court, Richard almost ran over Gat. In front of him the group had stopped. Beyond them, the torchlight had gone out, the only illumination a weak light emanating from the floor.

"Sometimes this happens," Hollick said. "Odd gusts, odd wind."

"Well, I don't believe in *sometimes*," Richard said, calling forth the Dark Thorn.

"No chances?" Bran asked.

"None," Richard said. "Ever again. What Guardsman Hollick did not tell you is more than just the coblynau live in these mountains. Didn't wonder where the silk came from to build the tents we passed through in the market, did you?"

Bran shook his head.

"The Gorryn," Henrick answered. "Man-size spiders. Very dangerous if prodded. They live deeper in the wild Snowdon, above- and belowground, spinning the silk for their webs. We collect it when possible. Gorryn rarely come into Caer Glain; they have no need, and when they do it is almost never this close to the surface."

"'Almost never' is still code for *sometimes*," Richard muttered.

The group moved forward slowly, weapons drawn, Richard leading the way with the white light of the staff fending off the darkness. It felt more comfortable in his hand than he liked, an extension of the anger he reserved for Merle. Henrick was close behind, his spear held at the ready. Both came to the first unlit torch sconce, set at a corner where a new corridor of gaping blackness to the right met the passageway they were in.

"This happened recently," Henrick pointed out, examining the smoking sconce.

"Light it so we can move on."

The coblynau moved to relight the torch.

Richard stepped into the junction, peering into the gloom—and had the wind knocked from him as a massive shadow slammed him against the opposite wall.

Fighting the swarm of unconsciousness, Richard focused on his assailant. Screams followed echoing chaos; the knight barely heard them. It was not a spider that attacked him. The bodach had found them. The Unseelie creature had him pinned, the white fire of the Dark Thorn enacted out of sheer instinct his only protection. The beast was relentless. It clawed and screeched at him, the smoky predator fighting to get at him.

Sweat and panic poured over Richard. There was nothing he could do to dislodge the bodach; it had him cornered with no intention of letting up until its strongest adversary to killing Bran was dead as well.

As Richard fought for his life, Lugh charged, roaring with Areadbhar lowered like a lance. The Long Hand followed their leader. Deirdre chased with the coblynau guards a step behind, rushing the Unseelie creature as well with weapons drawn and ready for the fight.

All fell upon the bodach.

All but Bran.

Claws grazed the knight's side but he ignored the pain, focusing on the Dark Thorn and the power it lent him. The beast screamed pain as multiple blades bit into its form. It did not relent its attack.

Even as it prevented Richard from dislodging it, the beast lashed out with a hind leg, kicking at any of his companions within reach.

Hollick and Lugh flew like tossed dolls into the intersecting passage, lost from view.

From the side, Richard saw Bran finally enter the fray. He held Arondight, the sword flaming azure more brightly than Richard had ever seen. With singular purpose, the boy drove the blade into the side of their attacker's darkened silhouette, the magic infiltrating the shadow like lightning. The bodach roared inhuman. Richard could feel the white-hot pain erupting within the monster, the unholy stench pungent in his lungs. Bran pulled Arondight free and sent its entire length at the head of the beast, thrusting beyond his means as he tried to deliver a deathblow.

The bodach recoiled. The pressure on Richard vanished.

It was all the space the knight needed. The power of the Dark Thorn exploded forth. The blast of white fire sent the bodach reeling. It twisted in the air, flame incinerating the beast as it hit the ceiling and jarringly crashed against the wall near Bran, flailing limbs and howls of pain filling the corridor.

The bodach righted itself instantly, its eyes fixed on Bran.

Adrenaline rushed as fear through Richard. He struggled forward, a wave of weakness from the expenditure of magic chaining him, roaring a warning Bran could not hear. The coblynau and others were running toward the boy, hollering with weapons raised.

Bran swung at the bodach.

It feinted and, with a dark laugh, knocked the fabled blade from the boy's hand.

Arondight vanished.

Eyes burning hatred, the bodach leapt.

Like a cat unleashed, his face's ferocity covered in crimson from a gash above his nose, Lugh reentered the battle, his spear held low to the ground. Unable to prevent its momentum, the bodach impaled itself, the spear penetrating its innards. Silver light exploded deep within the creature as did its howl.

It missed Bran to instead land feet away.

Seizing the chance, Richard sent the magic of the Dark Thorn toward the Unseelie beast. The bodach screamed further, surprised from the side assault. It fought the fountain of white fire, singeing, maddened to gain Bran and end him. Dizziness washed over the knight but he ignored it, keeping the fount of his magic focused on the bodach. The creature tore through the flames, unable to break through their intensity, the baleful eyes and biting jaws mere feet away but incapable of reaching Bran.

Buckling to his knees from weakness and Richard beginning to lose faith they could bring the creature down, an eruption of blue fire from Arondight burst from the corner of his eye and slammed the bodach in the side like a sledgehammer.

The fey creature landed witin the same corridor from which it had sprung.

"Pull the torch holder, Ardall!" Henrick roared.

Not hesitating, Bran grabbed at the sconce with all of his weight, not questioning the Master Guardsman.

The torch gave way as a lever. A series of snaps reverberated through the mountain. Boulders tumbled from the roof of the side passage entrance in a thunderous avalanche, showering Bran and the others with pebbles and dirt. Richard shielded his face from the destruction, worried the entire passage was about to come down. The stone beneath them shook like an earthquake and then became still.

Sudden silence hit the mountain.

Richard let the Dark Thorn dissipate to smoke.

The bodach was sealed away, unable to harm them now.

Richard pushed himself to stand. He felt drained of any authority that had been given him. A few paces away Bran stood, Arondight gripped tight, its length fiery and blazing angrier than ever before. It was odd for Richard to see the boy wield the sword he had spent so much of life regretting that he had accepted.

"What the hell?" Bran coughed as the dust swirled around him.

"We have fail-safes throughout all of Caer Glain," Henrick said, also coughing. "Never seen it needed before. The rock will keep that creature at bay, I warrant."

"By Ser Rhaith, what was that thing?" Charl growled.

"A bodach," Richard panted. "Unseelie."

"Why did it find its way in here?"

"It's after Bran," Richard said. "And it will continue until we find a way to kill it."

"It will not bother us for some time," Gat surmised. "That corridor leads to an exit abandoned long ago, unused by all but those who hunt game and pheasant in the lower reaches of the Snowdon."

Henrick glanced around. "Where is Hollick? Hollick!?"

No answer came.

Richard shared the stares of those around him as the realization struck; they all looked at the rubble-choked corridor from where the dwarfish guard had not returned after being kicked by the bodach.

"Hollick!" Henrick screamed, jumped up on the landslide. "Hollick!"

"He is already dead," Richard said.

"Gat, notify Master Commander Masyn of what has transpired here," Henrick ordered after a few minutes, his voice thick with emotion. "They must be made aware of this monster."

"Kegan," Bran breathed as Gat left. "If the bodach followed us into Caer Glain . . ."

Understanding hit Richard. "The Rhedewyr."

Finding a reserve of strength he didn't know he had, Richard chased after Bran. The others were close behind. If the bodach had entered the caverns of Caer Glain the same way they had, it could have killed the coblynau and their mounts. Kegan was in danger and without the Rhedewyr, the journey would be far more difficult.

After several twisting tunnels, Richard burst from the underground city into the glen, the sunshine of the late afternoon casting long shadows over the mountain.

The Horsemaster and the Rhedewyr were nowhere to be seen.

"Kegan!" Bran yelled.

"He's not here," Richard said. "Perhaps nearby."

"Wizard, ye owe me," a voice growled from the dark.

Llassar Llaes Gyngwyd stepped from the wooded blackness to their left and looked like he would fall over any moment. The giant had been in a fight. His patched clothing now hung in tatters, ripped apart so grotesquely it exposed the rent flesh beneath. Crimson slashes ravaged his forearms; chunks were missing from his beard as though forcibly pulled out. Eyes lost below a darkened brow, Llassar limped to stand before Richard with a painful smirk.

Lugh jumped to the forefront and lowered his spear at the giant in warning.

"Where is the clurichaun?" Richard questioned.

"I am here, Richard McAllister," Kegan said, appearing from behind the giant man's legs like a toddler to a father. "Safe and well."

"What happened?"

"The creature came. Attacked us. Llassar here held it off, along with the Rhedewyr. He saved us from death."

"Damnable right ah did," Llassar growled, standing a bit taller. "Nothing doin' really. Ah hate dem Unseelie folk. Evil skulkin' creatures, the lot of 'em."

"I am in your debt then, Llassar Llaes Gyngwyd," Richard said.

Henrick and Charl caught up to the rest of them, huffing.

"Ahh, the moles," Llassar acknowledged.

"The Rhedewyr are safe as well," Kegan added, then sounded a high-pitched whistle. "They put up a fight as only they can."

Willowyn, Lyrian, and the other Rhedewyr clopped from the darkness, manes tossing.

"You leave us to fend for ourselves, dungknight! And this is what happens!" Snedeker reprimanded, flying before Richard with arms folded in disgust.

"Fairy," Richard muttered. "Shut up."

Snedeker did just that, alighting on Deirdre's shoulder.

"There is much to discuss, Kegan," the knight said, not pleased about it.

"Not sure I like the sound of that, knight," the clurichaun said.

Richard filled him and the others in as quickly as he could, the distaste of admitting he was now the Unfettered Knight still rankling him. He shared what he knew about his new role, how Bran fit in, and how the boy had bested Lord Fafnir's grandson in a game of gwyddbwyll to win over the leader of the mountain city.

"Did you get what we needed from Lord Fafnir then?" Kegan asked.

"We did. One more lord to persuade though."

"You are the Heliwr, eh? The Lady remains mysterious in her actions, it seems," the clurichaun said. "I wonder what other tricks she has up her sleeve. And what of the bodach?"

"It won't be bothersome for some time," Henrick answered. "Blocked from this side of the mountain. It can get out but it will take some time. With any luck, Faric and Forrenhahl will cross it and kill it when they march from Caer Glain."

"March from?" Llassar glowered. "Where do ye moles go?"

"We march to Arendig Fawr," Henrick answered. "In three days, we go to war."

"A man of your . . . talents . . . would be useful upon the battlefield, Llassar," Richard said. "As Lord Fafnir and the coblynau have realized, Caer Llion and its king will come here in due course, and even this sanctuary will not be afforded you. You will die as the rest of Annwn. Would you not rather fight and prevent that from happening?"

"How much? Ah do not come cheap."

"Your death will be cheap then," Richard said.

As Llassar and Henrick haggled over the importance of joining Arendig Fawr, Richard met Lyrion and ran his hands over his sleek muscled neck. He looked deep into the dark pools of the horse's eyes and then patted him.

"I am happy you are safe, old boy."

A spark of curiosity entered the eye of the horse and he nuzzled Richard.

"He is beginning to like you," Deirdre whispered, hugging her horse close as they were also reunited. "I am pleased and so is Willowyn."

Richard patted the horse again. "I have few friends, it seems. Nice to know I may be making another who will not betray me."

"I am your friend, Richard McAllister," she said.

"I know. Thanks."

"Mount your Rhedewyr, knight," Henrick directed. "The

summit is not far. Tal Ebolyon is nigh, to be reached before true night falls if we press hard."

"We do not see in the dark as you do, Master Guardsman. It would be dangerous for us to ride at night," Richard said. He turned to Llassar. "You have a camp?"

"And a fire," Llassar said. "In the woods there."

"We will stay here for the rest of the day and night to recover from the bodach," Richard said. "At first light, we ride."

Llassar led them through a copse of twisted pine. The trail was wide, big enough to allow the giant through, and Richard soon arrived to a meadow where a fire fought its bonds of ringed stone. The flames were inviting. An enormous tent of mismatched silk was constructed under overhanging intertwined limbs—the place Llassar and his wife slept.

After the others had eaten and slinked into bedrolls, Richard decided it was time to speak to Bran. The knight stood where the light of the fire met the uncertainty of dark, the fringe of two very different worlds. He thought it appropriate.

Richard beckoned the boy over, unsure of how to begin.

"You are now the protector of the Seattle portal, Bran," Richard said, his weariness quickly driving him to his own bedroll. "You will train with Merle, who will teach you the various aspects of your craft."

"I know," Bran said simply, looking in perplexity at the hand that had held Arondight. "The power, Richard. Is it always like that?"

"It can be. It can also be dangerous."

"How so?"

"For starters, look at me," Richard said. "I am wiped out right now. The magic enacts a terrible price. No power is created without energy given, and in magic's case it is life energy. If you take it too far, it can kill you."

Bran nodded. Richard thought him hard to read.

"Does Arondight come from the same place your staff does?"

Facing away from the camp, Richard exhaled a deep breath. The boy was eager, maybe too eager. The world had already begun changing for him; it would change a great deal more before he knew everything Richard knew. Just like when he had accepted Arondight from Merle, Bran now had hundreds of questions for Richard, so many the former Seattle knight could not hope to answer in a night, let alone a year.

"I need answers, Richard," Bran added.

"I know you do," the knight said. "Nothing can be changed now at any rate. You've made your decision. I've had mine forced on me." He paused. "But, to answer your question, Arondight is held in safety here in Annwn, along with the other relic weapons held by the other knights. No one can steal them. You will be introduced to the other knights and learn more about this when we know how Lord Latobius decides. It is at that time I can contact the other Yn Saith and share what we know."

"And you are now the Heliwr."

Bran didn't say it as an accusation. Richard didn't know what to think. He wondered if the boy hated the mantle once belonging to his father.

If he did, he didn't show it.

"Yes, I am. Whether I like it or not," Richard said. "You and I were bonded in the glen when we became the tree. The Paladr took Arondight from me and replaced it with the Dark Thorn, born of the hawthorn planted by Joseph of Arimathea at Glastonbury Abbey. I do know the staff is called from some place other than Arondight. There is no place for the staff among the other relics. As the Heliwr, I am now responsible in ways you probably can't fathom—but you will, soon enough."

"You are angry," Bran said. "I can see it in your eyes."

"Go to bed," Richard said stiffly. "The staff took much out of me."

"I am tired as well," Bran said. "God, the intense power . . ."

"You'll get used to it."

Bran took a deep breath. "I do not feel any . . . different."

"And nor would you," the knight said. "Power does not change a person; a person lets power change them. It is there when you command it. Don't let it change you."

"Arondight failed your calling sometimes . . . because you

lacked faith?" Bran asked. "How can something so basic and simple overcome a direct command of your mind?"

Richard turned away. "It is not as simple as that."

"But how—"

"Bran," Richard sighed heavily, annoyed. "It is an extension of yourself. Arondight is a part of you now, like an arm or leg. It responds much in the same way. When you have need of the sword, will it. It will be there." Richard pinched the bridge of his nose. "No more on this now. Rest. More after we leave Tal Ebolyon, when we know more."

"What about the bodach finding us?"

"Not tonight," Richard said. "We have a few days. When it does, we will be ready."

More questions burned in Bran. Richard could see them. To the boy's credit, he moved away to his own bed near the fire.

Richard knew one thing. He would have to come up with a plan to kill the Unseelie. It was stronger than him. The next time, they would have to be prepared to finish it.

Or they would die.

With deep snores emanating from Llassar's tent, Richard threw a few more tiny logs onto the fire and got comfortable for sleep.

Deirdre watched him do so, her eyes finding his.

Richard turned away.

When he closed his eyes, he thought of Elizabeth and why his place in hell was assured.

Chapter 25

The morning dawned chill but clear.
Woken by a quick shake of his shoulder by Kegan, Richard wiped the sleep from his eyes, took a deep breath, and bundled his belongings for the trip to Tal Eboylon. He was sore and in a dark mood, his dreams during the night disturbed. After a quick meal of coblynau bread, tangy cheese, and few words spoken to the others, he mounted Lyrian and, with Henrick leading them, left the snores of Llassar behind. They passed the gaping door to Caer Glain and regained the trail leading to the dragons of Tal Ebolyon.

The group settled into the journey, Bran pulled Westryl alongside Richard.

"Do you really believe Philip will try to invade our world?"

"Perhaps. I don't know for sure," Richard said, thinking on it and still not arriving at an answer. "We still have not found the reason behind the attack on you, but I, like Merle, believe it to be related somehow to Philip wanting our world. But regardless, what I said to Lord Fafnir is true. Men like Philip crave more, their lives filled with insatiable greed. He will come one day to enslave both worlds."

"And then?"

"Philip will die," Richard said simply. "His army will die. And then this world will die. Annwn may have magic but the technology of our world will crush him. When that happens, those men like Philip in *our* world will destroy Annwn. We can't let that happen."

"We won't," Bran said.

"Why do you think Merle pressed me into this?" Richard snorted. "He knew a Heliwr was needed if we are to survive. If Philip is not stopped—if his desires are left unchecked—it could spell doom for both worlds. No matter if I hate the man for keeping this from me, a Heliwr is the only way to help maintain the integrity of the other portals. Merle pushed me here by using Elizabeth. For that, I will have a great many words for the old man."

"If I knew anything about Elizabeth in this, I would tell you."

Richard nodded guardedly.

"If he can view our world, wouldn't Philip know that our technology would be more than a match for his army?" Bran questioned.

"He should," Richard agreed. "And that's what frightens me."

While Lyrian strode on, Richard closed his eyes and reached out to the Dark Thorn. The staff was there, connected to him. Sighing, Richard opened his eyes and realized he might have a difficult time calling the staff: Arondight had answered his appeal most of the time, but his inability to control it completely had left him and others in danger. It was likely his past could also hinder his authority over the Dark Thorn.

The time for that test would come soon.

Of that he was sure.

The day grew warm. The Nharth disappeared to reveal the landscape—jagged barren slopes, the mountaintops around him too high for even the hardy lower clime pine and fir to grow. Short shrubs clung to pockets of dirt, and grayish grasses stabbed blades from crevices in the rock. The group passed drifts of snow, blinding beneath the sun. A hawk spiraled on what currents were afforded it, a lone act of life in the craggy reaches. It was hard to believe anything lived in the Snowdon heights, even dragons.

As the sun came to its zenith, the path leveled and the travelers came to Tal Ebolyon.

It was not what Richard had expected. Massive walls of eroded dark granite stood as high as a forest, dwarfing the knight and those around him. The stone blocks were seamlessly cut to fit while along the top of the wall the merlons were rounded nubs, scarred by weather and age. A circular doorway yawned in front of the company, the architecture similar in style to that of Caer Glain, a vast flat area beyond beckoning them forward.

"I hope Lord Latobius is here," Richard said. "Time is short."

"Will the dragons cooperate?" Bran asked.

"I do not know. Time to see."

"The dragons have had a rough time of it as of late," Deirdre said. "They are rarely seen in the skies. Travelers coming to Mochdrev Reach say they are dying. If that is true, I think this might be a great deal more difficult than Caer Glain."

"That means I alone talk then," Richard said. "And fairy, if you open your yap and piss them off, I swear I will put you in a jar and never let you out."

Snedeker frowned darkly but said nothing.

The Rhedewyr clopped through the opening into a different world. A lone snow-covered peak cut the blue sky, lording over a far-reaching lake as blue as icy steel. Large stone partitions like broken gray teeth grew from a carpet of finely cut green grass, the sudden vibrant color a shock. Oak trees as large as eight-story buildings shadowed every eroded wall, each symmetrical and healthy, while numerous trimmed hedges curved beneath them and met flowering vines snaking on stone trellises and hardy rhododendrons bursting with blooms. Several oddly shaped boulders littered the grounds like abstract art. It was a massive garden, beautiful in its layout and care, one the likes of which Richard had never seen.

Overshadowing the appearance of the green plateau and standing directly across the lake, a tower house like Dunguaire Castle jutted into the warm afternoon, the stone just as weathered as the wall they had just passed through. Towers with open windows grew from the corners of the fortress while a lone square keep squatted in its middle like a tree stump. No moat circled it, no gate impeded entrance inside. A white pennant hung limp from a lone pole at the keep apex, lacking a design of allegiance.

Nothing moved—not from within the castle or the garden.

"Dragons live in that castle?" Bran asked incredulously.

"No, no, no," Henrick answered with a laugh. "Lord Latobius and his dragonkin rest in the Garden of a Thousand Wings. It is the Fynach who reside in the keep of Tal Ebolyon, safe from the harsh winters that used to batter the Snowdon."

"Who are the Fynach?"

"Caretakers, of a sort," Richard said. "Coblynau devoted to the care and survival of the dragons. As Deirdre said, few dragons remain, only a handful. The Fynach work hard to discover the cause of the decline. They know more concerning dragons than anyone in Annwn—anyone anywhere, I believe."

"Why are the dragons dying?" Bran asked.

"No one knows, young Ardall," Henrick said. "Many believe the long summer the dragons have endured has altered them somehow. Others believe some kind of inbreeding has left them unable to produce offspring."

"Where are they then?" Deirdre asked. "Or for that matter, the Fynach? Should not one of them have met us by now?"

"I do not know," the guard said.

Arrow Jack let out a loud warning shriek.

Just as Richard clicked Lyrian into motion toward Tal Ebolyon, three dragons launched into the air from the far end of the garden, flying toward them like arrows shot from a bow.

"Lord Latobius will be difficult to persuade," Henrick offered. "The Yn Dri rarely come to agreement on anything, especially a subject of serious magnitude."

"Divisive bickering does not interest me," Richard said.

Lyrian snorted defiance but held his ground as the monoliths approached. Patting the Rhedewyr comfortingly, Richard watched with trepidation. Slinking through the air like serpents in water, the three dragons grew as large as houses, their scales shimmering in the sunshine. The lead dragon was the largest, charcoal hide rippling with golden highlights, black leather wings beating with strong, smooth strokes. Flying alongside the leader was a brownish-red beast, its limbs shorter than the others; to the other side and a bit behind, a shrunken gray-green ancient dragon flew. All were scarily formidable, claws like curved swords, long barbed tails, and horn-encrusted heads bearing jaws rowed with dagger-like teeth.

Richard wondered suddenly if he had overstepped boundaries by entering Tal Ebolyon uninvited.

He had little time to worry.

In a flurry of swift wing strokes that sent a sudden wall of air at him, the dragons settled gracefully to the courtyard on four legs and eyed the newcomers with suspicion.

"Prince Saethmoor," Henrick greeted, kneeling.

"Coblynau," the dragon rumbled. "It is an ill moment for you to visit Tal Ebolyon."

"I and those with me regret to hear of any ill befalling you," the guard said. "I am Henrick, son of Harrick, here at the behest of Lord Fafnir to escort visitors from Arendig Fawr to the foot of your father."

The dark blue eyes of Saethmoor probed the group, lingering on Richard and Bran. "Two knights I see before me," he said. "With an Oakwell fairy. A depressed clurichaun. A fair witch. And a murderous, *spear-wielding* hellyll."

"I am Richard McAllister, Knight of the Yn Saith," Richard said, dismounting and bowing. "My friends and I have come at great cost to ourselves and freedom, hunted by Caer Llion at every bend of our path. It has not been an easy path to trod. The Queen of the Seelie Court desires—"

"You are here, knight, because my Dragonsire responded to a letter received."

"We are, for that very reason."

"As I earlier professed, the timing of your arrival is unfortunate."

"The letter was not sent in vain, mighty prince," Richard said. "The survival of your race may depend on the contents of that letter."

The dragon growled deeply in thought.

"Maethyn?"

"By the laws of Tal Ebolyon, a response by the Yn Dri is necessary," the ancient dragon said, pondering. "The law is quite clear. No matter if the issue, once answered in the past, arises again."

"The Dragonsire will not be pleased," the reddish dragon disagreed.

"Unfortunate circumstances arise, Nael," Maethyn answered. "Guests to Tal Ebolyon will not be turned away without proper considerate discourse."

"Turning you away I cannot do apparently," Saethmoor growled to Richard. "Law rules our way of life and it blankets all, even non-dragonkin. You must understand, however, that hospitality may be hard to come by. Our lord suffers grievous pain. Can this be done with haste, Knight of the Yn Saith Richard McAllister?"

"I will be as succinct as possible, Prince Saethmoor."

"Maethyn, Nael, notify the Dragonsire of our visitor as I escort the group to the Ring of Baedgor."

"Your wish is my own," Maethyn nodded.

The two dragons leapt into the air with powerful wings.

"Come then," Saethmoor beckoned.

The prince led, striding between the hedges and trees. Richard marveled at the dragon. He was enormous but moved soundlessly like a giant cat, his four heavily muscled legs nimble and rippling, his wings folded protectively close along his back. Saethmoor held his head high, regally, even while his talons bit into the ground. It was the first time the knight had seen a dragon but he understood why the Morrigan desired Tal Ebolyon to return to the Seelie Court; Saethmoor and his kin were built for war and would make powerful allies against Caer Llion.

As Richard looked about the garden, he was startled to discover what he had mistaken as malformed boulders were actually sleeping dragons. Each one lay curled near a freestanding wall, burrowed comfortably a foot into the dirt, the shade of an oak tree overhead. Only a few such spaces were occupied. Hundreds and hundreds of other patches were grown over, unused.

"Dragons don't sleep in caves?" Bran asked.

"Dragons need little protection from the elements," Henrick said. "They have tough hide and an inner furnace for warmth."

"So few," Richard breathed. "Four dozen, at most."

"We dragons survive, one way or another," Saethmoor growled, stopping to confront the knight. "It has ever been and ever will be."

Richard nodded politely. He sadly didn't agree.

Saethmoor passed through a large square lined by numerous rose bushes, some grown as tall as the residents of Tal Ebolyon. The dragon did not view their beauty. Instead, he made his way down a set of wide, shallow stairs and into a lower circular area as large as a city block. Rectangular granite slabs like those at Stonehenge periodically grew from the circle's outer rim and glowed white, some forming trilithons while others stood alone. Power radiated from the area, born of some ancient mystique Richard could not identify but only feel. Maethyn and Nael sat perched atop two separate stones with three other dragons of varying earthy colors and sizes. All watched Richard and his companions enter the ring with vigilant scrutiny.

The scene at the center of the circle nearly brought Richard to a halt.

Lying on emerald grass and bearing hundreds of wounds, a green dragon lay stretched out, the rise and fall of its chest slow and laboring. The dragon was smaller than its kin, not fully grown as Richard could judge. It was dying and the concern Saethmoor had expressed upon their arrival became all too clear.

A man white like an albino but with raven black hair cradled the head of the dying dragon, soothing the fey creature as best he could. Short, stocky men who resembled Henrick but were bald and wearing white robes tended the wounds as best they could, examining the tears and rents in its wings while others patched the bleeding savagery with white cloth that turned quickly crimson. The man watched none of it, focused on the head of the beast, tears standing out clearly on his finely chiseled cheeks.

"Dragonsire?" Saethmoor said softly.

"What do ye desire, First Son?" Latobius snapped, not looking up.

"Visitors have entered Tal Ebolyon with a request for audience."

"What they request, I cannot give. Turn them away."

"Greetings, Lord Latobius," Richard intervened, dismounting to bow. "I am Knight Richard McAllister of the Yn Saith. I come on behalf of the Seelie Court and the Morrigan who leads it. My sincerest sorrow to you and your kin at the sight I see before me."

"What can ye possibly know of this or sorrow, *knight?*"

"More than you know, my Lord," Richard responded. "More than you know."

"The Queen oversteps her authority."

"She is pressed with war. And has need of your wisdom."

"As I wrote in my response to her, I care not," Latobius said. "The woes of this world have come to my domain and I must care for them first."

"Lord Latobius," Lugh interrupted, stepping forward. Richard withheld his desire to grab the hellyll back. "I am Lugh of the Long Hand, bearer of Areadhbar, hellyll of the lost Hinter Hills, and defender of Arendig Fawr. Richard McAllister speaks true. The destruction of Tal Ebolyon is at hand. To have ignored the letter from the Queen was to ignore your own safety."

"In no way will my kind take suggestions or accept criticisms from a *spear wielder,*" Latobius spat the last as a curse, shaking his head.

"I—" Lugh began.

"Saethmoor," Latobius commanded, waving them away.

Before the charcoal dragon could guide them away, Lugh slammed the butt of his spear against the grassy carpet. The golden point of Areadbhar glowed pristine white even under the sunshine, drawing all attention to him.

The dragons sitting upon the stone blocks growled low.

Tension filled the air.

"We mean you no disrespect or harm, Lord Latobius," Richard said, glaring at Lugh to stay his hand. "The Morrigan has need of your might in this trying time."

"Such spears have killed many of my kin," Latobius said, ignoring Richard.

"But not by *my* hand," Lugh argued.

"By steady hands possessed of ill wills," the dragonsire hissed. "Murderers. Perjurers. We dragons have long memories . . . long memories."

"How did your son come to this, Lord Latobius?" Richard questioned, changing the course of the conversation in hope of having any chance of success.

"Something flying, some evil from the lowlands," Latobius replied, still massaging the head of the enormous beast. "Tearing claws, a swarm of some bird unknown. His brothers found him struggling to regain the heights of Tal Ebolyon days hence. The Fynach work hard . . ."

"I know how this happened," Richard said. "But more importantly *who* did this."

For the first time, Latobius looked up. Eyes as black as coal fixed on the knight and the anger mirrored there simmered in depths grown deep from centuries of life and sorrow survived. It was all Richard could do to not look away.

"Who?"

"Philip Plantagent of Caer Llion."

Latobius nodded almost imperceptibly.

"How?"

"Caer Llion has bred halfbreeds of terror in a war he plans against the whole of Annwn. By the multitudes, half-eagle and fey-cat beasts are rampaging across the countryside and skies, killing livestock, Tuatha—whatever they can. It is clear Philip plans to weaken your allies while strengthening his campaign. He will stop at nothing until the breadth of Annwn is under his total control, including the Snowdon and Tal Ebolyon. The Morrigan gathers the remaining lords of the Seelie Court one last time to defend your right to exist. It is for this reason I have traveled to these high reaches, to ask your help in the conflict to come."

"The letter again, is it not?"

"The letter."

"My answer is the same. Maethyn, who oversees the laws we live by, and Nael, who guards those laws, both agree. The dragons of Tal Ebolyon cannot invest in a war that will undoubtedly kill more of my children."

"The letter arrived before this tragedy, my Lord," Richard pointed out. "I do not wish to see any more of your precious kin ravaged in this way. But Caer Llion comes and will not stop until all is under his rule and dominion, including Tal Ebolyon. Is it not better to fight alongside the many rather than alone with few?"

"Dragonsire," Maethyn whispered. "It is a difficult decision."

"Perhaps we ought to revisit our earlier decision," Saethmoor added. "This is not as clear as it once was. Not after the halfbreed attack."

"First Son, do not ask this of me," Latobius said, his mien tortured. "To lose any of ye would kill me as any spear."

"What happened to the son in your arms will happen to you," Richard said pointedly.

"He speaks a certain truth, Dragonsire," Saethmoor said.

"Enough!" Latobius thundered. "I will not tolerate it!"

"Retribution for this grievous assault must be considered," Richard pressed.

"Do ye not think I want vengeance?" Latobius said, gesturing to the damage done by the griffins. "For this? I want it more than anything. Anything!"

"Then bring your might, rejoin the Seelie Court."

"I will not. Cannot! The risk is far too great, I say!"

"My lord, you must," Richard insisted.

Anger flooding his eyes, Latobius gently put the head of his son down on the soft grass. Standing, his thin form immediately shimmered. The body of the lord expanded and elongated as it gained height, his skin developing scales, limbs growing longer and ending in razor-like claws. Clothes became leather wings, scarred with ancient healed rents. In a matter of moments, the fey lord had transformed into a dragon as formidable as any Richard could imagine.

The eyes of Latobius burned into the knight.

Richard gave no ground, conviction burning inside.

"Ye reek of loss, of uncertainty," Latobius growled in his new form, his massive head mere feet from Richard. "Ye care nothing for anyone, or the world. Why ye are here at all is an enigma."

Richard said nothing, unfaltering before obvious danger.

"Those who have nothing to lose make unwise and poor leaders," Latobius said.

"You do not know me," Richard challenged. "Nor my reasons for being here."

Muscles rippling in his dragon chest and neck, Latobius fixed his gaze on Bran. "And untested as a new faun, this one," Latobius snorted. The dragon returned to Richard. "Ye are an affront to me, to my wishes. Permit that I will not. My youngest son dies before me at the hands of war. Only seven decades old, a baby still in many respects. No eggs hatched since his cracked, with none on the horizon. I hurt as he does, yearn for revenge as those of my brethren around me. But I *will not* risk one more death like this. Too few, we are. To lose even one of us would undo us further."

"Lord Latobius?"

All eyes turned to Kegan as he dismounted from his Rhedewyr.

"Clurichaun," Latobius greeted, eyes narrowing. "Yer sadness is written on ye."

Kegan bowed. "Sad. And true. Days ago I lost my oldest son to the wiles of Caer Llion. Connal was his name, brother to Kearney. Connal was a better son than I had ever hoped to have. He died protecting us in the lower passes, but he died for a cause larger than us. He died to remind us all what the Dark One has planned, and it is our choice if we let that happen."

Latobius said nothing but watched Kegan closely.

"I tell ye this now not to persuade ye or anger ye further," Kegan said, eyes shining. "Ye are entitled to your pain. As *I* am. But I want ye to know some of us have suffered losses at the hands of the evil that expands from Caer Llion. I would do anything to prevent others from feeling this way—from feeling the way ye do right now."

"The pain in yer voice, clurichaun, I hear," Latobius said. "Ye have a large heart to share it with me. But sharing will not keep my children safe on a battleground, now will it?"

"But they *will* come here to kill you," Richard said angrily.

"Then let them come!" Latobius roared, smoke seething from

nostrils. The Rhedewyr and their riders shied. Richard did not move. "Let them come and witness our power!"

"It is best we leave," Henrick whispered, pulling at the knight.

Richard did not budge, his mind working fast. The meeting with Lord Latobius was on the brink of collapse. To stay meant possible annihilation at the fiery breath of dragonkind; to leave meant failing to return Tal Ebolyon to the Seelie Court. Richard had only one course left him, an admission he hated all the more for having to give it.

The knight called the Dark Thorn and knelt.

The dragons surrounding them watched closely as Richard bowed his head. The silver grains of the staff's dark wood sparked under the sun and white fire ran its length. Richard stared at the ground, hoping he wasn't losing his soul for what he was about to say, the conflicting parts of his entire life coming together in one moment that would define him forever.

"I swear an oath of fealty to your people, Lord Latobius," Richard offered in his loudest, booming voice. "Bring your people to the Seelie Court. Fight Caer Llion with all of your might. Help kill Philip Plantagenet. Send him and his abominations to the lowest pit of the lowest hell. In exchange for your return oath to rejoin the Morrigan, I will walk the ends of Annwn and my own world to find what ails dragonkind and cure it."

Silence fell over the mountain. Richard kept his head bowed.

He did not get up.

"Ye may possess the Thorn, knight," Latobius said. "But ye have yet to become it."

"I just did, I think, Lord Latobius."

Long moments passed. Richard awaited the verdict.

"It changes nothing, Knight of the Yn Ssaith," Lord Latobius finally said. "I know ye are sincere in yer oath. It is not enough; it is not time. First Son, these guests have outstayed their welcome. The path here has taken a toll, I see. Guide them upon barges to the lowlands where they desire to go. It will aid them in ways I cannot."

"Yes, Dragonsire," Saethmoor said.

Anger at his failure visceral within, Richard rose and let the

Dark Thorn vanish.

Lord Latobius looked closely at him.

"Knight, forgive me my choice," the great dragon rumbled. "Give the Morrigan my apology. I pray she is strong enough for the breadth of the Tuatha de Dannan."

"You cannot mean to betray Annwn," Richard snarled. "Betray your Queen!"

"It will not be so!" Latobius roared. "At great distances my kind can see, better than all other fey. But no one can view the future. It is that future I fight to protect."

Henrick pulled on Richard, but still the knight did not budge.

"Leave," Latobius said lowly.

"Very well," Richard said curtly. "I hope you reconsider. I hope you remember those who wounded you so, those who would see your kin wiped from this mountain. With courage we go to combat Caer Llion. I hope you regain your own."

Latobius ignored the rebuke and stared sadly again at his wounded son. The Fynach continued their efforts. Richard mounted Lyrian once more and, cueing the others, followed Saethmoor from the Ring of Baedgor. Richard did not look back.

It would do no good.

"You have a stubborn sire," Richard said to Saethmoor.

"He is in pain," the prince said, guiding them from the gardens to a flat stone yard bearing large wooden square platforms with posts at the corners like a bed. "He speaks wisdom but pain has chosen his direction in this. Perhaps he will think on what you have said."

"What do you think?" Richard questioned.

"What you have said, I believe," Saethmoor said. "I would rather fight."

"I failed then."

"No, Knight McAllister," Henrick said. "You do not know that."

"The lord may regain his stones," Snedeker said.

"More is what will be done now. It is time we visit Caer Llion, Bran," Richard said, the realization of his failure blooming into a flame of resolve.

"To do what?" Bran asked, clearly surprised. "I thought we would—"

"Fight with the Tuatha de Dannan?" Richard asked. "That will come. The Morrigan now owes me a favor, although a small one. It is time we exercise it."

"Why Caer Llion then?"

"To end the threat of Philip Plantagenet before the war even begins."

Chapter 26

Bran stared into the afternoon sky where the four dragons and the barge they carried flew, disappearing into the ether of the Snowdon.
In minutes they were gone.
What had taken days to ascend had taken an hour to undo.
Upon landing in Arendig Fawr, Richard ordered Bran to soothe Westryl and Lyrian before disappearing into the Cadarn to seek out the Morrigan and the lord of Mochdrev Reach. Bran remained with Arrow Jack, whose piercing eyes watched the mobilization of the city. The Tuatha de Dannan scurried about, dozens of races—short clurichauns and feline cait siths, ugly spriggans and hairy woodwoses, pointy-eared hellyll and many others. Fairies buzzed through the air, relaying messages. A few companies of coblynau had also arrived, adding their stalwart presence. From the depths of the forest, carts of armor and arms rolled passed, coming from Mastersmith Govannon. Even leprechauns tottered about, drunkenly trying to help.
All carried weapons of some sort, ready for the coming conflict with Caer Llion.
After the Rhedewyr were once again at peace from their

chaotic journey through the air, Deirdre and Snedeker returned from the Cadarn, steely determination in the redhead's eyes.

"That was an interesting ride, eh?" Deirdre commented.

"No kidding," Bran agreed.

"Looks like we go to war."

"So many races here."

"The Tuatha de Dannan are proud," Deirdre said. "This fight has long been needed. Even without Tal Ebolyon, the force gathering should be formidable."

"When Richard spoke in Tal Ebolyon, the dragon lord said something odd," Bran said. "He called you a 'fair witch.' Why would he say that? Are you really a witch?"

"My mother was a witch," Deirdre said, looking toward the Cadarn with an eagerness that annoyed Bran. "She died when I was very young. I know a few small spells she taught me, nothing that powerful. A levitation incantation. A song to change the color of leaves or control ivy. That's about it." She smiled sadly. "She would usually put back right what I had done."

"I'm sorry to hear you lost your mother so young."

"Life has a way of severing love sometimes," she said sadly.

Bran nodded, thinking. When his own mother died, he had changed dramatically and knew of what Deirdre spoke. Upon entering Annwn he had changed again, this time for the better. He no longer felt lost to the streets. Despite only being in Annwn for a few days, he had become a part of something much larger than himself. He had always wished it and, like his father, he now possessed a relic of great power in Arondight, giving him the chance to matter in a world where normalcy was sought and highly overrated. He may not understand Arondight or everything that transpired around him, but he knew he would never let the sword go.

And unlike Richard, Bran would use the magic blade to the best of his ability and never let it change him as it had the knight.

No matter who he fell in love with.

"Do you love him?" Bran blurted, suddenly annoyed at himself.

"Who do you mean?"

It was all Bran could do to meet Deirdre's green eyes.

"Richard," he said. "Why do you care for him?"

Deirdre looked away. "That is none of your concern."

"He is a broken man," Bran pressed.

"He is. But he will not *always* be."

A pit of sorrow mixed with anger sank into his stomach. The feelings Bran had felt from the moment he had met the redhead had blossomed into much more. She was a few years older than him but he did not worry on that. There was something about her, an intoxicating rush of emotions she drew out of him. He wanted to kiss her, hold her. He wanted more. Confusion about how to act left him paralyzed. She had barely looked at him, the feelings Bran experienced also present in her eyes but not sent his way.

They were instead for Richard.

Frustration built inside. Bran didn't understand.

He was about to say something he knew he would regret when Richard burst from the entrance of the Cadarn, striding with a resolve Bran had not seen in the knight before.

"We leave," Richard said simply. "Now."

"What happened?" Bran asked.

"The Morrigan is assembling what might the Tuatha de Dannan possess. Soon the entirety of those sent by Lord Fafnir will join the rest here. The clans outside the Carn Cavall are also amassing, near the headwaters of the Wysg River. In a matter of hours, the Seelie Court will again be gathered, even without Tal Ebolyon, organizing in the Forest of Dean, to march through the plains of Morgannwg province toward Caer Llion."

"Well, that is good news, isn't it?" Bran asked.

"It is. It will make what we must do all the easier."

"The more people the safer we'll be, I guess."

"No," Richard said. "We travel alone to Caer Llion, ahead of the army."

"Shouldn't we be with the bulk of the Queen's army?"

"The Morrigan and I want answers," Richard said. "The only place for them is inside Caer Llion."

"If that is true, I am coming with you," Deirdre interceded.

"No," Richard said curtly.

"You will need my help," Deirdre said. Bran could tell she was thinking quickly, as if her life depended on it. "The Rhedewyr you ride forth must be cared for. You do not plan to ride them through the front portcullis of the castle or leave them grazing alone in the plains, do you?"

"Still, it doesn't matte—"

"I'm coming," Deirdre said. "That's that, knight. I knew this was coming before you did. My father has given me leave to go my own way in this madness and I will do as such. If you do not like it, take it up with him."

Richard didn't look at her. Bran could see the struggle going on inside of him.

"It will be dangerous," Richard said.

"Kegan cannot go," Deirdre said stubbornly. Bran hated how she fought. "And my family knows the plains from Arendig Fawr to Vyrridin to Caer Cleddyf. I am your best chance at success."

With a grunt, Richard mounted Lyrian.

"Is this wise, Richard?" Bran asked.

"*Apparently*, I have no choice."

Deirdre smiled, ignoring Bran, her eyes fixed on Richard. Without another word, they both mounted and rode after the knight who trotted southward through the melee, Snedeker a blur chasing the merlin. As Bran watched the city fade behind him, he saw Caswallawn emerge from the entrance to the Cadarn. Their gazes met. The former lord scowled after the three, the hatred he had for the outworlders palpable. In a swirl of practiced deftness, Caswallawn whirled what could only be his invisible cloak about him.

In a second, the lord disappeared.

Bran hoped the surly lord made it to Govannon's armory safely enough to drink himself into oblivion.

Dusk settled in on the woodland after an hour, the final birdsong dwindling until silent. The path was wide and easy to navigate, the Rhedewyr plodding forward without hindrance despite the growing darkness. They did not speak, Richard leading, with Snedeker flying ahead, Bran and Deirdre coming after, and Arrow Jack a darting blur in the trees overhead. Nothing else moved. All of the activity was taking place in Arendig Fawr, leaving a world of sudden peace.

The trails wound downward, the Carn Cavall diminishing with every step the Rhedewyr took. The sticky warmth, once lost to the upper reaches of the Snowdon, had reformed around them amidst the pooling shadows that enveloped the land at the day's end. The gloom plagued Bran, made him suspicious. The memory of his encounter with the Erlking resurfaced, crawling over his skin with electricity. If he had learned anything from being in Annwn, it was to not trust the moments he felt safe.

After several hours had passed, Deirdre turned suddenly to scrutinize the forest behind them, worry darkening her beautiful features.

"What is it?" Bran asked.

"We are being followed," she said.

Bran shot a glance backward. Nothing appeared amiss.

"I know," Richard said, barely flinching. "The forest went quiet behind about half an hour ago. Probably not the bodach. It would have caught us by now. Keep aware. Could just be another traveler but no reason to take a chance."

The trail began to level as glimpses of the far-reaching plains came to them through the trees. The last glimmers of purpling light diffused the flatland. With the stars overhead slowly twinkling to life, Richard stopped to camp on the outskirts of the grasses where windblown pine sheltered a tiny bubbling brook, giving minor protection from prying eyes. Frogs nearby croaked their song while fireflies roamed the deepening darkness. All was still. The night drew peace like a blanket, a reprieve from the chaos Bran hoped would not come but knew would.

Settled near a small fire, Richard ate a meal while Snedeker puzzled over a blade of purple grass. Bran also sat by the fire and watched Deirdre care for the Rhedewyr, the redhead giving them a careful brushing after days without it.

"I do not know how much time we will have to speak in the

days or even hours to come," Richard said finally. "The time has come to share a few things."

Bran nodded, waiting.

"After I spoke with the Morrigan, I went in search of a waterfall in the Cadarn. It did not take long. Through the water, I contacted the other Knights of the Yn Saith. No, don't ask how yet. It is a magic Merle or I will eventually teach you when this business is finished. The important thing is they know about you, they know that I am now the Heliwr. They also know to be watching their portals far more closely than they have been for the last few years."

"You actually spoke with them?" Bran asked. "Like some kind of telepathy?"

"When you get on a roll, the questions are unending," Richard sighed. "Yes, I actually spoke with them. In person. There is a lake on the north side of the Carn Cavall that surrounds a small island, the Isle of Achlesydd. Achlesydd is an ancient tree that wards our weapons. When not called by the knights, the relics reside on massive stones. You are now tied to one of those stones. Even now, Arondight rests there. In this way they are safe."

"No one tries to steal them?"

"The isle is more guarded than Fort Knox," Richard snorted.

"What of the other knights?" Bran asked. "Will they aid us?"

"It is too late for that."

"Why?

"Scouts of the Morrigan have discovered the great amassing of an army at Caer Llion," Richard said. "In mere days, maybe even hours, it will leave and travel to the Snowdon or one of the portals. Regardless, the knights lack the ability to get here in time. Their portals are spread all over Annwn, days away. It is just as well. It is better they protect their respective cities. There are failsafes like Dryvyd Wood in our world. Even if Philip does bring his army through, it will not be easy for him. It will buy us the time we need." He paused. "Now call Arondight."

With a thought, Bran held the blade in his left hand.

"Arondight is one of Govannon's oldest creations," Richard said. "The sword was forged long before Lancelot. You wanted to know more about it. I will tell you the most important lesson you will learn, right now. Can you feel its power, where the sword calls its fire from?"

"No."

"Close your eyes, think it through."

Bran gripped the blade, letting his thoughts flow along its length. He felt it then. A part of the power came from Arondight but most welled within, from his chest into his hand. The fire he had used against the bodach lingered just below the surface, a caged animal ready for release.

"I can, yes," Bran answered, feeling a bit lightheaded.

"You and the blade are now one," Richard said, peering closely at Bran. "While possessing it, you have the ability to protect yourself from those who would see you dead. That protection comes at a cost. The magic comes from you, but nothing comes from nothing. If not careful, you can be consumed from within, be bled empty. The power can also be addictive for some. I have seen it. I am sure Merle will have more to say about this *if* we return."

"What do you mean *if?*"

"I won't lie to you, we may not return, not amidst the hell we find ourselves in at the moment," Richard replied. "Entering Caer Llion is a dangerous prospect even for the most trained. You are *not* trained. It's unfortunate timing. The risk might be too much." He paused. "But whether I like it or not, you are a fellow knight now and I need your help."

"Being untrained, I don't have to go in, you know," Bran said.

"You do," Richard said simply.

Bran was going to ask why when Snedeker, who had suddenly lost interest in his oddly colored blade of grass, flew to where the two knights were, sat on a rotting log, and listened to Richard with an intensity Bran almost found comical.

"What do you want, fairy?" the knight asked lowly.

"Nothing at all," Snedeker answered.

"You've been acting strangely toward me ever since that night with the Lady in the fairy glen," Richard pressed, clearly annoyed. "Watching me. I know you don't like me. I don't like you much. But I have to know. The Lady told you something, didn't she? That night."

Snedeker stared at Richard as if trying to figure out a puzzle.

"Answer me!" he demanded.

"Why does it matter?" Deirdre asked, having finished caring for the Rhedewyr and sitting at the fire.

"Oh, it matters. A lot. Every Heliwr has had a guide, a fairy, one that watches the knight's back in time of need. Bran's father had a fairy guide as well. Berrytrill, his name was. I think the Lady spoke to Snedeker there, asked him to serve. He has been quiet ever since that night and it has been grating on me."

"Snedeker, is this true?" Deirdre asked.

The fairy glanced at the redhead, an iota of guilt crossing his woodland features.

"Red, I meant to tell you . . ."

"So it's true? You are to guide Rick?"

"The Lady spoke to me, yes," Snedeker said. "Asked me to serve the Heliwr. If I had known it would be McAllister here, though, I never would have agreed. Thought it would be Ardall. The lesser of two cow pies, that one."

"Dammit," Richard growled low. "Just my luck. What else did the Lady say?"

"That was it, darktard," Snedeker snapped.

Richard looked as though he would call the Dark Thorn and incinerate the fairy immediately.

"So my father had a fairy guide?" Bran asked, trying to alleviate the tension. "What else haven't you told me about my father, Richard?"

"There is much I haven't told you," the knight said, still staring hard at the fairy. "Not because I didn't want to but because I didn't want you to feel obligated to follow in his footsteps. To tell you more about your father would have accelerated what I had hoped to prevent. Turns out Merle is a tricky bastard, and he pulled the wool over my eyes."

"Why keep me from anything?" Bran asked, a bit angrily. "It isn't your place."

"It *is* my place to protect those who can't protect themselves," Richard replied pointedly. "That was you. You had no idea what you were getting yourself into, just as right now you *still* do not. Sadly, I need your help in Caer Llion and that cannot be avoided."

Calming himself, Bran let Arondight vanish.

"Did you know my father well?"

"I knew him vaguely." Richard leaned back into his bedroll. "You look a bit like him, but he had a kinder heart than you have. No doubt due your time on the streets. He had a hard work ethic and believed quite strongly in what he was doing. Few ever bested him and those who did didn't last much longer afterward."

"I have few memories of him," Bran admitted.

"Died before you grew up, for sure."

"I asked this of you before," Bran said. "Do you know who killed my father?"

"No," Richard said stoically. "It literally could be anyone or anything, from this world or our own. I know his time came in the United Kingdom. Other than that, Merle was not willing to share much more."

"Then he didn't die in a terror attack in Ireland?"

"Ireland, maybe. A terror attack, like the IRA?" Richard scowled. "No. Whoever told you that is either ignorant or lying. Whatever murdered your father had to possess a potent magic to do it. Overcoming the power of a Heliwr is not easy."

"What magic did he have, as Heliwr?"

"You mean what magic do *I* have, eh?"

"I guess."

"That depends on ability," Richard said. "Remember what I did to Llassar?"

"Yes, the grass holding him firm. He called you a wizard."

"A weak wizard, at best."

"So you *are* a wizard?"

Richard smiled with no warmth. "You are as well now."

"What do you mea—"

"In due time. In due time," Richard repeated. "Tomorrow maybe."

Settling back into his own blankets, Bran tried to picture his father with the staff, when he saw dozens of gimlet eyes glittering from the darkness, surrounding the campsite at the edge of the firelight. Bran couldn't make out anything more than that.

"Richard," Bran whispered.

The knight followed his eyes. "They have been there for some time."

"What are they?"

"Llithiwch," Deirdre answered, looking at the shadowy wraiths from her own bedroll. "Skittish little creatures, rarely seen. They are Unseelie, but do not hurt anyone or anything. My people consider them a blessing of sorts; if they are here, no other Unseelie are nearby."

"Are they what follow us?" Bran asked.

"Could be," Richard said, but he didn't sound convinced.

"Spies?"

"No, not at all," Deirdre said. "Odd so many are gathered here though."

"Drawn by the power of Arondight," Richard observed. He hunkered back down into his bedroll. "Sleep. They can't hurt us. We are going to have a long day tomorrow."

Bran relaxed, as Deirdre followed Richard's example. Soon the soft snores of the knight and the even rise and fall of Deirdre's chest left Bran with the first watch. The luminous eyes from the darkness still watched. Bran kept the fire going, distrustful of the creatures, his thoughts straying to home as he stared into the fire. Seattle seemed so far away. Merle had put Bran between a rock and a hard place, having maneuvered him to the exact spot he wanted. Bran knew one thing—Merle had a lot to answer for, not only for his machinations but also the hundreds of questions Bran had concerning his father, his new role, and what it all meant for his future.

When Bran looked up from the fire, the Llithiwch were gone.

As he was about to settle back and relax, a new set of eyes appeared in the night, flaming crimson with utter hatred and growing larger by the moment.

"Bodach!" Bran screamed, leaping up and calling Arondight.

Richard gained his feet as though he hadn't been asleep, the Dark

Thorn filling his hand in white flame just as the bodach jumped.

With a shriek, the Unseelie beast bulled over the Heliwr.

Richard rolled with the assault, letting the creature blow mostly over him and then blasted it with white magic. The creature reeled away, the flames licking at its shadowy form as it fought to break through. Richard did not let up. Regaining his feet in that afforded moment, he kept his staff between them. The shadow tore at him even as the knight backed away. Richard parried every swipe, keeping the Dark Thorn held before him, his eyes burning with concentration.

"Bran!" Richard roared, falling to the ground.

As it had in Caer Glain, the fey creature fought to pin Richard to kill him, going after its most powerful adversary.

As the bodach leapt ferociously upon the knight, Bran charged with Arondight.

Deirdre beat him to it.

Hurdling the fire, Deirdre had her sword in hand, charging the fey. Her red hair manic, she sliced at the occupied bodach with wild abandon, roaring at the top of her lungs—to little effect. Annoyed by the woman, the bodach lashed out finally with one massive clawed paw, connecting with Deirdre.

She landed on the fire, the embers setting her clothes ablaze.

When Deirdre rolled away, on fire, something snapped inside Bran. In slow motion, he witnessed another attempt on their lives and his own weak inaction. Anger turned to righteousness; passion crystallized into deed. The screams of the Rhedewyr faded. The roars of the bodach vanished. All that remained was his desire to see Deirdre safe and the bodach destroyed before it could kill another and the blame be put squarely on him.

Arondight grew incandescent, flaming wild magic.

Before he could reach the bodach though, reports echoed in the night all around them, explosions in rapid succession. Pinpricks of light bloomed inside of the bodach, dozens and then hundreds permeating every aspect of the Unseelie beast. The bodach pawed the air, angry, screaming as if struck by thousands of spears at once.

It took Bran a moment to realize what was happening.

The bodach was being shot by gunfire.

Bran spun about, searching.

From the darkness soldiers emerged, each one carrying assault rifles and pistols. There were two dozen of them, each dressed as black as the night around them. The odor of burnt gunpowder on the air, they unleashed bullet flurries into the bodach. The creature could not prevent it; the lead from the gunfire, anathema to the Unseelie creature, ripped through its smoky being.

Finn Arne, Captain of the Vatican's Swiss Guard, ordered his men to press forward.

The warriors did. The bodach raged. With no thought to his own safety and the power radiating through him, Bran sent the magic of Arondight into the side of the bodach. The fire tore into the Unseelie beast, casting it off of the knight as though struck by a gigantic fist.

The shadow careened across the clearing, singed and smoking.

"Arne!" Richard roared. "Don't let it flee!"

The noose of Swiss Guard tightened about the bodach. Sensing it was outmatched, the creature tore across the clearing to escape into the night.

Richard was too quick. He sent the power of the Dark Thorn into it. The bodach fell to the earth again, smoking, flames licking its insubstantial body. It regained its feet, eyes glowing hotter. With Deirdre behind them, Bran and Richard faced the circling fey assassin together, the guards from the Vatican preventing escape.

White fire ran down the Dark Thorn, and Bran held Arondight before him, ready.

The bodach tore at the sod, bounding toward them.

"Go after it with everything you have, Bran!" Richard yelled. "Into its deepest part!"

Bran gritted his teeth, bracing his feet. The attack didn't come. Richard flung fire to one side of the bodach, forcing the beast away from Bran and instead toward him. It strayed from the blast and slammed into the knight. The bodach ravaged the magical shield Richard had readied—but suddenly the knight let the shield vanish. The bodach tumbled forward. As Richard let the Unseelie beast fall, he lashed out with a quick low swing, using the Dark Thorn like a sword. The fire severed the forelegs of the bodach, the limbs evaporating into the ether. The bodach dropped to the earth, screaming, scrambling in panic, using its remaining four legs to retreat in hopes of escape and regenerating its body.

"Now, Ardall!" Richard roared, diving aside.

Bran was on the bodach immediately. With all of his might and ignoring his own safety, he drove Arondight into the very center of the beast, letting the magic flow as it hadn't yet.

The blade penetrated deep, burning so blue it became white hot. The bodach let loose a deafening screech, one of anguish and loathing. It fought the sword, biting at the steel as it squirmed to be free. Bran sent all his will through Arondight and into the creature, trying to incinerate it from within, wishing the evil assassin forever gone from world. The injustice of the things he had seen helped him wield the justice to do what was right. Images of Connal dying, the tears of Kegan, Hollick disappearing within Caer Glain, and Deirdre being tossed onto their campfire like a doll seared Bran like a cauterizing iron, bolstered his resolve, and lent him power he had never known.

Light shattered the night, intensifying, as blinding as the sun.

The bodach howled, pinned, screaming and thrashing from the onslaught. The shadow dissolved in the brightness, losing what corporeal form it had. Bran did not let up. He twisted Arondight deeper, its fire penetrating farther into the center of the creature, even as euphoria he had never before experienced but frightening in its delicious taste gripped him. Bran reveled in it—fierce glee at seeing the beast destroyed reinforcing his conviction.

Like a conduit, he sent his heart into Arondight.

The bodach shuddered, unable to flee, and in a final scream of unrequited rage disintegrated to ash.

Chapter 27

"I will *not* continue to discuss this with you, Finn Arne," Richard said angrily.

Deirdre listened to the knight argue with the other outworlders, but the pain racking her body sent darkness before her eyes as Bran cleaned her burnt back. Deirdre remained focused though. Finn Arne, the captain of the warriors, stared hard at Richard, his arms crossed, his one good eye appraising the knight. With the bodach dead, the soldiers now surrounded them, each one a bar in a new prison. The redhead should have been pleased by the death of the bodach. She knew they were lucky to be alive, and she had Finn Arne to thank for it.

But events had taken a turn for the worse, it appeared.

Snedeker sat in Deirdre's hand, lending what sympathy he could, all the while giving the outworlders his darkest look. She didn't know who they were but she knew for certain she didn't like what they proposed.

"My orders are clear, McAllister."

"Damn your orders then," Richard said. "There is a great deal more going on here than you or your so-called *superiors* know. War has come. Not *maybe*. Not *possibility*. It is here *now*. I go to end it before it escalates into *our* world."

"By traveling to Caer Llion, I know, I know," Finn Arne said. "I still have orders."

"Who sent you? The Cardinal Vicar?"

"It does not matter."

"It does matter. Cormac O'Connor is only interested in attaining the services of the Heliwr, nothing more, nothing less," Richard said. "He wanted the boy because Bran Ardall is the son of the last Heliwr, Charles Ardall. In the time since you tried to kill us, I—"

"I didn't try to kill you."

"I don't care!" Richard said, cutting Arne off. "The point is . . . I am the Heliwr."

Finn Arne frowned. "You are?"

Richard called the Dark Thorn. White light fell on Deirdre and the clearing. The soldiers raised their weapons but the knight ignored them. The staff shimmered darkly in the early dawn, the silver grains of the black wood catching the light and releasing it.

"You must have seen me wield it during the battle," Richard said. "It wasn't a trick. I will make a bargain with you, one we both will benefit from."

"I am listening."

"If you let us go, we will willingly return with you to Rome. Once we return from Caer Llion and destroy Philip and his ability to see into our world."

"How do I know you don't go to join him?"

Richard barked a laugh. "I go to *kill* him."

"Who is the redhead?"

All eyes fell on Deirdre. She did not flinch. She had been surrounded by warriors all of her life, knew them as she knew herself, and despite their weaponry, those gathered were no different than any she had known.

"She is Deirdre Rhys, a lady of Annwn," Richard replied. "She is our guide."

"Is this true?" Finn Arne asked her.

"It is," she said. "I go with the knights to watch over their mounts while they are within Caer Llion. If they went to join the enemy, they would have had no need for me. Nor would I be wasting my time."

"What of my men?" Finn Arne asked finally. "I cannot bring my men into harm's way. We are *not* to become involved in any direct confrontation here in Annwn."

"I will tell you something, Shield of the Vatican, and you listen good," Richard stated, his anger plain. "For you to *not* become involved is the real travesty. The Seelie Court gathers to the east, where the Forest of Dean covers the approach to Caer Llion. They do so to counter an army bred to destroy this world and our own, one filled with aberrations of nature more deadly than the Kreche you met in Seattle. It is you who should join that war, bring your firepower and training, to protect the last defense to our world."

"It is not our place to become involved in the politics of Annwn," Finn Arne said, although without the surety he previously possessed. "And what if my men and I don't let you leave? We outnumber you."

Richard let white flames run up and down the Dark Thorn.

"I will kill every one of your men," the knight whispered, Deirdre barely able to hear. "You know how I feel toward your masters, toward your doctrine. I may not be able to kill you due to Prydwen, but your men are not so protected, are they? I will burn them away, your weapons and clothing away, and leave you naked as a jaybird. *Then* how easy will it be to bring young Ardall and myself to Rome, eh?"

Finn Arne and the knight stared one another down, neither giving way. Whether the knight would fulfill his promise and kill the warriors who surrounded them, Deirdre couldn't tell. Richard clearly did not fear the captain. With Bran behind her and ready to protect Richard, they had far more power than their aggressors.

"You go to the east after you finish with Philip?" Finn Arne asked after much time had passed.

"Coming through the Rome portal and traveling across the south of Annwn, you must have witnessed the army amassing at Caer Llion."

"I did."

"Then you know what I speak to be true."

"What does your wizard say about this?"

"I care not what he says, although we have not spoken since our battle in Seattle," Richard replied. "Knowing him though, Merle probably has wheels within wheels turning right now that are changing how all of this is going to end up. The one thing I've learned is to not trust him and how he uses people around for his own benefit."

"I don't trust you any more than I trust your wizard," the captain said. "I am not here to start or take part in a war. We are not equipped. I will wait for you to return, hold you to your oath, and take you back. If you do not keep your oath, I will rip Seattle apart to find you."

Richard nodded.

At that, Finn Arne gave several orders to his men. They disappeared through the plains in the east as the sun just broke the horizon.

In minutes, they were gone.

Richard sighed and turned back to Deirdre and Bran.

"Bran, would you start packing the camp," he requested. "We must leave here in all haste and gain Caer Llion by nightfall."

Bran handed the damp cloth he had been using on Deirdre to Richard, giving the knight a dark look. Deirdre ignored the obvious animosity between them. Bran left to roll their beds and pack their things.

Richard sat down next to Deirdre and continued what Bran had begun.

"You risk infection," Richard said flatly.

Deirdre grimaced as the knight cleaned her charred flesh. Her back and left arm were badly burned; the coals of the campfire had turned her skin to crimson and blackened wax. It could have been worse; the leather vest she wore had absorbed much of the fire.

It was clear, though, she needed weeks to recover from the injuries done her.

"You should go back," Richard continued, dabbing brusquely.

"No," Deirdre rasped. "No. I will see this through."

"You are incredibly stubborn."

Deirdre smiled through the pain. "I knew there was something you liked about me."

Richard kept scowling, removing as much grit from her back as he could. She let him, happy for his attention. The heat of Richard sitting so close warmed Deirdre. She kept the growing feelings she had for the knight inside. It was difficult to do. From the moment she had sat at his bedside in the Cadarn, she knew he was the outworlder in her mother's vision. It made no rational sense but there it was. He was strong, tempered by life, and intriguing. He was an unknown. While his past haunted him, he still possessed honor to see this business to its end. She had been with men, even thought she had been in love before, but nothing compared to this.

She thought back on the vision. It cooled her thoughts. The shade of her mother had said her future was intertwined with Philip Plantagenet. Knowing visions were riddles unexplained, she worried what the reality would be.

Especially given she traveled toward Philip willingly.

Lord Gerallt had been more supportive than her mother. Upon returning to Arendig Fawr, her father had seen the look in her eyes and knew she would never marry Plantagenet. He made the decision then to fight. Deirdre would aid the Morrigan while he returned to Mochdrev Reach to bolster what guard they had in the fight against Caer Llion.

He had no idea she had chosen to lead Richard and Bran.

"Damn creature," Richard growled as he cleaned her arm. "Should have been more ready for this. I just didn't imagine the beast could cross the distance from Caer Glain so quickly."

"You could not have known, Rick," Deirdre said softly, gritting her teeth. "A bodach is a formidable creature. Besides, I know this area and even I was misled. It is not your fault. That belongs to someone else."

"Plantagenet," he said. "At least it is gone."

"Who were those men?"

"Trouble from our world. They are gone now though."

"You have a knack for protecting us."

"Juding by your back, not enough, apparently," he said.

"I appreciate it," Deirdre whispered. "And you."

Richard did not respond, still focused intently on her arm. The two were mere inches apart. Deirdre had never wanted to reach out to someone more. The tickle of his shaggy hair on her bare shoulder. The musky odor of travel emanating from him. The act of his caring enough to see her wounds cleaned, to touch her. It all made him more desirable.

Before she knew it, Deirdre was leaning forward, seeking out his lips.

Richard gripped her stronger as she fell into him. Her lips brushed his briefly before he jerked back suddenly, obviously figuring out she did not faint from the pain but instead had other ideas. She looked deep into his eyes. He stared back. She saw the past and present of the knight mingle there and the former win.

"We must be going," Richard said, standing.

"It will take us most of the day to cross the plains," Deirdre said, cursing inwardly at her weakness and readjusting the remnants of her clothing. "We will be exposed unless we revisit the outer folds of Dryvyd Wood and take the long way."

"Circling the plains will take us an additional day we cannot afford," Richard said, looking away from her. "Best we get a move on."

After Bran finished packing their bedrolls, Richard mounted Lyrian. Bran and Deirdre mounted their steeds as well, and together they rode through the bars of trees and into the plains beyond. The day had dawned as those before it, blue sky littered with tiny white clouds, the world heating as the sun climbed. Rolling grasses as tall as Willowyn's legs swished around them, bleached golden by the hot summer. Tiny birds erupted from their business as the Rhedewyr startled them into the skies. On their distant left, the outline of short mountains sat on the horizon like bruised lumps; on their right, the green stain of the Dryvyd Wood grew, an invitation back to the place Deirdre had met Richard.

The day progressed and with it more pain. Even the memory of the brief kiss could not dampen Deirdre's burns. With the last few trees long behind them though, a growing uneasiness also built up in her. She felt exposed, as if she were being watched. It was the first time she had been out in the open since actively choosing to defy Caer Llion and an uneasiness grew. Occasionally the group passed ruins of weathered stone foundations, Annwn slowly reclaiming the castles and keeps men or fey had built, but furtive movement caught her eye and disappeared just as quickly. Richard led, never looking back at her. Arrow Jack cruised high above them, ever vigilant, and Snedeker rode on her shoulder, still unsure of his new role as guide to the Heliwr.

Halfway through the day, after crossing the thin ribbon of the Tywi River, a dark stain filled the horizon, coming toward them from the south with an unsettling rapidity.

"What is that?" Bran asked.

"Deirdre?"

"I do not know," she said. "Nothing Unseelie though, not in the daylight."

As the mass grew near, swarming individuals became evident, some a hundred feet in the air, others hovering at the height of the grass.

"Fairies," Richard said darkly.

"That is quite odd," Snedeker noted.

"What do you mean?"

"What he means is what comes our way is a whole clan of fairies," Deirdre said. "Something encroached upon their home to make them leave."

"And they are obviously not afraid of us," Richard observed.

The fairies drew closer and deviated from their path, slowing as they flew nearer to halt altogether before Richard and his companions—some settling to the grassy plains below, others continuing to hover high in the air as if on watch. Other than being of a similar size, they were not at all like Snedeker. Instead of twigs and leaves, the tiny newcomers appeared to be made from bits of the prairie, with bodies of straw, arms and legs of greener needle grass and plains flowers. Wings of incandescent gold held each fairy aloft.

One broke from the rest and flew straight for Richard.

"I am Richard McAllister," the knight said, as the fairy stopped in the air.

"Grallic of the Grastolls."

"Where do you go in such numbers, Grallic?"

"North, into territory less hostile," the fairy answered in a dry voice. He had a short beard of grayish moss, and the wheat comprising his body was crinkled with age. "Where 'tis safe."

"Dark creatures roam the world," Richard agreed.

"One was out here in the plains," the fairy sniffed. "Scouts crossed it in the foothills as they sought a new home for my clan. 'Tis now gone though."

"Not gone. Slain!" Snedeker interrupted. "Killed by these knights here."

"Knights?" Grallic asked, surprised. "I see no armor, no weapons of any kind except what the redheaded lady there carries."

"A knight of a different sort," Richard answered.

"That is well," the fairy said. "Ye have an Oakwell with ye."

"Snedeker is one of our guides."

"Driven from his clan, more like," Grallic snorted. "A fairy without a clan is a fairy who has betrayed his clan."

"The fairy is of no consequence," Richard asserted, cutting off what Snedeker was already beginning to say. "From where do you hail?"

"The area north of Caer Llion," Grallic grumbled. "The plains are full of men, men with their iron and anger. They camped on our lands, unsettled our home, and we had no choice but to leave. Hidden we have remained for centuries but no longer. Now we flee for our lives."

"How many men did you see?" Bran asked.

"Like the sea," the fairy said. "Do not go that way. 'Tis very dangerous."

"A war comes to the land, one like none of us have ever seen," Richard warned. "In a matter of days, if not sooner, the dying will replace the living. You are wise to leave."

"Wisdom has nothing to do with it," Grallic said. "Farewell to ye and yer clan."

"And to you, Grallic of the Grastolls."

Grallic gave Snedeker a dark look before flying around the Rhedewyr and heading toward the Carn Cavall. The swarm followed their leader. After a few moments, they vanished as though they never had been.

"What was that about, Snedeker?" Bran asked. "You told me the Firewillows came after you. You never told me why your clan kicked you out."

The fairy crossed his arms and ignored the question.

"He has never told me either," Deirdre said. "Says it is none of my business."

"Pigcrack right, it's not!" Snedeker shot back.

"I bet more than anything that this fairy deserved being kicked out of his clan," Richard said. "Guide or no guide, sent by the Lady or not, when it is their neck on the line, a fairy will never do what is right or courageous. Remember that, Bran."

Snedeker looked away into the distance, ignoring the knight.

Richard clicked Lyrian forward. The others followed. The plains grew humid as early afternoon pressed in. They passed down the length of the Tawy River, the waterway wider than the Tywi River but slower moving through the grasslands. The odors of the plains mixing with the musk of the horses settled in Deirdre's nose. Sweat trickled into her clothing, uncomfortably, but it was the burn that worsened, the heat from the fire seared into her feverish body. She kept a wary eye on the horizon, dreading what it may bring. A sporadic crow or prairie falcon circled, the only life they had seen beyond the fairies.

Arrow Jack kept to himself, an untiring scout. As the day's light purpled into sunset, the tall golden grass receded slowly and became greener, hearkening a new change to the land.

When the emerald smudge of Dryvyd Wood had devoured half the sun, Deirdre brought Willowyn alongside Lyrian.

"What is your world like, Rick?"

Richard raised an eyebrow, surprised by the question. "The only word I can think of is *busy*," he answered. "It is filled with people rushing from home to work and back again. It isn't like

Annwn, where people live off of the land—maybe it used to be a thousand years ago, but no longer. Magic has no place there, as it so obviously does here, and machines are everywhere. Everything happens at such a fast pace that often people of my world don't appreciate what they've just passed. People don't believe in . . . any of this." He waved his arm around. "Annwn is a myth only found in Arthurian tales and other such stories."

"The Forever King," Deirdre said. "*Not* a myth. We still recount the history behind his war with the Mordred, Medraut, and his other exploits in the Misty Isles. The people of your world seem to have a hard time believing things they cannot see."

"Very true."

"Sounds scary," she said. "I could not live that way."

"I used to be like them," Richard said. "Before Myrddin Emrys ruined my life, I was a student at a university. He proved those legends to be all too true. Now a day doesn't pass that I wish I could still be ignorant like the rest in my world."

Deirdre turned away. "Do you have a . . . woman?"

Richard looked away, the line along his jaw hardening. "Once I did," he said simply. "Long ago."

"What happened to her?" she asked.

Richard ignored the question. Deirdre thought he was avoiding it—and maybe he was—until she realized his interest in the horizon. In the distance, a column of diffuse gray smoke broadened toward the cloudless sky. She knew what it likely signaled and its frightening import.

"What is it? A wildfire?" Bran questioned.

"No, a far worse animal," Richard said. "See how the column has such a wide base?"

Bran nodded.

"That is smoke from hundreds of cook fires," Deirdre said. "And thousands more men sitting around them."

Arrow Jack cruised overhead, screeching, to land on a blasted tree in front of them.

Richard pointed out what the merlin warned. Just over the top of the plains, giant pointed structures of white, gold, and crimson erupted from the far-off line of emerald grass, their total height lost in the distance. They were the top of massive tents. War tents, Deirdre knew. The tents, coupled with the smoke, indicated what the Seelie Court and its allies were getting into.

"What are they for?" Bran asked.

"Tournament tents," Deirdre replied. "For the games of jousting and arms Philip is fond of watching. It is how he picks his guard."

"No longer," Richard disagreed. "That time has come and gone. Philip has chosen his men and they now cover the plains, waiting for whatever he has planned. Smoke that thick only comes from an enormous host, and we must give it a wide berth."

"If what you think is true and the numbers are that large, then Philip has amassed all of Annwn to Caer Llion," Deirdre surmised. "They could not have come from southern Annwn alone. The men of the northern cities have joined him here. Philip must be planning a battle of epic proportions to empty his strongholds in the north."

"Why no scouts?" Bran asked.

"You don't need scouts when an army is as large as that one." Richard squinted. "It seems we best turn westward."

The tents faded from view as they headed for the border of Dryvyd Wood, avoiding the pillar of smoke. The last dregs of the day swathed them in stale light, and the promise of night solidified as they continued to ride south and west. Insects buzzed and sang to one another, an old song for a new night. Salted air like that found on the coast washed over them suddenly on a soft breeze, reminding Deirdre of trips to the ocean when her mother still lived. Stars twinkled into being. The coming night would be pleasant; it would help her forget the pain that ravaged every jostle upon Willowyn.

Regardless, she kept an eye to the east where the smoke faded into darkness; it was hard to believe a host as large and lethal as the one she knew existed waited mere miles away.

When they crested a rolling hill, even Deirdre, who had been raised around hosts of men, was ill prepared for the sight.

Caer Llion unfolded like a dark promise, a monolithic structure lording over the group from a purpling horizon. Dozens of towers stabbed the sky, connected by numerous parapets at varying levels, and a high wall as tall as Mochdrev Reach protected its innards, unyielding. Rectangles of yellow light flickered from top rooms, alive with inhabitants. At the castle's base, a town of smaller buildings spread like beggars before a king, pushing up against the wall as if in need. To the north, hundreds and hundreds of giant campfires danced until they vanished over a rise where more assuredly awaited and each undoubtedly had dozens of men surrounding them. It was an awe-inspiring, terrible sight.

"Caer Llion," Richard said.

"Now what?" Bran asked.

Richard dismounted. "Time we leave Deirdre. And time for *me* to find our way in."

"How are you going to do that?" Deirdre asked.

"I am the Heliwr."

"So?"

"Once, in the early days when Bran's father was the Heliwr, a banshee slipped by me and into Seattle," Richard said. "Charles found a patch of bare earth and jammed the Dark Thorn into it. After a few moments he came out of his reverie and knew the direction the woman had gone, up toward Capitol Hill. It didn't take him long but he found her and ended her threat." Richard paused. "I have that same power. To find things hidden from me. Like an entrance. Like a creature. Like an artifact. As long as they aren't masked by magic. I only hope I am capable of doing it and that Philip has not guarded his entrances with spells."

"At least we aren't going through the front gate," Bran mumbled. "That would seem to be pretty asinine, if I do say so."

"I agree," Deirdre said. "The front is no good."

"Something else then," Richard said. "If I find an entrance."

"I am going with you, Heliwr," Snedeker said.

"You cannot," Richard responded. "Caer Llion has been warded by a series of curse tablet spells for centuries, placed at intervals in its walls. These won't allow Tuatha de Dannan entrance. How do you think the fey folk haven't been able to infiltrate and end the reign of the king? They can't. The moment one does, Philip is alerted. So no, not going to happen, fairy."

"Now, listen here, thornstick," Snedeker said. "I do not pla—"

"We'll be back soon," Richard said to Deirdre, ignoring the fairy.

Conflicting emotions warred in Deirdre. A part of her wanted to go and aid the knights despite no one caring for the Rhedewyr. Another part of her knew she would be worthless as a companion due to her throbbing burn and fever that grew within her.

"Be quick," she pleaded simply.

"Travel west to the outskirts of Dryvyd Wood. Hide just within the trees. It isn't far. Care for the animals," Richard said. "We won't be long. Bran, with me."

Bran gave Deirdre an encouraging smile before Richard traveled into the shadow toward the great castle, Arrow Jack disappearing in the distance with them. Soon Deirdre was alone with Snedeker to locate where their camp would be that night.

"You should have told me about guiding the Heliwr, Snedeker," she said, still a bit rankled the fairy hadn't shared everything.

"It felt . . . wrong, Red," Snedeker said. "The Lady would not have approved."

"So now you grow mindful of others' feelings?"

Snedeker turned away from her, as he always did when he didn't want to talk. Deirdre returned the favor. After a long walk she settled on a spot where several fir trees and mulberry bushes hid them from the plains. She cared for Willowyn and the others. She undid her bedroll. It would be a cool night, but she knew she couldn't build a fire. With the stars winking overhead and Snedeker a faint outline on a branch above, Deirdre rolled into her bed the best she could given her wounds and stared up at the heavens.

"You like him a great deal, do you not?" the fairy said.

"Who?"

"The Heliwr. Richard McAllister. I have never seen you like this. You stare at him constantly. You act like you have never seen a man before."

"I guess I like him. Yes. I do."

"Ardall does not like that," the fairy said. "Not one bit."

"The boy is infatuated, nothing more."

"Like you?"

Deirdre lay there, thinking. He had a point. She had tried to kiss Richard only to have him pull away. She had asked questions and received short answers. She had left her duty as lady of Mochdrev Reach in favor of helping Richard complete his role, and he hadn't so much as asked or said thank you. Bran Ardall had called him a broken man; Deirdre had said he wouldn't always be. Did she know that for sure? She could not help being drawn to him, but was it too much to hope that he would be whole again? What would it take for that to happen?

Could the shade of her mother have been wrong?

Could Deirdre?

"Red," Snedeker hissed. "Listen."

Deirdre broke her reverie, straining to hear what Snedeker did.

"I hear nothing," she said.

Then she felt it. It wasn't so much a sound as it was a periodic trembling in the ground. Something approached, something big, moving toward them from deep within the heart of the wild Dryvyd Forest. She got out of her bedroll and slid her sword free of its scabbard, backing against the tree Snedeker had taken as his bed. Long moments passed.

The shaking grew stronger until finally a rustle of limbs and movement gave way to reveal what approached. It stilled her breath. In the darkness she could just make out the outline of something mammoth, man shaped, far taller than she or any Fomorian she had seen, and as black as the night around it. Its features were hidden from her, the stars too weak, but the smell of fetid fish and oily tar came to her, pungent on the night air. Fear hammered through her veins but she held her ground, ready to give as good as she got.

"Lady Deirdre Rhys of Mochdrev Reach?"

"Who are you? What do you want?" Deirdre demanded, sword still held at the ready.

"We must speak, you and I," the monstrosity rumbled gently. "And a fairer woman to talk with I have not met. The stars have aligned this night and I will certainly make the most of it."

Deirdre already liked the newcomer.

"Why must we speak?"

"First, put that pig sticker away," the hulk said. "Before I take it from you and make a beautiful woman look quite a fool."

Chapter 28

Richard strode through the darkness, Bran a mere step behind.

They had been walking for half an hour, the lay of the land easy to navigate even in the night. The last remnants of the day's insects sang, the only witnesses to their passing. It was a gorgeous evening, the last colors of the sunset behind them, but Richard ignored all of it for the most part. What was to come sat tantamount in his mind; what was to come would require every magic ability he had learned over the years.

The memory of the attempted kiss by Deirdre distracted him, though, like a terrible thought that would not go away. The woman annoyed Richard. It had nothing to do with her specifically. Deirdre had shown herself to be an asset when it came to navigating Annwn, possessed of a keen intellect and a desire to see her future unfold as she wished, not what others wanted. Feisty in a way that Richard had lost with age, she hadn't backed down from any fight. She could have any man she wished.

It made no sense that she would want him.

But mostly Richard hated how she made him feel wanted when he deserved nothing from anyone ever again. Not after

Elizabeth. Not after her death.

He focused on the moment, growling inwardly at the whole situation.

"What are you thinking?" Bran inquired beside him.

"Mind your business," Richard said, more harshly than he intended.

"About the kiss, right?"

Richard stopped and turned to Bran. Even in the failing light he could see the jealousy burning in the boy's eyes.

"That's right, I saw it," Bran said defiantly. "Sent me to pack our things just to get some free time with her? How noble, *knight*."

In a rush of anger, Richard stepped before Bran, desiring nothing more than to bloody the idiot. It had been long in coming. When Bran didn't back down, the passion in his eyes not diminishing and almost pushing for a fight, Richard shoved him sharply aside and continued onward.

"I will only say this *once*," Richard snarled, striding away. "I am not interested in Deirdre. Not now, not ever. I am here to do a job. As you should be. Not to find a wife. Not to find a girlfriend. Not to make a new friend. Bring this up again and we are going to have a go of it. Seriously." He stopped and looked deep into Bran's eyes. "Understand?"

"Then stay away from her," Bran said with conviction.

Richard stalked away. "Youth knows all follies," he said under his breath.

"What did you say?"

"Nothing," he replied, shaking his head, as the boy followed. "Just ensure you are focused on what is to come. Thinking about her will not aid us this night. Philip Plantagenet does *not* care about her, and he certainly doesn't care about your feelings. Or about how you feel about me. One distraction can lead to our deaths. Make sure that does not happen."

After several tense minutes where neither of them spoke, Richard stopped. Caer Llion loomed before him, the outline of the enormous castle blacker than the sky around it. Richard felt impossibly close, exposed, the reality of his plan all too near and far too real. The bustle from the army camped to the north drifted to him, a thousand different sounds more than willing to end his life. If Bran kept his head about him and Richard could keep them hidden long enough, the chance that they would succeed increased from dismal to marginal.

"How are we going to get into Caer Llion?" Bran asked, breaking the silence.

"There are many ways into a fortress. Now is as good a time as any to find one," Richard said, stopping to call the Dark Thorn. "I might as well learn how to do this. We know Philip has some kind of seeing glass that aided him in going after you. I will focus on that."

"A glass, huh?"

"Yes, likely a mirror. Very powerful though."

"And finding it will show you where Philip is?"

"I don't know what I will do if face to face with him," Richard admitted. "Now be quiet. Let me do this."

Richard gripped the wood of the Dark Thorn, assured by its warmth. He had no idea what he was doing but failing to try would lead them nowhere. He drove the staff into the grassland and, with both hands wrapped about its might, Richard closed his eyes and concentrated on what he knew, bringing forth images of a nebulous reflective surface bearing awesome power. He focused on it to sense what was hidden. It didn't take long. As he did so, a part of the staff's magic met him halfway and tugged at him, answering his call, aiding his need. Richard trusted it, went willingly, and flowed out of his body. The magic carried him away from Bran. Drawn like a lodestone, he zoomed over the land in silence, speeding toward the western side of Caer Llion.

With the path discovered, Richard let the magic die and came back to himself.

"There," he said, pointing. "Some kind of opening into the castle, into its depths. Water. And a tunnel near the back of the castle. That's all I saw."

"What? Now?" Bran said. "But it's night!"

"Best time for us to attempt this."

"But we can't see!"

"Yet," Richard said. "Ready to learn a bit of magic?"

"Are you serious?"

"Focus on the ground and what you *cannot* see there," Richard ordered. "Just like you call Arondight into being, believe you can see what is there."

Bran concentrated. "I am."

"Stay focused on that and repeat after me—*yn argel*."

"*Yn argel*," Bran said once.

A flush of heat passed through Richard just as he knew it did Bran. It was gone just as quickly. The darkness drew back, as if a bright full moon had suddenly risen to highlight the world in silver. Every detail of the night sprang into sharp relief. When he looked at Caer Llion, even the darkest areas were in view.

"See now?" Richard asked.

"Wow," Bran murmured.

"You just called your first spell into being," Richard said, already striding toward the castle in the distance. "Simple but effective. Now let's get this over with, boy."

Richard hurried forward with Bran chasing behind, the new vision etching the night in relief. Caer Llion loomed and grew larger the closer they got, the walls stretching toward the stars as if trying to encase them. The sounds of drunken revelry, the clinking of armor, and the smells of cooking meat grew stronger, all too close for comfort. But no guards met them; no warning shattered the night. A rhythmic pounding reverberated through the air and ground, and Richard realized it was the crashing of waves against the rock of Annwn.

As they grew nearer the castle, the ground softened and muck sucked at their boots. A rivulet of trickling water soaked the sod, disappearing over the cliff edge.

"We follow this?" Bran whispered.

"Look."

A small half-circle opened in the castle wall where a grate emitted the sluice of water from Caer Llion.

"In we go," Richard directed.

After looking for security spells or curse tablets created

explicitly to keep people out, Richard tore the grate off, flung it aside in distaste, and crawled inside the gaping hole. Bran climbed in after him. The ceiling was low, the wall of Caer Llion thick. Water cascaded over his feet, icy as it soaked into his boots; their sloshing footfalls made the only sound. After a few steps they broke through the wall into a shallow subterranean cave, worn down by water, the air chilly after the long day of humidity. They pulled themselves carefully upward over a gently rising slope of damp, slippery rock and moss, the grade simple but the way difficult. Richard repressed a shiver. With the star shine absent, the darkness was far more complete. Without the spell, they would not have been able to see anything, let alone a way in.

The cavern meandered into the bowels of Caer Llion, twisting as Richard and Bran ventured deeper. The knight was unrelenting, moving ahead with a purpose that left Bran struggling to keep up.

Gaining the slope from where the water trickled, Richard froze.

The chamber he peered into was enormous. Stretching in a circle, a flat lake of black water spread like an ice rink made of obsidian, the bottom lost beneath its reflective surface. No ripple broke its stillness. The only interruption to the placid plane was a pyramid of stone in the middle of the cavern, erupting from the depths. Yellow light from a breach opposite where they stood flickered sentience, a promise of guards or worse.

An object of some kind glimmered from the pyramid of stones in the lake, too far away for Richard to discern it fully.

Richard shot Bran a raised eyebrow before moving on. He kept next to the wall where footing still seemed available, the water soaking through his boots. Bran followed. As they grew closer, Richard could make out a shore littered with worn boulders beneath torchlight and, past them, a passage vanishing upward into Caer Llion.

On their right, another tunnel disappeared from the lake, one that had been carved deep into the rock of the world.

Having circumvented the lake, Richard stepped to the gravelly shore on cat's paws.

He yearned to call the Dark Thorn.

"Where to now?" Bran whispered.

Richard searched the gloom, perplexed. The vision from the Dark Thorn had been completed and yet he saw no mirror or other device in the cavern. He was about to express as much when faint breathing stopped him.

"Who . . . is there?" a ragged voice croaked.

Richard suppressed calling the staff and lashing out as the lump of rock at his feet moved. An emaciated face camouflaged in grime shakily lifted toward him, eye sockets deep pits, their orbs removed forcibly at some point. The figure reached blindly for him, as if asking for aid.

"Get back!" Bran roared, spinning around.

Before Richard could even respond, a flurry of steel ringing to life screeched through the cavern as four soldiers detached from the shadows, confronting them with weapons drawn. They wore Templar Knight garb and sneers of hatred. A leather bag hung like a backpack from each set of shoulders, a tube running from the pouch to within inches of the warriors' mouths.

The Dark Thorn flamed to life in his hand, sudden light flooding the chamber even as Bran called Arondight.

"Surrender. There is nowhere for you to go," a grizzled soldier ordered.

Richard gave his answer. The fire of the Dark Thorn exploded into the midst of the Templars, white hot and angry. The magic burned like an animal unleashed, casting three of the warriors aside like a battering ram as their leader leapt away. The men flew through the air to crash against the cavern. Bones snapped. Screams of pain followed. The leader shielded his face with his forearms as he rolled to bring his sword against the knight.

Angry that they had been discovered so easily, Richard parried the blade, and with the deft motion of someone who has warred for a lifetime, he spun and jabbed the end of the Dark Thorn into the guard's throat, shattering his larynx. The man toppled over backward, clutching at his neck and at a tube that lead into the leather bag on his back.

"Where do we go?" Bran hissed.

"This is where my vision told us to go!"

"Well, try again! Now! Before more guards come!"

Just as Richard was about to drive the staff into the shore, the soldier he had just bested regained his feet, sucking on the tube. Surprise filled the knight. The man should have been dead but instead he appeared whole once more, his throat healed.

A tight grin spread across his face. He raised his sword and charged again, screaming hate. The other warriors who Richard thought were shattered against the stone of the cavern also struggled to their feet, their bodies working as though no damage had been done to them, each man sucking down the contents of the bags on their backs.

Putting it all together far too late, it dawned on Richard suddenly what the glimmer in the center of the lake had been.

They were in great danger.

As were two worlds.

"What have you done, Plantagenet?" Richard breathed.

Bewildered, Bran sent the fire of Arondight into the soldier ranks. It burned at their clothing, but the men beneath were untouched, fighting through the hot affront as though the flames were merely a warm wind. Still sucking on the tubes, they raised their weapons to attack.

Within moments, Richard and Bran were put on the defensive, fighting for their lives.

"My pretties," a voice cackled loudly. "Ye've returned to me."

The Cailleach emerged into the cavern from the glowing passage, covered in filth. "Came back to me, ye did," she laughed and made a lewd gesture. "Want what dat wife could not give ye, eh knight?"

Richard maintained the Dark Thorn despite the guilty memories rising to greet him.

"Best ye stay put," the Cailleach intoned, her hands weaving.

Richard found he couldn't take a step to confront the witch. Ice crawled from the damp shore up and into the waterlogged boots about his feet, crystallizing him into stasis. The same happened to Bran.

"Richard!" Bran screamed.

"Now, now, younglin', no need to worry," the Cailleach purred. "I want ye alive!"

As Bran fought to free himself, Richard sent the fire of the Dark Thorn over his boots, hoping to free himself, but the ice of the witch barely melted. The warriors bore down on the two companions, surrounding them with steel. Both Richard and Bran sent their magic into the soldiers but they weren't fazed by it, the flames washing over them as the contents of the bags kept the Templar Knights from any harm.

Two of them fought Richard to the ground, binding him with sheer strength, punching the breath from his lungs and leaving him gasping.

The Dark Thorn disappeared from his fingers.

As the knight struggled, he watched the boy fight like a tiger. Bran sent fire into the faces of the warriors, slashing at them with his rune-encrusted blade. It did no good. The soldiers grabbed at him, also bearing him down to the cavern floor, but he didn't stop fighting, stabbing. Snarling rage, the youngest of the soldiers who had been impaled by Arondight brought his broadsword down on the prostate Bran.

"No!" Richard screamed.

The boy howled in pain, his left hand severed at the wrist. Arondight vanished instantly.

The soldiers swarmed Bran to the hard rock of the cavern then, the young knight gone mostly limp, sobbing and cradling his ruined arm.

"Do not damage them much, me pretties," the witch said gleefully. "The play-king will owe me a few children for dis."

"Leave the boy be!"

A sharp cuff on the back of his head sent Richard spinning.

He could not believe what he had discovered. What Philip Plantagenet had done. It no longer mattered though. Darkness wrapped its nets over him, tightening about his awareness as it pulled him down, stealing every care he ever had, until even the fact he had failed fled him.

"Dis will be over soon, cully," the Cailleach crowed.

Unwilling to believe what Philip had done with the most important relic in the history of mankind, Richard fought his slide into the unknown.

Until he became one with it.

Chapter 29

Wet Seattle in his nose, Richard enjoyed the sudden sunshine.

The squalls of the late afternoon moved east, leaving patches of baby blue sky among blackened thunderheads broken apart by the setting sun. Smith Tower, its square heights glowing white, stood across the street from Richard among a backdrop of more modern skyscrapers reaching to the heavens. People bustled by, running after buses and cabs, their workday finished. Night came upon the Pacific Northwest with a fast glove.

He breathed in the damp air, exhilarated. It felt like a long time since he had been this happy, and he whistled it into the early evening as he waited.

The velvet-lined box bearing his promise waited in his jeans pocket.

"Rick, why do you always wait for me?"

Richard turned. In the day's final sunshine stood a woman of medium height with flawless skin, her black hair accenting a face of high cheekbones and blue eyes. She smiled at him; it was inviting in its simplicity.

It felt like he had not seen her in years.

"That's easy, Elizabeth," he said, and kissed her.

She returned his kiss after her initial surprise, her lips soft, her tongue warm and inviting as he breathed her in. It was a simple pleasure but one he hadn't grown tired of over the last two years, one he knew he would never grow tired of.

Elizabeth broke the kiss off reluctantly and stared into his eyes. "How was your day at the store?"

"The same," he replied, their fingers interlocking to begin the walk down into Pioneer Square. "Tourists looking for the newest best seller. Merle would make more money if he began selling novels seen on the *New York Times* list—like those by Stephen King or Terry Brooks. The old books he sells don't garner much interest, especially from tourists."

"Do you think he honestly cares about making money from the store?" Elizabeth asked, laughing.

Richard grinned back. He guessed not. Being a wizard had its benefits. When one could sense the future, adjust stock market money in the present, and know the outcome, there was no shortage of funds.

Over the Puget Sound the day ended, the sun sinking toward the Olympic Mountains, casting the sky in pinks and ever-darkening purples. Pushing his anxiety down and hoping what he planned would go smoothly, Richard stared at the sunset, perplexed. Déjà vu tugged at him. He could not remember the last time he had seen a similar sunset, but he could not shake the feeling he had already seen it.

"A beautiful evening," Elizabeth said.

Richard nodded, not sure what to say. With his other hand he wrapped his fingers about the box. A light nervous sweat broke out over his body.

He was a knight, but he had never been so scared in his life.

The slope flattened and the couple entered Pioneer Square, the century-old buildings of red brick illuminated by the soft glow of yellow lamps flickering on. Richard tried to nonchalantly guide Elizabeth where he wanted to go—not back to their shared apartment but to the odd little triangle where Yesler Way and First

Avenue met, at the heart of oldest Seattle. He floated as if above himself, his feet barely touching the sidewalk. As he grew closer, Richard could feel the portal beneath his feet less than a block away, thrumming with the magic that bound both his world and Annwn together.

When they came to the triangle, with its large iron pergola, Tlingit totem pole, and towering ancient maple trees, he gestured to one of the benches that offered tourists and the homeless a place to relax.

"Let's sit."

"Okay . . . ?" she agreed curiously.

He sat next to her, his palms damp. He suddenly felt oddly solid again now that he was sitting. "This is where we met, remember?"

"Doesn't seem so long ago, does it?"

"Feels like yesterday."

She cast him a worried smile. "Is everything all right?"

As he slid off the bench onto his bended knee, he stared into her eyes and pulled the jewelry box from his pocket.

"I have loved you from the moment we met, here in this very place, a grad student giving directions to a new girl in town," Richard said, the practiced words spilling out of him "When you said yes to a drink, I had no idea how lucky my life was to become. Now I do, and I want that luck to last to the end of my days."

He paused, regrouping his shaky voice, and opened the box for her to see the glimmering diamond set in a simple band of polished white gold.

"Will you be my wife, Elizabeth Anne Welles?"

The glow from her cheeks spread over her entire face. Eyes shimmering with tears that were threatening to fall, she nodded vigorously.

"Yes," she said, smiling brighter. "Yes I will, Richard McAllister."

Fumbling in pleasurable panic, Richard took the engagement ring and slid it over her finger. Almost before he had finished, she pulled him up by his shirt and kissed him tenderly, joyful tears now staining his cheeks as well as her own. The dampness that had broken out over his body gone, Richard embraced the moment and the love of his life, the fear he had had replaced by giddy completion.

As the colors of the sunset faded to black, the two intentioned just sat and reveled in the moment, watching people lost in their own thoughts and dreams walk by.

Elizabeth stared at the ring. "It is odd, not having any family to call and tell."

"I am your family now."

"Merle will want to know, I'm sure."

Richard looked away, toward where Old World Tales presented its wares to the public. Merle had warned him about falling in love, marrying, trying to have a family. The life of a knight in any age of the world was difficult, made more so by connections to loved ones put in danger by the close proximity of creatures that would see the knight and those close to him dead. Merle worried about the growing relationship between Richard and Elizabeth and how it would put her life at risk, but it was ultimately Richard who had made the choice to marry. Merle could do nothing to prevent it.

"You would give me anything, right?" she asked suddenly.

Richard nodded, hearing the earnestness in her voice. "You know I would."

"Well, I've always wondered . . ."

He smiled. "Yes?"

"I've always wondered what it would be like to hold the weapon you carry."

"You know I can't do that," Richard said, suddenly serious.

Elizabeth leaned closer to him, her blue eyes mesmerizing, hypnotic. She smelled like lilacs and vanilla, intoxicating. Fire stirred in his loins like he had never felt before, electric and passionate. He grew dizzy, lost deeper in her eyes with every breath. The triangle and greater Seattle dropped away, fading into a gray soup. Only Elizabeth remained, needful of his full attention, and he desperately wanted to give her anything and everything her heart desired.

He had never felt like this before—drunken yet functional, wanton but paralyzed.

The power of her eyes compelled him, made him want to obey.

As soon as he was about to answer her request and draw

Arondight from the ether, caution screamed. Something was wrong. The memory of Merle warning against allowing anyone to touch Arondight surfaced and stayed his hand, fighting his impulse to give her what she requested. It dampened the power of her gaze, cleared his mind enough for him to think about what he did. If anyone other than Richard could take the sword away from him, it would no longer be his, his tenure as a knight ended.

"Darling, give me the weapon you possess," she purred. "It is time for me to understand what it means to be you."

The same compelling force rose again, fighting his will.

He wanted to make love to her.

He needed to do all things for her.

The warning in his heart disappeared, and he brought his hand up to call the weapon that bound him in knighthood.

But as he began to bridge the worlds to call it, the face of another Elizabeth superimposed itself over the heat and need of the Elizabeth sitting next to him. The new Elizabeth had the same eyes, but they were loving and lacked the passionate fire that accosted him. Somewhere in his depths, the memory of a girl teasingly smiling at him amidst hundreds of stacked books on her day off coalesced and woke a part of him that had been swept away.

None of the avarice or commanding nature pummeled him; she was pure and clean and everything he remembered about her.

Remembered? Past tense? But she is right here.

"Elizabeth?" he murmured.

Grasping onto the more real image of Elizabeth like a safety line, the life Richard had forgotten came swirling into him with painful clarity. He fought against the stirrings of his blood, awakening to what had been done to him; he wondered for a second why he sat in Pioneer Park with Elizabeth as a rising past threatened to tear him apart. Then it all came flooding back—his quest in Annwn, Bran Ardall and the Dark Thorn, the Queen Morrigan and her war, the dragons, the fairy, Philip and John Lewis Hugo.

The death of Elizabeth.

"I want you," Elizabeth said from the bench. "Give me your knight's weapon so I may understand your work better."

Anger like a flooding fire burned away any confusion that remained. Arondight flared to life in his hands. Lusty greed filled Elizabeth's eyes at sight of the blade, a dark need he had never seen her have in the time he had known her. All of the people around him ignored the sword as if it didn't exist.

"No," he defied.

Her blue eyes, once so inviting, turned as hard as stone.

"Give it to me," she commanded.

Richard stood, lifting the weapon once ordained to him but no longer his. He did not hesitate. As part of him screamed resistance, a scene he had replayed over and over in his mind for years but had never come to terms with came to the fore, falling out in agonizing slow motion.

Not again!

Elizabeth grabbed for the hilt of Arondight.

Richard reacted on instinct.

Rage at what had been done to his mind drove him as he plunged the long blade deep into her chest, all of his strength and weight behind it.

Shock fell over Elizabeth as Arondight disappeared into her body, driven deep by righteous wrath—the hilt coming to rest against her breast, the blade exiting her back, slicked in crimson.

Pioneer Park and Seattle wavered like a mirage and vanished.

The light in the blue eyes he had loved so much grew dark, changing to emerald and elongating to a foreign facsimile of the woman he had loved, even as the Caer Llion dungeon became clear, cold, and real. Arondight changed to the Dark Thorn, which lay driven through the dead body of a thin korrigan in simple green forest garb, the staff's light accenting the battered iron shackles that chained his wrists and ankles to the stone of the castle in which he was imprisoned.

"Witch," an unseen man growled.

The Cailleach, who had also been similarly hidden next to a lone Fomorian giant, placed her spotted hands to the stone of the wall, mumbling archaic words Richard could only guess at.

The walls of the cell glimmered white.

The Dark Thorn disappeared instantly from his grasp.

"The tablet is restored," the Cailleach muttered.

"Leave us," John Lewis Hugo ordered, stepping from the shadows. The ancient witch frowned darkly before giving Richard a lurid wink. She left through the cell door.

"I told Philip you would not submit," John Lewis Hugo said, his ruined face glimmering red in the wavering torchlight. "Told him you would not succumb to the wiles and illusions."

"Give the staff back," Richard said. "And I'll prove you wrong one more time."

"You are not worthy," John Lewis Hugo snickered. "Have never *been* worthy."

Richard hung from his chains. "You think I don't know that."

"Still, it is remarkable you possess the Dark Thorn, the weapon of the Unfettered Knight," Philip's advisor observed. "How did you come by the staff? I was under the impression it was meant for the boy, not you. Not you at all."

Richard wanted to laugh. "Just lucky, I guess."

"Did the wizard err, I wonder?" John Lewis Hugo said.

"Hasn't he always."

"Killing your wife the way you did, killing the love of your life with the sword carried by Lancelot, arguably one of the most romantic and heroic men history has ever recorded," John Lewis Hugo prodded, grinning. "Poetic tragedy, would you not agree? Even the wizard would agree in his own false sense of irony."

"I didn't know it was her," Richard said, mostly to himself.

John Lewis Hugo stared hard at Richard. Memories from a day long gone but all too fresh stabbed the knight's chest. A korrigan similar to the one that lay dead on the cold dungeon floor had slipped by him. It had taken him hours to track it down to just outside of the apartment building where he lived with Elizabeth. Sneaking upon the creature with the lethal calm the knight had embraced, he slew it with Arondight before anyone on the street had an inkling of what had happened. Before incinerating the small korrigan to ash as was his custom, he knelt to watch the embers of life dim unto death.

But as he watched, the features of the fey creature melted away, revealing a human woman beneath. Panic seized him, tearing at his heart. Nothing would be as it had been. The glamour that had fooled him dissolved completely.

It was not a fey creature Richard had run Arondight through.

It had been Elizabeth.

"That is the problem I have with your world," John Lewis Hugo drawled. "Its degradation. Its unaware peoples. Its lack of moral compass. You did not know because you killed first to ask questions later. Wisdom has never been successful in such ways."

"What do *you* know of wisdom?" Richard growled.

"*You* are at the heart of that wisdom, puppet."

"You intend to invade Seattle then," Richard said, hanging his head. "I have seen your army. I have seen the desire written on you."

"That I will not tell you. You will discover quite soon enough."

"What do you mean?"

"You will either join the king in his efforts and lead his army with the Dark Thorn at its head, relinquish it to my authority, or be ultimately destroyed by years of torture," John Lewis Hugo said. "I hope for the second of course."

"Kill me then," Richard offered. "I will not help him *or* you."

John Lewis Hugo frowned, only one side of his face moving. He then turned and grabbed from the shadowy alcove one of the leather packs, bringing it into the light. Liquid sloshed within and John Lewis Hugo made sure it did so.

"Those things are blasphemous!" Richard said.

"No! They are providence!" John Lewis Hugo shot back, nodding to the Fomorian. "They are the means to end the sin that has populated your world since my leaving!"

The Fomorian pulled on a massive chain behind him that led into the ceiling. A hidden mechanism running in the walls pulled the chains binding Richard taut, splaying him wide open.

"The Holy Grail was never intended for destruction!" Richard yelled. "The Word would neve—"

"What written Word have you read, *Sir Knight?*" John Lewis Hugo drawled. "The Word punishes the wicked. It has ever been so. He lends His power to those who possess His truest intentions. Your world has become a rotten egg, now split open and spewing its putrid ilk upon innocence and virtue. The Graal will wash away those who have become an evil on the world."

"You are screwing with powers you cannot even possibly comprehend, let alone control, you ass," Richard spat. "The Grail has never been a tool of conquest."

"Not for humans, no."

A sinking feeling overcame the knight, one he could not ignore and knew to be suddenly true.

"No," Richard whispered disbelievingly.

"Yes."

John Lewis Hugo stepped in front of him, his face a cold, twisted mess. The knight looked into the heart of the black eye that sat in the malformed remains of his enemy's face, and a red light blossomed to expand into an iris of inferno. Long interred malevolence stared, holding him fast, showing him the truth; it was a sinister intelligence far older and much greater in scope than any man could possess, even having lived eight centuries. The smell of rotting mulch, mushrooms, and old death embraced Richard.

John Lewis Hugo was not in control but an entity far more ancient and dangerous.

"You see the truth, Knight of the Yn Saith."

"Arawn," Richard said in fear for what it meant, the realization damning. "You are the one—"

"Who sent the korrigan," the fey creature residing within the human body sneered. "John Lewis Hugo *died* the moment he tried to imprison me. I turned his magic against him—and Philip Plantagenet. You as well, since it was *I* who brought you here, who has controlled your life, who put your wife beneath your blade. How do you think I crippled you in Dryvyd Wood? I have been watching you for a long time, my Knight of the Yn Saith—and make no mistake, you *are* mine."

The implications bore Richard down in a fast spiral. John Lewis Hugo no longer existed. Not in a way that mattered. Arawn lorded at Caer Llion, and Philip Plantagnet, like Richard, was more than likely a puppet as well. The fey lord that stared with fury at Richard had once ruled the Tuatha de Dannan with an iron fist, kept the Seelie Court together through will, and helped thwart the initial efforts of Philip to take over Annwn. Powerful beyond legends, the loss of Arawn centuries earlier had crippled the Tuatha.

But Arawn had never been evil. Not like this. If the ancient fey lord went along with Philip's plans—raising one of the largest armies ever conceived—he did so for his own gain. The motives of Arawn were a mystery, but Richard knowing what he did about the thought-dead lord of Annwn, revenge had to be part of it. A plan that longstanding and intricate did not bode well for Richard, Bran, or the two worlds they hoped to protect.

And Arawn had drawn Richard into it, killed his wife, and ruined his life.

Anger filled Richard with fire.

He strained his shackles, enraged, trying to call the Dark Thorn to avenge the death of his wife and end the menace standing before him. Nothing happened. The giant Fomorian took a lumbering step forward as if not trusting the chains that bound Richard but he stopped once he saw the knight was powerless.

"*Why did you kill her?!*" Richard roared.

"To prepare my way into your world, of course," Arawn said, his eyes lightning. "Weakening the Seven, even if only one or two of you, gave me the opening to soon return home and set wrongs of old right."

"Then you killed the Heliwr Charles Ardall too!"

"No, no," the fey laughed. "Ardall did not matter. Not to me, anyway. He was an idealist with a pure heart. Having everything, he had want for nothing. It is difficult to bribe people of that nature." He paused. "His son, on the other hand. His son, has spent his life wanting. He will be easier to persuade."

Richard wanted more than anything to be free to rend the fey lord with his own hands. "Bran Ardall is too stubborn and too smart to join you."

"We will see," Arawn replied, grinning darkly. "We will see, my dear knight. If he survives. It was a grievous wound dealt his hand in the bowels of Caer Llion. Even right now, as we speak, Philip is with the lad, making him an offer. When the lad agrees, I will gain Arondight. Think on this. You should join the side of victory, not slaughter."

"Then you do want what Philip desires," Richard said. "Dominion."

"Not his father Henry II's call, but my own."

"Does the Morrigan know of this?"

"Shades, no," Arawn guffawed. "The Tuatha de Dannan know nothing of my plan. They would not even be able to comprehend it. They want to be left alone in their precious Annwn. But as I learned when we fey left the Misty Isles, your human world will forever keep intruding on our sovereignty. War will continue until one side wins. That time has come by *my* hand, using Philip to gain entrance to Rome and the relics it contains. The Tuatha de Dannan will be all powerful, with me as their returned leader."

"Why tell me all this?" Richard asked.

"Because after what is about to happen to you, it won't matter, I think," Arawn said, stepping aside and offering Richard to the Fomorian. "You see, I have no further use for you if you will not grant me the Dark Thorn. Therefore, I give you Duthan Loikfh."

The giant lumbered forward, a grin splitting his boulder of a head. Arawn sunk back into the shadows, eagerly watching. With meaty hands the size of roasts, the giant gripped Richard's left forearm in bark. Gritting his teeth, Richard knew what was coming and waited for the inevitable.

"My Fomorian is deaf as any good torturer should be. And more effective for it," Arawn said darkly.

The Fomorian snapped both hands in opposite directions.

Searing pain lanced up Richard's entire arm and into his body, the broken bones grinding against splintered ends. The agony was excruciating as black dots danced in his vision. It was only the beginning, he knew.

When the giant stepped back, the knight's arm hung at a crooked, unnatural angle, the momentary shock wearing down to a full-body throbbing ache.

Arawn stepped forward with the bag. Water suddenly danced against Richard's face, cold and inviting. The droplets infiltrated his mouth, wetting his tongue and lips. Swallowing, he fought through the haze of pain. But as he did so, the crooked arm knitted itself, straightening by a power unseen by the world for more than fifteen hundred years. The other wounds he had received while in Annwn also healed. The memory of what had been done to him remained, but after a few seconds, no pain existed in his body.

"It will get much worse," Arawn said with an evil smile.

"Kill me and be done with it."

"I do not think so, knight," the burned figure countered. "I, with the aid of the water in that basin, can keep you alive forever—and visit excruciating pain upon you the entire time. It will drive you mad, like this body has driven me mad. Bequeath the Dark Thorn to me, and I will end you quickly."

Richard snorted. "Then bring your worst, you asshole."

Arawn lost his smile. He nodded to the giant, who then pulled free a hot iron poker from the stoked red coals of the fire and approached Richard with a malicious look.

Richard tightened, snarling with rage.

The first scream made him hoarse for those that followed.

Chapter 30

Bran fought free of nightmares trying to anchor him forever to the darkness, feverishly sweating, his left hand throbbing fire.

He came groggily awake. He lay sprawled in a cell not much larger than his bedroom in Seattle, the stone floor leaching what warmth he still had and a lone torch offering none. The straw beneath him presented little cushion. As he sluggishly moved to push himself up off his moldy makeshift bed with both hands, he immediately fell back to the cell stone, pain the likes of which he had never known shooting up his left arm.

He realized an icy cuff bound his right wrist to the wall behind him. His other arm needed no such manacle.

Bran had lost his hand.

The memory of the strike cut through him like a razor blade. He sat up and nearly passed out. The Templar Knight had severed the hand at the wrist. He had no way of knowing how long he had been unconscious but the stump still oozed blood. The hand felt as though it were there, being stung by hundreds of fiery bees.

Weakness washed over him. He fought it. He knew if he did not get medical attention for his arm soon, he would bleed to death or die slowly from an infection.

Wrapping his arm in his shirt, Bran closed his eyes to think.

Richard had been right.

Bran should not have trusted Merle.

The realization maddened him. As he fought the darkness threatening to overwhelm him, he took a deep, steadying breath. The Cailleach and her Templar Knights had caught Richard and Bran with magic. Somehow the warriors, with the bag contents they had carried on their backs, had been invincible against the power of the two knights. Bran had been arrogant to believe he could handle Arondight and anything Annwn sent at him.

Richard had warned him.

And Bran had paid a steep price.

He wondered suddenly what had become of Richard and what would become of him if he didn't try to escape.

Not wanting to wait and find out, Bran tried calling Arondight.

Nothing happened.

He reached across the space he had become familiar with, seeking the sword and its power. Nothing again. Fear filled his soul. Arondight had come so easily before. He probed the void that connected him to the magic, knowing something must have been done to him. He encountered it immediately. It was as if there was a wedge between him and the sword, a thick iron plate preventing him from drawing Arondight. He fought it, forcing what will he had left to break through or get around it, to call the power and escape.

But it was no use.

The magic was beyond him.

Bran sat against the wall, as defenseless as a child. The iron chafing his wrist left him cold and alone. He fought tears he hadn't shed in years on the streets.

He looked around the cell, trying to discover anything that could be helpful. The room only contained a three-legged stool out of his reach and an alcove with a series of empty shelves. Nothing was hidden in the straw. The stone wall was mortared fast where his chain was attached. Through the bars of the cell door window, the yellow light of a torch down the hallway flickered, casting its light of unattainable freedom. No sound other than his own breathing and the slow drip of an unseen water source met his ears; he might as well have been in Limbo, frozen in time, reduced to nothing more than a discarded afterthought.

"Help me," Bran croaked to the universe.

"Do you indeed wish it, young Ardall?"

Startled, Bran looked up.

Beyond the bars of his cell door window, a redheaded man bearing a close-cropped beard and hard eyes stared at him. He disappeared as the locking mechanism of the door rattled, clicked, and allowed him entrance upon squeaky hinges of rusted disuse. He was tall with a square jaw, serious demeanor and, wearing all sable from neck to boot. The silver insignia of a lion blazed across a broad chest; at his hip, a broadsword of simple, elegant design rested within a scabbard displaying a jewel in its curved hilt. He had the look of one who was never denied—and if challenged, always won.

"Well? What say you?"

"Who are you?" Bran asked. "Why am I here?"

"Ahh, questions. When I was young, my mentor taught answering a question with more questions shows a shallow mind unworthy of proper discourse. Of course, I did the same when I was around your age."

Bran watched his visitor closely but said nothing.

"Yes, I know of you—and you me. I am the High King of Annwn, Philip Plantagenet, son of Henry II of the lion line and Eleanor of Aquitaine." The king stared harder. "As to why you are here, you have that answer for me."

Bran swallowed the distaste in his mouth. "If you know me, why am I in chains?"

"For a few reasons, by your own device. First and most pressing, you trespassed into my castle. I do, however, see that as a great boon."

"Why?"

Philip moved the stool from the corner and sat upon it, his

focus never leaving Bran as he kept his clothing from touching the dingy cell floor. "It saved me having to find you again. The moment you stepped foot upon Annwn soil became the moment I wished to speak with you at length. After you fled from the care of John Lewis Hugo, my only recourse was to find you once more. And now... now you have come to me."

"I would hardly call how your witch dismembered and shackled me as *care*."

"Well, both the Cailleach and John's methods have grown darker over time, warranted, but they have ever obeyed my orders," Philip said. He rubbed his bearded chin in thought. "And I do apologize for any misdeed by my Templar Knights that may have caused you harm. It was not my intention. Forgiveness will have to come in time for the loss of your hand."

"So what was trying to kill me?" Bran asked. "An order or a darker method?"

The man laughed. "I would never try to kill you. You would be dead if I wished it but that has never been my intention. No, no, I have far grander hopes for you than death."

"Then who tried to kill me in Seattle? Sent the bodach?"

"If a bodach was indeed sent after you, I marvel at your strength," Philip said. "As to who tries to kill you, I do not know. When I discovered the son of the last Heliwr would be visiting Annwn, I knew I had to speak with you. Regrettably, I never imagined it like this, in one of my dungeons. But life sometimes teaches humility."

"Well, as king you can have this chain removed," Bran urged. "As king you can release me from this dungeon and reunite me with my companion."

Philip leaned back. "Perhaps. Your power has been stripped from you, for the moment at least. I do not trust you, of that I will not lie. You planned a sinister deed by breaking into my Caer Llion, on some mission from that heretical wizard, no doubt, and in company with a very powerful knight whose doctrine states he should never leave his gate. I wish to know why you entered Annwn."

"What has become of Richard McAllister?"

"The Knight of the Yn Saith recovers from his injuries," Philip said. "I cannot say the same of you yet, sadly."

There was something about how Philip mentioned Richard's injuries—a glint in his eyes and a tone in his voice—that suggested a very different truth.

Then Bran figured out what bothered him.

It sounded like something Merle would say.

"You lie," he said.

"I do not. He is being healed as we speak," Philip said, the glint gone. "I repeat. What did you come here to accomplish?"

"We came to destroy some kind of seeing glass, an object you use to view my world from this one," Bran said, deciding to play along and hopefully learn more about his situation.

"The Cauldron of Pwyll? But why?"

"To prevent you using it. That's all I know."

Anger darkened the king's pale features. "What the wizard said is true, John *does* use it to peer into our birth world. But as is the case with wizards throughout time there is more behind the words of Myrddin Emrys than teeth. I may control the Cauldron but the Knights of the Yn Saith have the Fionúir Mirror, another such glass with similar attributes. It helps them view Annwn and keep it repressed." He snickered. "Their audacity is astonishing. Using what the wizard knows of the future combined with the knowledge from the mirror, they twist events to suit their own desires. It is control Myrddin Emrys craves, to see his will done and his future come to pass. The knight aids him when that was never the function of his station."

Philip paused a moment. "He and the knight said nothing of that, did they?"

Philip was right. Bran had not heard of the mirror, or thought of Merle and Richard as the worldly meddlers the king painted them to be.

Except when Richard warned Bran of Merle.

"I see they did not," Philip commented. "They wish for you to remain ignorant, to keep even *you* under their control. And that is the very reason why I sit before you right now."

"What do you mean?" Bran asked, feeling more lightheaded every moment.

"First, let us find a bit of trust. You are gravely wounded, having lost your hand," Philip said. "The man who took it is dead. I do not tolerate such grievous incompetence when it comes to my commands. You have lost a lot of blood—it is everywhere—and I doubt you have much longer to live. Let us trust one another."

Bran said nothing, unsure of what to say. Philip undid a water pouch at his side though, its contents sloshing like those on the back of the soldiers that had attacked Bran.

He undid the stopper and offered the pouch to Bran.

"Take a drink."

Bran took it with his right hand. He realized for the first time he was thirstier than ever before, probably due to injury done him. He also knew Philip had no reason to poison him.

Bran drank.

The moment the water went down his throat, he almost spit it out, not from choking but from how he felt. Warmth spread throughout his body. It built from his stomach and spread through his chest out into his limbs, growing in heat until it felt like it would consume him with a well-intentioned tender touch. He ignored the taste of minerals in the water; there was something else mixed in that made him feel more alive, stronger, than ever before in his life.

Bran gained clarity, his mind clearing of the fog that had suffocated his thinking since waking. He looked down. The stump of his left hand, bloody tissue and fevered with purple veins, began to heal over, the skin knitting anew. He couldn't believe it. The healing continued until only pink skin covered what had a few seconds earlier been a mortal wound.

"How did you . . . ?" Bran managed, dumbfounded.

"It is not important, young Ardall," Philip dismissed, replacing the stopper and pouch on his hip. "Now, to my proposition, one given me by my father and the Word."

Still amazed at what had happened, Bran looked up from his healed arm to Philip. "What word? I thought you are the king and your word is gospel."

"I *am* king. But my lordship does not extend over the Word."

"The Word being . . . God?" Bran asked, almost laughing. "I think you are drinking the Kool-Aid or something even stronger."

"I know not what that is but I can see you know nothing of me," the king scoffed. "I am not the villain your friends have cut me to be. I follow the tenets of the Word. It is for that reason I came to Annwn all those years past. My father had a vision of sweeping the infidels from the world, cleansing it as Saint Peter decreed. The fey are an unholy evil. Soon they and the evil that fills the world of my birth will be undone—at my hands. I wish you to embrace that calling and be an ambassador of sorts."

"But you said you couldn't trust me . . ."

"I see strength of character in you," Philip admitted. "You would not possess Arondight if you were not an honorable man, fighting evil. I want you to lead my armies, be my general, protect the innocent from the dastardly."

Bran did not know what to say. Based on what he had already seen of the king's rule in Annwn, he could no more trust Philip than he trusted a bully. Bran might not be able to fully believe or explain the intentions of Richard or Merle, but he knew he definitely could not take Philip at his word.

He would have to be as wily to be released.

"What would this entail then?" Bran asked carefully.

"When the sins of existence begin to outweigh the virtue of the Word, the Lord calls on those with extraordinary gifts to set His work aright. Saint Peter died to ensure his Lord's faith took root within a pagan Rome. A sacrifice. In the fourth century, Christianity overcame those repressive pagan ways by the strength of a visionary emperor, Constantine the Great, who took the first difficult steps to allow Christian worship a safe place. Once again, sacrifice. King Edward the Martyr died to keep the Benedictine monasteries safe from the greedy nobles of England. Another sacrifice. Even my father fought against the eastern infidels, losing much of his power and wealth to maintain the integrity of the Holy Land. I carry on that tradition. And as the world spirals all too eagerly into its own excesses, I will bring the light once more and push the darkness back.

"I have ever been a student of history. I know I need strong people of faith and strong character, men who are willing to sacrifice their lives for the greater good as so many have done before. I wish you to be a sort of ambassador, between Annwn and our world, to use your power to smooth the transition. I cannot do this alone, young Ardall."

"I don't think the army outside of your walls makes you alone," Bran remarked.

"That may be true, but virtue is not always won with arms."

"What do you really want?" Bran asked.

"I invite you, as a new knight, to use your power to help with that edict," Philip offered. "Think about it, Ardall. You will have everything that you have ever desired. Food. Drink. Wealth. Land. A beautiful woman. All the pleasures that a life in my service would guarantee. It can be your own, if you but join me."

Bran drew in a deep breath. What Richard had thought was true. Philip intended to attack the world, to return home with an army, to force people to embrace his rule.

The king also offered Bran all he had ever wanted and more.

It didn't take long for Bran to come to a choice. Those material things would not matter. Because the war that Philip planned to unleash would destroy everything.

"If you attack the world we come from, Philip, and that world finds out about this one, which it surely will, Annwn ceases to be," Bran said. "The power wielded by the governments will crush whatever you are planning. They outmatch anything you possess."

Philip barked a mean laugh. "You think I care about Annwn."

"I would think you care about your life."

"You are a coward, if you are not willing to die for grace," Philip said, frowning darkly.

"You don't comprehend. Listen to me—"

"No! You listen to me!" Philip roared, standing, redness rising in his cheeks. "The world of our birth has become corrupt. It takes strong men, men who are willing to do what is right before what is popular to save the souls of those who are truly worthy."

"Killing is not the answer!" Bran reiterated.

"Do not presume to know me, nor what I do," Philip sneered. "People will die, of that I have no doubt. Those who live will come to know the Word through proof of His existence."

"How were you ordained to do His will?" Bran questioned, growing angry. "Did you receive some kind of sign? You said something about proof?"

"I possess the Graal, the Cup of the Word."

It took Bran a few moments to register what Philip had just said. Then the realization hit him. The Holy Grail. No matter how crazy the notion sounded, Philip was telling the truth. The warriors who had subdued Richard and Bran in the cavern had risen instantly, healed, sucking on some kind of liquid in bags on their backs. Bran had thought it some kind of magic but the truth was far more real—and chilling. It explained how the hordes of halfbreeds had survived their conception. It explained how the king had lived for centuries beyond his mortal death and how he could keep every man in his army alive, even during battle.

It explained how Bran's arm had healed so quickly.

Lively arrogance danced behind the king's eyes, a flicker of burning certainty. If Philip possessed the Holy Grail and used it to bolster his army . . .

"When the sinners realize the power of the Word upon the world, they will be moved to obey the scripture of the Word," Philip continued, the snide assurance in his voice maddening to Bran. "Those who do not are evil, in the face of such truth, and killing them will be the Word's work, through my blood, my sacrifice."

"And those of your army," Bran added.

"They are willing," Philip said simply. "And worthy."

Heat inside Bran grew into a blistering furnace. The conviction of the worldview Philip shared and his need to place it upon others scared Bran. It reminded him of people on the street who had nothing else to lose. It made them volatile, dangerous.

If he could have called Arondight, he would have torn Caer

Llion apart, stone by stone, and brought it tumbling on top of Philip and his army.

"Will you join the power of Arondight to my own?" Philip propositioned.

Bran couldn't show his disdain for what the king offered.

That would likely mean his death.

"I will think on it," Bran said noncommittally.

"John has informed me that the last regiments of the northern cities will join the army here at Caer Llion by tomorrow," Philip said. "Once gathered under one banner and organized, I will march toward our destiny and the birth of a new world. It will be best when you realize who it is that holds the mercy."

Bran nodded. There was nothing for him to say.

"When I lead my army from Annwn, I want you to be at my side, young Ardall," Philip offered. "I will give you the night to think on it."

"And if I refuse?"

"To let you roam free would be an egregious error," the king said. "I cannot let that transpire—not from those chains and not in the release death would serve Myrddin Emrys and a new carrier of Arondight. You will remain here, shackled, until you come to believe what I say." He paused. "Think what we could accomplish, Ardall."

Philip turned to go then and without a look backward walked out of the cell. The door relocked with quick, firm turns, and the footfalls of his leaving faded to nothing.

Silence became Bran's only companion.

WHILE ON THE cusp of dozing, Bran thought of the Holy Grail. He still had a hard time believing Philip possessed the famous cup. Bran knew of it, knew of it from what Richard had told him and what he had read at Old World Tales. After the Grail left the Holy Land and made its way to the British Isles, it had come to King Arthur at Camelot. Wounded during the Battle of Camlann by his son and mortal enemy Mordred, Arthur sailed away upon a barge to heal in Avalon until Britain needed him once more. Ever since that time, men had hunted for the fabulous life-granting cup with no luck.

What if the reason the Holy Grail hadn't been found was because it was not in his world? What if the Cup of Christ had gone with Arthur to Annwn?

And what if Philip had discovered it?

It all made sense.

"Wake up."

Bran snorted from his reverie, opening his eyes as he huddled amidst the straw, looking around for the source of the childlike voice.

No one was in the cell; no one was at its door.

"Huh?" Bran grunted. "Who's there?"

"In the cell next to your own," answered a deeper voice of calm authority.

Bran looked to the wall of stone on his left. In three spots the mortar bracing the stones had been chipped away, leaving tiny gaps. He tried to peer through to the other side, hoping to see whoever it was that spoke to him, but he saw nothing.

"Lad, you there?" the deep voice questioned.

"I am."

"Good, good, I am pleased to make your acquaintan—"

"Of course he is there," a third, angrier man rasped. "You heard him, did you not, Uter?"

"Leave Uter be, Ambrosius," the boyish voice squeaked.

"My apologies, Sir *Wart*," Ambrosius mocked.

"How long have you guys been here?" Bran asked, suddenly happy to have someone—anyone—to talk to.

"Too long."

"Indeed," Uter agreed with Ambrosius. "Far too long. With any hope in the Lady, you will not be imprisoned for as long as we have been. Still, all those throughout Annwn under the boot of the false king are as we—in need of retribution from his ills and evils."

"My sword Caledfwlch shall deliver more than retribution," Ambrosius spat. "If I am freed, I will speak an oath on it!"

"You heard my conversation with Philip then?" Bran asked.

"We heard it," Ambrosius growled. "Could not help but overhear that *prat*."

"His time will come, Ambrosius," Uter allayed. "As surely as our own will. Now is not the time for anger however. Now is the time for planning."

Bran didn't know what to think. The two men and young boy had obviously known one another for some time, imprisoned together. Uter seemed to be a highly educated man, possessing the calm demeanor of diplomacy. Ambrosius sounded the opposite, driven by emotions, an impatient warrior. Wart could not have been more than ten; why Philip had need to jail a youth was beyond Bran. He could not believe the three of them could fit comfortably in the shared cell if it was the same size as the one Bran occupied.

"Why have you all been imprisoned?" Bran questioned.

"For the knowledge we possess," Ambrosius mumbled.

"How so?"

"Caer Llion is our castle," Uter responded. "It was taken from us."

"Your castle?"

"We saw the first stone laid, lived in it, lorded over it," Uter answered. "The knights of my table were chivalrous and courageous, and the lay of the land respected the law of love. The false king stole it and Annwn when he brought his ilk here, quite uninvited. Plantagenet has ever kept us here, in his dungeon, to revel in his victory, I believe."

"Damnable Plantagenet," Ambrosius hissed.

Bran once again didn't know who to trust. From what he had seen of it, Caer Llion was an ancient fortress. For Uter to have seen its creation meant he had lived for a very long time.

Then again, Philip had lived a long time.

"Philip took Caer Llion from you then," Bran said thoughtfully.

"He is an ugly, ugly man," Wart said a bit petulantly. "Not very nice at *all*."

"True words, Sir *Wart*," Ambrosius concurred.

"You cannot join with him," Uter added. "He would use you as he uses all. With the power of Lancelot's blade granted you by the Lady, it would increase Philip's power a thousand fold. He will keep you alive as long as it suits him. Word and Lady willing, freedom will be your own and you can fight his evil once more."

"And gain the pretty cup back," Wart piped in with a tiny voice.

"Cup?" Bran asked, startled. "You mean the Grail?"

"Wait," Ambrosius said sharply. "Listen!"

Bran did so, straining. He heard nothing.

"I hear noth—"

Then Bran did hear it. It was a sound but also a tremor in the wall behind his back, growing in intensity until the castle darkly hummed with it. It sounded like the great stone blocks of the castle were toppling above, as though a bulldozer drove through them.

"It comes," the Ambrosius said.

"What does?" Bran questioned, bewildered by what could be happening.

"Freedom."

The rumbling continued like an avalanche and became still. Shouts of bewilderment and pain followed. Outside his cell the manic voices of warriors echoed, the soldiers Philip had placed in the dungeon not far away. Whatever was going on up above had set Caer Llion ablaze with confusion, arousing the occupants of the castle into a frenzy.

The sounds of far-off battle filled the silence. And came closer.

Minutes passed.

Before Bran could figure out what was happening, the locking mechanism to his cell clicked. Suddenly the door opened.

No one entered.

Bran stood still, trying to get a glimpse out into the hallway, when an invisible vice encircled his forearm and held it in place.

Bran tried to pull away. "What the hell—"

"Relax, outworlder," a voice smelling of beer growled. "Let me free you."

"Ardall, you are alive! Amazing that!" Snedeker exclaimed, hovering at the cell entrance. The fairy watched the hallway, worry etching his features.

The shackle holding Bran's wrist fell away.

"Who is there?" he asked.

The light before him shifted as if through a rippling prism. It cleared and Bran stared at a floating grizzled face with a smirking, unwashed smile.

Caswallawn stared right back.

Chapter 31

Richard hung from the cell wall by chains, in absolute misery. The Fomorian stoked the fire pit for what must have been the hundredth time, heating several irons to white-hot intensity. Richard had no idea how much time had lapsed. It didn't matter. It was the torment that splintered his awareness, left him unsure of every instance the giant rammed a hot poker into his abdomen, broke a bone, or slashed him with a knife. Overcoming the pain skewed his understanding; every agony pushed him toward oblivion. But with every splash of water into his mouth from the Holy Grail he was reborn, brought back to his situation, forced to endure more torture.

Physically, he was fine, his injuries healed. Emotionally he was coming undone from the inside out, his mind sundering.

He was being driven mad.

Arawn had no interest in keeping Richard alive. The knight had brought Bran Ardall to Annwn as a worthy consolation. Whether Richard died or joined Arawn, it did not matter. Either way, the knight was not an obstacle—and Arawn had won.

His left arm broken and the Fomorian set to return with his next evil deed, Richard cursed himself. The Holy Grail. He had seen it with his own eyes. It had been within his grasp in the lake. The Grail was a source of unimaginable power. In the hands of Arawn and Philip, it made whatever army they raised a thousand times more powerful.

The Dark Thorn had called him to the cavern because the lake was a powerful mirror. If Richard had thought about why the magic had called him to the lake, he would have investigated further. If he had spent more time investigating, Caer Llion would have been deprived of the Holy Grail, a weapon Plantagenet planned on using against two worlds.

If he had taken the Grail from Annwn, the war would be over.

If he only had a chance to confront Arawn and kill the creature responsible for Richard killing his wife . . .

If. If. If.

Just as the Fomorian pulled a glowing dagger from the fire, the door to the cell opened. Richard raised his tired head to view the newcomer.

Bran stood in the doorway, alone.

Richard blinked, unsure if what he was seeing was real or the result of maddened hope. The Fomorian torturer turned, alerted by Richard's look. Blunted pale features peeled back in a ferocious snarl and it charged Bran with the dagger raised high.

With Arondight glowing in his hand, Bran waited for the giant.

"Run, Bran!" Richard roared.

Before the giant could finish crossing the room, it fell forward, tripped, and crashed to the stone, the knife flying out of its hand and air whooshing from its lungs.

"Now, Ardall!" a voice screamed in the cell.

Bran unleashed the magic of Arondight. The fire stabbed the Fomorian in its back and pinned it to the ground, incandescent flames unyielding as they inundated the huge creature. The giant roared in pain. Bran did not let up. A curling hand reached up but Bran ignored it, his eyes focused and filled with wrath.

Richard could not believe what he saw. Roaring as flesh burned away and the smell of charred meat saturating the room, the Fomorian pleaded with frying eyes to be let free, to survive.

Bran did not yield.

The giant struggled on until its protestations weakened. Movements slowing until only smoke rose, the Fomorian finally stilled.

Bran ended the torrent of flaming magic. The torturer lay unmoving. A surge of adrenaline rushed into Richard. Snedeker flew into the cell to hover before the prisoner.

"Today luck is with you, McAllister," the fairy said. "What did that asscudgel do to you? Are you alive?"

"No," Richard said. "But I'll live."

Caswallawn materialized suddenly in front of him. He fought the manacles that held the knight. Richard tried to gather himself. With his arm still broken and his mind and body weak from the repeated torture, he knew he would have to get ready for an attempt to escape Caer Llion. No matter how Caswallawn had broken into the castle—a distraction from the sounds rumbling above—there would be Templars after them as soon as Richard and Bran were discovered gone.

He knew one thing. His broken arm would not stop him from unleashing hell.

Finally freed by Caswallawn, Richard moved past the dead Fomorian toward the door.

"What are you—"

"Doing here?" Caswallawn finished, parts of his body in flux. "Is it not obvious?"

"But how did you know where we were?"

"I have followed you from Arendig Fawr, at request of the Queen," Caswallawn whispered, pausing at the door to peek out quickly. "We will speak of my time after this night."

"Time to go, knights," Snedeker said, whirring ahead.

"We must free the others imprisoned here," Bran said.

"I have already done so," Caswallawn said. "Hear the chaos above? Better luck in escaping we will find if the guards are trying to capture all of you."

"What happened to your arm?" Snedeker asked.

"Never mind," Richard spat, looking at Bran's stump. "Bran, grab that leather bag."

On the floor beside the dead giant lay the soccer ball-size pouch holding the water from the Grail. Letting Arondight vanish, Bran entered the room and grabbed the bag. He then held it out to Richard.

"Don't give it to me, dammit!" Richard grimaced. "Just carry it."

"Take a drink," Bran insisted.

"No! It's our proof!"

Bran slung the leather pouch over his shoulder, its contents sloshing, and called Arondight once he stepped out of the room.

"What takes place above?" Richard asked weakly.

"You will see," Snedeker answered. "At times, even I am smarter than the smartest."

"A diversion," Caswallawn said simply. "Let us move."

The four entered the torchlit hallway. Two Templar guards at either end of the corridor slumped lifeless to the stone—weapons not drawn, throats cut, surprised horror freezing their features. Richard moved down the hallway, following the lead of Caswallawn up a new flight of stairs. With every step the sounds of the above conflict grew until it permeated their entire world. Calling the Dark Thorn, Richard put more weight on it rather than Bran as they moved through the castle. Bran would need freedom to use Arondight soon judging by the battle raging above. Caswallawn wrapped his invisibility cloak closer and crept on until they climbed another set of stairs, eyes alert, making no sound, the promise of war ahead.

Snedeker kept ahead, a tiny scout, watching for enemies. There weren't any. Around nearly every corner more guards lay dead, the effective deeds of Caswallawn.

Just as Richard thought the invisible lord had killed everyone in the castle, four soldiers appeared, weapons drawn, surprise etching their faces.

Bran did not hesitate. With Caswallawn flattening against the wall, the boy sent the blue fire of his sword into the Templar Knights. They scattered like leaves on the breeze, bits of fire hungrily fighting for purchase as they screamed in terror. Caswallawn was on them like a sleek cat, knives opening the exposed neck arteries between chain mail and helmets.

In a matter of seconds, all four were dead.

Saying nothing, Richard and the others stepped over the bodies on their way upward. After what felt an eternity, Caswallawn edged into a passage where a door, flanked by thick lead plates bearing faintly pulsing green Celtic runes, waited.

He pushed through into the cool night air.

Into a courtyard of chaos.

Caer Llion loomed overhead. Yelling echoed, conflict all too close. Across from them a giant hole gaped in the outer wall of Caer Llion; through it, dozens of Templar Knights streamed from the plains without, scrambling beyond his view, focused on what had entered the castle. Richard kept himself pressed against the tower wall, propped up by his staff, trying to become one with the shadows. The others did the same.

The battle taking place nearby gave him pause; he did not know where to go now.

Arrow Jack swooped out of the night, screeching.

"How do we get out?" Richard screamed to Caswallawn.

"The hole," Caswallawn said. "And slowly. We are gravely outnumbered."

The invisible lord moved from the door along the rounded tower wall. Richard followed Bran, sweating freely, nausea from the pain sickening him. As they came around the corner, the melee across the courtyard came into view, and Richard nearly stopped in his tracks.

In the midst of the castle warriors, a massive creature stood above all, thick and heavily muscled, destruction raining down from its enormous fists even as spears and arrows punctured its body like a pincushion. Horn-like nubs grew from a rounded head where lank dark hair hung. The juggernaut roared at all quarters while pummeling those adversaries who came too close. The carnage at its feet was complete, bodies twisted and broken from its rage.

"The Kreche," Richard breathed.

"Halfbreed," Caswallawn rumbled. "Doing his job."

Richard stood thunderstruck. The Kreche must have come all

the way from Seattle. Had Merle known what transpired in Caer Llion at all times? Had he known Richard and Bran had been captured? That Richard would be tortured and Bran would lose his hand? If so, Merle had a lot to answer for.

But sending the Kreche had been a Godsend.

Richard turned back to the battle. He did not worry for the Kreche. If bullets could not take it down, the medieval weapons of Annwn surely would not.

"What of Deirdre? And the Rhedewyr?"

"She has already made her way to the Morrigan," Caswallawn answered. "So must we."

The lord whistled loudly, the sound shattering the din. The Kreche spun, staring directly at Richard and those with him. It took a final roaring swipe at those who attacked him, scattering the warriors like gnats, and then charged across the courtyard, the ground thundering.

The warriors of Caer Llion chased after but lagged behind. Caswallawn was already nowhere in sight, invisible once more.

"Get ready, Rick," the Kreche bellowed as he closed in. "Carrying you out of here."

The Kreche rolled over the last of those who stood in his way until he picked Richard and Bran up in his massive arms like rag dolls without missing a step. The breath flew from Richard as the rushing wind of their flight increased.

He let the Dark Thorn dissolve as the world eddied.

"We go now," the Kreche rumbled. "Keep your head down."

Richard did, tucked in the left arm of the Kreche like a football. Arrows and spears zipped by as they approached the broken wall. More warriors gathered there, swords and axes drawn as if trying to build a new wall of flesh to keep the prisoners from escaping. The Kreche gave them no mind. He leapt through as if nothing could hurt him. At the last moment the warriors of Caer Llion gave way from terror or died on impact, the heavy muscles of the Kreche unforgiving and the force in which the beast ran into the hole decimating all in its path. When the Kreche hit the ground beyond, his legs tirelessly pumped through those who tried to stop them until nothing but open ground spread into the dark.

The night embraced them as they ran into it.

Richard protected his broken arm and slept.

As the pink tinge of morning light peeked through breaks in canopy foliage, Richard awoke to a new day and to freedom.

He glanced around at the plains. Caer Llion was long behind them now, the orange glow of the army's campfires outside its walls a memory. No one was about; the stars were giving way to day. The Kreche still carried him and Bran, the halfbreed a machine, unstoppable, despite the dozens of arrows sticking from his body like a porcupine. After about an hour he took them across a wide river and into a part of the land that gently sloped upward where rounded mounds slowly gave rise to trees that thickened into a forest, blotting out the sky.

Richard perked up to get a better view. A hellyll wearing the armor of the Long Hand stood poised with a spear pointed directly at the Kreche.

"I have come with the two knights," the Kreche rumbled.

The guard lowered his weapon. "Follow me."

The Kreche lowered Bran to the ground. The boy stretched the kinks out of his muscles while looking at his absent hand. Richard remained in the cradling arms of the Kreche, not sure what to say to Bran about his amputation. He had warned Bran about Merle and about coming to Annwn. In his heart, though, Richard felt pain for him. Bran had learned his lesson the hardest of ways and had paid the gravest of costs.

With the Kreche unwilling to put Richard down and Snedeker hovering nearby like a nurse of some sort, the hellyll guard brought them through a screen of trees into an open forest encompassing thousands of warriors, each fully armed and armored for war, each watching the Kreche with a mixture of open curiosity and fear. Upon first glance Richard thought they were all hellyll, but as they made their way through the throng he realized they were dozens of fey—merrow, sprites, clurichauns, leprechauns, wood nymphs, fairies, minotaurs, bugganes, coblynau, and many more.

The Queen of the Tuatha de Dannan had called for war.

And that call had been answered.

As the Kreche carried Richard deeper into the forest, a pointed sweeping tent grew out of the land, its height almost as tall as the trees around it. The pavilion was a huge construction of thick silk and ornate planning, shimmering beneath the lightening sky and blending in with the green foliage and brown bark. Fey came and went from it, the center of command.

Guards waited stoically at the wide entrance.

They nodded access to the Kreche.

When Richard, Bran, Snedeker, and the Kreche entered, dozens of eyes shifted toward them. Orbs hung high within the interior of the tent, casting warm white light over the gathered Lords of the Seelie Court. The Morrigan stood before a map displayed on a broad oak table, the leader of the Tuatha de Dannan wearing sleek black armor, her eyes hard. Horsemaster Aife and Lord n'Hagr stood near her, listening to what she said. To the side Lord Eigion spoke to two other merrow and the stocky coblynau Lord Faric, grandson of Lord Fafnir of Caer Glain. Lord Finnbhennach and four very tall minotaurs discussed their armor with Mastersmith Govannon, who examined the steel and straps with diligence. Kegan looked up from a plush divan where he whittled a piece of wood into the shape of a Rhedewyr and honest happiness covered his features at seeing them. Deirdre and her father, Lord Gerallt, were also present, standing apart.

Out of all those who had been present at the Seelie Court meeting, only Lord Caswallawn was absent, unable to keep up with the Kreche while fleeing Caer Llion.

"You found them," the Queen said, nodding her approval.

When the monstrosity put Richard down upon the soft rugs, the Morrigan called for Belenus immediately. The ancient healer appeared from the depths of the tent and rushed to his side, the wizened old man's eyes soulful and worried. He immediately began to probe for injuries.

"Stay your place, healer. I have a broken arm," Richard said. "Bran. The bag."

"You need aid," the Morrigan asserted.

Bran unslung the leather sack he had taken. He gave it to Richard who uncorked it and drank from its contents.

The change was instantaneous. Richard felt vitality flow into him. The broken arm, at an odd angle and purpled down its length, straightened itself, the bruising vanishing as the bones grew back together on their own. The smaller wounds, bruises, and the weariness on Richard melted like ice under the sun. After seconds, no injuries or scars marred him.

Those around him stared in awe, and whispers filled the tent.

"Welcome back to the living, Rick," the Kreche rumbled.

Richard took a deep breath. "Thank you, old friend."

"How can this be?" Kegan breathed.

"Deirdre, come here," Richard commanded.

She gave her father an uncertain look but went over to Richard anyway, the burn damage done to her back and arm hindering her movements despite the aid she had already received.

"Drink," Richard ordered.

Deirdre gripped the pouch uncertainly but did as she was told. Surprise came over her face the moment the water hit her lips. She returned the bag in order to lower her tunic and the bandaging that covered the deep burns she had sustained. The skin of her back, once melted and blistered, smoothed until all remnants became healthy pale skin.

Richard handed the pouch to the Queen. "The water in that bag has been blessed and consecrated by the power of the Word's savior, from the chalice of the Holy Grail itself."

"The Graal," the Morrigan murmured. "How did it come to the Usurper?"

"I do not know, although it does explain his longevity," Richard said. "But I do know this, and the entire Seelie Court must listen. When Bran and I snuck into Caer Llion we entered through a small cave carved from the rock of the cliff face by a hidden spring beneath the castle. That spring forms a small lake, and at its heart glimmered some kind of object that captured the dripping water and fed it into the pool. At the time I had no idea what it was. When the Templar Knights of Caer Llion attacked Bran and me, we could not defeat them. They captured us easily. Every time we ended their threat with force, they rose to come at us again. Burns, broken bones, didn't matter. These warriors were invincible."

"But how?" Lord n'Hagr questioned.

Richard pointed at the bag in the hands of the Queen. "Each of them had one of those."

The members of the Seelie Court shared looks of concern.

"My cattle," Lord Finnbhennach muttered.

"Exactly right," Richard said. "The griffins did pick clean your cattle but not for the reasons we thought. The griffins stole their hides so that they could be cured and become thousands of those leather bags." Richard let what he was saying sink in. "Somehow Philip has taken the power of the Grail and given it to his warriors and, undoubtedly, his entire army. It explains how the halfbreeds we've seen survived their infancy when they would normally die natural deaths, and how those warriors could rise against Bran and me beneath the castle and be just as strong after being hit with all the magic we possess."

"So when you tried to find this Cauldron of Pwyll Philip spoke of . . ." Bran started.

"I found the lake," Richard said. "I focused on a powerful mirror. The lake we saw beneath Caer Llion is a mirror of sorts with the most powerful relic in our existence at its heart."

"Philip admitted he had it," Bran said. "The Holy Grail, I mean. He healed me with it."

"What else did he say?" the Morrigan pressed.

"He intends to attack my world," Bran answered. "He is crazed. Extreme. Says he is doing the Word's work in destroying sin. Says he will prove to the world the Word *is* real."

"And in so doing destroy two worlds," the Kreche growled.

"The army began marching yesterday," Lugh said, gripping his spear. "Moving east."

"East?" Richard frowned. "Why east?"

"There is a portal within the Forest of Dean near Aber Gwy, directly to our south," the Queen replied, her demeanor grown cold. "It is a two-day march from Caer Llion. Philip and his force will be there late tomorrow."

"Where does it lead?" Bran asked.

"Rome," Richard said. "The heart of the old Empire."

The room went silent. Richard could hardly comprehend Philip's choice but it made sense. Annwn's despot intended to attack the Holy See and the birthplace of Catholicism. It was the center for organized Christianity the world 'round. When he brought his army into that ancient city, it would give him a huge platform like none the world had seen. The amount of exposure would be overwhelming. Governments would yield to the invading force, not because they condoned terrorism but because the revelation of the Holy Grail would give them pause. And with the dark creatures Philip used at the head of his army, the foundations of what it meant to be Christian would crumble, the belief that humanity was God's only creation destroying the belief of millions of people. The opposite of what Philip hoped would occur. Anarchy would ensue. It would devastate the world and destroy Annwn in the resulting violence.

"Philip has no intention of attacking the remnants of the Seelie Court," Richard said. "He instead will start a war worse than any that has come before it."

"He must be stopped! Killed!" Deirdre exclaimed.

"This is not our battle," Lord Faric argued. "The Queen called upon the might of the Seelie Court to protect what is our own, thinking the wayward king would attempt to bring his army against the Tuatha de Dannan. That is no longer happening. The coblynau protect what is their own and no more. Without that need, I do not see why we should place our people in harm's way. My grandfather would not be pleased. I say we let Philip leave, once more take control of Annwn, and defend the portals from future entrance."

"You can't do that!" Bran thundered. "Philip plans on leading this army directly into my world. Are you all so shortsighted? He will rouse others in my world, and when that happens all is dead here, no matter how you guard your portals." Bran looked to Richard. "You have to tell them this is true!"

The coblynau broadened, his muscles straining beneath his armor. "You know little of our world, no matter if you are a knight, scion of Ardall."

"The boy is right, Lord Faric," Richard countered, crossing his arms. "What knowledge Bran lacks about Annwn you lack about our world. The Tuatha de Dannan have been absent from the land of their origin for a long time. Much has changed."

"Still, the decision to go to battle against the army the Usurper has amassed is our own to make," the Morrigan said.

"You already made that decision," Bran pointed out.

The other lords grumbled their thoughts until it became a yelling match. Richard watched it all unfold. The bickering. The disagreement. The inability to come to a conclusion that would benefit all. These lords were the leaders of Annwn and they acted like many of those in his own world—selfish and unable to agree for the greater good. The voices of the lords grew louder until the entire tent was a cacophony of indecision and angst.

"Shut it!" a deep voice thundered.

Everyone turned to the Kreche. All grew silent.

"I am not from this world and yet I am firmly rooted within it," the halfbreed said, his voice lowered now that he had their attention. "The King of Annwn may not be attacking you now but that is the least of your worries. The fight Philip brought to you will be an ant attack compared to what will happen if the men of *that other world* discover this one. The men in that world are greedy and corrupt. They possess power and machines you cannot fathom. When they come here—and they will come here, whether it be Philip or another—nothing you do will be able to stop your extermination."

"And they *will* discover you if Philip goes through that portal," Richard added.

The lords looked back and forth between one another.

"Now we listen to a halfbreed?" Lord Finnbhennach snorted. "As if he knows something of our ways?"

"Considering one of your own begot me, I say I have a say."

Lord Finnbhennach grunted but said nothing.

"War is not an easy thing to entreat," the Morrigan said, her presence commanding the others into silence. "If what you say is true about the Graal and the Usurper harnessing its power, what will that do for our odds in this?"

Richard shrugged. "I do not know. It could make each of his demon wolves and Templar Knights as if they were five? Ten? Not sure exactly."

"That means if their army is fifty thousand strong . . ." Lord Eigion thought out loud.

"It is actually many times larger than that," Richard said. "And growing daily."

"What say you, Govannon? Lugh? Aife?" the Morrigan asked.

"The halfbreed speaks true," the Mastersmith said. "All we have fought to maintain, the peace we have wished for so many millennia, will be for naught. No matter the dice odds, we must do what is right, not what is popular. Better now than even more outnumbered later."

"The Rhedewyr are ready," Aife agreed.

"Lord Faric?" the Queen asked.

The coblynau leader nodded, if barely agreeing.

"We are united," the Queen said simply. "The future will be our own by our design."

"If Philip is as arrogant as I think he is, it may be his undoing," Richard said. "But first I must speak with the other knights." Richard paused. "And get some clothes. Then we plan."

"One moment, Knight McAllister," Govannon said.

Richard, Bran, and the rest of the Seelie Court watched Govannon move to the side of the tent where his massive sledgehammer lay against a large pack. He opened the latter and, after rummaging within it, pulled a simple wooden box from its depths.

"If we fight," he said, "Then young Ardall will need this."

Richard watched as the Mastersmith opened the box before Bran. Inside, lying on soft crimson velvet, rested a gauntlet. The steel glove was short at the wrist, with metal fingers and a thumb. A menagerie of runes etched into its surface swirled.

Govannon had crafted a beautiful piece of artistry.

"Give me your left arm, Ardall," the Mastersmith said. "Let me place it on."

Bran did so. Govannon attached the gauntlet where the boy's hand had once been. When the glove touched the stump, the runes came alive, azure fire like that of Arondight racing over its steel. The fingers twitched and then moved as wonder filled Bran's face.

"But how . . . ?" the boy began.

"The weapon you needed back in my Arendig Fawr armory had no reason to exist yet," Govannon answered. "The reason being, of course, you still possessed your left hand. Is the gauntlet to your liking? Is it comfortable?"

"How does it stay on?" Bran asked, mesmerized.

"Magic, of course. Partly mine, partly your own. It is linked to Arondight, although the sword does not need to be called for the gauntlet to stay on. If you hold the sword in your new left hand, the blade can never be struck from your possession. The two magics work as one."

Bran flexed his new steel fingers, grinning.

"A wonderful gift, Mastersmith," the Morrigan said. "May it bode well on the morrow."

The lords of the Seelie Court nodded and turned back to their own thoughts, contemplating the choice of the Queen to go to war and their role in it. Some nodded to Richard, others turned away. It was not difficult for him to understand how hard it had been for these leaders to subject their people to war. The lords were given the chance to face the cause of their centuries of hiding and fear. Philip had to pay for what he had done—for what he was planning on doing.

Richard flexed his arm, feeling it restored. Battle was coming and he would be in the thick of it on the field.

If he knew one thing, he *would* encounter Arawn there.

And enact vengeance for Elizabeth.

Chapter 32

Within the Forest of Dean, Deirdre roamed the outskirts of the Tuatha de Dannan army, ignoring the stares that a human aroused, in search of her father. While she had traveled with Richard, Bran, and Snedeker to Caer Llion, Lord Gerallt had gathered two companies of his most hardened warriors from Mochdrev Reach and brought them to the Seelie Court. The rest of their forces he left behind, to guard the stronghold and people he fought to protect. He had been displeased when he found out she had left Arendig Fawr to guide the knights; she had not repented her decision, making him all the angrier. Neither had spoken to each other since.

But, on the cusp of battle, Deirdre would not let the possible last words between them be those of anger.

"He will still be angry, I can tell you that!" Snedeker said, flying alongside her and annoying her more than usual.

"He gave me free will to aid the Morrigan and the fight against Caer Llion," she said. "The knights are a part of that. I was best suited to take them. He has no say in the matter."

"The knights almost *died*, by the way," the fairy snorted.

"They were going with or without me."

"And you received that awful burn."

"Good thing the halfbreed came through the portal then and helped save Richard and Bran," she said. "They in turn healed me, leaving me unwilling to put up with your sass. So watch it."

The fairy cursed under his breath about redheads and their stubborn natures. Deirdre was happy he kept it to himself for a change. She slipped through the fey, thinking about two nights ago. The Kreche had come out of the darkness to set her toward the Forest of Dean with the Rhedewyr even as he went to confront Caer Llion to free the knights at the behest of Myrddin Emrys. She had only seen two halfbreeds in her life but the Kreche was easily the most impressive, the heart of a poet within the body of a behemoth. If it hadn't been for his diversion, Richard and Bran would not have been freed.

"Why do you think the Heliwr hates me?" Snedeker interrupted suddenly.

"Never had a conversation with yourself, eh?"

"Hilarious, Red," the fairy said, dripping sarcasm.

"Richard doesn't hate you," Deirdre said. "He simply has impatience for those who add nothing to life."

"Hey, I add a lot to li—"

"As he sees it," she cut him off. "Why do you even care, anyway?"

"The Lady is not pleased with me," he said.

"How do you know that?"

"She mustn't be," the fairy said, glancing around him as if the Lady could hear. "I am not guiding her Heliwr, not that he has shown any interest in my help at all, of course."

"Maybe you need to reach out with more sincerity."

"He will probably fry me to ash," Snedeker said. "Just for talking to him."

"He could," she said with a smile.

Snedeker rolled his eyes.

After she thought she had seen every quarter of the army, Deirdre came to the camp of Mochdrev Reach. Two hundred of her countrymen prepared for the battle, some men sharpening their weapons while others checked their armor. All shared a look on their faces that bespoke the fear of not knowing what was to come. Deirdre navigated through them, feeling the tension, and eventually found her father's tent.

When she entered, Lord Gerallt stared hard at her before returning to the battle formation maps two hellyll members of the Long Hand shared with him in preparation for the next day.

"You should not be here, Deirdre," he said, not meeting her gaze. "My time is precious now that Mochdrev Reach is in the thick of *your* decision."

"Father, I—"

"You should not have left Arendig Fawr."

"Father, I did what I thought I had to do," Deirdre said.

"And almost got yourself killed."

"For a very good cause."

Lord Gerallt continued to speak to the two Long Hand soldiers as if she were not there. From where he sat on her shoulder, Snedeker tapped her shoulder with impatience. After she realized he would not respond, Deirdre walked up to his table.

"Why are you acting like this?" she asked.

When he didn't look up, her anger got the best of her and she slammed her fist down on the closest map.

"Why?!"

Lord Gerallt gave her a chilly look, his round face ruddy, before he turned to the hellyll. "Leave us for a few moments, Everle and Vay. You too, Snedeker. I must speak in earnest with my wayward daughter. Alone."

Giving Deirdre a dark look, the fairy flew from the tent along with the Long Hand warriors.

"Deirdre, you tax me all too often," Lord Gerallt growled.

"You are not telling me everything," she said. "You are never like this. There is something eating at you and I would know what it is."

Lord Gerallt took a deep breath and looked away. Long moments passed. Deirdre waited, knowing she didn't have a choice, but her father also had a habit of taking his time in formulating his words when they held import. As she watched, though, the man she had known all of her life changed from a confident military commander preparing for the worst battle he would likely ever be in to a man almost defeated and ashamed, wearing a mantle of hardship Deirdre rarely saw.

"Whatever it is, it cannot be horrible," she encouraged.

"After John Lewis Hugo met you at the Rosemere, he came to find me within the castle," Lord Gerallt said, taking a deep breath. "We spoke. At length. It will not please you to hear this but I gave him my oath you would be brought to Caer Llion to marry."

"I knew that, father."

"Even if it went against your wishes," he added.

The support she had brought with her vanished. Deirdre didn't know what to say. In all the years she had looked up to her father, especially after the death of her mother, she now felt she didn't know him. At no time had he disrespected her in such a way.

It left her feeling hollow.

"You gave me no choice?" she asked. "You lied to me?"

"It was the only way to ensure our safety," he said, still barely able to look at her. "When you spoke to the shade of your mother and grew adamant we visit Arendig Fawr, I didn't believe the Seelie Court would rise again. I thought the only way to prevent death for our people would be to take the honorable path for all of the lives we oversee—and knowingly upset you most as a result, my daughter." He paused. "I am ashamed by my actions. I was wrong to speak on your behalf."

"How is taking the honorable path *right*?" Deirdre demanded, her disbelief replaced by wrath. "You betrayed my heart!"

"I regret not telling you sooner," he said. "But now things have changed. I can no longer play both sides. And the innocent people of Mochdrev Reach may pay the price for it."

Deirdre bit back a furious reply. She did not know what to think. In her mind, she knew her father had a difficult role to play in Annwn, one that required making difficult decisions. In her very depths though, she felt deceived by the man who had been her foundation for so many years.

When he had seemed so behind her for the last few days.

"You love him, do you not?" Lord Gerallt asked suddenly.

"The knight, I mean?"

"I do," she stammered, unable to hide her surprise. "I . . . cannot explain it. Richard McAllister is like no one else I have ever met. How did you know?"

"I may be old and fat but I'm not blind, Deirdre."

Embarrassment overrode her anger, but only for a moment.

"Would he tell you to protect the many?" Lord Gerallt continued. "Or do what made you happy?"

"He would never advocate being untrue to myself."

"Are you sure?" he asked sadly. "Why do you think he is so dark, Deirdre? I know his kind, all too well. Men become like him by betraying the deepest chambers of their hearts with selfishness. He is ashamed of his life in some way." He paused. "I did not want to be like McAllister, to destroy a part of myself or the love I have for you. Guilt will follow me to the end of my days, despite not fulfilling my oath to Caer Llion. For that, I apologize, and shall be judged accordingly in the afterlife. It is McAllister's role to give up his life to protect the lives of millions between our two worlds. I am sure he would tell you to do the noble thing as well."

The knight would at that, no matter how much it galled her.

"I know why you did it, even if I do not agree," Deirdre said. "I guess we both have lied to one another these last days."

"Your mother had a saying," he said. "'Forgive love its transgressions, for it forgives just as readily.'"

Deirdre nodded. "I like it."

"As do I."

Missing her mother terribly at that moment, Deirdre looked around the tent, the realization of what was to come settling on her like heavy armor. Preparations for battle were everywhere. On the morrow, death would come to many within the Forest of Dean. Centuries of tension would bleed upon the field.

Coldness settled in her belly. She fought its uncertainty.

"Tomorrow I want you to not be involved in the battle," Lord Gerallt said as if reading her thoughts.

"I *will* be part of the fight," she stated adamantly.

"I thought you might say that. Stubborn like your father," Lord

Gerallt said as he walked around the table to stand before her. He gripped her hands warmly but the smile he often displayed was buried beneath the gravity of his words. "I must further complete my knowledge of the Morrigan's battle plans but, before you go, know that I love you. You have been strong for a great many. Tomorrow will not be pleasant. Come what may and despite our decisions, we are still bound by love. I hope you can forgive me."

"I already have, father," she said, giving him a kiss.

"Keep that fairy out of trouble," he said, his smile finally returned.

She returned it. "I will try."

Lord Gerallt nodded, and after asking the hellyll to return, continued his study of the maps and the fey techniques for battle.

Deirdre left to care for Willowyn.

AFTER PREPARING WILLOWYN and several other Rhedewyr mounts for the next day's war, Deirdre walked through the moonlight to find Richard.

The sun had long since set, the members of the Seelie Court adjourning to their own areas. It was an army larger than any she had seen in her life; many of the Tuatha de Dannan could not sleep, still roaming the Forest of Dean in nervous anticipation. Deirdre felt the same way. With Snedeker flying ahead of her, she navigated clurichauns, spriggans, cait siths, and other fey in search of the Heliwr, hoping to see him one last time before conflict tore them apart.

After Lugh of the Long Hand pointed out the direction Richard had gone, she found him alone in a glen, just east of the army. It didn't take long. An ink stain in the shadows, he leaned against an enormous fir tree, looking upward through a break in the canopy at the stars.

She approached on silent feet, unsure of what to say.

"You should not have found me," Richard said, turning, wearing new clothing. "Your father needs you right now more than he ever has."

"That may be," she said defiantly. "Snedeker wishes to speak to you though."

Richard followed her gaze to the fairy who flew to hover before the knight.

"What do you want?" he asked.

Snedeker folded his arms, staring directly at the knight, his wings a blur in the silver moonlight. "The Lady requested I be your guide," he said.

"Yes. I know that, fairy."

"Look, let us cut the tail off the cat as my gramps used to say," Snedeker sneered, pointing at Richard. "I gave my promise to the Lady I would guide you in your duty. You do remember what duty is, right?"

Richard studied the fey creature darkly. "That tongue will be your death one day, Snedeker."

"As long as it is not tomorrow. I want to talk abo—"

"Being my guide as the Lady ordained, I know," Richard interrupted. "Then do your job."

Snedeker looked confused. "But I thought you wanted nothing to do with me."

"It is not *my* role to make you fulfill *your* role," Richard pointed out. "Watch my back tomorrow and do what I tell you, and maybe you will impress me. You can prove yourself that way."

Snedeker nodded.

"Tomorrow we hunt John Lewis Hugo," the knight continued. "You will be my eyes above the battle. Together we will find him. And kill him."

"What of Philip Plantagenet?" Deirdre asked, thinking it odd Richard failed to mention the Usurper in his plans. "Would he not be a better target?"

"Philip will meet his end. John Lewis Hugo is the one I want. In this my guide can prove his worth if he has the courage," Richard said. He then eyed the fairy. "Leave us now, Snedeker. Wait for my return in the Morrigan's camp tonight."

Snedeker gave Deirdre an inquisitive look before darting through the night back toward the camp.

In a moment he had vanished.

"I meant what I said," Richard said. "You should not be here."

"It makes you . . . uncomfortable," she said, moving to stand before him.

"It does."

"Because you care for me?" she asked, staring into his eyes.

"Not the way you want."

Deirdre found herself looking at her boots, thinking about the failed kiss. Richard said nothing either. The night shrunk around them, the moonlight highlighting the tension on their faces. She thought about her mother and her assertion Deirdre would meet the love of her life soon. What she felt for Richard was strong, his life intriguing, the depth of his soul a mystery. Even now she wanted to reach out, to lessen his pain, to find peace for him in their sharing.

"What happened to you?" she asked finally. "My father says only a man who regrets what he has done can have so much pain."

"You don't really want to know, lady of Mochdrev Reach."

"I do," she pressed.

The night seemed to coalesce around Richard, the darkness under his eyes growing, the sorrow permeating every line of his face. The stars moved overhead as time passed. Deirdre waited, knowing if she said anything he might run.

"My wife was an amazing woman. I killed her," Richard stated flatly. "When I was in Caer Llion, John Lewis Hugo revealed the role he played in that murder. Tomorrow I plan on correcting it."

"You did not really kill her?" Deirdre prodded, hoping.

"I was tricked, but it was my blade that slid through her chest," he answered. "I can still feel it, still have the odor of that night in my nose, still see the look of betrayal in her eyes as her light faded from them. I was meant to protect the people of Seattle. But I could not protect my very own wife from myself."

Horror filled Deirdre. Richard had killed his wife. Saddened by what he had gone through, understanding dawned. He would carry the hardship for the rest of his life.

All she could do was be there for him.

"Self-hatred has eaten my soul," he said. "Now revenge rules it. I'm not sure I'm capable of loving again."

"I see," Deirdre said. "Then my mother was wrong."

"What do you mean?"

"Nothing. I do not believe it. One day you will love again."

"I am a broken shell of a man, Deirdre," Richard said. "I have been for so many years I don't know anything different. You would do better to embrace young Ardall. He is quite smitten with you. As for me, tomorrow a part of the pain I carry will be silenced forever. Or I will die."

"You felt nothing when we kissed?"

"Nothing."

Her heart sank. Unfamiliar tears stung her eyes. She suddenly felt a fool. For days she had hoped to trap his heart but in turn had only hurt her own.

"I am sorry that causes you pain," he said. "As I said, Bran wou—"

"I *do not* want Bran Ardall," she breathed, aggravated. "I am in love with *you*."

"I'm sorry," he whispered finally.

Crossing her arms, Deirdre said nothing. There was nothing *to* say. When Richard moved to console her, she turned away, hiding her shimmering eyes.

"Leave me be," she sighed.

Richard gave her a final silent look before he turned and walked from the glen. His fading footsteps were the saddest thing she had ever heard.

Deirdre let him go.

She didn't want him to see her tears.

Chapter 33

"I will not evacuate the Basilica!" Clement roared.

Cormac stared hard at the Pope, watching the color rise in the other's cheeks despite the chill in the chamber of the Seer. A newly lit fire crackled in the hearth but offered only light. The Vigilo convened not in their usual private room but instead in the depths of St. Peter's, where Donato once lived. It was unchanged. It still held his books, his clothing, his belongings, and it all reminded Cormac the loss he suffered. The Cardinal Vicar hated being there. The feeling of holding his lifeless mentor stayed with him. It would never leave.

"Never in the history of Rome has St. Peter's been evacuated!" the Pope yelled, his anger filling the caverns.

"Your Eminence, there is no choice," Cardinal Villenza said.

"There is always a *choice*. Always."

The Vigilo stood in a half circle around the Fionúir Mirror, the relic draped with its sable cloth. Like Cormac, the men gathered did not wear their ceremonial dress of office; they wore simple attire beneath black rippling robes bearing the crest of St. Peter's embroidered onto each breast, the clothing more functional and useful if they had to move quickly to respond to the poised threat on their doorstep.

"How did it come to this?" the Pope demanded harshly, directed at Cormac.

The Vigilo grew silent under the penetrating glare of Clement. Cormac returned his stare, unflinching. He would not give the Pope the benefit of turning away. Clement blamed Cormac for what was happening. The Cardinal Vicar kept his silence. He knew voicing his anger would do nothing for his future plans and put him at risk for further lamentation by his peers.

"I wish to speak to the knight," Clement barked. "Now."

"He is just outside, Your Grace," Cardinal Tucci said.

"Well, show him in. I would hear this from his own lips."

Cardinal Tucci did as he was commanded, opening the door leading into the catacombs. Ennio Rossi entered, his gait smooth, his eyes dark pools of youth. He was young, younger than any Cardinal by decades, but Cormac had seen him age over the last week in ways a twenty-year-old shouldn't. Ennio too had looked upon the Cardinal Seer as a mentor and he too grieved. In place of innocence, a perceivable weight hung. Only hardship in life could reduce one in such a way—like the death of loved ones—and it was apparent Ennio now suffered life's vicissitudes.

Ennio Rossi knelt before Clement and kissed the Ring of the Fisherman.

"Ennio Rossi, Knight of the Seven," Clement announced formally, allowing Ennio to rise. "What I hear is disconcerting. A massive army the likes the Vatican has never seen marches against us. The Vigilo would hear what you know. Let nothing keep you from telling me all."

"It comes, Your Grace," Ennio started nervously, the crackling of the hearth the only other sound. "As I explained to Cardinal Vicar O'Connor, I was called before the other knights mere hours ago by Richard McAllister. All Seven came, including the new knight of Seattle, Bran Ardall. Richard informed us of the impending invasion of the Vatican. Plantagenet has built an army of incredible size, one of Templar Knights and savage halfbreeds. Richard almost died twice while he fought to learn more. The army marches toward the portal leading here. Richard believes Philip intends to bring that army through and begin some kind of new world order."

"But that is not all, is it?" Cardinal Tucci asked.

"No. Richard says Philip commands the Holy Grail."

Grumbling once more broke out among the Cardinals.

Like those around him, Cormac could not believe the Grail had been found let alone had fallen into the hands of a man like Philip. It explained much about Annwn and how Philip had been able to quell that land while remaining alive for centuries.

And McAllister had become the Heliwr, the power now beyond Cormac. It grated on him like salt in a wound.

"Do you believe McAllister, Rossi?" Clement asked.

Ennio Rossi looked down at his feet, his features pale.

"Well?" the pontiff growled. "The answer isn't down there!"

"Richard McAllister was quite clear," Ennio stuttered. "And yes, I believe he speaks truly. He has seen with his own eyes the army *and* the Grail. He saw the effects of the Cup of Christ on several soldiers. No matter how he beat them down with the Dark Thorn they rose to fight again. The Grail makes each of their soldiers like dozens."

"McAllister," the Pope whispered. "The Holy Grail."

"It matches up with the death of the Cardinal Seer," Cormac admitted. "Philip would not want the Vatican peering into Annwn while he moves an army toward the Rome gateway. Maintaining his element of surprise would be one of his foremost strategies."

"It almost worked," Cardinal Smith-Johnson said. "If McAllister had not abdicated his duty in Seattle to enter Annwn, we may *still* not have known of this threat."

The other Cardinals nodded their agreement.

"What of the other knights, Ennio?" Cardinal Tucci said. "Will they aid the Vatican?"

"They lack the time to travel to Rome," Ennio replied. "And each of their portals are too far away to join Richard and the Tuatha de Dannan at the portal in the Forest of Dean."

"So knowing has not improved our situation much," Clement said.

"Ennio will be prepared," Cormac said. "Swiss Guard too."

"You mentioned the Tuatha de Dannan," Cardinal Villenza interrupted. "What role are the fey folk playing in this?"

"The Queen of the Seelie Court has brought together her lords and a massive army of her own. They are poised near the portal, waiting. The Queen apparently knows if Philip enters this world, the destruction of Annwn will be assured. The ultimate plunder at the expense of the fey. The Seelie Court desires the defeat of Philip as much as the Church does."

"Two armies then," the Pope pondered. "All too near."

Ennio shifted his gaze away from the Pope. Cormac was proud of the boy. The scrutiny being sent him by the Vigilo would have wilted lesser men.

"And what of Ardall?" Clement asked.

"He is near my age, I think," Ennio answered, standing straighter. "He was quiet but nodded and gave his agreement with Richard when others of the Seven pressed him. He lost his left hand but has gained a magical gauntlet. Richard had confidence in him, although I do not know how much aid he will be able to give. Sal pointed out Ardall is untrained and virtually useless."

"It is true then," Clement said. "The boy has taken up a knight's mantle."

"He has. For him to be there, with us, makes it certain."

"Myrddin Emrys," Cardinal Villenza hissed.

Pope Clement looked hard at Cormac. He had failed in gaining the power of the Heliwr. Now, it seemed, the Pope blamed him for not gaining *two* knights for the Church.

"It is settled then," Cardinal Smith-Johnson said. "The facts of the matter do not lie. It is time to leave St. Peter's. Time to bolster our defense here in the warrens. Too many souls work and pray and visit the hallways and buildings above, the *city* above. It is our role to protect them. It is our role to do what must be done."

The Pope looked into the blazing hearth. He did so for long moments. No one interrupted him. The group waited for Clement, the pontiff having the final say in what was to come.

The call to evacuate St. Peter's would soon come.

"How will this be done?" Clement murmured.

"One of the foremost reasons Pope Gregory IV called for the current placement of the portal beneath the Basilica was to ensure sufficient defense could be brought to bear against such an invasion from Annwn. We do have options, Your Eminence."

"No such invasion has ever occurred in our history."

"True," Cormac confessed. "But as the Cardinal Seer was fond of saying, time comes for all things."

"Bolstering our defense is paramount then," Cardinal Tucci said.

Cardinal Villenza nodded. "What has become of Captain Arne?"

The Pope returned his hot gaze at Cormac.

"No word," Cormac divulged. "Still in Annwn."

"On a fool's errand," Clement said. "He who possesses the Shield of Arthur was ever meant to protect the Church and the Vatican."

"I felt it more wise to send him to Annwn and gain the Heliwr before Myrddin Emrys could complete his plans, Your Eminence," Cormac argued. "I could not have known the intentions of Philip or how they would enter our lives here."

"Wisdom!? You know not the word!" Clement thundered.

The room fell silent. The anger of the Pope infused the air. Cormac had never seen the pontiff so enraged—and he understood, to a point. Clement felt trapped by circumstance that he had no control over. Events he was barely privy to were directly threatening all he had come to shelter and grow. Few courses of action were available to him. Cormac could deflect the fury of Clement; the Cardinal Vicar only hoped the Pope would choose to fight back.

"It might be best for Your Eminence to vacate the Vatican," Cardinal Diaz suggested, breaking the silence. "The Lateran Palace on the other side of Rome, perhaps?"

"And present our faith to Plantagenet on a silver plate? No."

"Your safety is more important than—"

"My safety is tied to that of the Church, Cardinal Diaz," Clement said. "And the Church is in danger. Those of you here represent many souls around the world. It is you who must find sanctuary, weather the storm that comes into our home."

The Cardinals spoke their protestations at once.

"I will not hear it," Clement said loudly, raising his hand. The others fell silent. "You will leave St. Peter's immediately and find safety from what comes. There is nothing any of you can do in the midst of this danger, but you must remain to keep the hope the Lord instilled in each of us alive." He paused. "Cardinal Tucci, organize the Swiss Guard. Call all to arms and order them into the catacombs. They must be outfitted with the entirety of firepower the Vatican has at its disposal. Cardinal Villenza, make preparations as if the Vatican will be besieged—food caches, water, medical needs. You understand?"

The Cardinals nodded, but they were not pleased.

Clement turned to Ennio. "Do you have the power to destroy the portal?"

"I do not," the young knight admitted, fidgeting under the scrutiny. "It takes a wizard of immense power to achieve an event of that magnitude. I can, however, bring the catacombs down upon the portal, closing it off for the time being."

"It is settled," Clement said firmly. "Carry out my wishes and then find sanctuary." He turned to Cormac. "Cardinal Vicar, come with me."

Cormac frowned. "Me, Your Grace?"

"You will remain by my side in this," Clement said resolutely.

Ice filled his chest. Clement spoke a quick prayer, asking the Lord to watch over the Cardinals and keep all who required it safe. He then gave the members of the Vigilo his farewell before striding from the chamber with an urgency Cormac had never seen the Pope possess.

With the murmur of Cardinals discussing how events had unfolded and the choices the Pope had made fading behind, they both ascended the stairs into the upper levels of the Basilica.

Cormac wondered where he was being taken.

Once the two men had gained the upper corridors of St. Peter's, Clement glanced over his shoulder.

"I know you desire the papacy, Cormac."

Cormac walked a step behind Clement, unprepared for such a statement and unsure of how to reply. The two men made their way quietly, their soft boots barely making a sound on the polished granite floors. No one was about. The wing they were in was private, several rooms holding treasures from centuries past and housing the secondary suite of the Pope, offering a place of refreshment if he was uninterested to return to his primary Papal Palace apartments.

Cormac had rarely been here—few had—but Clement guided him with earnest purpose.

"I hope to serve the Lord in any capaci—

"No!" Clement cut him off and stopped, a finger raised like a sword. "When I say you desire it, I mean the darkest filament of desire possible runs through you. You wish the authority to protect the Church and all souls who comprise it, of that I have no doubt, but personal reasons guide you. I know of your past. The death of your family so long ago has never left you, and the revenge in your heart has been tempered over time into a driving force. The Seer knew it just as I do." He paused. "You have done well in overseeing the spiritual needs of Vatican City during my tenure, but I fear for what you will do if given the chance."

Old wounds opened for Cormac. "I have no reason to provoke anyone," he said.

"I truly doubt that, Cardinal Vicar."

Clement continued down the hall. Cormac did not know what to say. With a few pointed words, Clement had peeled back and exposed the lingering pain Cormac had carried with him for decades.

It would never die.

The two men eventually entered a suite, Clement locking the door behind them. Sunlight flooded multiple rooms through tall stained glass windows, casting various colors upon rugs, small statues, and ancient oak furniture that glowed as if newly waxed. Walls were adorned with large bookshelves laden with books; vases holding fresh flowers sat upon the tables. Several architectural maps of the former Basilica hung in encased glass. Marble, gold, silver, and other highly polished stones and metals flashed, artisanal perfection at every corner, but the beauty of the room felt sterile to Cormac. Cold. It was a suite for kings who flaunted their wealth.

Cormac looked around, drawing it all in. The suite would be his one day. If he survived whatever the Pope had in mind for him.

"I know you hoped to the gain the seed for yourself," Clement said, moving through the vestibule into the rooms. "It explains the secrecy you employed. I am not daft. Controlling the Heliwr would make for the strongest of tools in whatever endeavor you made him embrace. You failed, however, and now the Heliwr has fallen to the wizard."

"I did nothing but try to protect the Church and its interests."

"If that is true, you did a terrible job of it."

"And now you wish to castigate my good faith by putting me in harm's way?" Cormac questioned.

"Maybe you aren't as incompetent as you've demonstrated in recent days," the Pope said.

Cormac let the rebuke fall aside.

"Then again," Clement added. "Perhaps I am acknowledging your eventual rise."

The Cardinal Vicar had no idea what the Pope meant. He followed Clement into an adjoining sitting room where six plush chairs surrounded a short round coffee table. The walls were draped in colorful tapestries depicting epic events from the history of the Church—the upside down crucifixion of Saint Peter upon a barren Vatican Hill, the Emperor Constantine with sword held high standing firm against paganism as he legalized Christianity with his other hand, the crowning of Charlemagne before Pope Leo III on Christmas day, and knights bearing the cross of the Crusades storming a fortress in the Middle East.

Clement walked to the bare wall beneath the Crusades tapestry. He stopped.

"It is paramount that what I am about to show you remain between us," the Pope said mysteriously. "You will either come to know it by way of the papacy or we both will die this day and another successor will come to the knowledge on his own. Will you bide my authority and keep this secret I am about to unveil?"

Cormac nodded, confused but curious.

The Pope grunted and stepped to the simple gray blocks comprising the wall. He ran his leathered fingers over the stone as if searching for something. After long moments had passed, he placed the palms of his hands flat to the rock and, pressing inward, closed his eyes and grew still. Sweat glistened on his wrinkled skin. Mumbling words Cormac thought were Welsh, Clement leaned in closer to the wall as if unable to hold his body up any longer.

Cormac was about to step in, worried despite his misgivings for the Pope, when yellow light began to emanate from the fingertips of the pontiff, first barely perceptible but growing in brightness. With the knights of the Crusade watching from above, the cold fire seeped into the stone as if it were porous, and shot outward in various directions like cracks in a broken pane of glass. The room became drenched in golden light. Soon the outline of a tall rectangle became visible, the fire in the wall changing, molten and alive, moving fluidly as if sentient.

Just when Cormac thought fire would engulf Clement entirely, a bright, soundless flash erupted from the wall and Clement disappeared. Cormac shielded his eyes but when he looked again the fire was gone. Replacing it was a tall rectangular doorway.

And beyond, a room shrouded in gloom.

Eyes still closed, Clement took a deep breath, standing in front of the doorway, and then looked to Cormac.

"What did you do?" Cormac asked, shocked. "How . . . ? What happened . . . ?"

"If the white smoke blows for you one day, you will learn it," Clement replied tiredly. "It is a very old power, one of a few passed down from Pope to Pope for several centuries. The right words, a strong will, and need."

"What is beyond?"

"Beyond? Our salvation, I pray."

Clement strode into the dark recess without another look at Cormac. The Cardinal Vicar followed. Air grown stale from years of being trapped washed over them, and darkness met him with a terrible chill. Cormac barely felt it. Somewhere in the chamber an unidentifiable entity stirred, thrumming with life that raised the hairs on the back of his neck. Unsure suddenly about the intentions of Clement, Cormac paused, wondering if he should defy the Pope and leave.

Then he realized what he sensed.

It was collected power unimaginable.

Clement struck a flame into existence in the depths of the dimness and lit a series of small torches placed in sconces at even intervals around the square perimeter of the room. The light revealed an armory of sorts. Clamps set in the wall held numerous swords, axes, spears, staves, lances, and various other weapons of war, each unique, most glimmering in the firelight as if alive. A series of shelves set in the left-hand wall stored folded blankets, robes, cloaks, and gloves, while another shelf on the right carried numerous leather-bound books and trinkets. A glass case in the middle of the chamber held the remains of hair, splinters of wood, urns, and a number of different bones, from fingers to legs to skulls. It was a macabre repository, one Cormac could not believe existed.

"What is this place?" he asked, mesmerized.

"It is the Vault. How did Myyrdin Emrys empower the Knights of the Yn Saith?"

"He gave them magical weapons," Cormac answered. "Given such great power by the wizard, the knights can decide for themselves how to best serve the promise of the Vigilo."

"Partly right," Clement said. "He gave them magical weapons possessed by one person in history—the Britannian King Arthur. Along with the blade of Lancelot, the wizard chose to give the weapons he had access to."

"And?"

"These are many *other* relics the wizard had no ability to gain and subvert," Clement continued, gesturing at the walls and glass case. "Each of the items you see before you hold a property that science cannot explain. Magic, if you want to call it that, imbued by the Word's will. Over the years, beginning in the fourth century with the building of Old St. Peter's, the Church has hunted for these items, the most deliberate effort carried out by the

Templars in the Crusades, invading the Middle East. Others have brought them to the Church, some out of goodness to see right done, others for political favor or financial gain."

"Why have I not heard of this room before?"

"The best way to keep a secret is for few to know it," Clement said. "In this case, the Cardinal Archivist also possesses the knowledge, in case of a pontiff's sudden death."

The Pope went to the wall of weapons. With a steady hand he reached up and carefully removed a sword, the blade shining like chrome in sunlight. It was a long broadsword, its hilt thick, golden, and slightly curved toward the tip, the double-handed grip wrapped in silver wire. The pommel glimmered gold, the disk bearing the image of an oak leaf. It was a simple piece of craftsmanship but it radiated beauty and might. Holding it upright to catch the torchlight, Clement looked it over from tip to end, admiring what he held.

"Here is Durendal," Clement said.

"It's a work of art."

"It was once the weapon of Roland, a captain of Charlemagne, slaughtered in the battle of Ronceveux Pass. Legend recounts Durendal once belonged to Hector of Troy, reforged from his sword after his death at the hands of Achilles, but that has never been proven. It is a powerful weapon, unbreakable, enchanted by several Saints. It should aid us at this time of need."

"Ahh yes, I know of it. Didn't that sword vanish . . . into a river?"

"Poisoned stream," Clement corrected. "And yes, it disappeared from the sight of man. Roland tried to destroy it, but when he failed he had to hide it from his enemies. As with many things lost, it was found—and eventually brought here."

Cormac nodded. "We are arming ourselves then?"

"Indeed. The knights are equipped with powerful talismans. Philip Plantagenet has the power of the Grail at his command and who knows what else. Even most of the fey creatures of Annwn possess magic. The only chance the Basilica has of withstanding what marches toward it is to even the odds."

"You know the potential of each relic here?"

Clement pointed at a lone book sitting on a pedestal near the door that Cormac had missed. "The Exsequiae Codex. All of the relics here have been documented."

"I assume you are showing me the Vault to equip me as well?" Cormac asked.

Clement found an oiled belt with a scabbard, and after tightening it about his waist he sheathed Durendal. He then pulled down a dark gray broadsword from its placement on the wall, its metal glistening like a darkened rainbow. It was longer than Durendal, longer than Cormac's legs even, but Clement held it as if it were light as a feather. The blade was the opposite of the one Clement carried on his belt; the entire sword appeared to be iron, its hilt wide jagged blades like sharp thorns, its pommel a dagger-like diamond, the weapon absorbing the light and reflecting none.

He handed the sword to Cormac, hilt first, all too carefully.

"This is Hrunting."

"Hrunting . . . ?" Cormac asked, unable to remember where he had heard it before.

"Yes, Hrunting. The Demon-nail."

"It can't be," the Cardinal Vicar whispered. "That's fiction!"

"Fiction to whom?" the Pope asked. "Those who lacked the ability to document the story originally as history? Oral traditions are corruptible; they can become history or tale quite easily. Beowulf was real. Hrunting is real. It is one of the oldest relics to have been brought to the Vatican. Roman Catholic monks recovered it in Northumbria, sometime in the eighth century I believe, and they brought it to Rome. Hrunting can slice through stone. No one knows how it does this, nor how its iron can be stronger than steel." Clement paused, prepared to release the sword. "Take it, now."

Cormac took the blade. Hrunting was as light as a feather but he almost dropped it anyway. A tingling immediately traveled into his hand and up his arm, a throbbing like his entire limb had fallen asleep. The feeling passed after seconds, but heat continued to emanate from the hilt.

Cormac tightened his grip. He did not want to drop it.

"None of my predecessors know what that feeling in your hand is," Clement commented. He handed Cormac a belt and sheathe. "But it matters not. Hrunting is powerful. It will keep you safe for what comes."

"I like the sound of that, Your Eminence," Cormac said, a bit sarcastically.

"This room must remain protected."

"It will be," Cormac said, belting Hrunting at his waist. "We will not fail today."

"It cannot fall to the fey or anyone else," Clement said. "For anyone to take these items could mean terror for the world. Philip may have the Holy Grail, but the relics here would make an army even more powerful."

Cormac nodded.

"Cardinal Tucci and Cardinal Villenza will have already started fortifying the catacombs around the portal," Clement continued, extinguishing the torches in the Vault. "The knight will have need of us. He is young and inexperienced. He will need our guidance."

Cormac left the room, with its ancient relics and musty smell. When Clement had cleared the entrance he whispered a few words under his breath. The wall reformed as if it were alive, the blocks of stone returning to their original positions, mortar joining them all.

By the time they left, the Vault had become hidden once more.

Clement exited his suite. Cormac once again followed. They traveled back downward, through the elegant halls of granite and beautiful tapestries, passed marble statues in piety, back to the nave of the Basilica and into the warrens carved out of the rock of Italy. All that Cormac saw he now fought to protect, with his life if it came to that. Both men did not speak; the time for speaking had ended. The exacerbated animosity they both held was relegated to the past and held no place in the present.

That might change after Philip Plantagenet. If they survived.

For now, they were willing companions.

By the time they had returned to the barren underground world beneath St. Peter's, much had changed. Hundreds of Swiss Guard flooded the catacombs, each fulfilling some order they were given, all bearing semi-automatic weapons, pistols, and additional ammunition. Clement and Cormac parted them like a sea, authority and purpose written on their faces and in their strides. The air grew cooler as they descended farther, and soon they were standing on the subterranean shore of the underground branch to the Tiber River. Provisions for a long siege had been brought to the catacombs and defenses erected to aid them.

None of the soldiers questioned their orders, but they all sent awkward glances at the shimmering portal from time to time.

Cormac fingered the hilt of Hrunting, standing behind the line of soldiers and next to the Pope. Power emanated from the sword, his at command. He was ready. He suppressed his fear with anger and memories. Someone in Annwn had murdered his mentor and friend, and it gave him renewed strength to see right done.

He hoped he would have the opportunity to avenge that death.

Hours passed. Nothing happened.

Just when Cormac began to wonder if Ennio Rossi had been misled, the gray sheen of the portal shimmered, darkening movement stirring within it.

Cormac tightened his grip on Hrunting and drew it forth.

And waited for the inevitable.

Chapter 34

The heat beat down on Philip, matching his will to see his crusade through.

The day was beautiful, as clear as any that had come before it the past eight centuries. He could not have created a better one for conquest. The way was clear, his course set. The army he had amassed trailed behind him. It had taken generations of population growth since entering Annwn with the initial campaign of Templar Knights to have enough warriors to overcome the fey and return home. It had taken even longer to discover if the Graal could be useful beyond his own longevity. Capturing Arawn and using his knowledge had been key. Weakening the portals had been the last event. Each plan lay complete.

Now Philip yielded unimaginable power. When night fell, he would be returned to the world of his birth, a conqueror of worlds.

The only thing he lacked was the power of the Yn Saith.

Philip suppressed rage at the thought. Losing McAllister and Ardall still grated on him. Neither knight nor their weapons were his. The attack on Caer Llion had been a bold one, bolder than he thought capable of the demon wizard. He knew the Seelie Court had not conducted it. The reports from his soldiers indicated the halfbreed from Seattle, which pointed at Myrddin Emrys. Philip still did not know how the knights had escaped—the huge halfbreed could not have entered the close-quartered dungeons and released them, let alone kill his guards unaware—but it did not matter. The knights were gone and beyond his reach.

Philip pushed the matter aside. He would not let the small setback ruin his day.

The portal mountain appeared through the heat haze of the plains, beckoning to him and his destiny. Formed of white granite that lay beneath the emerald carpet of grass, the mountain jutted out of the world as if a giant had pushed its thumb up through the land and left it there.

To the east, the Forest of Dean spread like a green stain.

"The Cailleach is prepared, my king," John said, riding up next to Philip.

"She had better be, if this day is to go as planned," Philip said sharply. "The halfbreeds under her rule must be controlled if we are to have full command of our power."

"You are still worried about the loss of the knights?"

"It would do you well to be as worried," Philip said. He forced himself to be calm. "A king must be wary. There are other powers at play in this besides the wizard. Arrogance could kill us. Even the fey cannot be discounted."

"They will not be," John said. "The Tuatha de Dannan would not dream of attacking such a large force as you have assembled. If they do, it would be like a fly to a lion. Once we enter Rome and gain the Vault in the Basilica, fortune will be yours. With the relics housed there, none will defy you. Not there. Not here. Time will prove me right."

"There is more transpiring here than what we know, John. My instincts roar at me," Philip frowned. He looked around at the day as if able to find the problem. "Something is not right. I can feel it. We have left enough warriors at Caer Llion to keep our interests secure, and you have assured me the fey are inconsequential despite gathering their forces, but still I worry."

"Battle apprehensions, my king," John consoled. "As you have said, the Tuatha de Dannan are a broken group, unable to rouse their former might. I tell you the same, based on what I have seen the last few weeks. After this day, it will not matter."

"I want you at my side during the entirety of today," Philip ordered, still uneasy. He held the gaze of his advisor meaningfully. "It will take our combined war histories to overthrow the Vatican. Those in command of St. Peter's know of their danger. They will be prepared. And they possess power that we cannot afford to forget."

"I will do what I can to remain at your side," John replied, looking at the sky. "As Master Wace used to say, there are no guarantees in war. Only glory to take."

Philip did not reply. John had grown increasingly distant in the last few days. There was a hollowness to him, as if he were thinking of events that had nothing to do with capturing Rome and returning home. There were times Philip wondered if his friend still held the same ideals as he did. The Vault seemed foremost on his thoughts, as if gaining it meant the end of war. Philip did not agree with that. Magical implements were important, but he believed what Master Wace had taught so long ago.

Through arms, came strength.

Philip just hoped John had the ability to see the day through to its end.

As the mid-afternoon came so too did Philip to the mountain portal, the heat an itch on the back of his neck. The peak was larger than the distance had displayed, thrusting into the sky. Twisted trees clung to its side, the soil too thin to grow much else. About halfway to its summit, Philip could just make out two dead stumps between which a void of air shimmered in the day, the portal waiting for the High King of Annwn. No wind blew. No animals stirred. It was as though only Philip and the portal existed, each drawing the other onward.

He dismounted and glanced up the mountain. The trail to the portal above waited. It was far too steep for horses but that did not matter. Horses were not required for conquering Rome. Philip curbed his instincts that continued to scream at him. He would climb. He would bring his army through. He would regain the throne of his family, the blood running in rivers if needs be, and fulfill what his father had ordained.

Unleashing Hauteclere from his hip, he said a prayer before turning to his friend.

"John Lewis Hugo, our destiny awaits."

Not waiting for a reply, Philip entered the trail, John a step behind. It was not as difficult as it looked, his desire to gain the portal driving him upward. It took only minutes for him to gain the large ledge where the portal shimmered between two oak tree stumps of immense size. He looked out over the plains behind him. His army spread as far as the eye could see, a dark stream of death for any who tried to get in his way.

Philip smiled. After more than eight centuries, it was time.

Sucking on the tube leading to the sack on his back, Philip entered the portal.

Time seemed to freeze.

The portal felt the same as the one he had entered in London. The gray swirled around him, a void of unsettling vertigo. The path before him was blank. He walked forward anyway. He had done it before and knew what to expect. When the light intensified and pressure built on his chest until he could barely breathe, he girded his soul for the battle he knew would come, one he had always known would be a part of his destiny.

Philip Plantagenet returned to the world of his birth.

Chaos and pain came the moment he tumbled free of the portal. The cacophony of weaponry pummeled him as soon as he stepped into the cavern, an assault like none he had witnessed against any person in his life. He grimaced but kept his fear in check, the contents of the bag on his back keeping him alive as he freely drank. John followed him, doing the same, as did the first Templar Knights to enter Rome. Before them hundreds of Swiss Guardsmen fired their weapons from all quarters, the projectiles threatening to drive Philip backward. He held his ground, sneering. With every bullet that entered him, the Graal pushed it out; the moment a bone or his skull was struck, it healed. It would take more than the weapons of man to kill him and his men.

The Templar Knights continued to swarm out of the portal wearing leather bags of their own; dozens upon dozens of soldiers came forth, until hundreds formed an arc around the portal, keeping their king safe from the Vatican defense.

All were invincible. All were ready to die if need be.

The gunfire ceased suddenly, the silence deafening, as the roar of a man beyond the Swiss Guards lorded over all.

"Philip Plantagenet!"

With the assault's reprieve, Philip gained a better look at who had called his name. Two older men and a boy of barely twenty years stood beyond the defensive arcs of soldiers, all focused on the portal and the Templars that continued to stream through. The boy held a flaming knife that marked him as the portal knight; the men gripped long broadswords and wore black robes, one of which bore the papal crest of arms.

"Pontiff of Vatican City," Philip greeted, his contempt thick. "It appears you have a wonderful welcoming party here. Have you brought more worthy warriors to my cause?"

"I am Pope Clement XV," the oldest of the men said. "Beside me is the Cardinal Vicar of Rome, Cormac Pell O'Connor. St. Peter's Basilica is a sanctuary, one for the devout and one for the good. This day has sadly long been in coming. The Vigilo has witnessed your rise in Caer Llion, the growth of your people, the construction of an army filled with dark purpose. We will not abide its existence in this world. You must return. Now."

"I do not believe so," Philip said. "I have spent centuries in Annwn. The fey have been quelled. It is time. Time to fulfill the promise to my father made so many centuries ago. Time to wash this world of its evil as I did in Annwn. Time for you to join me or die. There are no other options, Pope Clement XV."

"From what I understand, you have not completed your duty."

Philip smiled. "I control Annwn."

"The Templar Knights at your side were banished for heresy centuries ago," the Pope continued, his voice firm. "You will take them from these sacred grounds. Or we will see them sent to Hell where they—and you—belong."

"My king has come to fulfill Saint Peter's direction for the world," John said beside Philip. "You are both of the Vigilo. I sense that much. Embrace us as brothers, not as enemies! It is time we work together, to establish the world as God intended, to see the Word spread through this world as it has never been before."

"You are a rotted man, John Lewis Hugo," the Cardinal Vicar spat, his red hair almost as white as his companion's. "Your selfish appetites while in Annwn have been well documented over the centuries. The Cardinal Seers have witnessed much. The last Seer in particular."

"The dead spy, you mean?" John said, smiling.

The Cardinal Vicar crimsoned.

Philip half expected the man to charge them.

"He was . . . weak," John said, a grin pulling at his decimated face. "As was his faith. He died a traitor's death. I read on you his memory, Cormac Pell O'Connor. It was you with him, was it not? Do not answer. I sense it to be true. You ran from me like a coward who nears wetting himself."

The Cardinal Vicar darkened with fury, his grip tightening on the sword he carried.

The Pope placed a warning hand on the other's forearm.

"I will kill you, John Lewis Hugo," Cormac Pell O'Connor said.

"You will return to Annwn voluntarily—or in a casket," the Pope declared to Philip. "Even with your polluted use of the Word's most cherished remembrance of His power on this Earth, it will be for naught. The knight at my side will stop you."

"It is clear to me you both are as weak," Philip sneered. "This world is weak. It has lost its way. You have been poor caretakers. I am here to rectify that. The Yn Saith who entered Annwn have both been ineffective in their quests. One is so faithless he can barely call his power. The other has lost a hand and his way. Neither is here to protect you, and one portal knight cannot possibly stand in my way. The Vigilo is a shadow of what Saint Peter intended. I will see his glory done and Rome returned to its former heart of spiritual guidance."

"I will not let that happen," the Pope said firmly.

"We will see."

"Show them the Word's wrath!" the Pope yelled.

Gunfire erupted again, the bullets cutting into the Templar Knights in front of Philip. He was safe, the wall of flesh and Graal might between him and harm. The soldiers advanced, a few dying as bullets infiltrated eyeholes in helms or soldiers not drinking from their bag at the right time, but most pushed forward as they cut down any Vatican guard that got in their way. It was slow moving. But in time, Philip knew, the cavern would be in his possession.

The rest of the Vatican would fall as well.

Seeing the obvious, the Pope and his Vicar joined the fray. Alongside the portal knight, they slashed into the center of the Templar Knights. It was clear they were uneducated in the use of such weapons, but what they lacked in ability they gained in magic. The swords they wielded were not ordinary. They cut through weapons and armor alike, eviscerating the men of Annwn before the Graal could heal. Arms and legs were severed from bodies, heads were decapitated from necks; the two men were soon covered in blood and gore.

The Pope and his Vicar fought valiantly but Philip knew the Vigilo leaders would eventually fall. The army from Annwn was too large.

When they were dead, Philip would take the swords.

The first of many useful trophies

The battle was deafening, the close quarters echoing the chaos. The knight fought like an enraged tiger, lashing out with fire and lightning born of his Arthurian dagger, Carnwennan. The fire consumed the Templar Knights, incinerating those who did not protect themselves with the Graal. The greatest losses were near the knight, who had moved toward the side of the cavern in an attempt to flank the warriors of Caer Llion.

Before Philip could order a counterattack, John charged with a wedge of Templar Knights to the right side, his burned face snarling an inhuman rage. The armored group tore into the Swiss Guards there, swords, axes, and maces chopping down men whose last thoughts were of horror and death. John roared encouragement even as Philip tried to bolster those soldiers in the middle against the Pope. The portal knight fell back toward the middle again as the Templar Knights barreled their way through the Swiss Guards.

The defense there collapsed completely, giving John and several Templars the chance through. Carnwennan slashed in the air, lightning like a whip and blinding all in its path, closing the gap as the Swiss Guard regrouped and held the line once again.

Hacking through the last few soldiers, John and those with him made for the entrance into the cavern and vanished into the upper reaches of St. Peter's Basilica above.

Leaving Philip alone in the cavern to lead the assault.

Yelling orders at the knight to hold the cavern at all cost, the Pope and his Vicar chased after John.

John's disappearance irked Philip but it had also rid the cavern of the Vigilo. The battle continued, unchecked. Blood ran in rivulets down the embankment toward the river behind the glimmering portal, most of it from unmoving Swiss Guards who littered the stone floor like dead leaves in fall. Still, Philip was unhappy to realize the fight was not ending as quickly as he had hoped, his forces from Annwn needing to increase to finish the Vatican once and for all.

Gauging how best to ensure a quickened victory, Philip felt ice run through his soul.

He realized no more of his soldiers came through from Annwn. The portal was still open, shining its ethereal glow, but his army no longer crossed over.

Something was wrong.

Philip cursed, gripping Hauteclere tighter, angrier than he'd ever been before. The instincts he had ignored in the moment of his triumph rang louder—their warning all too real.

With John gone, he would have to discover the reason himself.

Philip knew the Templar Knights he had brought through could hold the inadequate power of the Swiss Guard. For every warrior who fell and needed time to recover, two more pushed forward, cutting deeper into the hundreds of defenders who tried to keep Philip from his birthright. With the Pope and Vicar gone, it would not take long for Caer Llion to control the cavern. Neither the Swiss Guard nor the wizard's knight had the power to drive his warriors back through the portal. It gave Philip the time he needed to learn what had become of his army.

Then the cavern would fall. St. Peter's would be his. Vatican City would embrace him for the hero of the faith they yearned for. Then Rome.

The world would be next.

Philip needed the rest of his army to do so though.

Barking orders at one of his commanders and taking a dozen of his Templar Knights with him, Philip strode toward the portal back to Annwn.

The shimmering void swallowed him again.

Chapter 35

The army of Philip Plantagenet spread across the grasslands like a black stain.

With Snedeker on his shoulder, Richard watched in horror as the army plodded forward, unable to take his eyes off it. The sheer volume of Templar Knights, unaffiliated warriors of the lords Philip had conquered, and various darkly spawned creatures staggered the mind. He had seen thousands of soldiers camped north of Caer Llion; it had been barely a twentieth of the host now on the plains. Philip led his throng around outcroppings of shattered white granite bursting from the ground, toward the hills fronting the Forest of Dean where a portal shimmered between two leafless oak snags upon the middle of a sentinel mountain almost a mile away.

Arawn rode up to join Philip as the despot led his army.

Hate like he had never known coursed through Richard.

The fey creature undoubtedly had his own plans. Richard had kept the knowledge of John Lewis Hugo's true identity secret. Arawn had once led the Tuatha de Dannan. Richard could not share the truth. To do so could splinter the unified fey army, old factions given new life, destroying any chance of saving both worlds—and getting revenge against Arawn.

He looked over at Bran. The boy looked scared. He fidgeted with his new steel hand as he watched the progress of the host with trepidation.

"What are you thinking?" Deirdre asked Richard, the redhead appearing beside him.

"I am thinking . . . this is the day of your true freedom," he said, hoping he sounded stronger than he truly felt.

"I hope so."

"Confusion and surprise are our only weapons, I fear."

"They will have to do," Deirdre said, pausing. "No matter what occurs today, know that I care for you, Richard McAllister."

Richard looked into her eyes. They were a dark green like a deep sea. He had been hard on her the previous night and a part of him regretted it. He had no idea why she felt the way she did—the wiles of youth or a deeper connection he no longer understood—but it didn't excuse his harshness. Still, it was best he not give her hope for love. Not with him anyway.

He looked at Bran. The boy stared at them hard.

"Deirdre, I hope we survive the day," Richard said simply.

She squeezed his arm and smiled, her freckled face lighting up. She returned to where her father held Willowyn and his own Rhedewyr mount.

"She likes you," Snedeker said.

"Shut up. I know this," Richard growled. He looked around. "Are you prepared, fairy? We will have to be swift if we are to kill John Lewis Hugo."

"Prepare *yourself*, Heliwr," Snedeker said tersely. "I am ready."

"I hope so. Today is likely the day of our deaths."

Snedeker said nothing. Richard did not continue. In his heart, he did not care about the outcome of the battle, not in a way that would affect his decisions on the field. He only wanted a chance to kill Arawn. He had spent the entire night thinking about it. Despite the horrors he had endured in the dungeon of Caer Llion, he had risen that morning stronger in some way. Tempered steel now ran through him.

Nothing during the fight would stand in his way.

The Morrigan stood at the forefront of those who watched from their forest cover, her chin held high, eyes stabbing her enemy. Even though dryads, with their fists thrust into the ground and lips humming an alien song to the foliage, were shielding the Tuatha de Dannan from the locust-like horde, the Morrigan stood just beyond, seeming to invite the coming fight.

The rest of the Seelie Court watched nearby, lost to their thoughts. Caswallawn glowered behind his Queen, sullen and silent. Lord Eigion crouched with fellow Merrow, gills fluttering, eyes wide. Lord Faric stood with Commander Masyn and Captain Henrick, whispering tactics for when the battle began. Lord n'Hagr waited next to Lord Finnbhennach, each dressed in full battle gear, the former carrying large swords and a pole axe strapped to his broad back, the latter leaning on a giant mace, his horns shimmering. Lugh sat in a tree above, gaining a better look at what they faced.

Closest to Bran stood Lord Gerallt and Deirdre, father and daughter, both humans out of place amongst so many fey. Only Aife and Govannon were absent, the centaur vanished and the smith still producing armor and weapons deeper within the Forest of Dean.

The Kreche had left with the dawn, to take up his position according to the plan.

Richard knew what they all were thinking.

The growing army before them was far more powerful in numbers and magical protection than the Tuatha de Dannan.

Behind him, spreading into the far-reaching depths of the forest, the majority of the Tuatha de Dannan army lay silent. All of the fairy creatures were present, beckoned by their lords to fight for Annwn and their freedom, awaiting the command that would send them into conflict. Others had joined as well—massive hairless trolls from the coast with skin like rock, and spriggans hiding under bridges with dirty matted hair and wild wiry dispositions. With the addition of the coblynau and the men and women Lord Gerallt had amassed from his province—all wearing armor hammered together by the Mastersmith—the Queen of the Sarn

Throne's army was formidable.

It was an army composed of dreams.

And nightmares.

But it was nothing compared to the hellish creatures Philip and the Cailleach had bred in the depths of Caer Llion. Fairy and pixie scouts had reported the approach of Philip. It had been hard to believe the reports but now, seeing the horde trail west for miles, they all did. Upon returning, Caswallawn had corroborated it.

Richard had given what opinion he could but the members of the Seelie Court now saw with their own eyes.

Now he waited.

Like the rest of the Tuatha de Dannan.

"How did you find us?" Richard asked the fairy. "In Caer Llion."

"The halfbreed met Deirdre where you left us, after dark," Snedeker said, wings fluttering. "Appeared out of nowhere. Caswallawn, the man with the magic cloak, met us almost at the same time. Deirdre was unsure of them both but they spoke a long time. The halfbreed said much, like it knew the drunk lord would come."

"And then what happened?"

"Then they left and asked me to aid them. Smart asking me, do you not think?"

"But why send Kreche?" Richard murmured to no one.

"Caswallawn knew he could not enter the castle," Snedeker explained. "Magic in the walls that would detect his magic cloak, he said. But the halfbreed created a diversion. Smashed down the wall, just so, and that nasty drunk lord and I snuck in. He is worth his salt, that one. Then we found you."

Richard cursed inwardly. Merle knew too much and hid all of it. Had the wizard seen Richard and Bran in danger? He must have, if he sent the Kreche. Merle would know curse tablets warded Caer Llion and the moment the Kreche broke in, Philip and Arawn would think their alarm tripped by the halfbreed rather than the real culprits—Caswallawn and Snedeker.

It was a simple plan and it had worked. But, as he had done with so many others, Merle had used the Kreche.

One day, if Richard survived the coming battle, the wizard

would have to answer for it all.

It did beg questions though: What other wheels could Merle be setting in motion, particularly on this day?

Separating from the others, Bran came over to Richard.

"I know you are ready for this," Richard said without preamble.

"What will we do?"

"Try to stay alive," Richard snickered. He crossed his arms. "What happens to a snake when you cut its head off?"

"It dies," Bran replied.

"No," the knight said. "The body lives but no longer functions rationally."

Richard pointed out into the plain. The undulating ribbon from Caer Llion wove toward the small mountain granite outcropping at the edge of the Forest of Dean. Philip, Arawn, and the Templar Knights who made up the forward battery had already begun their ascent. The portal glimmered, waiting. It would not be long before they would pass into Rome.

"Why are we allowing this?" Bran questioned.

Richard ignored the question, an unsettling sight to the north. "Look at that."

Bran turned and peered through the canopy leaves. In the far distance black specks flew, miles away. Richard could not make out what they were but he was fairly certain he knew.

"Damn griffins," he growled.

"Why are they separated from their host?" Bran asked.

"I don't know. Perhaps Philip feels they have no use in the crypts of St. Peter's. To be honest I don't care," Richard answered. "The dryads shield us as best they can and at this distance the halfbreeds can't know we are here anyway. If those griffins are that distant they won't be in our way and won't alarm their master to our presence."

Bran said nothing. Richard gave the tightly packed groups of griffins another cursory glance. Instincts grown comfortable with time set alarms. Something was not right. The half-bird, half-fey creatures were Philip's power in the sky. It made no sense for them not to be patrolling over the massive host.

"Can't the Nharth help us? Conceal our attack?" Bran asked.

"The mountain fog fey cannot leave their heights," Richard said and then pointed ahead. "It is as you said, Bran. Look."

Philip left his horse at the base of the rocky pinnacle and traversed the trail upward. Arawn walked a step behind. Templar Knights followed, several thousand strong, their white mantles and gray steel forming a walking wall of death upon the outcropping. Philip, Arawn, and their Knights all possessed leather bags. Richard had wished to attack them early, kill the leaders quickly, but the power of the Grail would let no such plan succeed. Below, the two standards that had led the army now stood to the side of the trail entrance, each bearing a golden lion against a field of crimson. The Cailleach remained far back in the ranks, still within the plains and among the creatures she had bred, controlling them with her magical arts. To the side of the host galloped Lord Gwawl and the other men and fey who made up Caer Llion.

Philip stepped into the portal, absorbed by the gray light—and leading his army just as he had told Bran he would.

A flutter of wings above heralded the return of Arrow Jack.

"It is time," Richard said, patting Lyrian. "Get mounted, Bran."

While Kegan helped Bran mount Westryl, Richard swung up on Lyrian. The Rhedewyr pawed the ground, anticipating what was to come. The former portal knight marveled over the fiery energy beneath him. Lyrian had been a husk of an animal when Richard had met him. Now he lent strength to the knight instead.

"He has become your own," Deirdre said from Willowyn. "He would die for you."

"I hope it never comes to that."

"We all hope for that, McAllister," Kegan said as he and his son Kearney aided the lords to mount. "Best of luck to ye."

The lords of the Seelie Court dispersed, disappearing into the depths of the Forest of Dean to lead their respective peoples. The Morrigan remained while Lugh climbed down from his tree and brought up the bulk of the Long Hand.

Electricity infused the air and the Forest of Dean.

"Wait for my signal," Richard cautioned Lord Faric, who held a silver horn that glowed in the shade's diffuse light.

Almost a quarter of the Templar Knights, most being the command elements of the horde, had ventured into the swirling mass, the remaining soldiers entering two at a time and vanishing like they never existed.

"Wait..."

Lyrian shivered beneath him, muscles shaking and tense. Several hundred more Red Crosses entered Rome.

"Now!" Richard hissed.

The coblynau lifted the ornate Caer Glain horn skyward and blew. The clarion blast shattered the stillness of the day. As the sound diminished, Richard watched the Kreche drop from the heights above the portal upon the Templar Knights below. The bluish-black behemoth landed like a boulder, crushingly, killing the knights who had been about to enter Rome. The halfbreed was maddened and roaring, barring the way into the portal, unleashed and flinging knights from the granite pinnacle like a child throwing dolls. The warriors tried to fight back but it was useless; they screamed until the rocks below silenced them.

The Kreche had come down on the front of the army, unrelenting and loud, like a hammer striking an anvil.

As the halfbreed wrecked havoc, pushing the Templar Knights back down toward the plains, a sound like thunder grew in the forest, intensifying with every passing second.

"Let's hope this works," Richard said. "Ready?"

Summoning Arondight, Bran nodded.

Richard called the Dark Thorn, gaining strength from the magic flowing through him. The reverberation from the forest intensified until the ground shook, the mulch quaking and the leaves overhead trembling.

From out of the trees near the portal, a centaur rushed into the plains, her sword held high in anger and pride.

"For Annwn! Annwn!" Aife screamed, swinging her blade.

She was not alone.

Rhedewyr streamed after, almost a thousand powerful horses tearing up the sod of the plains and sweeping toward the advancing army. The men and creatures on the plain reacted immediately, spinning to confront the stampede, weapons raised in protection. It was to no avail. The horses were upon the army quickly, tearing through the ranks of the host like a scythe through wheat. The Templar Knights on the plains vanished under churning hooves, trampled into Annwn—their blood, armor, and separated limbs flying into the air.

Hundreds of lives were extinguished in moments beneath the charge of the Rhedewyr.

The silver horn erupted again, this time at the command of the Queen, and with Richard at her side and the might of the Tuatha de Dannan at her back, they charged from the Forest of Dean to be free.

Richard did not wait to see if Bran joined.

The Cailleach screeched shrilly, aware of the danger, knowing the king and his second in command were gone, leaving her with lords too far in the rear of the train to make an immediate difference, all exposed to the Tuatha de Dannan. With sharp barks, she released the halfbreeds from her restraint. The unnatural beasts came at once. They bounded across the turf to meet the fey folk, jaws slavering and red eyes glowing. Demon wolves of all shapes and sizes—some tiny and mewling from all fours like cats with human faces, others charging on two feet with sharp claws and canine heads—intermingled in a sea of rushing nightmare. Larger creatures, humans bred with animals much larger than a wolf, came after, the same hatred mirrored in their actions. All growled and spat venom as they came, a tide of unbroken, unnatural evil.

"For Annwn!" the Morrigan yelled, driving directly at the Cailleach.

The witch waited, an inhuman sneer darkening her features, robes pulled back and arms already spitting wicked green pestilence. Almost upon the crone, the Queen brought her own power to bear, her sword burning white.

It was the last thing Richard saw.

Dark, twisted bodies swarmed over him, a tidal wave of biting teeth and tearing claws. Most of the Tuatha de Dannan vanished from sight. Richard kept the Dark Thorn before him, protecting Lyrian as best he could, already sweating from exertion. His steed fought against the demon wolves like a rabid wolverine, fore- and rear legs shattering skulls and limbs and opening up bodies with ease. Richard sent his magic lancing at any dark thing that came, killing dozens of the manic halfbreeds, keeping them at bay with white fire. Black blood and ichor splattered him but he ignored it.

The world he knew fell away, the sun almost gone from his view by the unending torrent, his awareness reduced to adrenaline, twisted limbs, and bony spikes.

The need to stay alive, to enact revenge, burned through him, lending him strength.

Chaos ruled.

Like death, it had consumed Annwn.

As he charred the aberrations dead, flashes of the familiar came to him from other quarters at his peripherals. One moment a brigade of coblynau led by Lord Faric would push their way through the malformed bodies, hacking with axes and hammers, the fighters gruesome in their precision before disappearing again. Another moment the mighty Lord Finnbhennach appeared, his white horns caked with blood and gore, his mace a blurred weapon as it crushed all who came within reach. From far away he gained glimpses of the Merrow slinging tiny balls of white light that concussively exploded into the demon wolves until the water folk were chased down by a division of Templar Knights; Lord n'Hagr drove his buggane to their aid, unable to outright kill the Grail-protected warriors but pushing them back from the deadly Merrow.

The other fey lords swam in and out of his vision, fighting, killing, and dying. Together, they had dropped age-old animosities to save one another.

Richard got a glimpse of the portal. The Kreche had massacred until he had reached the plains, the huge halfbreed killing the Templar Knights despite the Grail water they carried.

No one else entered the portal.

Though hundreds of Templars had gotten through, Rome was safe—for now.

Then the Dark Thorn was almost ripped from him.

He held on, barely, his fingers clamping down on the warm wood as he confronted his assailant. A werewolf-looking creature gripped the staff, snarling as it wrenched on the source of the knight's power. Lyrian kicked out, panicked, but the creature was too close. Other demon wolves came on, bolstered by what their brethren had done.

Richard did not hesitate.

He sent magic coursing through the staff into the beast. The creature absorbed it, hair curling, flames vomiting forth from its gaping, fanged mouth, its muscles rigid in apoplexy.

The beast exploded, bits flying in all directions.

Richard kept his seat, if barely. Cursing his distracted carelessness, he continued to mow through the dark masses. A bit lightheaded, he swallowed dust from the air, and appraised the battle. The Tuatha de Dannan were mostly emptied from the Forest of Dean, trying to keep their lines from folding beneath the overwhelming numbers. Richard was now deep into the plains, overextended. Lyrian navigated the uplifted white granite with uncertain steps, even the surefooted horse having a hard time with the natural minefield.

Fearful his Rhedewyr might trip, Richard fought to return to the fey, knowing if the Caer Llion army broke through the Tuatha de Dannan, all would be lost.

Just as he began to fight free, a monstrosity almost as large as the Kreche roamed into view and came right for him. It shook the ground, its wide head shaped like that of a bear, its foamy roar of anger filled with long saber-like teeth. The brown shaggy fur acted like a shield, but the monster bled from numerous wounds. It ignored the dark kin around it, until it picked up one of the smaller catlike demon wolves and threw the beast at Richard.

Lyrian reacted instantly.

The Rhedewyr reared in challenge, killing the creature with its hooves even as he knocked it out of the air—and tripped upon a molehill of broken granite.

Lyrian stumbled backward.

Richard fell into demon horde shadow.

The ground almost paralyzed him when he struck it. Fear coursed through his veins. He pushed it down, sending fire in a broad circle from the trod grass of the plains. Enraged by their failures and sensing an advantage, the smaller halfbreeds rushed the fallen, mewling and spitting their hatred, breaking through the fire of the Dark Thorn to rend his life and end it.

Lyrian fought them, his whinny terrible.

Struggling to regain his feet, Richard knew the end was near.

He had failed.

As he hurled his magic in a last prayer, a massive man with sword held high leapt over the knight in defense, hacking at the demons in unbridled fury. Lord Gerallt was an unchained animal, joined by a dozen warriors from Mochdrev Reach. The men threw themselves at the oncoming mayhem, armor forming a barrier. With swords wielded and battle cries screamed, they blocked the tumult from Richard as a human shield.

"Get back, Heliwr!" Lord Gerallt roared. "Now!"

"Up, Rick!" Deirdre screamed, pulling him from behind.

Stumbling backward, Richard watched the demon wolves break upon his saviors like a tidal wave.

He sent fire at the creatures, a scream of warning frozen within.

It was too late.

Lord Gerallt and many of his warriors disappeared beneath the sharp teeth and rending claws of the coming onslaught. Without magic to aid their limited number, they didn't stand a chance. The wall swarmed with more bodies than Richard had seen before, black twisted things compacted into a tight space, their inhuman growls and ravening nearly drowning out the dying screams of Lord Gerallt and the rest of his men.

"Father!" Deirdre howled.

As the bear halfbreed shambled over the spot where the lord had once stood, Richard hauled Deirdre back with all his might but was unable, the woman enraged beyond control.

"He's gone!" he roared.

"No!" she screamed.

"Fall back!"

Richard brought the Dark Thorn up and willed fire passed the Rhedewyr into the bear above them. The beast roared but the fire barely had any effect. Snedeker screamed at the redhead, to flee, to find protection. It would be too late. The blackened noose tightened about Richard, Deirdre, and those warriors of her father's retinue who remained.

If they did not fall back, Richard knew they would join Lord Gerallt in death.

He would not fail—or at least die trying.

Then a familiar sound shattered the din of the battle.

The front ranks of the charging demon wolves dissolved into bloody mess, skulls blown apart, gaping holes appearing as if by magic. Unnatural limbs broke, splintered from bodies or bent back. The bear also stumbled, its matted fir parted in hundreds of small places, black blood spattering free. Snarls changed to howls of pain. The line of evil disintegrated, the initial threat destroyed, giving Richard room to help Deirdre and the others.

"McAllister! To me! To me!"

The Dark Thorn raging magic, Richard spun around.

Finn Arne leapt over dead bodies, his assault rifle pointed beyond Richard at the toiling mass of midnight. The two dozen armed soldiers the captain had brought into Annwn spread out in formation, their firepower unleashed. The odor of used gunpowder mingled with the sour musk of the demon wolves. With the soldiers aiding their flight, Richard pulled Deirdre forcibly back to safety as Lyrian shadowed them.

The Vatican guards fired at any halfbreed that came too close. They pulled their triggers often, shielding their rear as they fled the battle.

Tears streaked down the redhead's cheeks but her grip on Richard was steel. He held Deirdre up by his willpower and the Dark Thorn alone.

Somehow Finn Arne had found him.

"Where is Ardall?" the captain screamed over the clamor.

"No idea!"

"The portal is clear. We need to make for Rome."

"The Queen's army is scattering, being broken apart," Deirdre said through her grief. "Now is not the time to venture away from this battlefie—"

"Of no consequence," Finn Arne interrupted. "We must gather Ardall and return to the Vatican. It is the only important path at this time."

"There won't be a Vatican *left* if Philip's army makes the portal," Richard argued loudly.

"Why do the Templar Knights not die?"

"You see the leather bags on their backs?" Richard asked.

Finn Arne nodded.

"Water from the Holy Grail protects the Templar Knights, making them invincible," Richard said. He looked quickly about. "If this army enters our world, it will march over the entire earth and enslave humanity. It must be stopped here! Whether they take this portal or another, it makes no difference. The only way to keep our world safe is fighting now."

Then movement from the portal caught Richard's eye.

Philip Plantagenet, joined by a dozen armed Templar Knights, returned to Annwn, undoubtedly to discover why the rest of the army had not entered Rome. It was terrible timing. With the Kreche in the middle of the melee, Philip was free to reorganize his army. He was already yelling furious orders at his lords and pointing wildly at various areas of the battlefield. Even as Richard watched, Philip's army slowly congealed, regrouping, becoming an organized terror once more.

Soon the confusion that had been created by the surprise attack would be reversed.

When that happened, the Caer Llion army would reform.

And kill its much smaller foe.

"I must enter Rome," Richard said.

"What do you mean?!" Deirdre yelled, her eyes wild. "We need you here!"

"Captain Arne," Richard said. "Find Ardall. Keep the boy safe. He will help protect Annwn. You have to go after Philip! Now!"

"What will you do, McAllister?"

"Kill his second in command, kill the Templar Knights who have already gone through. Ennio Rossi will do his best on the other side, but it won't be enough against the Grail-infused Templar Knights," Richard shouted, gripping the shoulder of the Swiss Guard captain. "As Heliwr, I go after them to keep Rome and the secret of Annwn safe!"

"You should go after Philip!" Finn Arne roared.

"There is more here than I can tell you, Arne," Richard continued, burning with conviction as he pointed out into the battle. "We don't know what Philip and his second in command intend while in the Vatican! There are items to protect in St. Peter's. I must keep them safe. And bring down the cavern in the catacombs if needs be!" He paused. "Trust me. Now go!"

Richard expected the captain to fight back. He did not. "We have limited rounds," he said.

Fighting weariness, Richard mounted Lyrian.

"If that's the case, pick up a sword!"

After giving Finn Arne a nod, Richard gave Deirdre a sad smile. She just looked at him, sorrow and anger mingling in her eyes. Before he said something he would regret, Richard kicked Lyrian into motion. With the fairy flying beside him, the Rhedewyr shot like a dart around the melee toward the portal and Rome. The battle spread out over the plains from his higher vantage point, dust polluting the scene and the hot, sticky air. The whole event sickened him. When Merle convinced the knight to enter Annwn, Richard had hoped he could prevent the very thing he now witnessed. He had failed at that. Now it engulfed him.

He hoped he could prevent it from spreading into Rome.

He would not fail again.

"Snedeker, I need you to watch over Bran," Richard said.

The fairy frowned. "No, I will not leave your side."

"You cannot go where I go!"

"I am to be your guide!" Snedeker said, flying, barely able to keep up as Richard pushed Lyrian to faster speed through the tumult. "Keep you safe!"

"Bran needs to be kept safe," Richard offered, worried for the boy. "He needs *you* now. Protect him as best you can. I have faith in the Oakwells, faith in you. Even a portal knight needs a guide sometimes, right?"

"Where do you go then, McAllister?"

"Obey my command, Snedeker!" Richard roared. "Now!"

The fairy gave a quick nod before flying back into chaos.

As Richard battled his way through nightmare anew, hoping the fairy kept Bran safe, the shimmer of the portal and his revenge drew him on.

He would not be denied.

The white fire of the Dark Thorn raged like the sun.

As he broke from the maelstrom of battle and the sounds of the fighting and dying fell behind him, Richard turned away from it all, the staff clenched before him. He galloped Lyrian to the rocky base where the portal shone above. He dismounted and rushed up the trail, avoiding the bodies of Templar Knights killed by the Kreche. Philip had long since vanished into the host below, trying to regain control over it. Richard was alone and soon stood before the gateway. He turned from it and viewed the war of two very different nations as it ebbed and flowed over the expansive plains.

Keeping the staff in hand and bringing its protective magic to the fore, Richard took a deep breath and entered the portal. He went in hunt of Arawn.

But what he last saw on the plains filled him with ice.

The defeat of the Tuatha de Dannan was at hand.

Chapter 36

When Bran saw Philip Plantagenet reenter Annwn, he knew he could end the war if he was strong enough. The new portal knight was severely battered. After the initial charge by the Morrigan, Bran had lost sight of Richard, Deirdre, and most of the members of the Seelie Court. It had not been easy to enter the rending tide of halfbreeds created for Caer Llion's war, but before he had time to think on it, the wrath broke over him like a wave, reducing him to reaction. With Arondight a blur of azure metal and fire, Bran barely kept the death from himself, the euphoria from using the magic ebbing as he grew accustomed to it. Several times he almost lost his seat on Westryl, the battle on the plains threatening to end both their lives at every moment, but his perseverance saw him through.

As he rode away from the mayhem to catch his breath, Bran looked over the battle, not liking what he saw.

The plan Richard and the Tuatha de Dannan had conceived had worked—for minutes only. Without Philip in control, his army floundered beneath the surprise attack of the fey, causing leaderless pandemonium. It became clear to Bran it would not last. The Tuatha de Dannan were hopelessly outnumbered, and after the initial shock given by the stampeding Rhedewyr, they were losing. The Grail-infused Templar Knights coupled with thousands of halfbreeds were wearing the forces of the Morrigan down.

The lines of the fey were collapsing.

When they failed entirely, the final resistance would die.

Bran flexed his new hand. The blood-spattered gauntlet gleamed under the sun, the runes blazing. He could feel everything as if the steel had nerves, but the metal was cold.

He didn't care. The Mastersmith had made him whole again.

A unified scream erupted from the battle, drawing his gaze. A second later, a fountain of magic blew into the sky as if a bomb had gone off, tossing fey and the dark twisted things into the air like matchsticks. Other magic permeated the battlefield from sprites, leprechauns, sylphs, and other lesser wielders, but it was insignificant compared to the concussion that shook the battlefield. Flaring colorful energy crackled in the air, forming a dome, angrily alive until it dissipated. When the magic and dust settled, a barren circular area existed, lacking all combatants but two.

The Cailleach and the Morrigan.

The two women faced one another several dozen feet apart, their magic like electricity about them. Both were grimy and ravaged. The robes of the Cailleach hung in tatters about her, revealing her wrinkled, emaciated frame. The Queen had taken a beating as well, her black armor dented and rent open in places. Circling one another like cats on the attack, limping and lacerated from multiple wounds, they ignored those who watched, their eyes cold with wild resiliency.

Hate radiated from both of them, a heat Bran could feel in his very innards.

"Ye cannot kill me, Queen of Nothing!" the Cailleach screeched.

"Even the summer falls to winter, witch!" the Morrigan challenged back. "By your death, you will release summer before the sun sets!"

"Or I will piss on yer dead royalty!"

The Queen said nothing, her fey sword glimmering a faded purple under the afternoon sun. Only stunned from the magical detonation for those brief moments, the rest of the battle continued around the two enemies, but at distance.

With words of power Bran could not understand, the Morrigan threw her sword savagely at the witch. It fell short, sticking blade-first into the grass at the witch's feet. The Cailleach cackled again, ignoring the blade, bringing her hands up as wicked green fire gathered to attack anew.

The sword of the Morrigan erupted into a purple bonfire, engulfing the crone. She screamed, not from pain but in surprised anger, a nimbus of her own magic the only thing protecting her. Already moving, the Morrigan cut the distance between them. As the Cailleach tried to escape, the Queen leapt forward and, in one smooth somersaulting motion, pulled her sword free to slay the woman responsible for destroying the natural seasons of Annwn.

The hag regained her faculties in time. She wove her hands in the air until the spell she cast shook the land beneath Bran, a rumbling from deep in the earth. Just as the Morrigan raised her sword to strike down the Cailleach, a granite slab burst free from the grassy surface at the Queen's feet, showering all in sharp boulders, pebbles, and dark soil.

The unearthed granite caught the Morrigan unaware. She catapulted backward, sword flying from her grasp and arms flailing. She hit the ground hard, her armor absorbing most of the damage, her left arm caught behind her as she struck.

The shattering of plate and arm echoed through the din.

Snarling her hatred, the Cailleach screamed into the world. Vines burst from the soil around the Morrigan, thick with thorns the size of daggers. They wrapped about the legs of the Queen, digging into the steel of her armor, holding her fast. She fought against them but it was of no use.

Having quenched the purple fire about her, the witch approached, a snide grin on her ancient face.

"And now," the Cailleach said. "Finally."

The Queen glared with cold disdain, still fighting her bonds.

"Finally," the crone echoed.

Before Bran could vault Westryl into motion in an attempt to protect the Queen, the Morrigan grabbed the vines with both hands, closed her eyes, and began to hum, the sound overwhelming the chaos about her.

It was a melody of green things, a promise of protection and care. The vines reacted instantly. Tentacles from the same plant burst forth under the Cailleach with great force. The witch didn't have time to react. She screamed, horrified, the realization of what was happening coming to her all too late. The vines did not stop with her legs but went immediately for her arms, pulling them back, keeping them as far apart as possible. The hag fought but her restraints were stronger. They drew her down toward the ground until she was pinned, pulled flat on her back. Unable to weave spells, the Cailleach snarled her wrath, spitting and fighting like a caged beast.

The vines holding the Queen melted back into the earth.

"The Tuatha de Dannan are friends of nature," the Queen said, cradling her arm even as she stood over the witch. The Morrigan picked up her fey sword. "For too long you have been its tyrant. Pray you never join the wrong side again."

The Morrigan raised her sword high.

And with one arm, rammed the blade through the chest of her enemy.

Ribs snapped like twigs as the sword plunged into the heart of the Cailleach and into the ground beneath her. No blood emerged. The hatred on her face was preserved but the anger in her eyes faded. She soon melted into the land, hair, skin, and bones becoming dust, leaving only the filthy rags of her robe gathered on the gritty grass.

A moan of discontent and confusion erupted from the halfbreeds. With the death of their mistress, they were no longer controlled. They lashed out at anything or anyone, maddened and unleashed. It did not end there. Darkness spread across the sky, not from the north as Bran and Richard had seen before, but from the western fringe of the plains, where the griffins were suddenly free.

"You should be fighting, Ardall!"

Bran glanced up. Snedeker flew above him, wings beating furiously.

"Still alive, I see," Bran noted. "Where is Richard?"

"Gone through the portal, after that burned ass John Lewis Hugo!"

Bran stared at the portal. It made sense Richard would have gone into Rome. Philip had taken several hundred Templar Knights through to the other side. Even though the king had returned to Annwn, those warriors in Rome would not be sitting idly by waiting for the return of their master. Their mischief could not be ignored and John Lewis Hugo was a menace that needed to be dealt with as well.

Bran sat higher upon Westryl, looking for the other danger. He spotted Philip Plantagenet almost at once. The redheaded man yelled his orders across the battlefield, safely surrounded by dozens of Templar Knights and men from Annwn's northlands.

Bran pushed Westryl into a gallop.

"Where are you going?" Snedeker asked, flying alongside Bran.

Bran let the magic of Arondight course through him.

"To end this war."

But before he had made it halfway to Philip, Bran was spotted. Lord Gwawl appeared at his king's side and, mounting his horse, drove at the charging knight. Seven of his warriors followed, each with weapons and defiance drawn. Bran raised Arondight high, screaming his challenge, the magic building inside of him like molten lava about to explode. For years he had yearned for a life of meaning, and the fire for it consumed him as he pounded across the torn plains.

Here was his chance to make all the meaning for two worlds.

Lord Gwawl roared as he bore down on Bran.

Just before the charging warriors met, a black behemoth came out of nowhere and tackled the fey lord off his horse.

Bran pulled Westryl up to stop, not believing his eyes.

It was the Kreche.

The force with which the halfbreed hit Gwawl killed him instantly. Both flew through the air until finally crashing to the rocky turf. The Kreche didn't stop. He rained fists down onto Gwawl with such power the ground shook. The traitorous lord vanished beneath the assault, his upper body and head pummeled into the crimson-soaked sod.

While the Kreche looked for the next victim, grunting hard from exertion, his fists covered in gore, arrows flew through the air, striking several of the warriors who had been with Gwawl. Bran watched Aife ride into view, the centaur fluid and deadly. Two of the northland warriors dropped like sacks of grain. The others fled. Aife trotted to one of the warriors still struggling for breath through the holes in his chest. She notched her bow and unleashed the bolt into his neck.

He gurgled and stilled, his desire to get away forgotten in death.

The centaur nodded at Bran and rode away.

The Kreche stood, snorting his annoyance—the crimson crater and broken bones the only proof Gwawl had existed.

"There was no need. I had him," Bran said, suffused with magic.

"There *is* a need though, scion of Ardall," the Kreche rumbled, nodding toward Philip. "The man responsible for taking your hand awaits. The gift from the Mastersmith does not heal all wounds. And you cannot avenge if you are dead."

Bran fixed the halfbreed with a questioning look.

"I see you, see you clearer than you will ever know," the Kreche said lowly before looking to the portal. "Rick too. You both have something to prove this day, methinks."

Bran took one look at Philip before nodding.

"I will get you to your moment!" the Kreche prodded. "Follow!"

With a roar, the halfbreed tore down the slope, ripping up the sod, aiming directly for Philip and those who surrounded him protectively. Bran charged after the behemoth, flames running along Arondight, his need burning. They covered the distance to Philip quickly. The Kreche hit the defenders with a force that killed men and demon wolves on impact, sending them flying through the air, crushed by brute force. Bran rode Westryl a step behind, sending his magic into those who fought past the Kreche.

Soon soldiers and demon wolves surrounded them, attacking

from all sides. The Kreche was untiring, a machine of destruction, his thick arms annihilating all who came within striking distance. Bran kept safe the halfbreed's back, killing any man or creature that came too near. The closer the knight got to Philip, the hotter his magic burned, the faster Arondight became. He began to lose himself in the battle, the desire to prove himself driving him on.

When the day ended, people like Deirdre would look at him differently.

Then the Kreche went down.

It happened so quickly that Bran almost ran Westryl into the back of him. It took only seconds for the black writhing creatures to throw themselves at the halfbreed, swarming over him. Soon Bran found he was deep in a sea of unwashed clawed limbs, all trying to take him down as well.

"Go, Ardall!" the Kreche bellowed from the melee.

Only unsure for a moment, Bran kicked Westryl forward. The Rhedewyr barreled down any man or creature in his path and, using Arondight to keep his mount safe, Bran made his way through the army—right to Philip Plantagenet.

It didn't take long. The Kreche had taken Bran most of the way. When Philip saw Bran, the knight could tell the king was not pleased.

"You are alive, Ardall!" Philip yelled, darkening. "Come to join me at last?"

Bran said nothing, destroying the last few halfbreeds between he and his goal. Philip radiated annoyed arrogance. He wore all black as he did in Caer Llion, but also displayed a shining steel breastplate emblazoned with a crimson lion, gauntlets on his forearms, and greaves along his legs. Bullet holes littered his person but he was unharmed, the Grail water on his back keeping him safe. He held an elegant blade with a jewel in its hilt.

He did not budge, as if waiting for Bran to make the first move.

Bran gripped Arondight and felt the blade thrum with magic, even as the bloodied Kreche returned to his side.

"You hide behind a halfbreed now?" Philip snickered.

"Not at all."

"I see you got your hand back," Philip said. "It appears to be the work of the fey, a relic of some worth. I suppose this means you have become one of them."

"I do what is right," Bran argued. "What you desire has been attempted before in history. It seems every so often some nutcase tries to enslave the world. The world fights back."

"You willingly betray the Word then."

"On the streets, when confronted by a bully, there is no Word," Bran said, growing more annoyed by the king's grin. "There is only you against them. I have seen homeless beat the hell out of a bully enslaving them with fear. I see that bully in you."

"You are young. And naïve."

"And you are an extremist who needs to be put on his ass."

The arrogant smile on Philip's face dropped. "Apparently I should have let you die from your injury."

"Apparently," Bran agreed.

"Look at what you wish," Philip said, scowling. "The world of my birth is gone. The world it has become, *your* world, is a horrible cesspool. I have seen it from afar. Sin. Disease. Greed. Hatred. Sloth. God never intended Satan to have such firm control of his creation. Divine providence brought me a tool to see goodness returned. When the Word needs service, it sends His warriors. I am that warrior."

"Do not listen to him, Ardall," the Kreche snarled.

Bran kept Arondight leveled at the king, his anger simmering.

"Do not let the pagan wishes of the demon wizard or the weakness of the Church blind you to what is right," Philip added, ignoring the Kreche. "Join me."

Long moments passed. The dying continued around them.

In answer, Bran launched at Philip.

The king of Annwn sidestepped the attack easily and parried Arondight. "You *fool!*" Philip hissed. "You will join your rotting father for that!"

The king countered. Bran brought his sword up, his blade blocking the attack like an azure shield. The opponents circled one another. Bran could tell immediately he was outmatched. Philip had lived centuries, undoubtedly training during them, his movements nimble as a cat when it circled prey. Bran had no such training. He had the instinctual fire of the magic at his command and that was it. It was barely enough. For every injury Bran visited on Philip, it healed as quickly as delivered, the power of the Grail sustaining him. As the fight progressed, a part of Bran knew he couldn't maintain the magic for long. It wore him as nothing ever had and ultimately, with the Grail water, Philip would win.

Already wearied, Bran would have to do something soon.

As if understanding, the Kreche came suddenly at Philip from behind, a locomotive of inertia.

Bran sent flame at the Philip's feet, trying to trip him at a moment when the Kreche could fall upon the king and, like Gwawl, pummel him into obliteration. Philip was faster. He danced away just as the Kreche bore down on him. Lashing out with his sword, the king caught the halfbreed on the back of his leg as he passed.

The Kreche roared in pain, collapsing as he hit the ground.

The behemoth tried to rise but couldn't, his leg crippled.

Philip was on the Kreche instantly. He brought his sword down in a blur at the neck of the halfbreed, attempting to kill him with one stroke. Roaring, Bran blasted Philip in the chest. The fire sent the king flying through the air. He hit the ground hard. Without a word, he was back on his feet, drinking the water on this back, made whole again as if nothing had happened.

The fight continued, dust from their tumult thick in Bran's nose. He weakened.

Biding his time, Philip countered every attack, barely flustered.

Bran burned with frustration. He knew the magic was not infinite. The inexhaustible need to win lent him more power than he had ever known but it had begun to wane. Philip on the other hand was unchanged; he had not tired or slowed. While Bran became more desperate, magic he had barely gained control over threatened to consume him, every use requiring him to dig deeper into areas of his soul, places he intuitively knew were forbidden.

The more he could not break through Philip's will, the exponentially more he gave to keep up.

Readying to charge at Philip, the world tumbled from view.

One moment he was standing. The next he was on his back, having gotten sloppy and fallen over the carcass of a dead cat-like halfbreed. He fought to regain his feet but it was too late. Philip pounced on him instantly, the blade of his sword pressed into Bran's chest faster than the knight could stop.

"If I would have known you would be this easy," Philip began, gloating, "I would not have tried to gain your services."

"You will not succeed in this!" Bran choked. "Richard wil—"

"Will stop me? Friendship avails one nothing."

The pit in his stomach went cold. Bran had failed.

As Philip brought his blade up for a killing stroke and Bran futilely fought to block the blade with Arondight, a figure hit the king in the side and sent him tumbling away from the knight.

Bran could not believe his eyes.

It was Deirdre.

The redhead held her sword before her, green eyes flashing lightning. There was a wildness about her that Bran had not seen before, a willingness to give up everything—even her life—if it meant killing Philip.

When the king spun on her, she waited, ready to fight.

"Get up!" Snedeker screamed, suddenly there.

Before Bran could gain his feet, Philip tackled the redhead. She tried to run her sword through him, snarling intense rage, but Philip knocked it easily aside and kept coming. He soon had her gripped from behind, holding the blade of his sword against her exposed neck.

"Daughter of Lord Gerallt," Philip sneered. "To think I meant to give you everything as a queen."

"My father is dead!" Deirdre screamed, thrashing to no avail.

"Another traitor I won't have to kill myself then."

"Let her go," Bran ordered, staring into Deirdre's eyes. The knight saw new fear there that matched his own.

"Not before I do this . . ."

Philip pulled the sword viciously across her throat.

Blood erupted even as he threw Deirdre to the ground.

The last dam broke inside Bran, magic rising up from depths

of his soul he did not know he possessed. He charged the last few feet, Arondight blazing brighter than the sun, his rage tempering his will and the fire within endangering his very humanity.

The battlefield dropped away.

Reason left him.

Thundering his anger, he slashed at Philip with everything he had, not caring if he lived or died. Philip spun as Bran hoped he would, as he had seen the king do several times before. Instead of trying to parry the other's sword and dance away, Bran let the sword fall exactly where he knew it would be.

And caught it with his gauntleted hand.

Surprise followed by fear crossed Philip's face. Before the king had a chance to disengage, Bran rammed Arondight through the center of the crimson lion on Philip's breastplate almost to the hilt. Eyes wide, Philip clutched at him, trying to drink the Grail water. Bran did not care if Philip drained the pouch dry. The knight sent the power thrumming inside through Arondight, incinerating the king from the inside out. The smell of charring meat accosted Bran. He did not care. He let the magic take control, become a living thing, a torrent that would not stop.

Philip looked down at his chest, eyes bulging in disbelief, skin blanching to white. He gasped and coughed weakly once, crimson coating his teeth.

"Father," Philip whispered.

Slumping to the plains, the light in his eyes went lifeless.

Philip Plantagenet lay dead.

Sudden weariness stole Arondight from Bran. With a shiver he drifted like a ghost to where Deirdre lay. The redhead did not move, blood covering her jerkin. Without knowing what he did, Bran fell to his knees, feeling hot tears trail down his cheeks. He held the woman, the horror he felt within growing into a ravenous scream he would never be able to release.

"Red, no!" Snedeker wailed, flying to Deirdre.

The Kreche limped to stand over Bran.

"She is gone, scion of Ardall."

"Get me one of the bags!"

The Kreche paused a moment but ultimately did as he was bid. Bran took the bag and splashed water in Deirdre's mouth, hoping for the miracle that had kept Philip alive for so long.

Nothing happened.

"Come on, Deirdre . . ."

"I am sorry," the Kreche said. "She has traveled beyond, into the dawn. She has become one with it."

Snedeker put his head down on her unmoving chest and bawled. Bran did not move. He held Deirdre close, keeping hope alive, willing her to move, to breathe, to do anything that would not be the reality.

"She is gone, Bran Ardall."

Through his tears, Bran looked up.

Finn Arne stared at him. The captain of the Vatican held pistols in both of his hands but had no need of them, the rest of his guard surrounding the plains and keeping them safe. The one-eyed man knelt next to Bran, his demeanor somber.

"The battle is turning for the worse," Finn Arne said. "We had best not be here when that happens."

"I'm not leaving her."

"You must if you are to survive. She would want that."

So weary he could not stand, the pain in his heart encompassing the entire world, Bran surveyed the battlefield with blurry vision. The captain was right. Without the witch keeping the half-breeds under control, they were frenzied, giving into a bloodlust that only made them stronger, both those on the ground and the griffins in the air. As a result the Tuatha de Dannan had splintered into pockets of resistance that were being consumed. It would not take long for the Morrigan to call a retreat or die fighting.

Bran let Deirdre down gently.

When he regained his feet, fighting the tears, he took his own appraisal of the battle— and could not believe what he saw in the northern distance.

The shapes he had seen earlier grew at an accelerated rate.

Richard had been wrong. The black stains to the north were not griffins.

Not at all.

"Snedeker!" Bran shouted.

The fairy looked up from his place on Deirdre, sorrow etching his wooden features.

"Do you see!?" Bran screamed, pointing. "Look to the north!"

Snedeker did so. Surprise turned to fear.

"Right!" Bran yelled. "They come to kill with flame!"

"The Tuatha de Dannan must take cover in the trees where the dryads can protect them," the Kreche advised.

"Snedeker, tell the Morrigan to pull her forces out of the plains!"

Face screwed up with determination born of anger, the fairy stuttered in the air, already looking for the Queen. Snedeker then shot across the battlefield like a released dart, dodging the numerous dangers of griffins and flying arrows.

With no one around, the battle raging closer and closer to the Forest of Dean as the Caer Llion horde overcame the Tuatha de Dannen with increasing ferocity, Bran sat and waited, watching his likely death descend.

"If that's what I think it is, we must flee," Finn Arne said.

"We can't make cover in time," Bran replied. "Too far from the dryads. And I know who comes. He won't risk harm to his children, preferring to kill from afar with fire indiscriminately. That probably includes us."

"Your father would be proud of you this day, for the fight you gave your enemy, young Ardall," the Kreche said, his small eyes bright but his face solemn.

"Thank you," Bran said simply. "You should try to get away."

"You go, I go," the Kreche said.

When the black shapes in the air lost altitude and rushed to meet the plains and those upon it, Bran called and held Arondight aloft, fire licking the blade, knowing it to be the last time he would hold the talisman. The first flames from the falling shapes erupted from between jagged teeth and opened maws, the wide wings of the descending beasts fanning the scorching heat into those caught out on the plains southward.

The dragons of Tal Ebolyon had come.

Latobius flew beside his son Saethmoor and Nael, all blazing fire in a wide swath that ignited anything it touched. The flames incinerated thousands on the first pass alone, the fire burning through the leather packs carried by the Templar Knights and northland men, evaporating instantly the life-saving water of the Holy Grail and reducing the men to ash. Those who survived the first rush fought to retreat into the west, but the halfbreeds formed a wall, the demon monstrosities induced to chaos. Griffins attacked the behemoth fliers but they died in midair, set afire before most could reach the dragons.

Bran felt himself screaming—at the dragons, at the world, at life, at death.

A cheer went up from the Tuatha de Dannan but was quickly silenced as a spear thrown by a Fomorian ran Nael through his left wing. The dragon tumbled to the earth, crashing into ranks of demon wolves. The evil halfbreeds leapt onto the enraged beast, some still on fire and maddened by the dragon assault. Nael fought, spinning in confusion, wings and claws tossing halfbreeds in the air. There were too many though. The dragon was being ripped to shreds.

Latobius and Saethmoor roared as they banked, too far away to save their companion.

Followed by other dark elves, a hellyll warrior wearing the golden armor of Arendig Fawr rushed into the fray and jumped from an outcropping of granite onto the back of Nael, stabbing demon wolves dead in a blur with his spear. It was Lugh. The captain drove Areadbhar with both hands at his enemies, protecting the dragon, roaring battle. The other members of the Long Hand followed. They swept the burdened beast free of the dark flood. The demon wolves did not even notice their dead brethren; they continued to swarm only to die, fighting to kill the hellyll and dragon alike.

In a heave of incredible power, Nael sent the next wave of demon wolves scrambling backward, leaving him and the Long Hand able to flee. With the dragon free, Latobius and his son kept at the halfbreeds until most had been consumed by the hellish remittance of dragon might.

The conflagration met Bran in a hot wind but that was all.

The wrath of the dragons hammered into the Forest of Dean as well where the Tuatha de Dannan fought to keep Philip's army from entering safe haven. The canopy of the trees caught fire but the dryads held back the worst. Soon smoke obliterated his view and the screams of the dying filled the afternoon, but Bran thought he heard the sound of fey cheering amidst the tumult.

Lord Latobius and Saethmoor passed overhead numerous times. The Caer Llion army was broken. Several thousands stragglers lived but they fled into the wild.

Bran breathed in death but he remained.

The army of Philip Plantagenet was no more.

The smell of charred bodies in his nostrils, Bran let Arondight dissolve and sagged to the ruined plains over Deirdre's body.

And wept.

Chapter 37

Richard stepped from the chaos on the plains into bedlam underground.

Ear-shattering bursts of gunfire and bullets whining passed, Richard ran for cover behind one of the rune-carved stone pillars that made up the gateway, his magic brought up in protection. The knight was on the shore of a subterranean river, the portal casting light upon a cavern filled with hundreds of Templar Knights fighting Swiss Guardsmen defensively positioned before a tunnel entrance. Dozens of the Vatican guards lay dead among fewer Templar Knights, the arms fire having little effect on the Grail-protected.

It was clear to him the fight would not last long; the Swiss Guards fought admirably but the Templar Knights outnumbered their foes and would eventually gain the city above.

Richard frowned. Arawn was nowhere to be seen.

Bringing the Dark Thorn up to attack the warriors of Caer Llion, he paused.

Two Templar Knight bodies lay slaughtered at the exit of the chamber, behind several dozen fighting Swiss Guards. It appeared as though some of the army had already broken through into the passageways beyond, possibly already gaining the city above.

Arawn undoubtedly one of them.

Richard looked about, formulating a plan to break through and go after the fey lord, when a sudden blast of magic shook the underground to his left.

Ennio Rossi, the portal knight of Rome, fought the bulk of the Templar Knights, his long Arthurian knife Carnwennan a blur as he wove countless spells and sent them against his enemy.

Even with magic, Ennio had little effect.

And like the Swiss Guards, he would ultimately fail without aid.

Decision made, Richard cocooned himself in stronger magic. The Templar Knights were spread out in an arc, trying to break through at any weak spot and exploit it. To hunt Arawn and protect the Vatican, Richard would have to do the same. He cast the magic of the Dark Thorn into a spot thinned of Templar Knights. Not expecting a rear attack, many of them wheeled about confused, weapons drawn and Grail tubes in their mouths. He burned away their white mantles to the armor beneath, going for the leather pouches, trying to maim those who lost their protection.

They responded quickly, rushing him, no fear in their eyes.

He saw his danger almost immediately. Even though several Templars succumbed to the flames, there were too many. As under Caer Llion, he would fall to the power of the Grail. And this time no one would capture him. He would be outright killed.

Ennio acted, taking advantage of Richard's surprise attack. He screamed orders, sending the Swiss Guard to help carve a path. Well trained to carry out orders, the Guards concentrated their firepower in one area—the weak link Richard had attacked. Templar Knights staggered back from the barrage. The Grail overcame the damage as quickly as it came but the dazed soldiers were frozen by the assault, unable to fight.

The opening was there.

Adrenaline lending him strength, Richard broke through, blasting the stunned Templar Knights aside, suddenly at the side of the Italian knight.

"Get out of here, Rick!" Ennio roared in a thick accent.

"What can I do?"

The portal knight's face was streaked with blood and his shirt was saturated with sweat. The long knife in his hand glowed. "There is nothing. Find John Lewis Hugo!"

"Where did he go?!" Richard yelled in the tumult.

Ennio sent fire into a group of Templars who had killed several Swiss Guardsmen at the same time, tossing them away. Reinforcements quickly filled the gap.

"He gained the catacombs long minutes ago, with others!"

Not knowing if it would work, Richard closed his eyes and slammed the butt of the Dark Thorn into the floor. The stone shattered as the staff entered it.

"What are you *doing*?" Ennio hissed.

"Hoping I am right."

As he had done outside Caer Lion, Richard focused, this time on the body of John Lewis Hugo, knowing more explicitly this time what he hunted. He focused on the ruined face, miscolored eyes, pale skin, and black clothing. In seconds he had his quarry firmly fixed in his mind. Concentrating, the knight called upon the Dark Thorn to locate the fey lord wherever he had gone.

The power snaked from the staff into the ground like a hound unleashed, upward into the catacombs and beyond.

He knew where Arawn now stood.

"Go!" Ennio yelled. "I will not last long!"

Richard hesitated for only a moment, nodded farewell to the young knight, and sprinted for the entrance. Giving a look back, he heard Ennio call out a retreat, ordering the Swiss Guard back into the catacombs to defend where the tunnel narrowed. The knight wove a spell as he went, his fingers dancing upon his blade. Pebbles and dust fell from the ceiling. With every word Ennio uttered, the cavern quivered more and more, the sound becoming a deep resonant rumble as if an earthquake gripped the underground.

The portal knight intended to bring the rock down upon the Templar Knights—and obstruct the entrance into Rome.

As the trembling in the rock quickened, a manic assault from a wedge of Templar Knights broke through the retreating Swiss

Guards. The red crosses on their chests broke through the purple uniforms to come directly at Ennio.

Richard started forward, a warning frozen on his lips, but it was too late.

"Ennio!" he roared.

Swords fell into Ennio Rossi, over and over again. The knife in his hand vanished. The knight crumbled beneath the Templar Knights and their weapons.

The shaking of the underground ceased at his death.

"Fall back!" Richard roared.

The Templar Knights were a white and red swarm, their clothing ragged and their armor beaten, but the men within alive and vibrant. The retreat of the Swiss Guard drove them onward. As the Templar Knights hacked their way through the front lines of their foes, the defense of the Vatican retreated toward him in the corridor, eventually blocking the way into St. Peter's like a cork in a bottle.

Richard fled the cavern, leaving the defenses of the Vatican behind. The Swiss Guard would have to be enough.

Following the path of the Dark Thorn, Richard ran. The world changed from bland cave walls to those riddled with chiseled holes bearing coffins or the dusty bones of the long dead. After numerous passages, the torches of the lower levels gave way to a flight of stairs highlighted by the soft glow of electric white light above. Richard slowed, knowing he had to be careful. It was a chess game, but one where a poorly decided move would result in death. Although the Dark Thorn had cemented in his mind where the fey lord had gone, he did not want to fall prey to a Templar Knight left behind.

Ascending the stairs, Richard kept his guard up.

He stepped from the dank quarters below into a warmer room with a rounded stucco ceiling. A massive white marble sarcophagus with decorative corners lay pushed away from the wall where he now stood, a rock door once concealing the entrance to the crypts below.

It was the tomb of Queen Christina of Sweden.

He followed the Dark Thorn into the next room where red

rope stanchions cordoned off another chapel where potted blooming plants surrounded a plain marble slab covering a grave. Richard read the Latin and the dates inscribed in the stone.

Pope John Paul II lay interred within.

Richard knew where he was. He stood within the Vatican Sacred Grotto.

The knight moved on. The Sacred Grotto was more elaborate in architecture and design as he went, a separate entity from what had been below. Various symbols from Christian antiquity joined sophisticated crypts, the importance of those interred humbling despite his misgivings for the Church. Popes and other dignitaries were buried within feet of him, men and women who had devoted their lives to the Catholic Church. The ancient world he had only seen in photographs unfolded, the birthplace of Catholicism in the bowels of Vatican Hill, a world tucked away from Rome and all Richard knew.

He breathed in the stale air and hurried onward.

Seattle felt a lifetime away.

Richard took a final flight of broad stairs and, stepping through a last doorway, entered St. Peter's Basilica.

He paused, dwarfed. Moonlight infiltrated the interior of the massive basilica through windows set in its dome, highlighting the beautiful artwork and statues beneath. Richard stared at the wealth, annoyed at the grandeur. Above the door he had emerged from the statue of Saint Longinus towered from its niche in one of the main pillars, the centurion who stabbed Christ carved by Bernini into marble relief, his sight restored and gripping the Holy Lance. Ahead of Richard the Baldicchino rose to an unprecedented height, its bronze canopy shielding Saint Peter's Tomb beneath it.

No one was about. It was deathly silent.

Moving on, he saw a bronze statue of Saint Peter, his left hand holding two keys to his heart, the right hand blessing those who looked upon him.

Richard gritted his teeth. Peter had formed the Vigilo. It was the Vigilo who had failed at protecting the Grail and its secret, leading to Plantagenet and his war. Richard hoped Bran could correct one of those mistakes.

Richard would correct the other.

He ran full out, his footfalls barely echoing in the vastness. Richard would have to risk entering into a trap to end Arawn quickly. The sightless eyes of a dozen different saints watched him pass. He paid them no heed. Tiny among the opulence of Renaissance and Baroque architecture, Richard kept the Dark Thorn before him, the details supplied by the staff fixed in his mind, revenge driving him on.

Before he got to the five massive doors leading into the vestibule and out into St. Peter's Square, Richard broke right under an arch where the monument to princess Maria Clementina Sobieska had been erected over a doorway.

Richard knew the door led to the roof and dome—and to the Pope's private attic story studies above.

The bodies of two Templar Knights blocked his path.

They were about twelve feet apart, one where Richard now stood, the other within the frames of the doorway. The horror of death was frozen on each face: the bodies had been dismembered by a blade that had cleanly cut through muscle, bone, sinew, and arteries—one had lost his legs below both knees, the other lacked an arm and had a large gash in his armored chest revealing torn metal, shattered ribs, and a bloodied lung.

The pouches containing the Grail water had been punctured.

Richard stepped over the Templar Knights, sweating freely now, and glanced in the doorway and up into the reaches above.

No one waited in ambush that he could see.

He climbed the staircase, leaving the gruesome scene behind. He took the stairs two at a time, eyes ever ahead. Bolstered by the magic of the Dark Thorn, Richard ascended as quickly as his legs would carry him.

Halfway up, he encountered another body: a Swiss Guard.

The soldier lay limply upon the stairs, eyes staring sightlessly, dead from multiple stab wounds.

Richard continued.

Coming to a platform where another set of stairs continued

to the roof, Richard deviated to a side entrance leading into the interior of the basilica and the multiple rooms not allowed entry to tourists that looked down upon the Square. The door, which appeared as though it had once been locked, had been pushed off of its hinges, hanging crookedly aside. Four bodies of Templar Knights and Swiss Guards lay intertwined, their lifeblood pooling together and drying upon the stone floor, the remnants of a battle that had recently transpired.

Richard stepped between hacked limbs into a grand hallway.

Like the eastern façade of St. Peter's, the corridor he found himself in was more than a football field in length. Beautifully wrought chandeliers hung from the high ceiling, chasing away shadows. The wall on his left featured luxurious tapestries and paintings; seven doors broke up the opposite wall, between which tall statues of previous pontiffs stood, bearing scepters of office.

Dead bodies lay strewn about in the hallway.

Leading to one door.

As he moved around them as best he could, a soft gurgling came from one of the bodies near a statue that had been sliced in half from shoulder to other knee as though it were butter. The Templar Knight died slowly, the man slashed through his abdomen, the rent armor and white mantle soaked in blood.

Richard knelt but there was nothing he could do.

"Pleeasse . . . millloord . . ."

Richard watched the man's passing. The warrior gulped his own blood, struggling to find breath, before finally dying.

The knight stood and ran his hand over the dissected statue. The marble had been hewn in two by some instrument that could cut through stone. Whatever had destroyed the effigy had also cut through the armor of the knight with ease.

"Open the Vault now!" the voice of Arawn raged from an open doorway nearby.

"We will not step aside!"

Gripping the Dark Thorn with conviction, Richard entered a room full of tension. Arawn and two Templar Knights surrounded two older men draped in black robes of the Church who were pressed against the only wall devoid of a bookshelf. Arawn gripped a kneeling Swiss Guard by the front of his uniform, holding a long dagger to his neck, but his harsh gaze never deviated from the older of the two Churchmen.

Pope Clement XV and Cardinal Vicar Cormac Pell O'Connor.

Danger pointed at the head of the Catholic Church. No matter how Richard felt about the Pope, his presence prevented Richard from unleashing the power of the Dark Thorn erratically. It added a risky dimension to the situation. Like the Cardinal Vicar, Clement held a sword in front of him, the length of the blade bright where blood slicked it. Both men were positioned defensively before the Templar Knights beside Arawn, far from any protection Richard could create.

"If you do not open the Vault, I will kill this man, his soul's death on your conscience," Arawn growled, twisting the point of the knife into the neck of the Guard. "The magic on the other side of this wall drew me here. Make way!"

"His sacrifice for upholding the laws of our Father in Heaven will be rewarded upon his entry," Clement grunted. "What of your own?"

Arawn said nothing. Clement noticed Richard then, his lined face filling with a mixture of annoyance and hope. Arawn followed the Pope's stare, his burned face darkening.

"Come to join me at last, Heliwr?" he asked, grinning.

As the Templars spun to confront the newcomer, Richard steadied his resolve.

"No. I have come to end your reign."

"You are late then," Arawn said. "I have survived to this room. By day's end, the Vatican and all within it will be mine."

"The Word will never allow it, John Lewis Hugo!" the Cardinal Vicar countered.

"Cormac Pell O'Connor," Richard explained. "What you believe to be Hugo is in fact the ancient fey lord, Arawn, having set wheels in motion centuries ago to destroy the Vatican and the world of man, using Philip Plantagenet to meet his own ends and build an army for a different conquest entirely." Richard paused, instead looking at Arawn. "Even now the Tuatha de Dannan fight *your* army in Annwn."

"You lie," Arawn growled. "The army I built would not be so easily spent."

"Where is Philip if I lie?" Richard asked.

Twisting the knife, Arawn did not answer.

"A fey lord killed the Cardinal Seer then . . ." the Vicar said.

"And he will not gain the Vault behind us," the Pope added. "Arawn, return to your world of Annwn. The relics in these walls will not be yours to possess."

"Within that Vault is the ability to expose centuries of Church lies," Arawn said to Richard. "I know you hate them as much as I. This world can no longer crusade against those it does not agree with. The Tuatha de Dannan are needed to the banish evil of those lies. Once mankind knows we exist, it will look for truths beyond their narrow noses. The relics are needed. The swords these men carry are part of that collection!"

"Only one man was ever meant to control that much power," the Pope argued. "And He has long since been martyred and become the Word."

"You hoard them for your own devices!" Arawn shouted.

"The Vigilo prote—" the Vicar began.

"Your Vigilo is an abomination!"

Richard kept the Dark Thorn before him, wondering what he'd gotten himself into again. The knight hated Arawn for what the fey lord had done, having killed his wife and used him for an advantage. Richard also hated the Church, the lies Arawn spoke of all too real. He knew he could not let Arawn gain the Vault, but the Vigilo were as culpable for centuries of murder. The world spun about him. For the first time, Richard did not know what to do. Arawn was a danger he had witnessed firsthand, but aiding the Pope and the Cardinal Vicar helped another side just as evil.

"Richard McAllister, look to history!" Arawn said, still holding the Guard by the throat. "Without the crusading desires of the Catholic Church pushing my kind from this world, there would have been no need for Annwn. Or the portals. Or Knights of the Yn

Saith. Your wife never needed to die, had the Vigilo been satisfied with their own place in the world. The fey seek balance. Ultimately, the men in front of us represent an evil that drew us here."

"Your wife is not the issue here, McAllister," the Pope argued. "This creature must atone for—"

"He will!" Richard roared, slamming the Dark Thorn against the stone floor. "Remember this though, pontiff. I am not here for you. Or your Vigilo. I come here to set right wrongs."

"Get the Heliwr then, Templars!" Arawn shouted.

The room erupted into pandemonium. Arawn was like a snake. He dodged the thrust and sent the dagger plunging into the neck of the Swiss Guardsman. Blood spurted everywhere. Richard barely had time to bring forth the fire of the Dark Thorn in defense as the Templar Knights charged with swords drawn. Steel rang. Grail bags gave life to the warriors attacking Richard. He barely had time to think. In the close quarters it was hard for him to move, but he gave the ground he needed to maneuver, releasing the pent-up magic inside of him, the fire of the Dark Thorn urgent.

As he gave ground, one of the Templars swung his sword in a broad arc even as the other attacked Richard from the side. For the first time the knight used the Dark Thorn as a club, parrying the sword even as he sent his fire directly into the man's face.

The Templar Knight fell backward, twisting away.

Richard incinerated the bag on his back.

He had only just ended the first threat when the second Templar Knight fought through the fire, roaring his battle call like a maddened bull and swinging with great force. Barely having time to dodge and wielding only enough fire to slow the warrior down, the Red Cross backed away until cornered against a bookshelf of massive tomes.

Grinning, the warrior brought his blade down to cleave Richard in two. The knight sidestepped. As he did so, the warrior overextended his efforts and was caught off balance.

Gritting his teeth, Richard smashed the head of the Dark Thorn across the left cheek of his attacker.

The warrior crumbled like a puppet cut from its strings.

The first soldier was back, sword in hand.

"Don't make me kill you!" Richard thundered.

Knowing he was no longer protected by the power of the Grail, fear entered the man's eyes. Richard feinted at him. The Templar Knight fled the room then, knowing he was bested before he even began.

Richard turned to discover the power in the room had shifted.

Arawn had overcome Clement.

The fey lord held the Pope against him like a shield, the edge of his dagger lying against Clement's wrinkled neck. The polished sword of the Pope now lay on the ground. Richard didn't know how to proceed. As he lowered the flame about the Dark Thorn to a halo, he walked slowly to stand nearer the three other men.

"Let me pass into the Vault," Arawn asserted, squeezing Clement by the throat.

The Cardinal Vicar did not move, his sword at the ready.

"Richard McAllister, we hate the same hypocrisy," Arawn said smoothly. "You do not let the Church command you. Nor do I. It is for the Tuatha de Dannan I do this. When Plantagenet had his lackey trick me, I thought my time over. The man who owned this body took my life. I was imprisoned for long decades before my spirit eroded that of John Lewis Hugo and his body became my own. Encouraging Plantagenet to reclaim his birthright was my first step against the very Church that drove us from the Misty Isles."

"You and I hate the same thing."

"But you are Tuatha de Dannan!" Richard shot back. "You sent that cait sith to his death into Seattle! You kill your own kin in Annwn even as we speak!"

"I did not bring them to this fight, knight!" Arawn seethed. "I do not wish their demise any more than you do. By the time I gained control of this flesh Plantagenet had built a large army and it was too late for me to aid my brethren. I use him as he used me, to keep my own safe. Help me regain balance!"

"I will not give into your wishes, Arawn!" the Pope growled. "The secrets and power beyond that wall will avail you nothing!"

"We will see. It is up to you, Cardinal Vicar. Let die your Pope?"

"Do not give in, Cormac," Clement insisted.

Arawn snarled, looking back and forth between the Cardinal Vicar and Richard. The knight could see the struggle within Cormac. It matched his own. To give into Arawn's demands meant giving him power; to not give in meant the death of the Pope.

Clement had no such hesitation.

"It is to you now, Cormac Pell O'Connor."

Clement twisted hard from Arawn, breaking the grip, even as a dagger appeared in his hand from the folds of his robes. The fey lord did not flinch from the weapon even as the knife plunged into his back. Sucking on the contents of his own Grail bag, Arawn rammed his dagger through the chest of Clement.

The Pope gasped and his eyes rolled toward heaven.

He went limp and collapsed.

"Neither of you can kill me," Arawn sneered. "The power of your Word is with me and forever shall be."

"No longer," the Cardinal Vicar said.

The grin on Arawn's face disappeared. Water gushed to the floor. Pope Clement had not only stabbed the fey lord but also the bag that offered him protective life over the body of John.

With a snarl, Arawn went for the sword the Pope had dropped. Richard did not wait. He vaulted in between the two men and jammed the butt of the Dark Thorn into Arawn's chest, slamming his body backward against the stone wall, pinning him there.

"Finish him!" the Cardinal Vicar roared.

"We will not *kill him*."

"He is evil!" Cormac raged, raising his gray sword. "Look what he has done! Step aside, McAllister. Now!"

Conflicting emotions swept through Richard like a wildfire. He wanted to slay the fey lord as much as the Cardinal Vicar did. He still saw Elizabeth as she died under the blade of Arondight; he still burned for vengeance at what had been done to his life.

"I will not," Richard said finally. "We don't know what will happen to the spirit of Arawn if we kill the body of John Lewis Hugo."

"If he is left alive, what then?"

"I will speak to Merle on this subject. He will know what is best when it comes to the fey," Richard answered. "Arawn will be tried with wisdom. Not by us."

"By whom then? The Morrigan or her ilk? The laws of the Holy See? Italy?" Cormac scoffed. "No. He has killed the pontiff. He has infiltrated the Vatican. He alone knows of Annwn, and the Seelie Court would more than likely let him off the hook for his affront. All that we have fought for—all that you have fought for—would be put at jeopardy by not killing him now!"

"If you try, I will kill *you*," Richard said flatly.

It was the hardest thing Richard had ever had to say. The Cardinal Vicar was taken aback. The dark brooding eyes of Cormac stared at Richard. The knight stared right back at his elder.

"Merle or the Morrigan will know best how to punish the spirit inside of John Lewis Hugo," Richard repeated. "It is the only way to ensure punishment is given."

Breathing hard, the point of the Dark Thorn still pressing him against the wall, Arawn grinned. "My end will not come by your hand knight," he whispered. "Not like your wife."

"That may be," Richard said, unwilling to let the personal barb unseat his authority of the Dark Thorn. "But your role in this is over."

Arawn laughed, a sick sound.

And began to change.

Unsure of what he was seeing at first, a black fog clouded Richard's vision, the miasma swirling out of John Lewis Hugo's body and into the air. It hung suspended before him, diaphanous and cold, free flowing, unmoving.

Two red coals blinked in the ether.

The spirit of Arawn.

Latent rage at the escape attempt filling him, Richard sent the fire of the Dark Thorn into the cloud with controlled fury, wrapping the fey in coils of magic. Arawn struggled, fighting the staff, trying to invade Richard instead. The knight closed his mind to the offense. Bringing years of anger to the fore coupled with the memory of Elizabeth and her last few fear-filled moments, Richard tightened the magic of the Dark Thorn on Arawn like a vise, a dam of pain unleashed, crushing the spirit. Inhumanly wailing, the lord fought as the magic bit into him.

It did not matter. The mind of Arawn burned away as the fire of Richard's will incinerated it.

The final, terrible scream of Arawn echoed through the suite. Then all went silent.

Breathing hard, Richard looked upon the now palsied body below him. The fey lord that had come close to destroying him had vanished, leaving a body wracked by spasms and twitches, hands clawed and twisted. A dull moan escaped the mouth, growing into choking gasps of pain.

"What is wrong with him?" the Cardinal Vicar asked.

"The pain . . ." the man mewed, teeth gnashing.

Richard stared at the body of John Lewis Hugo, unsure of what he witnessed.

"Kill me . . ."

The fire that had made Richard a killing machine became smoke. Arawn no longer resided in the body, leaving only one possibility for who spoke to them.

It was John Lewis Hugo, his soul no longer trapped.

Pleading for death.

"Kill me . . ." John Lewis Hugo cried.

"No," Richard said.

"Pleeeease," John sniveled, gulping in air. "Kill meee . . ."

"Do not do so, McAllister," Cormac ordered. "Or suffer damnation."

Richard ignored the Cardinal Vicar and knelt, grasping the shaking wrist. Like he had done to Al and Walker in Seattle days earlier, the knight went into the mind of John Lewis Hugo.

There he encountered fractured pandemonium.

The agony of the man overwhelmed Richard. The soul of Philip's onetime best friend was disjointed and broken, a shattered pane of glass. Richard had never felt such acute and traumatic memories in another before. John Lewis Hugo had witnessed every savage moment Arawn had been privy to—the mutation and breeding of thousands of children with fey and animals via the Cailleach to create a ghastly army of halfbreeds, orders given to assassinate countless political figures within Annwn to either gain favors or just to see them die, the torture and breaking of numerous jailed men and women in the Caer Lion dungeons merely to satisfy his insatiable curiosity about human anatomy.

John had screamed into the void where his consciousness lay, unable to alter the events his body took part in, until his very being frayed and snapped.

The distress was so poignant Richard had only one course.

Richard moved into what remained of the other's mind and massaged it, lending his strength to John Lewis Hugo. The emotional anguish was too much for Richard to assuage—too many years of witnessed abuses for the magic to wipe away. As he had done to the two homeless men, the knight erased the centuries of horrible memories, to a time before John Lewis Hugo entered Annwn when he loved a tailoring assistant on Threadneedle Street in London. It had been the last time he had been truly happy. Richard felt what John Lewis Hugo had experienced so long ago—the innocence and the love, the hope of a touch and the feeling of a kiss on blushing cheek, the first unfamiliar and anxious moments of sex. They were emotions Richard had long since thought dead within his own heart, and they left him sad.

There, in the past, Richard slowed the other man's pulse.

When the knight opened his eyes again, John Lewis Hugo sighed contentedly one last time—and did not breathe again.

"You are going to hell, McAllister."

Richard stood again, weariness finally catching up to him. He ignored the Cardinal Vicar and strode toward the door of the suite.

The knight turned back to face Cormac only once.

"If you had any doubt, you are too."

Chapter 38

"You realize, Bran Ardall, you have saved the world as we know it."

With the boy standing behind him, Richard sat across from Cormac O'Connor, a large desk and a gulf of uncertainty between them. He stared out a large office window overlooking stormy Rome. It echoed the unsettling feeling he had inside. Sitting in a plush chair, he and Bran were alone with the Vicar, Finn Arne having left the room after reporting that the catacombs had been cleared of the remaining Templar Knights and the portal was secure once again.

Cormac had changed into clothing more suited to his station—red vestments with white trim, a red zucchetto upon his head, and a gold cross about his neck. The sword he had carried, Hrunting, lay with Durendal in the corner of the room, both cleaned of the blood staining their blades.

A gloomy dawn was only an hour away.

Somewhere below in chambers Richard could only guess at, Pope Clement XV lay in secluded peace. Very few knew of his death. In time it would be announced as a heart attack to the world and his burial wishes would be carried out.

A new Pope would then be selected.

A clock in the room ticked the seconds of silence away. Hungry and tired, Richard had accepted the invitation to the Cardinal Vicar's office and brought Bran for two reasons only.

"Please, have some fruit and water," Cormac offered, gesturing at a bowl of apples, bananas, and grapes and a glass pitcher. "You must thirst after what took place. It is the least I can do. Without you, both the Vatican and Annwn would have falle—"

"Stop with the pretenses, Cardinal Vicar," Richard said bitingly.

The Cardinal Vicar stared hard at the knight.

Neither spoke, gauging one another.

"When has civility been frowned upon?" Cormac asked finally.

"When it is not sincere."

Cormac did not flinch from the unabashed insolence. "Let us speak frankly, McAllister. You have ever been a thorn in the side of the Vigilo. It is beyond rational reasoning why Merle has chosen you to be the Heliwr. That said, there is no reason we cannot begin anew. It will take strength and friendship to see the coming days set right. Rossi is dead. Dozens of Swiss Guards are dead. The survivors will need to have their minds cleared of their memories to keep Annwn safe. And with the knowledge that even some fey have the might to challenge the separation of our worlds, it is more pressing than ever that we work together." He paused. "Needless to say, you have no reason to fear our association."

"The loss of Ennio is great," Richard said. "The loss of your Pope is a hardship for you. Loss is nothing new to me though, Vicar. Loss is not foreign to Bran here either. You extend an olive branch. I have no desire for one."

"Why did you agree to meet with me then, McAllister?"

"There are two reasons. The first, I keep my promises," Richard answered. "You sent Finn Arne after young Ardall here, hoping to capture him at best, harm him at worst. I promised your captain upon meeting with him that I would bring Bran here with me after the death of Philip Plantagenet. That happened, so I am here to fulfill that oath."

"Now, you wait one minute. I meant no harm to B—"

"There is more," the knight interrupted. "I wanted him to meet you, to see your face, to know there are men in the world like you who use other people to their own selfish ends. Bran is now a portal knight. He has yet to fully understand the forces that move throughout this world. He now knows of you."

"You just described your wizard," Cormac said, face reddening.

"That may be truth. Bran now knows this too."

"I have no aspirations but to keep the two worlds separate," the Cardinal Vicar said. "The Vigilo maintains a valuable service. Sometimes it requires sacrifice and the best tools available. Sometimes those tools are people. I merely look for the best ways to keep the peace. Nothing more."

"You are a liar," Richard said. "I know you, Vicar. The rest of the Yn Saith know you. You are like Philip and Arawn. More will *never*, ever be enough."

The ruddy face darkened further in anger.

Richard did not flinch.

"How *dare* you accuse *me*," Cormac gnashed, the color of his face matching his robe. "I asked you here not to quibble about the lies and efforts of Philip but to extend my heartfelt gratitude and begin a relationship in these trying times. His Excellency lies in a cold room, murdered. My best friend and mentor already lies in his crypt, murdered. Countless Swiss Guards gave their life to stop Philip and his machinations. The Catholic Church and all who depend on her will soon be in deep mourning. Instead you throw that in my face? And question my motives?"

"You don't deny it," Richard snapped. "Who do you think *you are*?"

"I think you have not done the mathematics of the situation, *Heliwr*," Cormac spat vehemently. "Even now, as we sit here speaking, the College of Cardinals is convening in the Sistine Chapel to begin the election process. The white smoke *will* blow for me. It is best for you to understand this precept: Do not be quick to make an enemy who wears so much authority upon his mantle."

Richard sat forward. "Are you threatening me?"

"If that is what it takes for you to not make a mistake," the

Cardinal Vicar sneered before looking to Bran. "For one so *young* to not make a mistake."

"Would you have me murdered?" Bran asked evenly.

Cormac folded his hands before him. "Ever hear the adage 'One kills a man, he is a murderer; one kills millions, he is a conqueror; one kills everybody, he is a god?' I have no doubt you have. For centuries the Vigilo has kept the world safe from those who would subvert it. It was given us by Saint Peter to ensure Christianity remained strong after his passing and spread to all hearts. Once a part of the Church, the knights are now a rogue element, given an agenda by a *wizard* of all people," Cormac hissed. "You are part of the same hypocrisy."

"You sound pleased the Pope is dead," Richard said.

"Perhaps there is some truth to that," Cormac admitted. "But I see His will be done."

"He is nothing but a thug, Richard," Bran said.

"As I said, you are young and insolent, fool!" the Vicar thundered. "How dare you question *me*! A whelp! A boy who has never seen the world and the evil within it. I know more secrets about this longest of wars than you could fathom! I should have you shackled for your disrespect!" Cormac paused, his ire lessening as a grin tugged at the corners of his mouth. "I mean, after all, perhaps it was *you* who killed the Pope."

Before he knew it, Richard was on his feet. The Dark Thorn materialized into his hands, its magic angrily diffusing the room. The Cardinal Vicar leaned back in his seat, a modicum of fear dampening the fire in his eyes.

"You are nothing to me, McAllister," Cormac goaded as he stared hard at Bran. "You lost your ideals years ago when your wife died. The power that has been bestowed on both of you does not make you wise."

"That may be," Richard said. "But at least my soul is not stained."

With contempt, the Cardinal shook his head.

"For now."

"If I see you again—if you so much as send Finn Arne after me or Bran or the other Yn Saith—today will not be the last day you see me. And trust me, you don't want to see me again."

"Sounds to me like you are willing to bloody your hands by killing the innocent, as long as you believe it is done for your own rightness," Cormac remarked.

Richard let the Dark Thorn vanish.

"I will do what I must."

"As I've done ever since my family was murdered by heretics," Cormac said, smiling without any hint of humor. "As pontiff I will ensure that same pain does not happen to another person. You and I are more alike than you even know. In time that will become as apparent to you as it already is to me."

"Richard, we should go now," Bran said.

Richard held his tongue. Cormac stared at him with stoicism. The Cardinal Vicar suddenly looked older, the venom gone out of him to reveal the black circles under his eyes and the sagging wrinkles of his cheeks. Richard realized the power Cormac wielded had worn him down, but some inner fire kept him driven.

"I pray you will change your ways," Richard said simply. "Or we will cross paths again, and it will not be pretty for you if that happens."

"His will be done, right?" Cormac said.

Knowing he had proved what he needed to for Bran and having nothing left to say to the Cardinal Vicar, Richard turned to the surprise of Cormac and strode from the room.

Bran followed.

Neither looked back.

"I BURIED DEIRDRE myself, over there," Bran said, pointing.

Richard stood within the shadowy shelter of the Forest of Dean, looking over the dark carnage on the plains. The earth still smoked where charred dead halfbreeds rotted. The Tuatha de Dannan buried their own as well as the enemy, treating every corpse with respect and removing all steel so as to not poison the earth. Saethmoor worked alongside his smaller fey brethren, digging vast grave trenches with his talons. As Richard watched the hard work being done, the monumental loss of life and the reason for it burdened him.

He felt like he had failed to prevent the massacre.

Looking on the white granite bursting from the torn sod like shattered grave markers, Richard tried to understand what created men like Cormac O'Connor or Philip Plantagenet.

Snedeker sat on his shoulder, wings docilely fluttering. Richard was sad about Deirdre. She had died honorably, protecting Bran, and now she lay buried out beyond the battlefield where the plains had come to no harm—one sacrifice of many.

"You cared a great deal for her, didn't you?" he asked.

Bran drew in a deep breath.

"As much as she did for you."

Richard nodded. Bran had grown up during his short time in Annwn. The sadness written on him had gone deep into his soul. It would be a long time before Bran shuffled the sorrow off.

"Do you hate me for that?"

Bran shook his head but didn't say anything.

"I saw Ennio Rossi die," Richard said quietly. "He was young. Too young."

"Do you feel that way about me?" Bran asked.

"I don't," Richard replied. "Not anymore. This has aged you, more than you yet know."

Bran looked at the gauntlet where his left hand used to be. Richard knew what he was thinking. Change had come to both of them, change like the coming future. Even now the humid air that had suffocated their time in Annwn gave way to a cooling breeze washing in from the ocean. In the distance, dark clouds gathered, bearing with them the promise of unfettered electricity and rain Annwn had not seen naturally in centuries.

The coming storm matched the turmoil within both knights.

"It is time, Richard, young Ardall," the Kreche informed, limping from the tent where the Seelie Court had gathered.

"I know," Richard said. "What will *you* do now, my old friend?"

"I have never been built for politics," the Kreche rumbled. "The

Seelie Court has no need of my opinions. But I will remain here, in Annwn. The gateway to Rome is without a protector. I cannot fathom allowing a crossing of any kind."

"I understand. Your origins make it so," Richard said. "I hope you return to Seattle soon then."

"I will return to my piers along the Sound when I can," the Kreche grunted. He turned to Bran. "And Ardall?"

Bran peered into the dark eyes of the Kreche.

"Yeah?"

"I meant what I said to you on the battlefield," the Kreche said, giving him a short bow. "You are a great deal like your father."

"Kreche?"

The monstrosity paused from limping toward the shimmering entrance of the gateway to take up his post, head down, barely turning.

"Yes?" the halfbreed said.

"Call me Bran."

The dark behemoth grunted and continued on his way.

"We are wanted," Richard said, patting Bran on the shoulder.

They walked to the colorful tent where the remaining lords of the Tuatha de Dannan convened for the third time in two weeks. The fighting had not reached the tent, leaving it unsoiled, but the wind from the coming storm ruffled its sides. Above them, in the canopy of the trees, dryads swung from branch to branch in the slowly swaying trees as they healed the Forest of Dean as best as they could from the lingering effects of the dragon fire.

Two hellyll warriors stood guard at the entrance. Both nodded in greeting as the two knights entered.

All eyes of the Seelie Court turned to them.

"Welcome, Knights Richard McAllister and Bran Ardall," the Morrigan greeted from a high-backed chair a bit taller than the others occupied around it. Flowing silk had replaced her armor, her injured arm held carefully in her lap. Two fairies sat perched behind her again, awaiting any need she may have. The other lords nodded their welcome too, each bathed after the battle and in new clothing. Other than the Queen, the only other lord displaying any sign of injury was Lord n'Hagr, his brutish face pale, his left arm gone and bandaged above the elbow. Lord Latobius had also joined the Seelie Court, changed into his human form to sit within the confines of the tent.

With no hint of pain on her chiseled face, the Morrigan gestured with her other hand to a set of chairs set up near the table.

"We will not stay long, Queen," Richard said, sitting down.

"Are you both well?"

Richard nodded. Bran sat down beside him.

"There is a change in the air," the Queen began, her eyes scanning the lords. "In gratitude to the Heliwr and the efforts of Bran Ardall, the reign of Philip Plantagenet is finally at an end. Each and every one of you and your peoples surrendered life and blood for our freedom. There is power in that, a strengthening of the bonds of our Court that will stretch across the entirety of Annwn. And even now, as we sit here, the world reasserts its natural order once more, the first chills of a harsh winter long needed stirring within the bowels of stone and dirt and plant."

"The Cailleach damaged much," Lord Aife agreed sadly.

"It is our role to put our affairs in order and transition out of that damage," the Queen said. "How soon may we leave these environs, Mastersmith?"

"The burial proceeds as quickly as it can, my Queen," Govannon replied, his demeanor weary. "The reclamation of all iron and steel items has continued all morning but it will be some time before we may fully inter our kin to nature. Late tomorrow. Or perhaps early the next day."

"I see. Unfortunate. The rains will come as we travel home."

"What of the Graal that started all of this?" Lord Eigion asked.

Lugh stood, still wearing his scarred armor. "When my men overcame the force the Usurper left behind in his city, we ventured into the castle. Women and children were mostly left behind, posing no threat, even if Lord Evinnysan attempted a defense. With the aid of Lord Faric and his coblynau, who see far better in the darkness, we traversed into the catacombs of dungeons as Knight McAllister related. I will not speak of the unnatural breeding pens we discovered, but the chamber where McAllister reported the Graal to be was nothing but a lake, the cup not found. I have my men hunting the plains surrounding Caer Llion in hopes of coming across it and the person who took it."

"Perhaps one of the prisoners Caswallawn freed during our escape from the dungeons stole it," Richard said. "Or a group of soldiers pilfering the city before the Tuatha de Dannan entered it."

"I do not know. It is not likely," Lugh said. "From what my men and I could discern, one person took the cup. Templar Knights were slaughtered at every turn from the dungeons. Signs pointed at one highly trained individual. From there, nothing was found."

"We have seen the Graal can be used for terrible evil," Aife said. "Finding it should be a top priority."

"It must not be allowed to enter into unknown hands," the Morrigan said, nodding in agreement. "The Rhedewyr will scour Annwn. And with them, my best and most able trackers."

"Why does not the Heliwr search for it?" Caswallawn beseeched.

All eyes turned on Richard.

"You are quick to put the knight through another quite dangerous ordeal, Lord Caswallawn," Lord Finnbhennach interrupted, his horns gleaming beneath the fey light of the orbs. "Especially after he helped return your stolen kingdom."

"I have no intention of disgracing his gift by suggesting he owes us more," Lord Caswallawn said.

"No, no, it is all right," Richard said. "I would do as Caswallawn suggested if I could. When I reentered Annwn from Rome the first thing I did was try to discern if it remained in Caer Llion. I failed. The Dark Thorn seemed confused, pulled in three different directions. I cannot explain why. One day I may aid in the retrieval of the Holy Grail. Until I learn more from Merle about the staff, it may be some time."

Frowns and dissatisfied grunts filled the tent.

"It will be as you say, Knight McAllister," the Morrigan said before turning to Aife. "How fare the Rhedewyr then? Are they recovering from their stampede?"

"The Rhedewyr graze upon the grasslands to the west," Aife

reported, returned entirely to her nude human form. "Almost two dozen died in the initial rush against the army of Caer Llion, more than a hundred injured. Kegan and his remaining son aid them now. They will be ready for whatever you require, my Queen."

"What will become of Caer Llion?" Lord n'Hagr rumbled.

"It will go to the remaining family of Lord Gerallt," the Morrigan said. "First, I must say with great sadness, I am sorrowed by the loss of the lord and his daughter. Without men and women of honor, the Tuatha de Dannan would barely have anything to trust in mankind. They will be missed and never forgotten. Caer Llion shall exist as a monument to Lord Gerallt and a center of power here in the south. The remaining descendents of man—including the Templar Knights who survived the battle—will have sanctuary within its walls and the plains about it."

"Lord Gerallt leaves behind no direct heir," Snedeker said sadly. "I believe he had a younger brother, though, with a family of his own."

"If Lord Caswallawn can abstain from Govannon's brew, I wish him to help guide Lord Gerallt's brother until he is fit to rule on his own," the Queen said. "Lord Caswallawn, do you accept this great honor?"

"I do, my Queen," Caswallawn said.

"It is settled then." The Morrigan nodded to those around her. "Caer Llion will maintain the peace in the south. Lord Fafnir, his grandson Faric, and the coblynau will once again entreat trade relations between Caer Glain and the rest of Annwn, as is their right now that they have returned to the Seelie Court. Lord Latobius, his brethren, and their Fynach caretakers will undoubtedly remain in Tal Ebolyon where they have ever resided."

"We will continue in our snowy reaches as long as we are able," Latobius assured. "It is home."

"Lord Latobius, those gathered here owe you and your kin a debt as well," the Morrigan added. "If it had not been for you and your intervention, our demise would have been at hand."

"Took him long enough to arrive," Caswallawn snorted.

Everyone looked around uncomfortably. Richard wanted to

strike Caswallawn. It appeared even after the survival of the Tuatha de Dannan and the expulsion of Philip, old wounds refused heal.

"My people die, Lord Caswallawn," Latobius whispered. "Surely, you of all the lords present know what that means. Each life among my people is far more precious than I can relate. Nael will heal in time. The wounds visited upon him are mending in a shaded glen not far from here, and we were fortunate to not lose him. To die is to give meaning to that death, but when a people are as few as we are, no death holds meaning."

"I did not mean to offend," Caswallawn conceded.

"It is ever in your nature to do so, Lord Caswallawn," Latobius said sadly. "I decided it best to view the battle and its progress from a safe distance before offering our might. After all, no reason to become involved if Tal Ebolyon was not needed."

"It was," Lord Eigion pointed out. "Those sitting here are very much in your debt."

"You have my oath to discover what ails dragonkind," Richard reminded the dragon lord.

Latobius nodded to the knight in appreciation.

"Richard McAllister and Bran Ardall," the Queen addressed, moving on. "What is it you desire from the Seelie Court, though I cannot offer title or land?"

"There is nothing you can give us, Queen," Richard replied.

The Morrigan nodded. "Then a favor at another time. What will come of the portal in Rome? A Knight of the Yn Saith has perished there, which saddens us all a great deal for his sacrifice. It will take time for Myrddin Emrys to promote a replacement."

"The Kreche will oversee the portal from this side until such a time he is relieved by a new Knight of the Yn Saith," Richard said.

"A formidable warrior. I am pleased to hear it," she nodded, her eyes hard. "Men from the Church of your world were a part of the battle, having come into these plains before the battle had even begun. They aided the Tuatha de Dannan, although I believe they did so at their own gain. They must never again bring their beliefs or their weapons into Annwn."

"The Seven and I will do what we can to prevent that."

"I am sure once you return to your home and meet with Myrddin Emrys that your future will become clearer for all," the Morrigan said. "Long have our two worlds lacked a Heliwr to give balance. We must restore that which we have lost. It will take your help and it will require strength. I hope your knighthood lasts decades."

"I will be what I decide," Richard said noncommittally. "Bran and I will begin our trip back to Seattle this afternoon. Before doing so, however, I will contact the surviving members of the Yn Saith and inform them of the events that have transpired here today. I will do what I can to honor the two worlds."

"I know, Richard McAllister," the Morrigan said with a brief smile. "Do any lords here wish to speak?"

Silence filled the tent.

"The Seelie Court will separate in two days," the Queen ordained. "May many days of peace be visited upon Annwn."

Chapter 39

A chilly breeze ruffled unruly hair as Richard stared across the water. It was a crisp late fall afternoon; the maples lining the Seattle waterfront were skeletal. Clear skies lorded over the Pacific Northwest, giving a rare view of the sun as it dipped toward the snow-covered Olympic Mountains in the far west, but the light wind stole what little warmth the day offered. Cars rumbled behind him, some upon the Viaduct overhead while others ran along Alaskan Way at his back. The rush hour had begun, the day at its end, and downtown employees were making their way home. None of them had any idea what had transpired in Annwn, their lives kept blissfully ignorant to the truth buried in the bowels of Pioneer Square nearby.

Returned to Seattle, Richard already felt more at ease than he had in a long time.

"A beautiful day," Bran noted at his side.

Richard leaned against the rail of the pier and folded his hands. "Elizabeth and I used to walk here in the summertime. Eating ice cream. Laughing at the tourists."

"Good memories then."

Richard drew in the salted air. "Yeah."

They both went quiet, not looking at the other, each lost to his thoughts. Richard missed Elizabeth, the ache within almost unbearable in one of their familiar places. The confrontation with Arawn had reopened harsh wounds, and although Richard had ended the creature ultimately responsible for the slaying of his wife, a large void remained that the knight now sadly realized would never fully heal.

Loneliness would always be a part of him.

"No secrets between us," Bran said then, his gauntleted hand hidden within the pocket of a coat given him by the fey. "If I am to fully take on this role of portal knight, I need to know I can at least trust someone. I want it to be you."

"I will not be Merle, Bran."

The boy nodded. "I have to know, why didn't you share the truth about the identity of John Lewis Hugo with the Seelie Court? Did they not have a right to know, Arawn being one of the fey lords and all?"

It took Richard a few moments to organize his thoughts.

"Arawn was well respected in the Seelie Court," he began, watching a sea gull float on the breeze above the docks. "He was quite powerful, like the Morrigan, and the other lords followed his direction often. When Philip imprisoned the essence of Lord Arawn and all his knowledge of Annwn within John Lewis Hugo, the Seelie Court lost a driving force from their midst. For centuries the Tuatha de Dannan were without Arawn, and for centuries the benevolence of the Morrigan was all they knew."

Richard paused. "Arawn was broken, or at least some part of him was broken. I saw it in his eyes. Madness had set in after struggling with the will and soul of John Lewis Hugo. That insanity made him unpredictable. Arawn would have done what Philip planned but for different reasons. He wished to bring the Tuatha de Dannan back to prominence. He wanted retribution for millennia of Church aggression against his kin. He would have become as fanatical and dangerous as Philip, the Church, or any religion willing to sacrifice lives for a particular brand of truth.

"To tell the Seelie Court of this would have planted a seed I'd rather not see grow into future hardships for you and I. If the lords discovered Arawn meant to return them to the Misty Isles, who knows what that seed could become. Look at the Court. Caswallawn believes strongly in restoring the glory of his house. How far would he take that? Lugh controls the Long Hand, who miss their Elven brethren in our world. Even Lord Latobius may believe the antidote to what ails his kin is in England where they once were fertile. Any one of those lords would reenter our world if they thought they could do it.

"And since Arawn came so close to accomplishing that very feat, I feel it best to not evoke such possibilities," Richard finished, shrugging.

"You hide the truth then," Bran said. "As Merle would."

"Perhaps," Richard said, thinking on it. "Perhaps I'm more like the old man than I wish to admit."

"The Church. The fey. Plantagenet and those he led," Bran snorted. "All of them were willing to kill thousands for what they believe. Even on the street, nothing like that happens. This is the insanity I've been brought into, eh?"

"Thousands can die at the behest of the world's powerful, yes," Richard said. "But make no mistake, even the low man can succumb to extremism. I have learned over my life that the simplest and most well meaning thoughts and emotions can become an evil—whether they be from the man on the street or the highest religious Church member in the world. It does not matter. Religion becomes fanaticism. Love can become jealousy. Food and drink can become gluttony. Taking anything to the extreme is an evil."

"Like your need to avenge the death of your wife," Bran noted, his eyes piercing Richard's own. "No matter if your leaving put the rest of us in Annwn in danger."

"Like your feelings for Deirdre despite knowing her for only hours," Richard retorted pointedly.

The boy stared hard at Richard before looking away, the pain he felt etched deep on his features. The older knight watched him before turning back to the Sound. Neither spoke. They both knew they had stung the other; they both knew the truth the other spoke.

"What of the Holy Grail?" Bran asked finally.

"What of it?"

"You really can't use the Dark Thorn to find it?"

"I couldn't," Richard said. "A very old magic resisted my attempt. It is like the cup is in one place and two other places at the same time. I do not know how or why. I do know we must keep it from others who would use it for their own gain. Merle will speak more on that when we begin our training, I would imagine."

"Training, huh?" Bran said unenthusiastically. "Schooling."

"You already passed one helluva test in Annwn, Bran."

Bran turned away from the Sound, hands still in his pockets. "We should walk to the bookstore," he said. "Find Merle."

"He will come," Richard grunted. "When he is ready."

As if on cue Merle appeared, the old man walking down the boardwalk with his hands buried in khaki pants pockets and customary pipe in mouth. He wore a light jacket that rippled in the breeze. Richard watched him come, wondering how much the wizard had actually known about Arawn and the truth behind the death of Elizabeth.

"Come from a Renaissance Fair, I see," Merle commented with a twinkle in his eyes as he walked up, looking over the clothing both Richard and Bran wore.

"Very funny," Richard growled.

Merle looked over at Bran and gave an almost imperceptible bow.

"Knight," Merle greeted.

"Hello, Merle."

"I am pleased to see you both returned whole and healthy," he said. "It was not the easiest of paths you both trod."

"Cut the crap, Merle," Richard demanded.

Merle removed the pipe from his lips and tapped its charred contents out against the rail of the pier.

"Okay then."

"Did you know how Elizabeth was really killed?"

"I knew well enough not to tell you," the old wizard declared.

Before Richard could protest, Merle raised his hand. "Be kind, Richard. You know, as well as I, if I had told you the fey lord Arawn had orchestrated the death of your wife, you would have left Seattle, abdicated your post, and ventured into Annwn with vengeance in your heart. It would have driven you beyond rational thought and ultimately would have led to your own demise—without atonement for the wrong. No, the way for you to gain what you wished required time and a sacrifice of the truth."

Richard curbed the bitterness he felt. "And you expect me to trust you after this?"

"You have not trusted me for years," Merle said.

Richard frowned hard. The whole world around him had dropped away with the exception of the icy blue gaze of Merle. The wizard was right. Trust between them had died when Elizabeth died. Trust with almost anyone had.

He turned away, swallowing bile.

"And you, Bran Ardall," Merle addressed, ignoring Richard and digging in his pocket for tobacco. "What of you?"

Bran looked at Richard before turning back to the old man.

"Did you know I would accept Arondight?" Bran asked.

"I did not, actually," Merle replied. "Contrary to what Richard may think, I am not as gifted as many stories make me out to be. I see future *possibilities*. I see inside of hearts. Nothing more though. The possibilities inherent in the future are not the actual future, only a thought of what could be. There are infinite paths, and although I am fair at deciphering the paths we might one day tread, it is not something I can prophesize."

"You are saying some possibilities you see never become real?"

"That is exactly right," Merle admitted. "With you, I knew your potential and helped place you upon a path, but that path had crooked tributaries and you had to chose those on your own. You chose to accept the Paladr. The Lady had other plans, plans I too had foreseen possibly happening. You chose to infiltrate Caer Llion and you chose to hunt down Philip Plantagenet. You stood up to tyranny in Annwn, actions you would have done with or without Arondight. Like your father, you have an honorable heart.

If by that you still think I orchestrated events, by all means, believe as Richard does."

"But you are one of the most powerful beings—in history!"

Richard snorted. "Do not let him lie to you. He saw enough to send the Kreche into Annwn. Without doing so, we'd still be locked in the dungeons of Caer Llion."

"I did, you're correct," Merle confessed. "There are times when multiple paths hold *mostly* the same event. That was one of them. Wisdom, knowledge of what is true or right coupled with just judgment as to action, has little to do with clairvoyance and more with insight. Is that magic? Is that knowledge of what *will* happen? No."

"You know more than any single person ever," Richard growled.

"That's right," Bran said.

"But I still do not know *all*," Merle insisted. "If there had been a way to prevent the pain in your life, Richard, or the death of your father, Bran, I would not have hesitated. These paths were kept from me. Do you have any concept the frustration those events—or countless others over the centuries—have caused me? How the loss of those I have cared about over the years begins to weigh a man down, even a man like me?"

Bran looked down to the sidewalk. Richard bit his tongue.

With deft hands, Merle repacked his pipe as he gazed at the purpling sunset. Richard knew the ancient wizard was right.

Merle was not the enemy.

The old man gave Bran a piece of paper.

"Think on your left hand, Bran, and read those words aloud."

"What is it?"

"You will see."

Bran did as he was instructed. The moment he finished speaking the gauntlet where his hand had been vanished, replaced by what appeared to be his human hand."

"What did you do?" Bran breathed.

"I did nothing. You did," Merle said. "In effect, you just called your first illusion into being. It will hide your hand from those who come into the shop."

Bran was quiet as he flexed his hand anew.

"You seem pensive?" the wizard remarked.

"When I use Arondight, I feel as though I lose a part of myself in the magic," Bran said, his voice worried. "Thinking about it, I am almost scared to call it into being."

"All power corrupts. To what degree depends on the person," Merle answered, his face solemn. "Politicians. Kings. Everyday folk. Even a Knight of the Yn Saith with the purest of hearts can succumb to the allure of ultimate power. Some have, to be honest. The loss of control can make a man or woman over into something dark and ugly. You have that within you as well. All do."

Bran nodded. "How do I—"

"Learn to control it?" Merle offered. "Knowledge of yourself and knowledge of the power you have been given. You have barely begun to examine what you are capable of. I will teach you. Richard, if he is willing and able, will guide you, as he has studied some of the Wards you will be studying. You will discover your own limitations and, in so doing, discover how to control the burgeoning power inside. In time, Bran. In time."

"What am I to do until then?"

"Right now, nothing," Merle said with a small smile. "In the coming weeks, months, and years, you will grow into the man I have seen."

As the sun set behind the Olympic Mountains, the chill of fall gripped the pier. Richard remembered what it had been like to accept Arondight and begin training to be a knight. Bran had a great deal to learn, but from what Richard had seen, the boy was quite capable and would not have a problem with the Wards.

Integrating his own new role into his life might be a different story altogether.

"Your father would be proud of you," Merle added finally.

"I feel closer to him now than ever before."

"It was meant," Merle said. "Charles Ardall was an amazing man. There are many stories I would like to share with you. He loved you and your mother very much, would never stray too far for too long from Seattle. Some Heliwr roam the world, having no want or need, but Charles was rooted here. He protected you and the two worlds that his life would be centered around—without error or bias."

"How did he die?"

"That is a tale for another time," Merle said.

"Already playing games," Richard mocked. "Typical."

"It is an incomplete tale," Merle conceded. "The act itself was beyond my sight for reasons I cannot fully explain—only speculate at. There are other forces at work in this world beyond my own, Bran. I do not see all, as I've said. I sense another soul, such as my own, who took part in the murder of your father."

"What do you mean?" Richard asked. "A saved demon soul."

"No, another wizard."

Richard was surprised. He had not heard that before. Bran seemed to accept the news, but Richard could already tell the boy was gearing up for a barrage of questions he would ask Merle later.

"Knowing won't bring my father back," Bran sighed.

As Bran took a deep breath, the cogs in his mind clearly spinning, Merle pulled a few dollars from his jacket and offered them to Bran.

Bran took the money. "What's this for?"

"You are starving," the old man said. "Get something to eat. I would speak to Richard alone."

"All powerful *and* poor," Bran said, showing off the dollar bills. "Is that it?"

"Goodness has never been a profitable business."

Bran pocketed the money.

"Rick!"

Richard and his two companions turned.

Al and Walker walked toward them, their bedrolls hiked upon their shoulders, each carrying change cans that jingled all too lightly. They were as disheveled and dirty as usual, but each bore a grin that dispelled some of the hardship they experienced living without a home.

"Where ye been, Rick?" Al asked. "We were worryin' about ye."

"I've been . . . around," Richard said. "How are you healing?"

"'Tis nothin', nothin'. Takes more than some hoodlums to kill ol' Al," he answered. "We headin' up the hill to the shelter for some grub. Care to join?"

Having removed memories from both Al and Walker and being reminded of John Lewis Hugo and his last moments, Richard shook his head sadly. "No, I'm not hungry right now, Al. But thank you for the offer," Richard said, looking to Walker. "You okay after the other night? Fighting those drug dealers must have been scary, especially when they knifed Al."

"Yeah, 'twas," the addict answered. "I was so freaked I can't even remember what dey looked like."

"Scary, for sure," Richard said.

"I know dis sounds nuts but I feel . . ."

"Yes?"

"I . . . I feel like I owe yeh my life in some crazy bat shit way."

"No, Walker," Richard replied, returning the sad gaze of the addict. "It was all you and Al. You saved yourselves."

"See ya tonight den, Rick," Al said.

Richard nodded.

Al gave Bran and Merle an aloof look. He then led Walker with a shambling gait away down the boardwalk, across the street beneath the viaduct, and into Pioneer Square. The inseparable two vanished behind the brick buildings and masses of people, their cups and bedrolls carried with hope, two friends keeping the dangers of the streets at bay.

Richard would see them again soon, no doubt.

"Come into the store when you are finished eating," Merle said to Bran. "There are things I would like to show you."

"I will," Bran said. "Thank you for the money."

Merle inclined his head. "Thank you for being your father's son."

"See you around?" Bran asked Richard.

"Yes," Richard grunted.

Shaking his head, Bran also walked away, into the city he now protected. Richard was concerned for the boy. Bran had cared deeply for Deirdre and now his heart suffered in her death. As Bran disappeared into the Bricks like the two homeless men before him, Richard recalled what it had been like when the wizard had bequeathed Arondight to him, knowing Bran's hardships to come.

He hoped the boy had an easier time of it—both with the weapon and his heart.

"He is a tough lad," Merle said. "You have no need to worry."

"He is tough. I shouldn't give him such a hard time."

"Or the fairy, for that matter," Merle said, glancing up.

Richard followed where Merle looked, into the boughs of the maple tree where Snedeker hid among several obstinately clinging leaves against the coming winter.

"Is it a poor choice to let him reside here?" Richard asked. "He has nowhere else to go now that his only friend is dead in Annwn."

"I do not see why not," the wizard said. "Charles kept his guide Berrytrill near at most times, including in this world, with little problem. I think it will keep you anchored to your new role and give you someone to talk to about all of this beyond just a sad and grumpy cockamamie washed-up wizard."

Richard nodded, not quite sharing Merle's confidence.

"Did Jack return to the store?" he questioned.

"He did," Merle said simply. "It's how I knew you had returned."

Richard nodded, staring at the water.

"You did well," the old man whispered.

Richard knew what Merle meant. Long moments passed. The confidence the bookseller had shown him did little to change how he felt about his past and his future. The death of Elizabeth remained an ache deep in his soul. Richard knew it would never heal and the atonement in Rome did little to assuage it.

"I miss her," he said simply.

"I know you do, Richard," Merle murmured. "I know you do."

Both men watched the golden light of the setting sun purple toward evening and eventual darkness. It was the end of another day. Neither said a word. Both knew it was not necessary. They had spent enough time with one another to know silence had more meaning than words sometimes.

After a while Merle turned to depart, leaving Richard to his own thoughts.

"I will open in the morning," Richard offered suddenly.

Merle stopped and squinted.

"There *are* several dozen new books in need of repair and cataloging. Old books, centuries old, from the heart of Romania as well as ancient Germania and Gaul." He paused to light his tamped pipe, pulling on the smoke. "Your room is how you left it."

"Perhaps I can find jobs for my two homeless friends?"

Merle exhaled a white puff into the fall air.

"Perhaps."

Richard watched Merle stroll across the busy street, his pipe emitting quaint puffs of smoke upon the salty breeze. Soon the city swallowed him too, lost to the busy ruckus of rush hour.

The sweet odor of the wizard's leaf, however, lingered.

Richard waited a few minutes, breathing in cold air, and let the end of the day wash over him with its finality.

If he were to be lonely now, it would be on his terms.

Ignoring the growing darkness, feeling the Dark Thorn and its reassurance at being only a call away, he turned from Puget Sound, a man with more peace than he had experienced in years, and made his way back into Pioneer Square.

Back toward Old World Tales.

The
DARK THORN

ABOUT THE AUTHOR

SHAWN SPEAKMAN grew up in the beautiful wilds of Washington State near a volcano and surrounded by old-growth forests filled with magic. After moving to Seattle to attend the University of Washington, he befriended *New York Times* best-selling fantasy author Terry Brooks and became his webmaster, leading to an enchanted life surrounded by words.

He was a manager at one of the largest Barnes & Noble Booksellers in the country for many years and now owns the online bookstore The Signed Page, manages the websites for several authors, and is a freelance writer for Random House.

He also contributed the annotations for *The Annotated Sword of Shannara* by Terry Brooks, published in 2012.

Shawn is a cancer survivor, knows angel fire east, and lives in Seattle, Washington.

www.shawnspeakman.com